I0742273

WHILE THE CITY NEVER SLEEPS

WHILE THE CITY NEVER SLEEPS

ALEX BLEDSOE

Copyright ©2025 by Alex Bledsoe

Cover Design by Sarah Macklin

All rights reserved.

No part of this book may be reproduced in any form or by any electronic or mechanical means, including information storage and retrieval systems, without written permission from the author, except for the use of brief quotations in a book review. No part of this book may be used for training of LLM systems or any type of generative AI without express permission from the rights holder.

To Mark Bloodworth
Although we're the same age, when I was staggering in and out of Cadillac's pool hall in the Eighties, Mark was single-handedly creating one of my favorite titles of the indie comics boom, a multilevel story of a city and its inhabitants called <u>Night Streets</u>. Alas, it only ran for five issues (of a six-issue story arc), but it stayed with me ever since. This book would not exist without that long-percolating inspiration, and I hope when he reads it, Mark enjoys it as much as I've always enjoyed his work.

I have never felt salvation in nature. I love cities above all.
—*Michelangelo*

THREE DAYS BEFORE
THE FESTIVAL

DAWN

The Mendicant, a man of indeterminate age, ethnicity, and socioeconomic level, opened the door to the roof. He knew how to do so quietly, despite the hinges being rusted and corroded by years of neglect. He also knew better than to do so if he was the least bit unsure it was safe. In Ratway, rooftops were as dangerous as streets and alleys.

The night air blew chilly this high, even though it was summer, and carried the tang of the polluted shipping channel known as the Smoke River. In the distance, sirens from a variety of city vehicles wailed in a dissonant, quintessentially urban chorus. Below, on the streets, cars streaked from light to light, drivers itching to break free.

A young woman, arms folded impatiently, waited for him. She wore a dark hoodie over a black baseball cap, the combination shadowing most of her face. Army surplus boots, fingerless driving gloves, and worn jeans created a look simultaneously striking and yet generic; dozens of young women with her same basic appearance filled the city. Her lower face, all that was visible under the hood, was pleasant without being striking; she was pretty but not memorable. It was also impossible to guess her age with any accuracy; she could be as young as fifteen, or as old as thirty.The Mendicant appreciated such imprecision. In a world where everyone tried to be distinct, both he and this woman strove to be vague. It suited them both, for very different reasons.

"Good morning," he called.

The first gray morning light illuminated her face under the hood and revealed the upper half was painted with black greasepaint, making a crude but effective mask. "What have you got for me?" she said, her voice flat and unfriendly.

The Mendicant headed an organization of child thieves, pickpockets, and con artists. They were orphans, both boys and girls, capable of turning on tears in an instant or slipping through crowds so that they were impossible to follow. No one knew his real name or background, but he knew everything about everyone. Well, *almost* everyone.

"Is that how you greet me?" he said with faux outrage. "No asking after my health? No inquiries about my family?"

"I could give a shit about your health. And your 'family' has my sympathy. Put up or shut up. It's late, and I'm tired."

"I'm sure you are. I heard about your little contretemps earlier. It's drawn quite the crowd, if the sirens are any indication."

"Yeah, well, it needed doing, and nobody else was going to."

"I'm not arguing about that. But you do realize they'll come after you with everything now that you've attacked two police officers."

"The ones who've been sexually abusing poor women and girls for months. Including a couple of yours."

The Mendicant frowned at this.

"Oh, don't pretend you didn't know, or that you cared."

"I'm not pretending anything."

"Yeah, well, let them come looking for me. That'll save me the trouble of looking for them."

"It's war against the cops, then?"

"It's war against anyone who hurts the people of Ratway. And that could easily include you, if you stop being useful. So, what have you got?"

He paused for a moment, trying unsuccessfully to read the shadowed, obscured face beneath the hood. Then began his recitation. "That dealer who calls himself Big Perm has moved over to the four hundred block of Tenth Street. Guess you made Marlin Avenue too hot for him."

"Or not hot enough, if he thinks just relocating will stop me. What else?"

"There's a pimp named Wogo. Asian, although I'm not sure from where. Works the block over by Torchy's. I've seen three of his girls with facial bruises in the last two weeks."

She nodded; this needed no comment.

"And finally, I have it on good authority that there's going to be a hit."

"By a pro?"

"Yes. Out of town action. On someone in the Kefali organization."

"Who?"

"I don't know. But it'll happen in the next three days."

"Why the deadline?"

"Because of the Festival."

"What festival?"

"*The* Festival. It's in Bay View this year."

"Never heard of it. And if it's Bay View, it's not my problem either."

"Are you sure about that?" He gestured at the borough below him, known officially as Rattaway after some nineteenth-century benefactor, but commonly referred to as Ratway. Once a rich community of immigrants all seeking the American dream, it was now rundown and crime-ridden, avoided by everyone except those who had business here, and those who couldn't leave. "Kefali has his tentacles all over Ratway just like he does everywhere else."

"Everywhere else can deal with him on their own time," she said. "I'm only concerned with what happens here."

"I thought superheroes stepped in when there was trouble anywhere."

"I'm not a superhero."

"Ah. Is it the river, then? Maybe you're like a vampire, who can't cross running water."

"You're giving me a headache. Anything else?"

"Just a suggestion: a cape. You need to wear a cape."

"I'm not wearing any fucking cape."

"Then that's all I have." He waited, and when she said nothing, he prompted, "And for me?"

"You still want to use that abandoned gas station as a hideout?"

"I prefer the term 'staging area.' And yes."

"Then you have it for the week. I won't bother you, and I'll do what I can to make sure no one else does."

"No one else would. But I appreciate the concern."

"But anything after that depends on what you have for me next time."

"Doesn't it always?"

"I'll send word where we'll meet next week."

"I'll wait with tingles of anticipation."

"Oh, and where's Sparrow?"

"He's working."

"I promised him a lightning trick this time."

"Mm. You do seem to take a shine to him, as they say down south, and that's bad for morale."

"How do you figure?"

"Favoring one over the others. I try to keep them all equal."

She scowled at him. "You're a piece of work, did you know that?"

Before he could reply, there was a flash of bright blueish light. The Mendicant smelled ozone and had to blink away the searing after-image. When he did, the woman was gone.

The sky grew lighter, and the hazy silhouettes of the East Side's skyline across the river conveyed the glamor people imagined when they thought of the city, while the lingering shadows hid the criminals, victims, addicts, the depressed and suicidal ones, and all the other secrets from those naive romantics.

Even after six months of passing tips to the Lightning Girl, he still wasn't sure if she was a realist like him, or a romantic like those dreamers.

As soon as he could see clearly again, the Mendicant descended to the streets, and back to his world.

7:25 A.M.

A famous city once claimed to have eight million stories. This city has at least that many, and this is one of them—or several, depending on how you count. And although the Mendicant and the Lightning Girl are both involved, this particular story starts on the other side of the city, and in the same way so many other stories begin— with a killing.

When Arthur Shawcross found the girl curled up in the passenger seat of his vintage Corvette convertible, he was instantly on his guard. He was middle-aged and very successful, but he also knew he was no great catch, and half-dressed pretty girls didn't wait for him in his car without some ulterior motive.

Whoever she was, she wore only a t-shirt and underwear, her multi-colored hair was disheveled, and mascara tear tracks streaked her face. He looked around, but this section of the parking garage was empty, not only of people, but also of other vehicles.

Why didn't I put up the top? he thought in annoyance. Aloud, he said, "Hey. You in the 'Vette. Wake up."

The girl opened her eyes and stretched. Then with a start, she sat up and huddled against the passenger door. "Don't hurt me," she blurted, knees drawn up to her chest.

"I won't hurt you, but how did you get in here? This is a secure building."

She blinked, pushed a mat of tangled multicolored hair from her face, and said, "I don't know. I can't remember."

"Uh-huh." He put down his gym bag in the backseat. "What's your name?"

"Delilah."

"Hope you don't do haircuts."

"What?" she asked blankly.

"Nothing. Bad joke. How old are you, Delilah?"

"Sixteen."

"Where are you from?"

"Why are you asking me so many questions?" She said this in a mixture of whine and pout that made her seem even younger.

"Because I'm a lawyer, and that's what I do. Where are the rest of your clothes?"

"I don't know," she said in a small voice.

Arthur sighed. Some GHB casualty picks *his* car to hide in, and now he'd have to spend the whole morning dealing with her, instead of playing tennis like he'd planned. "All right, come on, get out."

She opened the door and slowly exited. When she stood before him, he saw that she was indeed very shapely beneath her scant clothing, and her face was pretty and soft. She tried to pull her shirt down to cover her panties, which made a display of her cleavage. He suspected she was trying to present herself as sexy, a skill she'd probably learned as a form of protection. But Arthur saw a scared child.

"I'm not going to hurt you," Arthur assured her again. "I'm just going to call the police to come help you get home."

"Hey, pal, she's with me," a male voice said behind him. "What the hell are you doing to her?"

Arthur turned. The man had short, scruffy brown hair, two-day stubble and wore jeans, a black t-shirt, and a well-worn corduroy jacket. He pointed a small automatic pistol.

Shawcross sighed. "A shakedown? Really? Do you two have any idea who I am, and who I work for?"

"We know exactly who you are," Delilah said, all demureness gone. She skipped over to the man, no longer self-conscious, and stood beside him with a mischievous smile.

"Then you also know that this building has state-of-the-art security." Arthur realized as he said it that guards should've been here by now, and for the first time felt apprehensive.

The man raised the gun and pointed it at Arthur's chest. "We'll take that chance," he said, and shot Arthur through the heart.

The lawyer fell dead to the concrete.

"Good job, Delilah."

"Did you get a look at the car?" Delilah asked. "It's a 1990 ZR-1. It's got a 6.2-liter V8 under the hood. Do you know what *Car and Rider* said about it?" She looked up, as if searching her memory. "'It's the most civilized and least expensive sports car there is, because it's still a Corvette.'"

"That's nice," the man said patiently, "but we're only half done with our job."

"Oh! The bag!" She rushed to a shadowy corner and returned with a heavy brown satchel. She took out some penguin-patterned leggings, quickly pulled them on, and stepped into some worn flats. Then, from the bottom of the bag, she took out an enormous pair of surgical shears.

Arthur Shawcross's body was found by Josh Wilbanks, another resident of the posh condo tower, when he returned from an all-nighter celebrating the release of a new clothing line. He parked his Mini Hummer across two spaces, got out, and slipped in the blood trailing from the corpse to the nearest drain. Since Wilbanks was still relatively stoned, his first call was to his lawyer; he couldn't be *entirely* sure he hadn't been somehow responsible. Once reassured, he called the police.

Even before the victim was identified, the location of the murder assured that it drew a pair of experienced detectives, Laura Slade and Cole Slaughter, from the nearby 6th precinct. It also assured that someone, probably one of the uniformed officers swarming to block all the entrances to the garage, would tip off the media. In this city, nothing remained secret for long.

9:40 A.M.

Shawcross's body lay beside his Corvette. Yellow crime scene tape blocked off the whole floor of the garage, and technicians from CSU did their arcane work across every square inch of that protected space. Three junior detectives milled around, awaiting orders.

Nearby, lead detective Laura Slade spoke to Wilbanks. Thirty-five, of average height, Laura wore round John Lennon glasses. But suspects who assumed her bookish demeanor meant a woman meek and easily intimidated learned very quickly how wrong they were. She'd earned a brown belt in Krav Maga, the fighting style used by the Israeli Defense Forces, as well as finishing in the top five in the department's marksmanship competition for the past seven years. Soft-spoken and easy-going until it was time not to be, gossip said she could kill you in more ways than you knew how to die.

Josh Wilbanks, sobering rapidly after finding the body, was one of those wealthy young men who resembled nothing so much as the villain in an 80s fraternity movie, although at the moment he was so flustered he was barely coherent. Laura stayed extra calm, hoping it would rub off a little. She asked, "Just take a deep breath, Mr. Wilbanks, and tell me how you found him."

His pale face gleamed with sweat. "I was coming home after a party. My space is right across from that Corvette."

"Do you know the Corvette's owner?"

"Isn't that him under the sheet?"

Laura sighed. Whatever the guy was burning off, he still had enough in him to keep his pupils dilated. "I *mean*, did you know him before?"

"No, I'd seen him around, but we never spoke. It's kind of a status thing: the people who live here are too important to speak to each other."

"What did you do when you saw him?"

"At first I thought he'd had a heart attack or something, but when I saw all the blood, and what was missing…" He swallowed hard. "It was pretty obvious his heart wasn't the problem. So I called the police."

Laura nodded at the Mini Hummer parked across two spaces. "Tell me, are you better at staying in the lines when you color?"

It took Wilbanks a moment, then he said defensively. "I pay for both slots."

"I'm sure you do." Laura motioned one of the junior detectives over. "This gentleman will take you down to the station to make an official statement."

"I need to clean up a little first."

"We don't have a dress code. You can get in wearing anything."

The junior detective took Wilbanks' arm and led him toward the elevator, but he called back over his shoulder, "Did you find his…?"

"I really can't say," Laura replied.

When the elevator doors opened, Laura's partner Cole Slaughter emerged. A year younger and three years her junior on the force, he had neat blond hair, bright blue eyes, and a disarming smile that had suckered more than one perp into incriminating himself. He joined her and said, "Well, here's a coincidence for you. The whole security system was out for thirty minutes. Just shut itself off, then came back on. Guess what it didn't get?"

"Our killers coming in, killing the victim, or going out," Laura said wearily.

"You're almost as smart as your phone," Cole teased.

One of the crime scene technicians came over and handed them a wallet in a plastic evidence bag. "It appears the 'Vette's registration was right," the tech said. "Our boy was Arthur Shawcross."

Laura put on latex gloves and carefully removed the wallet. The driver's license confirmed the identity, but of course the photo couldn't be used as verification. "The Dodger," she said. She asked the picture, "Now who did you piss off?"

Arthur "The Dodger" Shawcross was a lawyer who represented only one reclusive client, yet in law enforcement circles he was as well-known as the ones touted in late-night infomercials. His courtroom skills were legendary; he was one of the few top defense attorneys who relished a jury trial. And he always won, usually through his rhetoric, although on occasion witnesses did change their minds about testifying, or mysteriously disappeared altogether. Still, nothing ever stuck to him or his clients. Hence his nickname.

And now, someone had killed him and taken his head.

"Was the beheading the cause of death?" Cole asked.

"Nah, he was shot," the CSU man said. He popped his bubblegum before adding, "There'd be tons more blood if his heart had still been beating when his head came off. But his head ain't the only thing missing. He's also is missing a ring."

"How do you know?"

"'Cause they damn near tore his finger off getting it."

"Wedding ring?" Laura asked.

"Judging from the indent on his finger, I'm guessing something bulkier. Like a class ring or something."

Laura looked at Cole. "I don't know many fifty-year-old men who still wear a class ring."

"Maybe a Masonic ring, then," the technician said with a shrug. "You know they run everything, right?"

"Slaughter and Slade," a woman's voice called. "Wondered who the lucky detectives would be. Should've known."

They turned toward the voice. Cole said, "Hey, Becca."

Rebecca Hutchcraft, crime reporter for the *Daily Standard*, the city's lone remaining daily newspaper, joined them. Forty, red-haired, and lean, she wore her press pass on a lanyard around her neck. Technically she wasn't supposed to be here, but she knew everyone in the 6th. "I hear through the grapevine that someone lost his head this morning. Can you confirm that?"

"How did you get here so fast?" Cole said suspiciously.

"I hit all the green lights. Have you identified the victim yet?"

"His identity hasn't been confirmed," Cole said.

"Oh, come on, Cole, by the time I get a story out, everyone will already know."

Cole exchanged a look with Laura. Hutchcraft was really one of the last of her kind: an honorable reporter. Laura shrug-nodded; nothing could be kept quiet for long these days, anyway.

"It's Arthur Shawcross," Cole said. "The Dodger. Shot once in the chest, then decapitated."

Rebecca didn't blink. "Any suspects?"

Cole waved his hand. "Right now, a whole city full."

"Think it was a pro?"

"Given where we are, I think we can rule out a random mugging."

"Thanks." Rebecca quickly scribbled notes on her pad. "Shit, guys. Does that mean there's a gang war coming?"

"If there is," Cole said, "it'll be an octopus war."

"What's an 'octopus war?'"

"Well-armed."

Laura sighed and rolled her eyes. "Cole. Damn."

"Maybe you should go over to Ratway and recruit the Lightning Girl," Rebecca said.

"Oh, come on," Cole said. "You don't believe in *that*, do you?"

"I didn't," Rebecca said. "Until she attacked those two cops last night."

10:19 A.M.

Twenty-five blocks away, in the top floor suite of an office tower near the river, Belinda June "B.J." Burr touched her Bluetooth earpiece. "Yes?"

The Kefali Corporation's senior vice president was statuesque and dark-haired, with a no-nonsense demeanor known to petrify lesser mortals. Rumor far downstream in the organization said she got the job by being *very* friendly to Stavros Kefali himself, the company's seldom-seen, never-photographed Greek owner. Those closer to the situation suspected B.J. was actually Kefali's daughter, and he kept the relationship secret for her own protection. The second allegation was closer to the truth, but missed some crucial details.

But however B.J. got her job, she occupied it with a steely competence seen as the living manifestation of Stavros Kefali's will. She wasn't mere eye candy or a powerless figurehead.

Now she listened to the voice of her personal assistant, Stefan Carr, his voice shaking. "You b-better check Channel 5's breaking news. It's about The Dodger."

B.J. brought up her internet browser and quickly navigated to Channel 5's page. The red banner across the top announced, NOTED ATTORNEY FOUND MURDERED. She clicked on the link, and it opened a video window with a live feed. A handsome Black newscaster with a microphone broadcast in front of an upscale residential building.

"...sources within the police department say Shawcross was shot from close range and may have known his assailant. Shawcross, known as 'The Dodger,' has been linked with organized crime, and those same sources warn that this could mark the beginning of a turf war between gangs."

B.J. realized she'd stopped breathing and forced herself to take slow, measured breaths. She swiveled in her chair and peered at the city through the office's floor-to-ceiling window. The bright morning sun reflected off the other buildings. The Kefali Building wasn't the tallest, but the view was still spectacular, a long clear shot down the famous boulevard that led to the oasis of Saginaw Park.

Occasionally, when she took in the scale of the bustling metropolis, she felt a massive rush of ownership, a sense that anything and anyone in the city belonged to her. Now, though, all she saw was a labyrinth of danger and betrayal, where whoever killed Artie could look up at the building and laugh at the impotent rage of the people inside.

The image grew blurry, and she wiped at the tears trying to escape. This wasn't the time. A list of necessary actions collated in her head, and the first one was easy.

Again, she touched her Bluetooth, which automatically buzzed her assistant. Her voice steady, she said, "Stefan, call Darren, please."

"I've already tried. I got his voice mail."

"Do you have his schedule for today?"

"You always said asking Darren to be that organized is the very definition of pointless."

"Well, keep at it, and as soon as you reach him, tell him I said to get his ass down here now."

"Yes, ma'am."

At that moment, Darren Flaxstone was hunched down in his parked car in the Hemingway neighborhood of Bay View, watching the bodega across the street. He'd been there for two hours already but was the kind of man who could wait indefinitely. In his experience, the other guy always cracked first.

Darren was twenty-eight years old, with shaggy hair and eyes that could go from twinkle to laser in a blink. Like B.J., his connection with Stavros Kefali went back to his childhood, which earned him entry to the boss's innermost circle. He didn't have an actual job title, but if he had, it would have been something like "Chief Troubleshooter." The Kefali organization was a well-oiled machine, and if something squeaked, Darren was sent with the metaphorical WD-40.

He watched the bodega for any sign of DeeDee Repent, a mid-level pimp who, Darren knew, had been running extremely underage girls at one of his houses. Mr. Kefali had no issue with prostitution, since it was one of his steadier income streams, but he absolutely drew the line at exploiting children. This was no secret, and DeeDee knew it. He just figured with such a large organization to manage, Kefali wouldn't notice.

DeeDee, bless him, clearly knew nothing about his employer.

And there he was, rounding the corner with a bounce in his step, projecting the confidence that was the pimp's main weapon. Unlike the cliche characters in Seventies cop shows, DeeDee wore a conservative suit and shiny, expensive shoes. His job was to convince his girls that no matter what, he was always in control. And the truth was always that he never had been.

He greeted the man sweeping outside the bodega with a fist bump and a smile. They exchanged pleasantries, and DeeDee picked up the morning paper. He did not bother to pay.

Darren got out of the car and called out, "Hey, DeeDee!"

DeeDee stopped and looked around.

Darren crossed the street through the morning traffic. At a taxi's irate honk, DeeDee spotted him and took off back the way he came, his hard-soled shoes clacking on the concrete.

"Shit," Darren muttered and ran after him.

The sidewalks were intermittently blocked by groups of people lined up for their mid-morning coffee or a late breakfast at food trucks. DeeDee barreled through them, pushing people aside and throwing curses left and right. Darren dodged into the street and ran parallel to the sidewalk in the narrow space between the parked cars and moving traffic. He quickly passed DeeDee, who was so busy checking behind him that he didn't see Darren until he ran smack into him.

"Let me the fuck go!" DeeDee screamed, thrashing.

"Calm down, DeeDee," Darren said, struggling to hang on to the squirming pimp. "I just want to talk, okay?"

"Bullshit! You're here to kill me!"

He finally pinned DeeDee's arms to his side from behind then winced as the pimp kicked backward at his shins. "If that was true, you'd be dead. Ow!"

"Help! *Help!* He's trying to kill me!"

A new voice said, "Hey, you two. What's going on?"

They both turned. A middle-aged uniformed officer regarded them with skeptical interest. Behind him, his younger partner nervously held two cups of coffee.

"Nothing," Darren said, not releasing DeeDee. "Just goofing around with my friend."

The cop was too experienced to buy this. "So your friend's idea of 'goofing' is screaming bloody murder?"

"Tell him," Darren said and shook DeeDee for emphasis.

"Yeah, man, I was just bullshitting, you know?" DeeDee said, faking it badly. "He's my best friend. Two peas in a pod, we are."

"Uh-huh. Let's see some I.D., both of you."

With no choice, especially as more people began to notice the confrontation, Darren released DeeDee and pulled out his wallet. He handed it to the officer. DeeDee pretended to look for his.

The officer sighed; the pimp wasn't fooling him. "Come on, fella. Hand it over."

"He's going to run," Darren said.

"Fuck you," DeeDee said. "I'm just looking for—" And then he took off.

"God damn it," the officer said. He dropped Darren's license and ran after him.

Darren sighed. It was pointless to be angry; sometimes things simply didn't work out. Dumb, bad luck. He'd catch up with DeeDee later.

"Why'd he run?" the younger cop said, still holding the coffee.

"He hasn't returned a library book in seven years." Darren picked up his I.D. from the sidewalk. "Did you need me for anything else?"

"Just hang around until my partner gets back, okay?"

"You know he won't catch him, don't you?"

"I know. But it makes him feel good to try."

A minute later, the older cop staggered back to them, gasping for breath, his face bright red. "Lost the… little fucker," he wheezed. He took his coffee and managed a sip. When his breathing was more normal, he said, "Now. Who are you again?"

Once more Darren handed over his I.D.

The older cop looked at it then at Darren. Suddenly his eyes opened wide. "Oh, Mr. Flaxstone," he said deferentially. "I'm sorry to bother you."

"No bother, officer," Darren said, taking back his I.D. "I know you're just doing your job."

"I hope we didn't interrupt anything too important."

"Nah. I'll find him. DeeDee's not smart enough to hide very well."

The officer, still flustered, offered his hand. Darren shook it then turned to leave.

"Hey, Mr. Flaxstone," the older cop said. "Can I ask you a question?"

"Sure."

He stepped close and spoke in low tones. "Do you know anything about that Lightning Girl over in Ratway?"

"Only what I read in the paper."

The younger cop chuckled and muttered, "Nobody reads the paper anymore."

"He's right out of the Academy," the older cop said, "so he knows it all.

Did you know she attacked some cops last night? Totally out of the blue and unprovoked?"

"I hadn't heard. Did she kill them?"

"Might as well have. Burned their dicks and balls off."

"Ouch."

"Yeah." He paused, mustering the courage for what he really wanted to know. "Your boss, uh...isn't involved, is he?"

"Absolutely not," Darren assured him. "That is *so* not his style."

He put a friendly hand on Darren's shoulder, thought better of it and said, "You have a good day, Mr. Flaxstone."

"You too, officer."

As he walked back to his car, Darren took out his phone and checked his messages. There was only one, and he quickly returned the call.

"Stefan, it's Darren. What's up?"

The junior cop scowled at his partner. "Did you scrape your knees getting up from that blow job?" he said derisively.

"Youngster, you have a lot to learn. *That* was Darren Flaxstone."

"Who?"

"Chief street fixer for Stavros Kefali."

The younger cop deadpanned, "Really."

"Really."

"He doesn't look that tough."

"Shows how little you know. You ever heard of Eyeless Archie Meadows?"

"No."

"He ran a gambling operation for Kefali, and the feds got enough on him to turn him. When Flaxstone found out, he took him out to an abandoned building, put his head in an industrial vise and squeezed it until one of his eyes popped out of its socket. Suddenly, Archie forgot everything he knew, and the feds had no case. He wore an eyepatch for the rest of his life. That's how he got the nickname."

"Why'd they let him live?"

"Because he was great advertising for what happened if you ratted on Kefali. Finally threw himself in front of a train."

"'Threw himself'?"

"So they say. And do you know what they say about Darren Flaxstone?"

"What?"

"Cross him, and he'll kill you twice."

The younger cop shook his head. "Huh."

"See? You got a lot to learn, Junior." They returned to their patrol car.

11:10 A.M.

Thirty minutes later, Darren arrived at the Kefali Building. He tossed his keys to the valet without looking. Sammartino, a former MMA fighter who was now the doorman, greeted him with, "Good to see you again, Mr. Flaxstone."

"Good to be seen, Sam," Darren said.

"Mr. Pawson is waiting to take you up to Ms. Burr's office."

"Do you know why?"

"He's afraid you've forgotten the way?"

Darren laughed, but understood that whatever the urgency, it was being kept under wraps. Sam usually knew everything.

Pete Pawson was the building's head of security, a veteran and former mercenary whose suits always appeared too small for his short, wide frame. "Hey, Darren," he said as the two men shook hands. "B.J.'s wearing a track in the carpet pacing around."

When they were alone in the express elevator to the penthouse office, Darren asked, "Do you know what's going on?"

"No, but it's some top-level shit."

Darren knew he'd get no more from Pete and was now even more concerned. When you kept your head of security out of the loop, it was a big deal.

The elevator doors opened, and Pete said, "You know the way. Good to see you, Darren."

Darren went to Stefan Carr's desk. He hadn't met this particular assistant in person before, but he was definitely of the type B.J. always picked: male, efficient, immaculate, with an earpiece and a practiced chilly gaze. "May I help you? Oh, you must be Mr. Flaxstone."

"Good thing I am, then."

"Ms. Burr said to send you straight—"

But Darren had already gone past him and through the doors into the palatial inner office.

He stopped dead at the sight of B.J. In a bad British accent he said, "Good heavens, Miss Burr, you're beautiful."

She stood and walked around the desk to him. They looked into each other's eyes for a long moment, until B.J. said, "Somebody killed Artie this morning."

"What?"

"He was shot in the parking garage of his building." She couldn't bring herself to tell him about the beheading; he'd find out soon enough.

Darren couldn't speak for a moment. "Christ, B.J., Artie and I were supposed to go fishing upstate this weekend."

"I know."

"Who did it?"

"We don't know yet. No one's claimed responsibility."

Darren swallowed hard. "Does the boss know?"

"Not yet, unless he's checked the news. I feel like I should tell him in person, either way."

"Do you want me to come with you?" Darren was one of the few allowed into Stavros Kefali's presence.

"No, I'll handle it."

"He'll be mad."

"No doubt. 'Mad' won't cover it."

"I suppose I should get to work on it, then."

"That's what he'd want."

"Stavros or Artie?"

"Both."

They fell silent, and Darren took her hand. For a moment they stood together, only their laced fingers touching. Then she squeezed his hand and let go. "You'd better get to work," she said.

Darren nodded and left.

When she was alone again, the tears threatened to pour, but her control was too strong. Right now, there was too much work to do.

Rebecca Hutchcraft sat at her desk in the *Daily Standard*'s cavernous city room. In the years before everything went online, the space would've been filled with reporters all talking at once, either to sources or each other, with the soft clack of computer keyboards in the background. Before that, in its heyday, she could only imagine how loud the thirty-odd manual typewriters had been. Now there were ten reporters left, although they were expected to do the same job as that room full, and for considerably less pay.

Rebecca scrolled through the paper's biographical information on Arthur "The Dodger" Shawcross, scanned and indexed in the paper's voluminous archive. A native of the borough known as Bowland, Shawcross had an extensive if petty juvenile record, and then sometime in his senior year of high school, he'd come under the influence of Stavros Kefali. The reclusive billionaire and alleged crime boss had, ironically, straightened out the aimless boy, sent him through law school and set him up in his lucrative, one-client practice.

"Hey, Eli," she called out to the reporter at the next desk over. "What's Greek for 'consigliere?'"

"Do I look like Google Translate?"

"No, but didn't you go to college in Greece?"

"Yes, but I didn't study Greek mobsters."

"Come on, 'consigliere' means 'adviser' in Italian, so what's the word for 'adviser' in Greek?"

He thought for a minute. "Sýmvoulos."

"How do you spell that?"

"B-I-T-E-M-E."

Rebecca gave him a hard stare, and he turned away with a laugh. She quickly typed a paragraph for her article:

Shawcross functioned as legal advisor for Kefali, defending his underlings in court, and was famous for his theatrical grandstanding both in and out of the courtroom.

She had a half-dozen similar paragraphs already composed. She'd figure out their order after she had more information from the police. In the meantime, she continued to read about the dead man.

The Dodger handled everything for Kefali: contracts, taxes, and legal affairs, along with criminal defense when one of his minions was caught doing something illicit. He had a stellar record, too: virtually no one in the Kefali organization had ever been convicted of even a minor offense, and she knew the police now considered it a waste of time to bring charges against any of them, let alone Kefali himself.

But now the Dodger was the victim. And the crime itself was far beyond the pale.

"Well, shit-fire," she drawled in the Texas accent that only came out when she cursed.

"Working on that obit on the Dodger?" asked Eli.

"Yeah. Stavros Kefali basically raised him from a pup. He never worked for anyone else. He even turned away the Marleys when they tried to poach him."

Caruso kick-rolled his chair over to her desk. "You think the Marleys smited him?"

"'Smited?'"

"I keep a list of synonyms for murder. That's today's. What about the Marleys?"

"Beats me. No incipient major organized crime trials in the works, no recent busts or arrests of anyone that would merit this kind of response. No ongoing turf wars or disputes, from any of my sources."

"This might start one."

"True enough. The Chodian Mad Dogs are always looking for an excuse to take on the big boys. And the Hawkclaws wouldn't mind expanding their territory."

"Wonder if it's payback?"

"If it is, it's not for anything recent."

"An old grudge then?"

"Could be. But against who? The Dodger himself, or Stavros Kefali?"

"Or a third party trying to *Yojimbo* in."

"What the hell is a '*Yojimbo*'?"

"Japanese movie. A samurai comes into a town run by two gangs and gets them to wipe each other out. That was last Wednesday's word."

"Anyway, there's no evidence of that yet, although I guess I shouldn't rule out anything."

"Might help if you talked to Kefali directly."

"Fat chance. He's like JD Salinger or Howard Hughes."

"Salinger and Hughes both opened up to teenage girls. So to speak."

"I thought it was the other way around."

"Can't help you, then." Caruso kicked back to his own desk.

Rebecca gazed at her screen. If the police made a quick arrest, then it was likely a small-time thing, a mugging or robbery gone askew. If not, it meant something bigger. Cops always knew more than they could prove, and a *whole* lot more than they said.

"Hutchcraft!" her editor, Ransom Wade, called from his office.

She went to his door. "Yes?"

"There's a press conference down at city hall this afternoon."

"About the Dodger's murder?"

"What? No. The cops wouldn't get that excited about some crooked lawyer. This one is about the Lightning Girl and those two cops she messed up."

"Are they planning to admit she's real?"

"I don't know. But I want you there. Two o'clock."

"I'll be there."

Back at her desk, she worked even more quickly, wanting to get this story done and filed before the press conference. After weeks of categoric denials that the mysterious Lightning Girl even existed, she wondered what made the police suddenly willing to talk about her.

She threw a paper clip at Eli to get his attention. "Any word on what exactly happened between the Lightning Girl and those two cops she killed?"

"She didn't 'kill' them. If you believe the apocryphal word on the street, patrol officers Morlette and Hogan were shaking down every hooker and junkie on their beat in Ratway. And they weren't exactly willing to discuss it if someone couldn't or wouldn't go along."

"If she didn't kill them, what did she do?"

"She burned them. In a place men would prefer not to get burned."

"Oh."

"Indeed."

"If you've got all the background, why aren't *you* covering the press conference this afternoon?"

"Ah, whatever they say won't amount to shit. They'll never acknowledge Morlette and Hogan as anything other than virtuous brothers in blue, injured in the line of duty by a vigilante lunatic."

"You still didn't tell me why you weren't covering it."

"Because Ransom flipped a coin, and you lost."

She looked over her shoulder at the editor, who just shrugged.

"Hell of a way to run a fish-wrapper," she muttered as she returned to her desk.

The building manager—a man far too polished for the slang term "super"—unlocked the Dodger's condo. "No, you wait here," Laura said when he moved to precede her and Cole inside. They left the manager under the watchful eye of the uniformed officer standing guard.

In addition to their latex gloves, they wore blue disposable covers over their shoes. Gun drawn, Cole turned on the light to illuminate a tasteful, expensively decorated living room with a great view of the city. The Kefali building was dead center, and he wondered if that had factored in the Dodger's choice.

"Police officers," Laura announced, pulling her own gun. "Anyone here?"

"He lives alone," the super volunteered.

"People have been known to have guests," Cole said. "And I bet they have to sign in, don't they? Would you check for us, please?"

He rolled his eyes in annoyance. "Sure. Just a moment." He took out his phone and spoke in low tones to someone.

Cole walked into the kitchen and opened the garbage can; it was only half full, and he saw nothing suspicious.

The one out-of-place thing was a pizza box on the marble countertop, with three slices remaining. The pizzeria was Little Lexi's, in Bowland. "Looks like you can take the boy out of Bowland but not the other way around," he said. "Wonder how much he had to pay to get it delivered all the way here?"

"*I* wonder if he's involved in those new luxury towers going up in Bowland?" Laura asked. "They're displacing a lot of low-income people. Maybe that's the motive."

"Possibly," Cole said. "But someone pissed about the changing face of their neighborhood wouldn't likely have either the smarts or the juice to take down the security system here."

"Good point."

"Excuse me," the building manager said. "No visitors have signed in since last week." After a moment, he added, "Do you need me to stay?"

"Why, are you in a hurry to leave?" Laura asked.

"I have other tenants who are still alive, you know."

"Sure, go. Just be where we can reach you if we need you."

When he'd departed, Cole said, "I like him. People say I have no taste, but I like him."

The bedroom door was closed. Laura knocked and said, "Hello? Police. Anyone in there?"

There was no answer.

They stepped to either side of the door and put their backs against the wall. "Whose turn?" Cole asked.

"Yours."

"On three."

He silently mouthed the countdown, then turned the knob and stepped aside so Laura could kick open the door. As she moved away, Cole jumped into the room, crouched low.

The bedroom was just as tastefully decorated. The bed itself was king-size, the covers in disarray. Laura checked the bathroom and said, "Clear."

They put away their weapons. "Nothing out of the ordinary," she said, "for a rich lawyer."

"Well, maybe that," Cole said as the bedclothes began to move. As they watched, a bare feminine foot extended from beneath the comforter.

Laura pulled back the covers.

A small Asian woman, dressed in a skimpy black nightgown, gasped and curled into a ball. She looked vaguely dazed, as if coming off some high.

"Just relax," Laura said. "We're police."

She stared from one to the other. Then, in a move as fluid as quick-silver, she rolled out and landed on her feet, in a fighting stance.

"Whoa, whoa," Cole said. He held up his badge. "*Jǐngchá.*"

She did not move, and her body did not waver.

"Not Chinese, I suppose," Cole said.

"Or she is, and she doesn't care," Laura replied. She holstered her weapon and stepped out of her shoes. "Block the door."

"Oh boy," Cole muttered and backed up.

The Asian woman attacked first. Cole couldn't quite follow Laura's moves, but they ended with the Asian woman on the floor and Laura upright and not even winded. She quickly handcuffed the woman and hauled her to her feet.

"Call some of the uniforms to get her," she said to Cole.

"You know it always makes me nervous to see you do that," Cole said as he summoned help. "What if you run across somebody tougher than you?"

"At my funeral the rabbi will throw my corpse into the crowd and whoever catches it will be the next to die."

The Asian woman, whose eyes were now clear, said in perfect English, "You're Mossad?"

"No, I just hang out with them from time to time," Laura assured her.

"I wish I'd known that," she said sincerely.

"Who are you?"

The girl said nothing.

"I bet she's a pro," Cole said.

"I don't know what it is that makes you so stupid, but it really works," the girl shot back.

"Look, we're not here to bust you," Laura said. "We're just looking for clues about who killed the Dodger."

Her eyes widened and instantly filled with tears. In a tiny voice, she said, "Artie's dead?"

"He is. I'm sorry."

She would've collapsed to the floor if Laura hadn't had a good grip on her arm. Her wail of sorrow filled the bedroom.

Two uniformed officers appeared and took her into custody. Laura stepped back into her shoes and gave Cole a wide smile. "Whew," she said.

"I'm curious," Cole asked. "Was that difficult?"

"No, but just because she didn't expect it. She knows her stuff, too."

"You can tell after fifteen seconds of fighting?"

"I could tell by the way she got out of bed."

They methodically went through the rest of the apartment, careful not to disturb any potential evidence. Nothing was suspicious or out of the ordinary.

"The CSU people can finish up here," Cole said. "Maybe we'll have better luck down at his office."

"It's in the Kefali building, right?"

"Oh, yes. The hottest real estate on the East Side."

11:30 A.M.

The shooter and Delilah sat in the window of a Starbuck's directly across the street from the Dodger's building. They watched police cars go into the parking garage, followed by an ambulance, none with sirens. They knew there was no urgency.

"Wonder what cops are doing in there?" Delilah asked.

"First, they'll check the garage, then go up to his apartment," the man replied. He was known as "Apocalypse Joe"; no one knew his real name. "Then to his office. Eventually they'll come here and canvass the staff, asking if they saw anything unusual. They'll also probably watch the security footage."

Delilah nodded, sipped her latte, and reached down to confirm that her satchel, now fuller than before, remained at her feet.

"It's still there," Apocalypse Joe said, amused.

"I know that," she snapped defensively. "When's our meeting to turn this over, anyway?"

Apocalypse Joe checked his watch. "Not for a couple of hours yet. Just relax. Are you hungry?"

"No. I'm impotent."

"Impatient," Joe corrected.

"What did I say?"

"Impotent. Which can't apply to you."

She snickered. "I guess not. I meant, 'impatient.'"

He grinned at her over his own cup. "I know. That's one of your best qualities, did you know that?"

She stuck out her tongue.

"I'm being totally serious," he continued. "That's why we make a good team. Your spontaneity balances out all my careful planning. Without you, I might never stop planning long enough to actually do anything."

"You don't think I'm *too* impatient?" she said like a demure young girl.

"Never. You're just the right amount of impatient."

This made her smile. He reached across the table and took her hand.

In the dimly, dimly lit study of an old, old house in the borough of Pigeon Hill, a young man prematurely gray with worry and stress sat behind a heavy desk and listened to his cell phone. When the caller finished, he said, "I see. Thank you." He ended the call.

Harrison Marley, Jr., known as "Harry the Less" behind his back, was not quite thirty-five. He was slender in the way of the genetically blessed and dressed in the kind of expensive casual clothes that the rich wore with such ease because they'd never worn anything else. He was also the acting head of the Marley crime family, the Kefali gang's biggest, and only serious, rival.

"Monte!" he called, and a moment later his second-in-command Monte Rissell joined him. Monte was big, middle-aged, and solid in the way only the naturally strong can pull off. He had a scar in his left eyebrow, a gold tooth, and a list of murders as long as his arm. He'd never been arrested for any of them.

Harrison asked, "Did you hear the news?"

"Since I have to ask, 'about what?' I guess that means 'no,'" Monte said.

"Arthur Shawcross was killed this morning."

"The Dodger?"

"Yes." Harrison sat back in the heavy leather chair.

Monte's eyes narrowed. "Boss, did we—"

"I didn't order it. And as far as I know, we had nothing to do with it. Do you know anything?"

"I wouldn't go behind your back, boss."

"Not even if my father told you to?"

"Not even then. You're the man now, not him."

Harrison nodded. "Do you think Kefali will believe we weren't involved?"

Monte shrugged. "Been a long time since we've had a real war. Everybody seems satisfied with the way things are. They'd have no reason to think it was us."

"So, if we didn't order it, who did?"

"Maybe nobody. Maybe it has nothing to do with his job, and it's one of those wrong-place-wrong-time things."

"No," Harrison said with certainty.

"How do you know?"

"Because they cut off his fucking head and took it with them."

That gave even Monte pause. That was old-school trophy-taking, something the city hadn't seen in decades. "Someone wanted to send a message to old Stavros, all right."

Harrison spun his high-backed office chair slowly, deep in thought. "Would the Dorestines do anything like that?"

"Not likely. They're strictly minnows in the shark pond."

"How about the Chodian Mad Dogs?"

"Street punks. So are the Hawkclaws."

"Somebody muscling in from outside?"

Monte shrugged. "News to me if it is."

"Well, then go find out who," Harrison said impatiently. "And what they want. If it's going to be a war, I want to know which side I'm on."

"Will do, boss." He left without another word.

Harrison looked up at the ceiling. Two floors above, his father lay in bed, a nurse continually by his side. And although the nurse was supposed to report any time the old man made a call or had visitors, Harrison knew his father could easily do an end-run around her, either with bribes or threats. The old man was devious to a degree Harrison could only aspire to, and in his lucid periods, he was as dangerous as he ever was.

Dangerous enough to start a war? Harrison wondered. Had his father ordered this hit, just to stir things up before he checked out for good?

Harrison wouldn't tell him about the Dodger, at least not yet. But he would try to head off any conflict with Kefali by taking care of whoever had ordered it done. It was the kind of conciliatory gesture the old man would never make, fearing he'd appear weak. But Harrison understood that sometimes, it made economic sense to appear a little weak. The enemy of my enemy, after all.

Harrison looked out the big bay window at the mansion's grounds and punched a number from memory, one that he'd never written down, into one of the pile of burner cell phones he kept in his desk.

11:47 A.M.

B.J.'s personal cell phone buzzed, and she picked it up from her desk blotter. She didn't know the number, so she answered guardedly, "Hello?"

"We didn't do it," Harrison said.

"Oh?" B.J. said neutrally. She recognized the voice but wasn't going to give anything away.

"No. At least, not under orders from the top. I can't speak to any loose cannons yet."

"So you *could* have done it?"

"I'll let you know what I find out. I just don't want a war to start over this until we know what's going on. That won't do either of us any good."

"I agree."

"What does Mr. Kefali think?"

"He's never *wanted* a war. The cost-to-income ratio is all wrong. But he won't take this lying down. If you're going to do something, I'd do it sooner rather than later."

"I understand. I'll be in touch." He ended the call before she could respond.

B.J. put down her phone. The word must really be spreading, if Harrison the Less felt the need to blow the dust off this seldom-used back door. She hadn't really thought the Marleys were behind it; the city had been peaceful for over five years, the territorial lines accepted without conflict and enforced without excess bloodshed. The only disruption had been the appearance of the strange female vigilante in Rattaway, and no one was sure she was even real.

"Ms. Burr?" Stefan said in her ear.

B.J. touched her Bluetooth. "Yes?"

"The police are here. They want to search Mr. Shawcross's office."

"Do they have a warrant?"

"No."

They could certainly get a warrant, B.J. knew, but that would place her, and the organization, in an adversarial relationship when there was no reason for it, save the fact that the Kefali Corporation was, under all the trappings, organized crime. But they weren't investigating the organization, they were trying to solve a murder. So it made sense to cooperate, up to a point.

"Send them in," she said, and stood.

Laura and Cole came through the double doors. The office, designed to dazzle with its space and view, did its job; for a moment the two detectives were speechless. Then Laura said, "Ms. Burr, I'm Detective Slade, this is Detective Slaughter. We're investigating the murder of one of your employees, Arthur Shawcross."

"Yes, I know," B.J. said. "We heard about it, though no details. We're all very upset. What happened?"

Laura and Cole exchanged a look, then Laura said, "He was shot once in the chest. Point blank range. In the parking garage of his condo."

"My God," B.J. said, not having to fake the sadness or surprise. "That place is a fortress. How did they even get in?"

"We're working on that."

"We'd like to look over his office," Cole said. "We can get a warrant, but we assume you'll want to help."

"Of course."

"We'd also," Laura added, "like to speak with Mr. Kefali."

"I'm afraid he's out of the country," B.J. said.

"Have you told him about the murder?"

"Yes. He took the news hard. He's known Artie since he was a child. It's almost like losing a son."

"When will he be back?" Cole asked.

"Not for some time. He has a lot of business in Europe."

"So, he's upset, but not enough to make him cut his trip short?" Laura asked.

"That's an awful thing to say," B.J. said.

"I apologize. I don't suppose you can get him on video conference? It'll save us the trouble of getting a subpoena, and you the trouble of having to respond to it. With your best lawyer out of the picture, it could get messy." Laura smiled with taunting faux innocence.

B.J. and Laura looked at each other hard for a few moments. To Cole it resembled the staring contest back at Shawcross's apartment before the women started fighting. Then B.J. said coolly, "Have a seat, then. I'll see if he's available."

"What's the time difference?" Cole asked.

"He's seven hours ahead," she said as she sat and began typing.

Laura and Cole took the two luxurious leather seats against the wall, far enough from the desk to allow private *sotto voce* conversation. Cole leaned over and said, "Seven hours puts him in western Europe."

"If she told the truth," Laura murmured back. "For all we know, he's in the back room."

B.J. said, "Detectives, I've got Mr. Kefali. Please." She stood and gestured at her now-empty chair.

Laura took the seat, and Cole leaned over her shoulder. On the screen, Stavros Kefali looked out with sad eyes. He sat in what appeared to be an expensive hotel room, an Eastern European cityscape visible in the window behind him. He wore a lightweight linen suit, open at the neck. He had curly black hair, pale skin, and a handsome unwrinkled face reminiscent of some ancient statue, all full lips and straight nose. He almost seemed effeminate, but when he spoke his voice was unmistakably masculine. "Officers," he said in unaccented English. "I'm sorry I can't be there to answer your questions in person. I'm quite upset, as you can imagine."

"You have our condolences," Laura said. "I'm Detective Slade and this is Detective Slaughter. I'll get right to the point: did Mr. Shawcross have any enemies that you know of?"

"He was a lawyer," Kefali said. "I suppose anyone he ever beat at trial could be considered an enemy. A lot of those are prosecutors with the district attorney's office, you know."

"We'll check into that," Laura said.

"What about other..." Cole pretended to seek the right word. "Organizations similar to yours?"

Kefali gave a wry smile. "I appreciate your diplomacy, Detective Slaughter. But my business is entirely legitimate. I can't say the same thing about my competitors, of course. And yes, I'm sure they bear grudges. But those would be against me, not my legal representative."

"He was more than that," Laura said. "Some people say you treated him more like your son."

"That's certainly the place he occupied in my heart," Kefali agreed. "I won't lie, his death angers me. But I'm not interested in any kind of revenge. That would be bad for business, and also wouldn't bring Arthur back. I trust the police to find his killers, and the legal system to prosecute them. I only hope they turn out to be people who simply picked the wrong victim at random."

"You said, 'they,'" Cole said. "What makes you think there's more than one?"

"I don't know, obviously," Kefali said smoothly. "I meant 'they' in the general sense."

"When do you plan to return to the United States?" Laura asked.

"As soon as possible. I have business to tidy up here first."

"I hope you'll let us know when you're back."

"Certainly. And if I can help in any way before then, please contact me through Ms. Burr."

"Thank you," Laura said. The call ended with three distinctive beeps.

Laura stood and faced B.J. "Thank you as well, Ms. Burr."

"As Mr. Kefali said, anything we can do to help."

"We'd like to see Mr. Shawcross's office now," Cole asked.

"Of course. And I'm sure you realize his client files are still confidential."

"Of course."

"Then follow me."

12:04 P.M.

Apocalypse Joe and Delilah walked down a narrow, trash-strewn alley between two tall buildings. Even on the ritzy East Side, there were places like this, where the city's sanitation workers never went and the sun never quite crested the buildings enough to penetrate to the ground. That kept it perpetually dim, damp, and a few degrees cooler than the surrounding streets. And just like any dark place, it brought out the insects, both the six- and two-legged kind.

He tapped on a faceless metal door and said, "It's Joe."

"Joe who? And if you say 'Joe Mama,' I'll open the door shooting."

Delilah pushed in front of him. "You don't recognize him? He's the Vladimir Putin of puttin' a boot in."

"In what?"

"Your ass! He's the Ed Gein of horror and pain, the Al Capone who'll kill you to the bone! He's Apocalypse Joe!"

Joe grinned and shook his head. Quietly he said, "I liked that Ed Gein one."

She beamed. "Thanks."

"I'm here to see Mummadabba," Joe added.

The door clanked open. A large bald man loomed over them, checked down the alley both ways, then allowed them inside. He closed and bolted the door behind them, and settled back onto a tall stool, resuming some game on his phone.

The hallway smelled of fresh paint and disinfectant, and the lights were harsh fluorescents. They did Delilah's pasty complexion no favors. Joe knocked at a closed door marked OFFICE, then turned the knob.

Inside, cheap shelves held rows of expensive, specialized electronic equipment. There were no visible prices or descriptions: if you had to ask what it was or how much it cost, you couldn't afford it in either sense. The illicit pop-up would be gone by this time tomorrow, only to appear somewhere else for a day.

Behind a small desk sat the man known as Mummadabba. He was of Hispanic descent, somewhere between twenty and forty; it was hard to be more specific due to the extensive tattooing that covered his neck up to his jawline. He wore a vest above his khaki trousers, exposing the tattoo sleeves extending to his fingertips. The motifs were all American: eagles, Harleys, baseball, strippers. Johnny Cash and Willie Nelson looked up from the backs of his hands.

"Hey," Mummadabba said genially, with a slight accent.

"Hey back," Joe said.

"A little bird told me you did your job this morning."

"Smart bird."

"And how did it go?" Mummadabba asked, as casually as if inquiring about a first date.

"Fine."

To the girl, Mummadabba asked, "Would you agree with that, Delilah?"

"Yeah, we were in and out in five minutes."

"And the items I requested?"

Joe tossed Mummadabba the ring taken from the Dodger.

Mummadabba turned it over in his fingers. "Perfect."

"What does the symbol on it mean?" Delilah asked.

"Oh, if I told you that, it would *so* complicate our relationship."

"So you don't know, either?"

Mummadabba smiled enigmatically. "Now, what about the *other* thing?"

Delilah put the satchel on Mummadabba's desk and unzipped it. Arthur Shawcross's blank, gray face stared up through the zipper's teeth.

Mummadabba winced and turned away. "Okay, okay."

Delilah zipped it back up. "And now our stuff?"

Mummadabba unlocked a cashbox on the desk beside him, put the ring inside, and took out a bunch of debit cards rubber-banded together. "Here you go. Ten thousand dollars on each one. Untraceable."

Joe took six and gave four to Delilah. "Pleasure doing business with you, Mummadabba. The Mendicant was right about you." He turned to go, then stopped. "Oh, and by the way, I know that people who traffic in cliches like to say, 'the first rule of assassination is to kill the assassins.' I've already taken care of the trail on my end, so in case you had something that obvious in mind, if anything happens to me, the press and the cops will get all the information they need to trace this right back to you."

Mummadabba scowled. "That's harsh."

Joe shrugged. "It's a harsh world."

In the alley outside, Delilah asked him, "'If anything happens to you'?"

"What?"

"In there. You said if anything happens to you, they'll get a world of hurt. What about me?"

"Didn't I say, 'us'?"

"No. You said 'me.'"

"I meant the royal 'me.'"

"Uh-huh," she said doubtfully. Then her mood made a one-eighty and she asked, "Can we go shopping now, Joe?"

"Sure."

She jumped up and down like an excited child. When they reached the street and headed toward the subway, she took his hand and danced around, drawing stares.

1:37 P.M.

After lunch, Darren Flaxstone lounged against the brick wall at the back of the East Side's Precinct No. 1 building, grateful for the shade. Crushed cigarette butts and the plainly disconnected security camera spoke to the fact that no laws would ever entirely eliminate smoking, especially among the people who saw the worst the city had to offer on a regular basis. The uniformed officers and plainclothes detectives stood with their own, puffing away with impunity, like the tough kids behind a 1970s high school.

Darren, in a suit and tie, looked enough like a stressed-out lawyer grabbing a smoke before an arraignment that he didn't seem out of place. He carried a briefcase packed with dummy files, so even if it was opened, it would back up his disguise. He checked his phone; his contact should've been here ten minutes ago.

A side door opened, and a hulking figure in hospital scrubs came out. Enoch Wiswell looked around, saw Darren but showed no apparent recognition. He was an assistant coroner and had been an inside source for the Kefali organization for years. He leaned on the wall beside Darren and said casually, "Warm enough for you?"

"It'll do 'til warm comes along," Darren replied.

"Can I bum a smoke?"

"Sure." Darren passed him the pack; he took out both a cigarette, and the folded bundle of money from inside.

Wiswell lit his cigarette and said, in a low voice, "I assume you're here about the Dodger?"

"Had a chance to look him over?"

"Yep. He was shot first, at close range with a small-caliber handgun. Bullet penetrated the heart, then lodged in the spine, so we have it, in case by some miracle the murder weapon shows up." He paused. "Do you know about his head?"

"What about it?"

"It was removed post-mortem."

Darren went cold. "They took his *head?*"

"Yeah."

Darren kept the true extent of the reaction off his face. "Anything else?"

"They took a ring, too."

The chill down Darren's spine grew arctic. "What kind of ring?"

"I don't know, man. I just saw the mark on his finger where it should've been, and the tear on the knuckle where it came off. Bigger than a wedding band, smaller than a Super Bowl ring."

Darren was glad he'd taken off his identical ring as part of his disguise. He, Artie and B.J. had all received them as gifts from Stavros Kefali, indicating they had been trusted with his biggest secret. "Anything else?"

"Toxicology won't be back for a few days, but there was no overt sign of drug or alcohol use."

Still without looking at him, Darren said, "Okay. Thanks, Enoch."

Enoch tossed his cigarette to the pavement, crushed it and went back inside the building. Another door opened, and a half-dozen shackled prisoners emerged and shuffled toward a waiting prison bus. Darren knew none of them.

As he walked back to his car, Darren mulled what the coroner had told him. Decapitating Artie's corpse might have been anything from a gang initiation to a bored serial killer but, combined with taking the ring, it confirmed this was no mere random crime. No, whoever stole the ring knew *exactly* what they were taking; and by also taking Artie's head, they were sending a very specific message.

But not just anyone could pull all this off. It required specialized skills, not only in killing, but in security, stealth, and escape. The era of simply snipping the phone lines to disable alarms was long gone; whoever did this understood how to hack into systems, bypass firewalls, and shut things down without leaving a trace. Theoretically, it could've been done from anywhere in the world with wireless access; but killing a man and beheading them had to be done on-site, in person. So he was pretty sure the alarm had also been disabled locally.

And if that was true, he had a good idea where they'd gotten the hardware, and software, to do it.

"Darren," a woman's voice called. "Darren Flaxstone."

He looked up. Rebecca Hutchcraft strolled toward him, smiling. He mentally kicked himself for being so preoccupied he hadn't even noticed the reporter until it was too late to slip away. *Smooth move, Flaxhead.*

He said casually, "Hey, Becca. What brings you down here?"

"Press conference."

"About the Arthur Shawcross killing?"

"Is that why you're here?" She looked him up and down. "Disguised as an ambulance chaser?"

"Disguise? I promise, I *am* an ambulance chaser," he said with a grin.

"Yeah, you might put someone *in* an ambulance," she shot back.

Rebecca and Darren's respective jobs caused them to cross paths over the years, and on occasion—when it suited his boss's plans—Darren fed Rebecca some exclusive tidbits. But neither of them had any illusions about the other. "Now that's harsh," he said, and put a hand over his heart as if he'd been wounded.

"Uh-huh," she said dryly. "Right. Well, I'm not here for the Dodger. Everyone's being super-tight about that, anyway. I'm here for the Lightning Girl."

"The one over in Ratway?"

"Are there other ones? Because *that* would be a story."

"Ha. No, I just assumed that was all rumors. You mean it's for real?"

"Real enough that a couple of cops got their dicks burned off."

"Not your best metaphor."

"What metaphor? That's literally what happened. So now the police have to say something, and they'll probably announce a special task force and a tip line and all the other bullshit they do when they need help but won't admit it."

"You're cynical, Becca."

"And you're not? So what are you doing here, then?"

"Contesting a parking ticket."

"Did you win?"

"Of course I did. I've got more excuses than a pregnant nun."

She narrowed her eyes at him, and he could practically hear her deciding if his presence here was worth pursuing. Finally, she said, "Well, it's been good to see you, Darren. Take care."

"You, too."

As she walked away, Darren realized he was actually shaking. Men with guns trying to kill him barely raised his pulse but talking to a smart woman? That forced him to watch his every thought, and *that* was exhausting.

Somewhere a truck beeped as it backed up, and the sound brought him back to the moment. He looked at the faces of people passing on the sidewalks, at the cars, and up at the skyscrapers. Millions of people surrounded him, but they were mere citizens, oblivious to most of what happened, lost in cell phones or video games or whatever their distraction of choice. They had no idea what sort of people dwelled in their midst, or what those people were capable of.

Whoever killed Artie, though, understood that. And then Darren realized something else: this was a professional, and a pro with that kind of certainty would want to mark it. And *that* meant Darren knew yet another way to find him.

2:00 P.M.

Rebecca made it a point to remember the name of every cop she met, and thanks to that she had a wide network of officers and administrators who could get her information that would never escape official lips. So she was prepared if the chief took questions.

The media briefing room was packed with people, mostly camera crews for broadcast and online news sources. A row of uniformed officers lined three walls, and in front of the fourth was the platform and podium for whoever was speaking. They had that grim angels-of-vengeance look that always popped up when something happened to one of their own.

Police Chief Frederic Fairbourne—"Fair Freddie," as he liked to call himself—stepped up to the podium, a tablet tucked under his arm. The chief of detectives, the head of the police union, and the mayor's assistant all followed and stood behind him, bolstering his authority with their own.

"Ladies and gentlemen," Fairbourne said, "I've got a prepared statement, and then I'll take a few questions."

He put on his reading glasses and looked down at the tablet's screen. "Last night, two officers with the 89th Precinct in Rattaway were severely injured by a criminal vigilante known as the 'Lightning Girl.' Although both will recover, they will have permanent disabilities and could have died." He looked up with grim, serious eyes. "This will not stand, not in

Rattaway, not anywhere in this city. To bring this criminal and any accomplices to justice, the mayor has authorized me to establish a special task force, based out of the 89th, consisting of a dozen full-time officers. We're also offering a $100,000 reward for any tip that leads to an arrest and conviction. The people of Rattaway can rest assured we will not stop until this criminal is caught."

So far, so predictable, Rebecca thought.

Fairbourne removed his glasses. "Now I'll take your questions."

A dozen voices rose at once, and Fairbourne pointed to the sexy blond news anchor of Channel 8. "You first, Astrid."

Astrid Tuttle said, "Chief, you mentioned 'accomplices.' Could you tell us more about that?"

"We don't believe this woman acted alone. We don't believe she could have taken down two experienced officers by herself." He pointed again. "Derek."

Derek Barnard, crime reporter for Channel 4 who specialized in exposes of corruption, said, "Chief, do you have any idea *why* these two particular officers were targeted?"

"We believe they were simply the first officers to cross paths with the criminals."

Derek couldn't repress his gotcha face. "What about the accusations that they were shaking down sex workers and drug dealers?"

"That's unfounded gossip, Derek, and frankly, I'm surprised at you."

"So, there's no truth to those accusations?"

"None at all. Officers Morlette and Holman are veterans of the force and good family men." He next pointed at Rebecca. "Ms. Hutchcraft?"

"Chief, the story on the ground is that whoever this woman is, she's able to somehow control electricity with her bare hands. Care to comment?"

"We don't believe she's some sort of mutant superhero, Ms. Hutchcraft," he said condescendingly. "She's just a criminal with an original schtick. She only comes out at night, when it's a lot easier to hide the smoke and mirrors. Likely she used some kind of modified taser or stun gun."

"But why?" Rebecca pressed. "What's the *point* of it all?"

"I tell you what: I'll let you ask her yourself, when we've arrested her."

Fairbourne moved on, but he was too experienced to let anything important slip. Rebecca had gotten what she needed, anyway: an admission that the cops had no fucking clue who or what this Lightning Girl was. But although they'd never admit it, they did know *why* she did what she did. Those two cops with barbecued dicks believed they were untouchable; this woman had shown them that they, and by extension any other dirty cops, definitely were not.

She didn't envy the girl, whoever she was. The retribution, she knew, would be both swift and terrible.

2:28 P.M.

The Ink Ink Nudge Nudge tattoo parlor nestled in the bottom floor of a packed tenement building in the Johnson Loop neighborhood of Bay View. The owner, Wingo, and his artists did top notch work, but only by referral; if you walked in off the street, you were told just as quickly to walk out. They specialized in gang signs and kill tallies for people who paid cash and liked their names forgotten.

The electric bell over the door chimed as Darren entered, and a heavily tattooed woman with bright blue hair emerged from the back of the shop through a curtain. When she saw him, she smiled. "Hey, Mr. Flaxseed. What are you all dressed up for?"

"For you, Crespa," he flirted. "Who did you think?"

"Ha! If it was for me, you'd be in leather."

"Maybe under all this, I am."

She giggled. "Then I hope you powdered up, otherwise you'll chafe something fierce."

He leaned on the front counter. "Mr. Kefali has a problem," he said softly, "and I think you and Wingo can help me out."

"You know we will if we can."

"Did you hear about the Dodger this morning?"

"No."

"Somebody decided he needed to lose about ten pounds of ugly fat. So they cut off his head."

Her eyes opened wide, and her surprise seemed genuine. "Oh, my God."

"You guys do all the kill tatts for everyone in the city who might have the balls to pull off this particular hit. Who's made an appointment?"

"Let me see," she said without hesitation, and stirred the mouse to awaken the computer. He came around the counter to peer over her shoulder.

"Loco Peretti is on the books, but that's a standing one, every six months. Not one he made recently." She scrolled some more. "Bobby Mavole is coming in tomorrow, but he's been overseas doing security work, and doesn't get back until tonight.

Darren tapped the screen. "What about this 'A. Joe'?"

"Never heard of him. I didn't take this appointment; Wingo must have. Either he knows him, or he's a vetted referral."

"He has an appointment tomorrow morning at ten."

"That's as much as I know, too. You'll have to ask Wingo."

"Is he working?"

"Yeah. Go on back."

Darren went through the bead curtain and followed the buzzing noise to one of the small rooms. The odors of green soap and A&D ointment mixed in the air. Not wanting to startle Wingo as he worked, Darren said quietly, "Hey, it's Darren Flaxstone. I need to talk to you."

"C'mon in," Wingo said, and gently pulled the needle away from his client.

Wingo had grown up on the West Coast, where he'd learned at the inky feet of some true masters. At the moment, he was working on the ass of a young woman who was either too stoned, or too terrified, to be self-conscious about showing so much skin. Another man, apparently her companion, glared from a stool in the corner. He was big, bald, and used to having his size do most of the work. Darren nodded at him, then said to Wingo, "Probably better if we do this in private."

"Who the fuck are you?" the bald guy rumbled and folded his arms.

Wingo sighed. "Don't get your balls twisted, all right? I'll be right back."

"You just going to leave her like this?"

Wingo inspected the girl. She was now asleep, drool pooling on the pillow. "I don't think she'll notice."

He led Darren out into the hall. When they were relatively alone, Darren said, "Tell me about A. Joe."

"Any Joe in particular?"

"The shooter you're inking tomorrow."

Wingo looked around, reassuring himself that they wouldn't be overheard, and spoke even lower. "That's Apocalypse Joe. How'd you hear about him?"

"I think he killed the Dodger this morning. And cut off his head."

Wingo was so startled he actually gasped. "No shit?"

"No shit. And I'd like to have a word with him."

Wingo thought it over. "My clients are supposed to be confidential. You of all people should appreciate that."

"They're not confidential from Mr. Kefali. Remember who keeps you in business."

It wasn't said as a threat, but Wingo knew it was one. He paid protection to Kefali every month, and in return he was never raided, and had no competition within ten blocks. And part of that payment was information.

"He's from out of town," Wingo said at last. "I didn't know him, either. The Mendicant referred him to me."

"The Mendicant," Darren sighed, as if the name were a curse. "I should've figured he'd be involved. Do you know who hired *him?*"

"No. He never gives anything away for free, man. He just told me the guy's name, and we set up the time."

Darren knew that was accurate; among his many, many other illicit schemes, the Mendicant often positioned himself as a middleman and broker for large-scale crimes needing specialized personnel. "So who's paying the bill? Not for the tat, for the job?"

"You'll have to ask the Mendicant."

"Then I'll do that. Oh, and Wingo? If the Mendicant knows I'm coming, I'll know where he heard it."

Wingo held up his hands. "Hey, I'm above the fray. I'm just an artist."

"Keep it that way," Darren suggested with a smile that wasn't a smile.

B.J. stood in the doorway of Arthur Shawcross's office, on the same floor as her own. It was filled with the kind of heavy, leather-bound books that, to a non-lawyer, represented the weight and power of "the law." She'd seldom seen him reference them.

She asked, "How's it coming?"

Cole and Laura, now wearing bright green latex gloves, paused in their methodical search. "It's a lawyer's office, all right," Cole said. "Everything here is either innocuous or missing."

"How do you know something is missing?" B.J. asked.

Cole smiled at her. "Because everything here is innocuous."

"We'll need his passwords, too," Laura added.

"I'm sorry, I don't have access to those. Only he does…did."

Laura said, "Convenient."

"Mr. Kefali trusted him."

"And so did everyone else?"

"Mr. Kefali is the final word."

"That doesn't answer my question."

B.J. scowled very slightly. It was clear she hated having to be polite to these people who'd invaded her space, especially on a day like today. "Isn't Arthur the victim here? It sounds like you're treating him as a suspect."

Laura came around the desk. "Either Mr. Shawcross was killed in a random act of violence by someone who didn't know or care who he was, or he was killed *because* of who he was. Until we know for sure about the former, we're assuming the latter. If he was a decapitated dentist, we'd be asking the same questions at *his* office."

Whatever B.J. really thought about this was hidden behind her practiced bland smile. "Of course. It's just all so much to take in. It's late, and I know you missed lunch. I'll have something sent in. Please, continue."

When she'd gone, Cole let out a low whistle. "My dad used to say, 'all women are the same, only some of them don't show it.' She's definitely got something. Any idea what?"

"Practice," Laura said dryly.

2:44 P.M.

B ack in her office, B.J. locked the door. She touched her Bluetooth and said, "Call Internal Security Program." When the automated voice answered, she said, "Begin protocol Burr Five."

There was no immediate change, but she knew a jamming signal now flooded her office that would disrupt any monitoring devices, including the company's own, and set up a scattering field on the huge windows that prevented anyone from peering inside with electronic lenses. No one outside her office could possibly know what was happening within it.

When the voice assured her the protocols were in place, she went to the wall behind her desk and put her hand against a particular spot on the paneling. The hidden palm reader confirmed her identity, and that section of wall slid aside. She stepped through, and it closed behind her, the seam invisible.

The small space beyond was filled with tiers of monitor screens, all aimed at the center of the room. They showed everything from the building's cameras to reruns of *Law and Order: SVU*. The sound, though, was muted on all of them, so that all she heard at first was the equipment's cumulative hum.

From the center of the room, Stavros Kefali's voice said, "Nicely done earlier, B.J. Where did you tell them I was?"

"I wasn't specific. Only that you were seven hours ahead."

"Good. They're searching Artie's office, I see." One screen displayed a high, wide-angle shot that showed Laura and Cole at work. "They're certainly efficient. Their files imply they're honest as well."

"There's nothing for them to find, of course," B.J. said. "Anything incriminating is password protected. Not even their best techs could crack it." After a pause she added, "You look tired."

"It's almost time for the Festival," he said, as if that explained it.

"I haven't had a chance to say it, but I'm really sorry, Stavros."

"Thank you. I'm sorry as well. I know you two were close. Any word from Darren yet?"

"No."

"Inform me immediately if he finds out anything."

"Of course."

"And now, the Festival. How is our special guest?"

"Enjoying his time with the five young men he selected."

"Good. And he has no second thoughts?"

"None." She turned to go.

"B.J., wait," Kefali said. "It can't be a coincidence that this happened so soon before the Festival."

"The police think it might be. They think it could simply be a mugging gone wrong. Totally random. Just bad luck."

"Then why are they searching his office?"

"Because they don't really believe it."

"Neither do I."

After a moment, she volunteered, "Harrison Marley reached out to assure me it wasn't them."

"Which Harrison Marley?"

"The Less. Senior's on his last legs. He suffers from a variety of things that you don't recover from."

"Do *you* believe they weren't involved?"

"There's nothing that points toward them. And no motive."

"Except to show us we're vulnerable so close to the top." He paused. "I want you to assure our people that the Festival will still go on as planned."

"I'm sure none of them doubt that."

"All the same, put out the word. Let's pre-empt any doubts. The Festival is too important."

She nodded. "Yes, sir." Then she left.

Once the panel closed, she said, "End protocol Burr five." There was no visible change, but she swore she could *feel* the barriers disappear. She sat down behind her desk and slumped wearily, exhausted by the need to appear unflappable for the staff.

She hadn't always been that way, of course. When Arthur Shawcross discovered her, she was twelve years old, living on the streets of Bowland and running a scam in which she lured grown men into alleys, then threatened to scream she'd been molested if they didn't give her their money. It was surprising how many men capitulated at once, and she often wondered how many child molesters were walking around free.

But then she tried it on the Dodger.

"Mister!" she called. "Hey, Mister, come here! I need some help, please!"

He wore a trenchcoat over a suit that cloudy day and carried a briefcase and umbrella. He appeared for all the world like a young investment banker on his way to a power lunch, and to B.J., those were the easiest marks of all. They were so unprepared for threats that they gave up almost at once.

Arthur paused, looking for the source of the voice. He stood still as the oblivious pedestrians went around him, most of them engrossed in their phones.

Now that she'd gotten his attention, B.J. set the hook by showing herself just enough to lure him off the street. In the dim, shadowy space between buildings, they might as well have been on another planet. Even the sounds of the avenue mere feet away were muted.

"Down here," B.J. called and ducked out of sight. From where she hid, she could see his silhouette reflected in the glass door of a discarded microwave she'd precariously balanced against a dumpster.

"Maybe you should come here instead," Arthur said warily.

"I can't," she groaned. "I'm hurt."

"Uh-huh." Arthur moved cautiously toward her. "Hurt how?"

"It's my leg. I think he broke it."

"Who's 'he?'"

"Please, I'm bleeding!"

By this point B.J. realized Arthur was no easy mark, so she readied the switchblade she kept for emergencies. It was old, and the rusty mechanism slowly snapped it open like a windshield wiper on low. But it still terrified most people in Bowland, especially when wielded by a wild-eyed girl in an alley.

Arthur had almost reached her hiding place behind the concrete steps that led up to a blank door. Then a cat scurried from a nearby bag of trash, jumped up on the microwave and shifted it enough so that she could no longer see him. B.J. waited, and when he didn't appear, she said pitifully, "Mister, I can't move. I'm really hurt."

There was no response. She was certain she hadn't heard him withdraw. Was he just standing there, frozen in indecision?

"Come out of there, you little monster," he said directly above her.

She found herself staring into the barrel of a pistol six inches from her face. He stood on the steps, the gun steady in his hand. B.J. realized she'd made a serious mistake.

"Drop the knife," Arthur ordered, and she did. He gestured with the gun, and she crawled into the open and got to her feet.

He looked her over. "How old are you?"

"Nine," she lied.

"Try again."

"Twelve."

"That's more likely. What's your name?"

"Mary."

"Well, it'll do for now until you tell me your real name. Who do you work for, Mary?"

"Myself."

"No pimp?"

She raised her chin in defiance. "I'm not a pro."

"That's good to know. What are you?"

"Self-employed."

He barked out a laugh. "Do you know who I am?"

"Some pedophile asshole who's going to rape me and kill me?"

"No. I'm Arthur Shawcross. They call me the Dodger. I work for Stavros Kefali."

Even on her bottom-feeding level of society, B.J. knew who *that* was. She no longer had to fake being scared. "L-look, Mister, I just wanted to rob you, not—"

"Shut up," he ordered, and she did.

He walked around her, examining her closely, never lowering the gun. *For someone who's* not *after my ass,* she thought, *you sure are giving me the eye.*

Finally he said, "I'm going to put this gun away, Mary. Then I'm going to walk to the end of the alley and call a cab. If you come with me, I'll feed you, get you some clean clothes and explain some things you'll find very interesting. I give you my word, I won't lay a hand on you. Nobody else will, either. So you have to decide quickly if you trust me or not."

She heard the gun click as he decocked it. He walked past her, picked up his briefcase and umbrella, and strode off without looking back.

She thought it over until he reached the end of the alley and stepped out into the open. Then she ran after him, calling, "Hey! Wait up!"

And that decision led directly to this moment.

She sat down at her desk. What would she do, she wondered, if the Festival didn't go on as planned, and something happened to Stavros? She ran the business, but when it came right down to it, she depended on Stavros for every crucial decision. Would she be able to hold the organization together on her own? Or would she be the first one to fall in the chaos?

2:54 P.M.

As he removed heavy law books from the shelves, Cole said, "What's the most disgusting thing you ever saw?"

Laura looked up from the filing cabinet she was searching. "I saw a woman at an outdoor music festival go into a port-a-potty barefoot."

"Which one?"

"Third from the end."

"No, which festival?"

"Bonnaroo."

"Really?"

"You surprised I didn't say Lilith Fair?"

"No, I'm surprised you went anywhere that crowded."

She shrugged. "I was young. I was experimenting. Why did you ask?"

"Because this is the most boring search I've ever done in my life, and if I don't watch it, I'll just fall asleep and keel over. I mean, what's the point? The guy's a lawyer, he's not going to just leave incriminating things lying around."

"He's the victim, Cole, not the perp."

Cole started to reply, but something he found made him stop. "I think I spoke too soon. Now *this* is weird."

Laura immediately joined him. "What?"

He held a two-foot-long tube made of some sort of light, gleaming porcelain, with gold-plated stoppers at either end.

"Where did you find that?"

"Behind some books, inside a niche in the shelves. There was a little door that was supposed to slide down and cover it, but whoever took it out last forgot to close it."

Laura gently turned it over and held it close to her face. "I think this is ivory."

"Isn't it illegal to have that?"

Laura gave him a deadpan look. He shrugged.

She carefully shook it. "Nothing loose inside."

She undid one stopper, reached inside and felt a rolled-up piece of something like stiff cloth. Carefully she tugged on one edge and pulled out a roll of some sort of paper, faded and fragile with age.

"What is it?" he asked. "A poster?"

"Dunno." She touched one corner and gently bent it away from the roll. "This isn't paper. I think it's papyrus."

"Papyrus? Like the Egyptians used?"

"Yeah."

She took it to the desk blotter and gently unrolled it. It was covered with lines and symbols that appeared to be Greek.

"It must be some kind of antique," Cole said, using a stapler and other objects to hold down the corners. "Our guy collects Dead Sea Scrolls. The rich really *are* different."

"Just a minute." Laura took out her phone and snapped a quick picture. Cole put the papyrus back in its holder and returned it to its hiding place.

Stavros Kefali, as bored watching the detectives search as they were searching, turned away from the Dodger's office video feed to watch a teaser for the next episode of the *Real Housewives in Prison Makeover Special.* If he'd seen them find and replace that scroll, so many things would have been different.

3:13 P.M.

Mummadabba rode his vintage '73 Norton Commando motorcycle through the Bowland traffic and ignored the irate honks and shouted insults. If they wanted to go fast, then the assholes shouldn't drive cars; he'd gone seven blocks before the ones that first berated him had reached the next light.

Tied securely atop the gas tank in front of him was a Styrofoam cooler that now held Arthur Shawcross's head, ice packs above and below it. Mummadabba had honestly never seen a severed head before, and he didn't spend a lot of time looking at this one; he was supremely glad he'd worked up the nerve to close its eyes.

The area's gentrification had spread even farther than the last time he visited, and his destination was in one of the old buildings newly renovated into offices and apartments. He pulled around to the back, to an employee entrance monitored by a security camera.

His parked his bike and waited with the cooler under his arm. Finally, the door opened, and he went inside. The only other way out of the room was a single elevator, which he entered. He pushed the lone button.

Three floors above, the door opened on the company headquarters of Wide Justice, Inc, a software and game design company. The entire floor was one big open room, painted white and filled with light from huge windows. Young designers rode Segways and scooters, played basketball and took turns trying out the latest VR software. The few who noticed Mummadabba paid him no real mind.

On the far side of the room stood the lone enclosed conference room, its ceiling open above the divider walls. He knocked on the door and called out, "Helen Pappas?"

A female voice said, "Enter," and he did.

The founder and president of Wide Justice was a woman in her thirties with the black hair, olive skin and brown eyes beneath thick brows that marked her Mediterranean ancestry. She looked up from the gaming maps spread on the table as Mummadabba entered.

"I've got what you want," Mummadabba said and held up the cooler.

"Close the door," she said. When they were isolated, she continued, "I saw on the news that he'd been killed. No one's mentioned his head."

"See for yourself." He put the cooler on her desk.

She opened the lid, removed the cold pack, and gazed at the face. The Dodger's features were now slack and rubbery, almost like a bad special effects prop. To be certain, she pushed up his lip and examined his teeth. Then she sighed with, if not relief, at least with acceptance.

"Was I right?" Mummadabba asked smugly.

"Yes." She replaced the cold pack and closed the lid. "And the killer?"

"Paid and sent on his way. After cleaning up."

Helen's eyebrows rose. "He cleaned up the Mendicant?"

"I assume, although I haven't heard anything. I wish he'd checked with me first. The Mendicant was useful."

"It's against my better judgement to leave your shooter alive, too."

"Like I said, if the people I hire start turning up dead, I won't be able to get anyone to work for me."

"And I agreed, despite my misgivings." She paused. "And the ring?"

"Right here," he said and took it from his pocket.

She turned the jewelry in her fingers as its gems sparkled in the light. Her expression, normally so hard and serious, softened for a moment. Then she sighed and opened a briefcase on the table. Mummadabba tensed reflexively, but she did not withdraw a weapon. Instead, she took out a sealed envelope. "Here you go. If you're smart, you'll invest it back into your business and not spend it on whatever vice you favor."

He tucked the envelope inside his jacket. "If I wasn't smart, we wouldn't be working together."

"That's true."

"What's the big deal about that ring, anyway?"

She just looked at him. Her gaze made him nervous, then downright scared. "Forget it," he mumbled and looked away.

"Goodbye, Mummadabba."

"Until next time, Chief." He gave her a half-salute and departed.

He knew better than to ask *why* she wanted the Dodger's head, or what she hoped to gain by antagonizing Stavros Kefali. If a gang war did erupt, the less he knew made it that much easier to stay out of it.

Mummadabba had no loyalties; or, that is, he was loyal to everyone. He worked in Kefali territory and paid the percentage without question; he also did work for the Marleys, and made sure they got their tribute. If he crossed into the Chodian Mad Dogs' area, he made sure they knew about it and gave them whatever they asked. He prided himself on never making a ripple on the underworld's scummy pond.

4 :15 P. M.

Darren was not the first to note the parallels between his own boss and the Mendicant. Both took in unwanted children, gave them a sense of home and family, and taught them a purpose in life. The difference was in that last item; Kefali's apprentices learned useful, and profitable, skills that helped them as well as the organization, while the Mendicant's were taught only the dodge, and benefited only the Mendicant.

Like Mummadabba's mobile electronics shop, the Mendicant's base of operations moved around, and it took Darren until late in the afternoon to finally find him. He'd settled into an old service station in Ratway near the area's last functioning subway stop, the 17th Avenue/135th St. line. From here, his crew of children and teens could quickly move to any part of the city. All around the station, half-abandoned public housing from the last century awaited either arson or a wrecking ball.

Ratway had never been the best part of the city, but over the last two decades it had been essentially abandoned by a city government more concerned with gentrification and a massive, ever-increasing debt. Its inhabitants were undocumented immigrants, junkies, petty criminals, the mentally ill, and the chronically poor. Of the two dozen people killed by the city's law enforcement in the past year, sixteen were on this battered side of the Smoke River. Potholes marred the streets and avenues, traffic lights hung unlit, and after dark the real predators roamed the shadows.

Darren tried the station's door, but it was locked. He wiped the dirt away and peered through the window into the pitted, dented garage. He could make out nothing. "Mendicant?" he called. "It's Flax. Need a word."

There was no reply. All those empty windows in the buildings around the station made him very nervous. Although Artie had been killed with a handgun, at close range, it didn't mean his killer didn't also have a sniper rifle locked on Darren right now. Also, four men had gathered at the corner and watched him with silent interest. He took his Colt from its holster, held it low and close, and tried again.

"Mendicant! No bullshit. Let me know you're in there."

There was still no answer. He bent and tried to lift the repair bay door, but it was locked or rusted shut.

He crept through the debris to the back of the station, where he found an *Employees Only* door obscured by a green dumpster. He carefully pulled on the door's handle, and it opened.

He was greeted by a strong surge of smell, and a loud buzzing sound. He recognized both. His stomach wrenched tight as he went inside.

It was worse than he'd imagined. A half dozen old mattresses had been arranged around the old oil change bay, and dead children lay on them. Each had been killed with a shot to the head at close range from a small-caliber weapon, some in the forehead, some in the back. The buzzing sound came from the flies that swarmed their wounds.

A lone adult lay face down near the door to the office, one hand outstretched. Unlike the kids, dispatched with one quick shot, he'd been hit a half-dozen times: in each calf, in the thighs, and finally in the back.

"You cowardly bastard," Darren seethed, realizing the Mendicant had been shot while running away, leaving his charges to their fate. Impulsively, he kicked the dead man in the side, dislodging a cloud of irate insects.

Calm the fuck down, he told himself. *Think it through.* There was always the chance that this had nothing to do with the Dodger's death, but Apocalypse Joe's trail led here, and Darren was willing to bet his hunch. There was one easy way to find out, of course. He put away the Colt and pulled out the Cold Steel Tac II knife he kept in a sheath on his right ankle. He examined the Mendicant's wounds, determining which would be the easiest to cut open. He chose the one in back of the left thigh and expertly dug out the bullet.

"You *killed* them," a voice said behind him.

Before he even fully formed the thought, Darren grabbed the intruder by the neck and placed the bloody knife blade against the jugular. Only then, when he saw the wide, terrified eyes, did he realize he held a child: a boy of about eight or nine.

He pulled the knife away but kept a grip on his neck. "No, I didn't. I'm trying to find out who did, though. I needed one of the bullets that killed the Mendicant." He shoved the boy up against a wall. "Don't run away. Understand?" He nodded. Darren released him. "I was coming here to see the Mendicant. I found them like this."

The boy said nothing. With his eyes open so wide, he looked like an anime character.

"What's your name?" Darren asked.

"Sparrow," he whispered.

"Sparrow, I'm Darren. Do *you* have any idea who might've done this?"

He nodded.

"Who?"

"A man and his girlfriend visited yesterday. The Mendicant sent us away so they could talk."

Darren wiped his bloody fingers on a piece of old newspaper. "Did this man have a name?"

"'Pork Lips Joe,' I think."

He put the bullet into a sealed plastic bag, which he stuck back in his pocket. "Could it have been 'Apocalypse Joe'?"

"Maybe."

Darren cleaned the knife's blade with the same old newspaper. "What did he look like?"

"I don't know. Average."

"White, Black, Hispanic, Asian?"

"White." Sparrow pressed himself back against the wall.

"Can you remember anything else about him?"

"No." Darren was about to ask more, but the boy continued, "The girl he was with, though. She was really weird."

"How so?"

"She was all…jumpy."

"Like she was afraid?"

"No, like she had some problems." Sparrow touched his temple to indicate where those problems dwelled.

Darren took out his lighter, touched it to a corner of the bloody newspaper, and watched it quickly burn. "Do you know why they wanted to see the Mendicant?"

"He was hooking them up with someone else. I don't know who. He did that a lot."

Darren stomped the last of the paper; the whole place would probably go up just as fast if there was a stray spark. "Okay, thanks. Can I—?"

He looked around, but Sparrow had already vanished. He ran to the door in time to see his nimble form zip out of sight around a corner. He thought about chasing after him but decided it wasn't worth the effort. He doubted the boy could tell him anything more.

"Good luck, kid," he muttered then headed back to the subway.

4:29 P.M.

W hat time is it?" Laura asked wearily. Searching an office, especially a big one like this, was both tedious and time consuming.

"Four-thirty-ish," Cole answered. He had the thankless job of pulling out every law volume on the huge bookcase and flipping through the pages to see if anything was hidden. So far, he'd found nothing.

Laura stopped for a minute and stepped close to Cole. Quietly she asked, "I don't want to sound paranoid, but did anything about that video call from Kefani look odd to you?"

Cole, without stopping his search, replied softly, "He looked sickly, didn't he? Pale complexion, dark circles under his eyes."

Laura began searching the shelf below his. Experience taught them to assume there were cameras and microphones in the office, so they each spoke softly, with as little lip movement and eye contact as possible. "That wasn't what jumped out at me. It looked like the scenery behind him was a green screen."

"Why would he need to do that?"

"Because he's not where he says he is?"

"Then why not just sit in front of a wall? Hotel paneling in Europe looks pretty much the same as it does here. We'd never know."

"I don't know, and that's what's bugging me."

"You think he had something to do with the murder, so he's overcompensating?"

"That sounds out of character."

"Yeah." She sighed in annoyance. "Fuck it, let's finish here and go home."

6:16 P.M.

Rebecca tucked her laptop into her bag and put it over her shoulder. Once again, she was the last to leave the press room. Seeing all the empty desks drove home her conviction that she'd been born fifty years too late; had she been around during the seventies and eighties, the era of Watergate and Iran/Contra, she would've been like a hog in slop. Now, even though she'd just turned forty, she felt like a dinosaur. The "informed public" was a myth; people believed what they believed, even when all the evidence was against it. Anything they disagreed with was dismissed as propaganda for the other side.

As she headed toward the elevator, Ransom Wade called through his open door, "Rebecca, can I speak to you?"

She detoured to his office. "What's up, boss?"

"That was a good piece on the Dodger's slaying. I assume you're staying on it?"

"Of course. Why?"

"Where does that leave your story on the Lightning Girl press conference?"

"You make it sound like she's announcing a new line of shoes or something."

"She's the biggest thing in town, you know."

"Ransom, seriously. There's no such thing. It's somebody's elaborate practical joke, or art project, or something. It's definitely not someone who can harness electricity like a superhero."

"What about those two cops?"

"You mean the two *crooked* cops taken out by someone who thinks it's funny to make it look like the Lightning Girl did it?"

"The police are taking it seriously."

"Yeah, and in Texas the police take it seriously that they can arrest you for owning more than six dildos. I wouldn't put it past the cops to have made the whole thing up to cover their boys' bad behavior." She paused. "Ransom, why are you so interested?"

"She sells," he said with a shrug. "Our circulation is down for the fourth month in a row."

Now she understood: Ransom was worried about his job. With three kids in school and a wife unable to work due to fibromyalgia, he needed it for the health insurance alone. And he was too old to start over as a beat reporter somewhere else. "Wow," she said seriously.

"Yeah," Ransom agreed.

"The press conference story's in your inbox. It's not much, but…look, even though I'm sure it's not for real, it doesn't mean there isn't a real story somewhere in this Lightning Girl nonsense. Let me do a little serious digging."

Ransom's eyes showed relief, even though his voice said, "Don't do me any favors. I don't want a half-assed expose."

"I promise I'll expose my whole ass."

"All right. And sooner is better, before some podcasting SOB scoops us."

"Got it," Rebecca said.

She rode the elevator down alone, deep in thought, pondering these two stories. The murder of Arthur Shawcross was real, with a dead body, a police report, and a missing head. The Lightning Girl, however, was a mere urban legend supported only by blurry phone videos and rumor. There was more hard evidence for the Loch Ness monster. Still, she knew Ransom was right; when their initial story about the sightings in Ratway had come out, they actually sold out for the first time in her memory. Online subscriptions went up as well. She had no explanation for this, except that a female vigilante who hurled electricity was so novel in the real world that people simply had to know more.

The elevator dinged open, and she crossed the lobby to the main doors.

Laura and Cole drove away from the Kefali building, Shawcross's desktop computer in a large evidence bag on the backseat. It was astounding, and a little suspicious, that B.J. let them take it without a warrant; she'd even offered it before they asked. They had no real hope of getting into its files; the department was notoriously behind the times on software crime. But they had to make the effort.

"If this turns out to be a regular old mugging," Cole said, "I'm going to be downright peeved that we wasted all day."

Laura, behind the wheel, said, "No, you won't. It's procedure to investigate all the angles. We'll feel annoyed but justified."

"There's an epitaph for you. 'Annoyed but Justified.'"

The evening traffic grew thick, and it was impossible to go more than a few car lengths at a time before being stopped by a light. The detectives were both used to it, though, and neither paid it any mind. It gave them both a chance to think.

"It's a message," Cole said out of the blue.

"Taking his head?" Laura asked, on the same wavelength. "Of course it is."

"And it's old school. Gangs used to send each other body parts as trophies back in the day. Remember that woman whose head was hacked off with a machete a few years ago?"

"*Almost* hacked off. I was a junior detective on that case, so I saw it. It was still attached, but just barely."

"Okay, almost," he conceded. "What about that time they mailed a guy's heart to his brother?"

"That's apocryphal."

"What's his religion got to do with it?"

She looked at him sharply, unable to believe he was so clueless, only to be greeted by a wink. "Anyway," he continued, ignoring her scowl, "it's got to be a message specifically for Kefali."

"You think his head will turn up at Kefali's office?"

"I'd almost guarantee it. It may be there already."

They pulled into the garage beneath the 6th Precinct. Although the 1st Precinct was the figurehead, where the chief and commissioner both had their offices, the 6th was no slouch: it was modern and clean, as befitted an East Side bastion of law and order. Laura and Cole had transferred in from different outlying precincts and were made partners after each had done time with an established detective to learn the ropes. Not to solve crimes—both had amply demonstrated that skill—but how to get along with the rich and powerful. Even when it was open-and-shut, there were no simple crimes on the East Side.

Cole carried the computer, and Laura the boxes of the Dodger's files from the trunk. At the elevator, a uniformed officer nodded at them when he emerged and asked, "New computer? Fancy."

"We thought we'd bring the tech boys a challenge," Cole said.

"The Cube Farm? They'll just use it to play *Overwatch*. Have a good one."

When the elevator doors closed, Cole asked, "What's 'Overwatch'?"

"A game we don't have time to play," Laura said.

On the seventh floor, they carried the evidence through a door marked *Forensic Lab*, and underneath that, *Electronic Crime*. They'd called ahead, so Max Fenn, the IT guy they knew and trusted, waited for them. He led them to a conference room, away from the other cubicles, with an empty table waiting for the computer.

"It's a Pearl," Max said as he looked it over, sounding like a kid who'd just discovered a lost treasure. "I've only read about these."

"Should we be impressed?" Laura asked.

"You sure as hell should," Max said. "This is the most secure hardware out there. It costs more than all three of us make in a year, combined. Not only is the hardware designed to foil every common trick to break into a computer, the standard software sends viruses back at the attempted hacker."

"I assume you know some *uncommon* tricks to break in?"

He gave her a sly grin. "I sure do. I'll call you as soon as I know something." He ran a finger along the top edge of the screen. "Soon, my little friend, you'll learn who is your master."

Cole followed Laura up the stairs to the next floor and the regular forensics department, where she dropped off the box of paper files with the evening shift examiners. The sun had fallen behind the buildings so that the view through the windows was gray with dusk. Back at the elevator Laura said, "It's my night with the car. Can I drop you somewhere?"

"Nah, I'll take the train. I like having the time to shift gears before I get home."

"Okay. Tell Anna I said hello."

"I will."

Cole got out on the ground floor and gave Laura a farewell wave. He said good night to the desk sergeant and emerged onto the street. The sky was red and yellow to the west, and the city lights already stood out against the encroaching night.

A block from the station, he passed a busker. The man looked about fifty, wearing overalls and singing in an exaggerated country twang. His guitar case held a few bills and a lot of change. Cole thought nothing of it until, stopped at a crosswalk, he caught some of the lyrics.

> *"I want a woman in the kitchen, and some kids in the yard*
> *I want to eat when I'm hungry and fuck when I'm hard*
> *I want a gun that shoots 500 rounds a minute*
> *And big ol' boat with an Evinrude in it..."*

Cole went back to the man. He just stared until the man stopped playing and said, "Fella, you're making me nervous. Do you have a request or something?"

"I'm curious. Is that really what you think of women?" Cole asked.

"You a feminist?" the busker said, in the same way Joseph McCarthy might've asked, *Are you a Communist?*

"Yes, I believe women are people," he said dryly.

The busker smiled. "Look, it's only a song. I have to get people's attention, you know? I mean, I'm competing with the whole city."

"Do you have kids?"

He nodded. "And grandkids."

"Is this how you want them to remember you? As the old asshole who thinks women should be barefoot and pregnant?"

"Fella, you're taking this song much more seriously than I do."

"Maybe you should think harder, then," Cole said. He tossed a dollar into the guitar case and resumed his walk.

On the train platform, he texted Anna that he would be late, that he had to work surveillance until midnight. She texted back a sad face but didn't argue. She was used to his hours by now.

When his train arrived, it wasn't the one that led home. Instead, it was the Rattaway 17th Avenue/135th St line that led straight into the heart of the most dangerous part of town.

6:48 P.M.

Rebecca Hutchcraft's husband Mike put a plate of lasagna on the table in front of her. "It's a little spicy, like you like it," he told her. The little boy at the table started to say something, but Mike pre-empted him. "And I have plenty of non-spicy for you and your delicate palate, young man."

"Thank you," Rebecca said genuinely. "This is exactly what I need today. Sorry for getting here so late."

"Did something happen?" Mike asked as he took his seat.

"Did you see a dead body, Mommy?" their son Tim asked eagerly.

"As a matter of fact, I did. And no, I won't tell you about it, at least not while we're eating."

"*Thank* you," Mike said sincerely, while Tim let out a disappointed sigh.

Rebecca felt a rush of warmth. All her doubts about marriage, career, and parenthood now seemed like the dreams of a silly girl. Mike took care of the house, and Tim, with hardly a complaint; if he missed his hedge fund career, he never let on. Tim, nine years old, was both bright and blessedly normal, a child who needed very little correction and discipline.

Unless he's fooling us both, Rebecca thought, remembering the occasional mischievous glint in her son's eye.

But she had to admit that a big part of her happiness was finding

Mike, who had no problem becoming the stay-at-home parent and leaving her free to work. Some of her friends teasingly questioned his masculinity, but if she'd been so inclined, she could've assured them it had made no impact; in fact, now that he wasn't constantly stressed and overwhelmed, he was actually more demonstrably virile.

Now she caught him watching her inquisitively. "What?" she asked.

"You seemed like you were somewhere else," he said.

"Yeah, maybe you were remembering that dead body," Tim said through a mouthful of lasagna.

"Don't talk with your mouth full, or I'll be looking at *your* dead body," she teased. "I'm sorry, guys, but I need to do some more work tonight. I thought I didn't, but it's going to gnaw at me unless I do, and I won't be any fun at all. Will you be too mad at me if I go back out?"

"Of course not," Mike said. "You do what you need to. Tim and I will be fine."

She stood, came around the table and kissed him. On its own, it went from a simple peck to a warm, deep kiss, prompting Tim to moan, "Oh, come *on*, yuck. I'm eating here."

She kissed Tim on top of the head. "I expect a good report on you from Dad."

"I'm an angel," he said, with an exaggerated eye bat.

7:15 P.M.

The old fish market in Bowland had been closed for three years, its clutter and smell no longer desirable to the gentrifying dilettantes. At one time, it had employed almost one-third of the borough's population, but now its buildings stood empty as the zoning board sorted through the backhand payments and legal chicanery to clear the property for development.

But like nature, crime abhors a vacuum. So these deserted buildings, with their huge freezer rooms, berths for ships to deposit their cargo, and loading docks for tractor-trailer trucks had found a new life in the smuggler's trade.

Although she ostensibly ran a gaming company, possibly the most insular of industries, Helen Pappas also had connections that would surprise and appall her Millennial and Gen Z software teams. They guided her to the right part of the sprawling market, where a small crew unloaded and cataloged illegal elephant ivory and rhinoceros horn prior to it being moved to more secure storage. The workers, mostly men, uncrated the pieces and aligned them on a long table still reeking of the generations of fish gutted on its surface.

A big man with a shotgun blocked her path. "Downtown's that way, sweetheart."

"I'm looking for Lobotomy Eyes."

"Look somewhere else."

Helen met the man's gaze with her own. Something passed between them that left the man suddenly cowed, and he stepped aside. Helen strode into the building until she spotted the tall woman with spiky white-blond hair.

"These tusks go to the Denver buyer," the woman instructed a group of men. "Hold the rest until I get back to you."

"Lobotomy Eyes," Helen called. "I need to speak to you."

The woman turned to her. She had a real name, but Lobotomy Eyes suited her perfectly. She had a pale face and big, round, expressionless brown eyes. Some rumors about her said that, if you got close enough to see under that hair, you'd find an actual lobotomy scar, but as far as Helen knew, no one had ever verified that and lived to tell.

Lobotomy Eyes was a finder: whatever you wanted, if you wanted it bad enough, she could track it down for you. How expensive it was depended on how difficult it was to find, and how quickly you wanted it. Someone clearly wanted a stash of black-market ivory.

She stepped away from the table and said flatly, "Helen Pappas."

"I have another job for you."

"I'm listening."

"Do you know the Mendicant over in Ratway?"

The glassy stare that gave Lobotomy Eyes her name didn't change. "I've heard of him."

"He runs children. I need a half-dozen of them. Male or female doesn't matter, but they should all be virgins."

"Planning a sacrifice?"

"And if I am?"

Lobotomy Eyes shrugged. "Where should I bring them?"

"Call me when you have them." Helen passed her a card. "Twenty thousand per. Unhurt."

Lobotomy Eyes tucked the card away. "When?"

"As soon as possible. If it's more than two days, I can't use them."

"I'll be in touch." And with that she returned to her sorting as if she'd never left. Helen turned and strode out, wishing all transactions could be so trouble-free.

8:05 P.M.

The boy Sparrow stood on the roof of a fifteen-story building watching the sky fade to gray, then black. He had no idea what else was in the building below him, but he knew that the roof sported the one thing no other building did—an ancient television aerial, its aluminum shaft bent but not broken. It was a touchstone for him, in a city where everything else was always changing.

He had escaped the massacre at the garage by the thinnest of margins, and for a long time, he didn't know what to do. His best friend Corvus, almost his big brother, always ran interference for him at times like this, when he was too freaked out to make any kind of decision. But Corvus was gone; he wasn't among the dead, at least, but neither had he made any effort to get in touch.

"Look," Corvus told him once, as they huddled in a dumpster to evade some excessively diligent uniformed officers, "you have to get over this whole freezing-up thing."

"I just can't choose," Sparrow protested. "Do I run or fight? If I run, which way?" He began to cry.

Corvus smacked him on the back of the head. "Stop that. Let me tell you a story. Before you came along, there was this boy, Heron. Big eyes, great pout, could make anybody take him in. But he couldn't make a goddamn decision. One winter day he's running away from another gang across the park, and he takes a shortcut across one of the ponds. It's winter, right? So it's frozen. He gets halfway across, when he sees another bunch from the gang coming at him from the opposite direction. Can't go forward, can't go back. What do you think happened?"

Sparrow shook his head. "He ran sideways?"

"That would've been smart. No, he stood there trying to decide for so long, the ice cracked and he went under. They didn't find him until spring." Again, he slapped Sparrow on the back of the head. "The point is, *any* decision would've been better than no decision. Understand?"

Now Sparrow looked back on those words. Some things were just obvious: the Mendicant was the only parent he'd ever known, and his death could not go unanswered. But there was little a ten-year-old boy could do on his own.

Any decision is better than no decision.

"If you're up there," he said to the sky, "I could use your help. I don't have any way to pay you, but I'm quick and smart and I'll owe you a favor."

Under a clear night sky, lightning flashed nearby. Sparrow turned hopefully toward it, certain his prayer had been heard. After all, he hadn't been praying to God.

TWO NIGHTS BEFORE THE FESTIVAL

9 : 3 6 P . M .

The man in the driver's seat passed the joint to his friend. The marijuana had been soaked in liquid PCP; the euphoria helped settle their nerves.

Still, Antonio said from the passenger seat, "I don't know if I can do this."

"Don't be a pussy," his friend Seamus snapped.

"This is some serious shit, though. Killing a whole family."

"Look, man. That bitch disrespected me. A bitch don't do that and live."

"Then let's just kill *her*, man. Why her kids, too?"

"Because I don't leave fucking loose ends." Seamus checked the rearview mirror to make sure the block was empty, then reached under his car seat and pulled out a Glock. "You ready?"

"Fuck, no. Let's just get out of here."

Seamus grabbed Antonio by the hair. "Look, you say you're my friend, right? Then act like it. After what she did, she has to fuckin' *die*. People don't laugh at me and walk away." He got close to his friend's ear. "All you have to do is film it, man. I'll ice 'em all."

Antonio saw the cold glint in Seamus's eyes and realized he had no choice. Seamus had always been the big dog, and Antonio the puppy following behind. Antonio took out his phone and sighed in defeat, "All right, then. Let's go."

Seamus got out and immediately tucked the gun into the waistband of his jeans, the way he'd seen the gangsters on TV do it. He winced as the bulky weapon ground against his hipbone and shifted it to a more comfortable position. Antonio followed, so sick to his stomach he could barely walk.

The rundown lobby and stairwell were deserted. At the fourth-floor landing, Seamus opened the door and peered down the hall. The fluorescent ceiling lights flickered, giving the decrepit hallway an even sicker sheen. Shafts of yellow light leaked from under the apartment doors, while muffled voices and music came from behind them.

Seamus gestured for Antonio to hold up the phone. When he did, Seamus slunk into a tough-guy pose and said, "We're here to teach that Gonzalez bitch a lesson. Woman don't disrespect me and live. She thinks hiding in Ratway means I can't find her?" He flashed the sign of the Chodian Mad Dogs, the gang he was desperate to impress. Then he motioned for Antonio to follow.

At apartment 412, Seamus put his ear to the door. The bass blasting from a room across the hall drowned out everything else. Light shone under the door and through the peephole. That meant she was home.

"Wait, wait," Antonio whispered urgently. The phone's screen had suddenly gone all distorted, then blinked out. "Your phone just died."

Seamus was too far into the moment. He stepped back and kicked open the door. "Who do you think you are, bitch?" he yelled as he burst in, gun held sideways the way he'd seen on TV.

But except for a single ceiling light, the apartment was bare. No furniture, no pictures, nothing.

The sight froze both boys in their tracks. "What the hell?" Seamus said to no one. "Where the fuck is she?"

"She told me about you," came an unfamiliar voice. "So I helped her relocate."

From the darkened kitchen stepped a woman in a dark gray hoodie over a black baseball cap, jeans, and combat boots. Only her lower face was visible.

"Who the fuck are you?" Seamus demanded and pointed the gun at her.

"You must be Seamus," she said. "She did a pretty good job of describing you. Said you thought you were ten percent better looking than you actually are."

Seamus stepped forward and put the barrel of the gun against the woman's head. "I'm a goddam Chodian Mad Dog! Who the fuck are you, bitch?"

Her mouth turned up in a smile.

"Ow!" Seamus screamed, dropped the gun and jumped back.

"What happened?" Antonio cried nervously.

"Fucking thing *shocked* me!"

And then they both understood who they faced.

"Oh, shit," Antonio said.

The Lightning Girl held up one hand, fingers spread. Little arcs of electricity rose and popped between them. "You come down into Ratway thinking you're tough? Your lady friend is under my protection now, limpdick. That means if I hear you've made any effort to contact her, to track her down, to even speak her fucking *name,* I'll find you. If you try to get your pissant gang to do something, I'll take care of them first, *then* find you. Did you hear what I did to those cops?"

Both nodded, wide-eyed.

"Then you need to know two things about that. The first is, it was easy. The second?" She smiled again. "I enjoyed it."

Antonio and Seamus tumbled over each other in their haste to get out of the apartment, the building, and Ratway.

I nitiating back door handshake," B.J. said softly, the blue illumination from her screen bathing her thoughtful face. Behind her, the city's glittering nightscape filled the windows.

She sat at her desk, her hair loose around her shoulders. She had changed from her rigid work attire into a tank top and yoga pants, intending to stop off at the company's private gym three floors below before heading home, to work off some of the tension and grief she'd accumulated during the day. But then she'd been alerted that Arthur Shawcross's computer had been activated at the police station.

Darren stood behind her and peered over her shoulder. "And they can't tell they've been hacked?"

"We paid a fortune to develop this software, so they better not be able to. They probably think they're outsmarting us, breaking the encryption and everything." She watched the "load" indicator gradually slide to the right. When it showed complete, she said, "And now we're in. The entire police department is at our fingertips."

"For how long?"

"Until they hire someone smarter than our people."

"So, indefinitely?"

"Pretty much. Where to first?"

"Find the ballistics report on the bullet from Artie's chest," Darren said.

She expertly moved through the police department's slow, antiquated system, until she found the file. "Here we go. Says it was stuck in his spine. No match to the bullet striations in the law enforcement database."

"And I didn't expect one. Hang on." He handed her his phone. She touched it to the screen, and its transferred image appeared. It was a ballistics report on the .22 caliber bullet he'd dug out of the Mendicant, done by a firearms expert on the Kefali payroll. B.J. put the two bullet images side-by-side on the screen. They were identical.

"I knew it," Darren said. "Apocalypse Joe killed them both."

"Who or what is 'Apocalypse Joe?'"

"I'm not sure yet."

"But he killed Artie?"

"He pulled the trigger, but somebody else aimed him."

"Do you think he has a record?"

"Doubt it. No point in checking, anyway. I know where to find him."

"Where?"

"He's supposed to show up for a kill tattoo at Ink Ink Nudge Nudge tomorrow. I plan to be there."

She turned to him. "Will you be careful?"

"Of course I will."

"You promise? You won't try that macho 'I'm too tough to worry about covering my ass' stuff, will you?"

He kissed her cheek. "B.J., you know you don't have to worry about me. I was born with two umbilical cords, red and blue."

She frowned, puzzled. "And?"

He winked. "And the bomb squad cut the wrong one."

She giggled. No one else in the Kefali organization other than Stavros himself had ever heard her do that.

"Besides," he continued, "I may not know this Apocalypse Joe, but I definitely know his type. Plans out every detail, leaves nothing to chance. He knows that even the slightest mistake might trip him up."

"Why is he getting a tattoo, then? Shouldn't he have already left town?"

"Ah, you see, that's *marketing*. The next one to hire him will hear that he's so good at covering his tracks, he's not even worried about sticking around after the hit." He stood, stretched and walked to the window, where he gazed out at the city night.

She waited, but he said nothing. "What's wrong?"

Without looking at her, he said, "Dead kids. Six of them, along with the Mendicant, the man who brokered the deal between Apocalypse Joe and whoever hired him. They were executed. That's where I got that bullet."

"You plan to kill this Apocalypse Joe?"

"I can probably find out as much from his corpse as I can from his words."

"That's not what Stavros wants."

"He wants to know who killed Artie and why. This is how I find out."

She came up behind him, put her arms around him, and lay her cheek against his back. "Stavros thinks this is intended to disrupt the Festival."

"He might be right."

"He usually is."

He turned in her embrace until he faced her. Her arms went around his neck, and he put his hands on her hips. "It'll take more than one unexpected death to derail something that's been around for so long."

For a long moment they looked into each other's eyes, each seeing their shared history mirrored back at them. They had been close, then distant, then close again several times in their lives. Now, it seemed, closeness once again called.

"This feels familiar," she said softly.

"In a good way?"

"In a... oh, fuck it." She put her hand on the back of his head and pulled him down into a kiss.

In his private chamber, Stavros Kefali watched on a screen as their kiss grew more intimate. It made him neither angry nor pleased; although he considered them both his adopted children, he certainly didn't require that they see each other as brother and sister. B.J., especially, needed this occasionally; she had very little time for an actual social life, so this allowed her to, as they say, cut to the chase. This sort of emotional release probably kept her sane.

He recalled his early organizations, ruled by the fear and intimidation common to criminal gangs. It had been exhausting, on constant guard against duplicity and betrayal, never knowing who might turn on him next. How, he'd wondered, do you find people you can actually *trust*?

And then he realized: you don't *find* them, you *raise* them.

And he'd been doing so ever since, most recently with Arthur, Darren, and B.J.

He left the latter two to their activity on the office couch and turned his attention to another screen, one that displayed three young, naked men writhing together in bed. One of them, a handsome second-generation immigrant from Corfu, was crucial to the Festival, and Stavros wanted to be sure the boy got what he'd been promised. It certainly looked like it. And considering the ultimate outcome for the boy, it was a small enough price to pay.

Now he turned to a third screen, one that showed the street outside his building. When he learned that Artie had been beheaded, it confirmed two things he'd already suspected: one, the death was a message meant for him, and two, it had been timed to disrupt the Festival.

It also meant that, more than likely, Artie's head would arrive here soon, along with a message, or perhaps *as* a message, from his killer.

But who? Who could be behind this?

Only one impossible name came to mind.

Cole Slaughter had to push hard to get the rooftop door open. Like everything else in Ratway, it was neglected and dying, its lock mechanism long gone and one hinge so rusted he could barely budge it. It made a loud scream of metal against metal, announcing his presence if anyone was around to hear.

He emerged onto the roof and leaned against the wall of the stairway entrance to catch his breath. He dripped with sweat beneath his suit. Twenty-five stories up would tax the legs of even a professional climber, and with stops for rest, it took him half an hour to reach it. And God, the smells along the way!

As his breathing returned to normal, he looked out at Ratway's buildings, several taller than the one he stood atop. The illuminated windows showed apartments where people existed on the fringes of society, in poverty and unemployment, but not hopelessness. In one window, he watched the silhouette of a young woman as she danced, oblivious to anything but her music.

He walked to the edge and peered down at the street. Headlamps leapfrogged from traffic signal to signal, and pedestrians cast long shadows as they moved through pools of light. A car's thumping bass did a Doppler shift as it passed below. If it was this loud two dozen stories above, it must've been deafening on the street.

Easily a hundred crimes were being committed just on this block. But even if he somehow arrested every single perpetrator, it would make no difference. He wondered if anything would. Then he reminded himself he was here because something actually seemed to be making that difference.

He settled in to wait; now it was just a matter of patience. And no one got to the rank of detective without a massive supply of it.

R ebecca Hutchcraft now wore the kind of old, well-worn clothes that made her look less conspicuous on the streets of Ratway. It wasn't technically a disguise, but she doubted anyone would recognize her unless they looked at her directly. And the chances of that, down here, were slim. Too often eye contact was a prelude to violence, so most people kept their gaze straight ahead or down at their feet.

There was an element of danger in this, too, but that was part of the fun. A single woman on the streets of Ratway was, by common sense, asking for trouble. But she had a name to drop in case that trouble came.

She emerged from the subway station and drifted into the pedestrian Brownian motion past the liquor stores, pawn shops, and adult emporiums that powered the local economy. A few men called out to her, but when she didn't respond, they moved on. There was, she realized, a tactical advantage to being a woman of forty. When she reached forty-five, she'd be invisible.

Her destination was in the middle of the next block. The sign for the City Free Clinic, in a storefront that used to be a hardware store back when Ratway was thriving, glowed with pure white light against the night and neon around it. Its front was behind bars and security glass, and through them she saw a handful of patients seated in the waiting room.

People had to be buzzed in, so she hit the intercom button on the wall. "Yes?" a woman's voice said.

"I'm here to see Dr. Parashar."

"What's the nature of your illness or injury?"

"It's Becky with the bad hair."

There was a snort-laugh, and the door buzzed. Rebecca went inside.

The people in the lobby all tensed up at once, like a herd of prey animals worried a predator might be near. Small children huddled close to their mothers, single young women tried to disguise terror as courage, and one old woman just sagged further into his chair. Once the surprise faded, they gave Rebecca nothing but dead-eyed suspicious glances.

The receptionist, a young Black woman named Tinley, said, "Doc's in her office. You can go on back."

"Hey, how come she gets to go and we have to sit out here?" one of the single women demanded.

"Your ass isn't glued down," Tinley shot back. "The front door's right there. You think you can find a doctor who'll see you cheaper than free, you go find her."

The woman folded her arms sulkily but didn't leave.

Tinley buzzed Rebecca through the inner door. Brutal experience confirmed the tight security was necessary; many an irate husband, father, boyfriend or brother had tried to storm the clinic to take back what they considered "theirs"—women and children with the temerity to tell these males, "no." There was even a separate waiting room for men, smaller and with an impenetrable connecting door. And Tinley kept a handgun within easy reach.

Rebecca passed the exam rooms until she reached the office of Saraya Parashar, the physician who owned, operated, and occasionally defended, the City Free Clinic. She was tall, of Indian descent, with stylish glasses that only amplified a glare that could melt steel. She'd earned a Silver Star as an army medic in Afghanistan, and nothing rattled her.

She smiled when she saw Rebecca. "It's the queen of the fourth estate!"

"Only a lady-in-waiting," Rebecca said as they hugged.

"I always meant to look up what the other three estates were."

"The clergy, the nobility, and the commoners."

"That sounds very...British," Saraya observed.

"Very."

"What's new in your world?"

Rebecca sat on a corner of the desk. "I saw a headless body this morning."

"Your husband?"

"Hah! No. Some ritzy uptown lawyer. Someone cut off his head right in his parking garage."

"Why?"

"That's the question. I've covered enough organized crime to know his head didn't just get loose and fall off. It was a message. *What* message we won't know until we see where it turns up."

"Somebody took it?"

Rebecca nodded.

"What brings you down here tonight? Do you think I've got his head in my freezer?"

Rebecca and Saraya had been friends since high school, and although their career paths separated them for a decade, they stayed in touch. When Saraya opened her clinic, Rebecca did some free publicity for her to help secure the funds. She also volunteered whenever she had time.

But Saraya knew her friend wouldn't just drop by unannounced, not this late. No one was ever "just in" this neighborhood after dark.

Rebecca said, "I need to meet your friend."

Saraya sighed. "I should never have told you that I'd met her."

"Yes, you should. It's the only reason I think she's not just an urban legend. I *do* know she's the only thing that makes people read the news these days, especially since she fried those two cops last night. So, if I want to keep my job, I need an exclusive."

"That doesn't sound like you," Saraya said perceptively.

"Stop reading me so well, dammit. The real reason is that my editor, who's a decent man in an impossible situation, will lose his job if we don't up our circulation."

"Now, *that's* the Rebecca I know."

"So how do I get in touch with her?"

"Why do you even think I'd know?"

"You know everyone and everything." Rebecca leaned close. "Unless *you* are secretly the Lightning Girl."

"Okay, first? If I was, I guaran-damn-tee you it would be Lightning *Woman*. Second? When the hell would I have time for that? And third? Have you ever seen me shoot sparks from these?" She held up her fingers to display her short but immaculate nails.

"I've seen daggers shoot from your eyes."

"Those were scalpels."

"Come on, you're the only lead I've got. You've met her."

"Yeah, when she brought me a boy who'd been beaten. It wasn't a social call."

"You must know something."

Saraya sat back. After a long, thoughtful moment she said, "I might."

"I knew it. So you can get me an interview with her?"

"I can't promise that. I can put the two of you in proximity, but I doubt she'll talk to you. She's very taciturn."

"Good thing I'm charming."

Saraya looked at her seriously. "Look, Beck, I don't know who or what she is, but she helps the people down here. It's the first time a lot of them have had any hope. She stood up to the cops, who are worse than the criminals in Ratway. Whatever her reasons, whatever her methods, it's her results that matter to me."

Rebecca understood that. The first reports of the Lightning Girl recounted the way she interceded on behalf of sex workers against their brutal pimp; she shocked the guy so hard he flew into a chain-link fence. Next, she protected a liquor store owner from some would-be robbers. She never made a statement, never presented any kind of manifesto or list of demands. She simply arrived, took care of business, and vanished back into the night. Any attempt to photograph her, or take a video, could only be done from a distance; when they got too close, they recorded nothing but static. The police blew her off as some kind of hoax or joke, especially when she did their job for them.

But last night's encounter with two allegedly crooked beat cops quickly changed that.

The official report stated that two patrol officers, Morlette and Hogan, had stopped a suspect for suspicious behavior; an unseen accomplice had attacked them with something like a cattle prod or stun gun. By the time the two alleged perps were gone, a crowd of locals had gathered to cheer the cops' misfortune. They knew that Morlette and Hogan were the worst of the worst, empowered bullies with twisted appetites for sex and pain. Their "suspect" had been a local trans boy named Leo, and if past experience counted for anything, the two cops planned to get their kicks by demonstrating that his biology was still definitely female.

The cops, predictably, put out the word that a dead Lightning Girl would be better PR than one who could make statements and explain herself. If any of them got the drop on her, she'd be killed by a cop who later claimed he "feared for his life."

So Rebecca had to find her first.

"I don't want to give away her identity or anything," Rebecca said. "I just want to give her a forum to explain what she's trying to accomplish."

Before she could reply, Saraya's desk phone buzzed. She picked it up, and Rebecca stepped out in the hall to give her privacy. She gazed down toward the waiting room door, mentally going over the questions she'd ask the Lightning Girl.

"You can come back," Saraya said. When Rebecca returned to her office, she added, "I really do need to see my next patient, so I'll cut to the chase. I'll ask. That's all I can do."

"Thank you," Rebecca said. "When should I come back?"

"Who said you should leave?"

It took a beat for Rebecca to register that. "Tonight?" she whispered.

Saraya nodded. "If at all."

"Well, if I'm going to be here, I might as well be useful. What can I do to help?"

"Disinfect room three while I see someone in room two."

"I'm on it."

11:11 P.M.

At home in her Bay View apartment, Laura Slade typed out a text message to a friend who worked in the Stilstand College history department. When she finished, she attached the photo of the strange scroll from Shawcross's office.

Laura lived alone, unless you counted the one-eyed cat she'd adopted, in a one-bedroom rent-controlled efficiency apartment three blocks from the house where she'd grown up. She sat at her desk in a t-shirt and underwear, a bag of organic baked potato chips open beside her. Other than her chewing, the only sound was the traffic outside and the soft bass from her wallmate's music.

She went through a list of criminal cases involving severed heads, looking for any detail that connected with the Dodger's murder. Beheading wasn't common because it was *hard*; cutting through all that muscle and bone took time, and expertise, and a fair bit of physical strength.

She found one case fifteen years prior in which a man used a home-made guillotine, but he'd brought the victim to it, not the other way around. It was plausible that Shawcross's killers shut down the security system and walked nonchalantly into the building without anyone noticing; it was less plausible that they did it with some kind of portable guillotine in tow.

Another case involved a piano-wire booby trap at a drug dealer's apartment; again, though, the victim came to it, walking blithely through the door where the device snared his neck in its loop.

She stopped for a moment as something struck her. Perhaps she was going about this all wrong. Instead of looking up victims with missing heads, perhaps she should investigate devices capable of committing such acts. If she could narrow that field, then it might be easier to track down those who had access to them.

The one-eyed cat curled up at her feet, and she raked her bare toes through its fur.

11:25 P.M.

Cole had almost fallen asleep standing in the shadow of a crumbling chimney when a bright flash of light startled him awake.

He stood very still, listening intently, smelling ozone. Soft footfalls crunched across the roof's gravelly surface, growing louder as they neared. He palmed his weapon and stepped out into the light.

It was her. He put away the gun.

"Hi, Sparky," he said to the Lightning Girl.

She sighed. "I fucking asked you not to call me that."

"And maybe eventually I won't."

"Uh-huh. What's up?"

As always, Cole tried not to stare at her, and failed. He was desperate for something, some detail that would identify her. But her simple yet effective disguise gave away nothing distinctive.

At first, he'd tried to get a clear photograph. But nothing electronic worked in her vicinity, and no one he knew still used film cameras. So he finally gave up and accepted that he'd know only what she chose to reveal.

"I don't know if you've heard," he began, "but this morning, over on the East Side—"

"The East Side's not my problem."

"Let me finish. A lawyer working for the Kefali mob was killed. Then he was beheaded. We haven't found his head."

She took this in thoughtfully. Ratway was her protectorate, but Kefali's mob was all over the place down here, selling drugs, sex trafficking, and strong-arming anyone who didn't go along. And if there was a gang war over the Shawcross hit, Ratway was likely to see the bulk of the fighting.

"What do you want me to do?" she said at last. "Go head-hunting?"

"I have a feeling it'll turn up. No one takes a head for no reason. What I'm curious about is who did the beheading and why. Is anyone moving in on Kefali's turf down here?"

"You mean other than the cops?"

"Yes," he said wearily. "Other than the cops."

"You're the detective, smart boy, you figure it out. Is there anything else?"

Her cavalier attitude annoyed him. "Look, Sparky, a full-on gang war is something neither of us want, right? Because they're not going to fight it out on the East Side or in Bowland or Pigeon Hill. It'll be on the streets right here. Lots of people will die, mostly the low-level thugs and innocent bystanders. Your people."

"Then stop it before it happens. That's what you're paid to do."

He clenched his fists. They had met a month earlier, on what threatened to be the last night of Cole's life. He'd been brought in to work undercover to break a gun-dealing ring operating out of Ratway's old Hellman's Boil neighborhood. Posing as a potential buyer, he'd arrived for the two a.m. meeting dressed in a confiscated suit he could never afford on his own and took his time looking over the merchandise displayed in the trunk of a black sedan. This wasn't the bust, so all he had to do was note the names, and faces, of the participants.

And then *she* showed up.

A flash of blinding light caused everyone to dive for cover and draw their weapons. By the time any of them could see again, a young woman in a hoodie stood before them. She was slender but not girlish; she carried herself like a confident, adult woman. The hood and cap brim hid her eyes, but she watched everything from beneath that shadow. Later he'd realize she'd also shaded the upper part of her face with black makeup.

The gunrunners quickly produced numerous firearms, some of them military grade.

She did not seem intimidated. "I guess if you guys had bigger dicks, you wouldn't need to compensate so much."

Cole did not see her move; she didn't dramatically point her hands and aim bolts of electricity. But all the men holding weapons suddenly screamed and dropped them, and then smaller bursts of light exploded right in their faces. Blinded, burned, they screamed and ran off into the night, some of them running full-tilt into cars and buildings.

Cole realized he was all alone, unarmed, and without backup. He slowly raised his hands and stepped into the open. "Hi. Er...don't... bolt me."

She turned to him. He could still only see the lower half of her face, but her lips were full and, he had to admit, luscious. "Well. Why didn't *you* pull a gun on me?"

"Would you believe I'm on the job?"

"Show me a badge and I might."

"It's inside my shirt." He slowly produced his badge on a chain around his neck.

"That doesn't carry as much weight down here as it does over in Pigeon Hill or on the East Side. And it doesn't answer my question."

"I'm not with them. I'm undercover, trying to bust them."

She glanced at the stray immobile forms on the ground, the ones who'd cold-cocked themselves in their haste to flee. "The direct approach worked pretty well for me."

"Yes, but you didn't find out who was paying them, either."

"I don't care who's paying them. Or who's paying you. I care that they stop hurting people in Ratway." Again she looked them over. "It appears they have. So, I'm done."

"Wait, don't...flash off," he said impulsively. He thought frantically for a way to keep her here and hated himself for the entirely non-police reason. There was something about her confidence, her ease, her absolute command of the situation that had him riveted. And those lips didn't hurt, either. "I'm Cole Slaughter."

She laughed. "No way."

"Yes way, I'm afraid. And you?"

"I don't need a name."

"What do people call you?"

"They don't, if they know what's good for them."

"Look, I...maybe we can help each other."

"I don't need your help."

"But I know what's going on in the rest of the city that affects Ratway."

Good one, Cole, he thought. *Blow your cover and make a deal with some crazy woman who shoots sparks at people.* But then another part of his brain, one more primal and direct, said, *Look at the way she fills out those jeans, Cole. And the way she owns the whole space she's in.*

His offer made her pause, and she thought it over. At last she asked, "And what do you get out of it?"

More time with you, he thought, but he said, "The same thing. You tell me what's going on here, I'll pass it on."

She laughed. "To the cops? The *Ratway* cops?"

"They're not all bad."

"Only another cop would say that."

"You're just one person. How much can you actually do?"

"All I can. Hopefully it'll help other people see that they can do things, too."

"Why?"

"Why, what?"

"Why do you do this? Why *you?*"

Again she paused to think over her answer, but this time she didn't reply. Instead, she pointed up at the buildings above them. "I'll meet with you for five minutes, once a week. Up there, on the roofs. You show up, and I'll come to you. We exchange information, and that's all. You try to trap me, arrest me, or kill me? You'll pay for it. Are we clear?"

"Clear." He offered his hand.

She looked at it and laughed. "No." Then a bright flash of light momentarily blinded him, and when he could see again, she was gone.

Now, despite the fact that he still fantasized about her almost every night, he was beyond being intimidated and well into being pissed off. "Nobody makes you do what you do. Nobody even knows why you do it, including me. For all I know, you're just some weirdo after attention. Maybe I should shoot you right now, and wipe that black grease off your face to see who you really are."

"Maybe this is who I really am. Maybe the face under the hood is the disguise."

"Don't get philosophical."

"You haven't asked me about those two cops that got burned last night."

"Do I need to?"

"They're your brothers in blue, aren't they?"

"Not if they were dirty."

He couldn't see them in the hood's shadow, but he felt her eyes on him. He'd just made a huge admission, one that carried ramifications for them both. He was condoning her actions, a sign of trust she hadn't expected.

"I'll keep my eyes open," she said at last, the snap gone from her voice.

"Thanks."

"Now here's something for you. There's an abandoned gas station at 145th and Logan Ave. If you look inside, you'll find a dead man, and a half dozen dead children, all shot."

"Wait, *children?*"

"Children."

Cole was speechless for a moment, then managed, "Fucking hell."

"I have it on good authority that the killer goes by the name 'Apocalypse Joe,' and that he travels with a younger female companion."

"Do you also know *why* he killed those people?"

"That's your job. But find him fast: if he shows his face here again, I'll burn it off." She paused, then added, "Don't make the mistake of thinking you're Commissioner Gordon and I'm Batman. You can't summon me with a signal, and I'm not here to do your legwork, just like you're not here to do my thinking for me. I'm here to protect the people of Ratway. Only you know why you're here."

"Maybe because now I understand why you do what you do," he said.

"You just think you do. Meet me back here three nights from now. Whatever I've found, you'll get."

"And likewise."

Without waiting for a response, she casually held one hand out. There was a sudden, blinding flash of light, a smell of electricity in the air, and she was gone.

Cole looked down at his hand, surprised to see his fingers shaking. *I'm not Commissioner Gordon to your Batman,* he thought wryly. *I'm Lois Lane to your Superman.* Then he left to follow up on the tip about the dead kids.

11:29 P.M.

After Cole left, the Lightning Girl returned to the roof. Sparrow, who'd expertly hidden in the shadows and watched the whole encounter, beamed up at her. "Thank you."

"Don't thank me yet," the Lightning Girl said, in a tone so gentle anyone who'd encountered her before wouldn't believe it. "I've just passed on what you told me about the Mendicant and your friends. The balls are in the air, the actual juggling will come later."

"Do you like him?"

"Who, Cole?"

"Yes."

"Not like you mean. We're uneasy allies."

"'The enemy of my enemy is my friend?' The Mendicant used to say that."

"He wasn't wrong." She knelt and put a hand on the boy's shoulder. "Do you have someplace to stay?"

"Lots of places. All over."

"No, I mean, someone to take care of you."

"I can take care of myself."

The Lightning Girl smiled with unexpected kindness. "I know that. But you're a kid; you shouldn't have to."

"And you shouldn't have to burn cops' dicks off."

The Lightning Girl laughed. "I *should* tell you to watch your mouth, but I like it too much." She stood up and ran a finger along Sparrow's cheek. "Watch yourself, my man. I'll be in touch."

Sparrow made a pistol shape with his hand and clicked his tongue. "Right back at ya."

The Lightning Girl's laugh ended with the flash that hid her departure.

B.J. straddled Darren on the office couch. Her eyes were half-closed, and her torso sweaty. The office lights were off, and her gleaming skin reflected the multicolored lights of the city outside. It felt gloriously, insidiously daring: she knew no one could see them, but at the same time, she had the delicious sense of being an exhibitionist, of putting on a show for the whole city. They would see her naked, see her fuck, see her come.

Which she did, the same way she did everything: quietly and with great intensity.

Darren knew her well enough to tell, and he smiled up at her. She pushed a strand of sweaty hair from her face. "Proud of yourself?" she teased breathlessly.

"Always nice to know I haven't lost my touch."

"Mmm, I'll say. Now it's my turn. Or yours, depending on how you score it."

She moved her hips in a slow rhythm, then faster and harder. He matched her with his own thrusts, lifting her from the couch when he arched beneath her. When he came, he cried out and his whole body tensed for a long moment. Then, with a gasp and a smile, he sprawled flat on the cushions.

"That was nice," she said.

"Definitely," he agreed, still breathing hard. "Remind me why we don't do this more often?"

She kissed him, then lay down atop him. "Because we're both too busy."

"It's not like it's a huge time commitment."

"This? No. But this leads to *that*. And *that* is something we definitely don't have time for."

They kissed again.

"Can I tell you something I haven't told anyone?" she asked.

"Of course."

"I'm incredibly nervous about the Festival."

"Why?"

"Have you seen the movies from last time?"

"Of course."

"I've got a huge responsibility. What if I…?" She trailed off, not wanting to put her fears into worries.

"You've organized the whole thing. You know how it works. You'll do fine."

"I've read about the old Festivals, when people did go crazy just from being there. I don't think I could forgive myself if I did."

"You won't," he repeated, then got to his feet and began gathering his clothes. "I need to go."

"Just to prove me right?" she teased.

He laughed. "No, I have to be ready to catch this Apocalypse Joe in the morning. He's careful as fuck, and I want to be in position so far ahead that he won't have a prayer of spotting me."

As he dressed, she lit a cigarette. The entire city was supposed to be under a "no smoking indoors" law, but like so many other laws, that one didn't apply to her. She blew a plume of smoke and said, "If you're just sitting there watching the place, doesn't that make him more likely to spot you?"

"Not with his psychology."

"You know him?"

"I know his type. Right now, he's been paid and he's probably celebrating. It'll be a low-key thing, he won't be flashing money at clubs or anything, but it'll still keep him occupied. He has a female companion, so he's likely doing something similar to what we were just doing."

"But not as well."

"Well, who could?"

She stood and buttoned his shirt for him. "Let me know when you've interrogated and disposed of him. So Stavros won't worry about you."

He knew *exactly* who'd be worrying about him. "Hey, if I had a dime for every guy I looked for who got away…"

"You'd have no dimes?"

"Precisely."

They kissed again, then she gathered her own clothes but didn't dress; she wanted a shower first, in the luxurious executive washroom hidden behind another office wall. As Darren stepped into his A. Testoni Oxfords, she was struck by the thought of carrying on this way in another office, for another organization. Would that even be possible?

Truthfully, this wasn't that different from any other office job: she managed payroll, supervised staff, and approved expenses. And most of Kefali's business was, in fact, legitimate: cargo ships, trucking companies, a few car lots, and even a chain of pop-up sunglasses retailers. But all those combined didn't equal the income from one week of their online sports betting, or dealing in the latest designer drugs, or supplying sex workers to some exclusive party. The mask might be pure, but the face behind it was as corrupt as Dorian Gray's portrait.

Darren came up behind her and rested a hand on her bare hip. "You seem lost in thought."

"Just imagining doing this same job for another company."

"I'm sure if you asked him, Stavros would let you. He might even help you."

"No, that's not what I mean. I was just thinking how lucky I am to be here."

He took her by the shoulders and turned her to face him. "Me, too." He kissed her softly, tenderly. "I'll let you know how it goes."

"Thank you."

He left her, naked in the dark, and slipped out her office door.

In his secret room, Stavros Kefali watched a screen that showed Darren descend in the elevator. Another followed him to his car in the parking garage, tapping into the new cameras installed just hours earlier. There were already security cameras in place, but someone clever had disabled the security system in Artie's building long enough to commit the ghastly crime, and Kefali had run diagnostic after diagnostic on *this* building's systems to ensure nothing similar could happen. For his own peace of mind, he had Pete Pawson install a second system, wired separately, known solely to him and Pete.

But that was only with part of his brain. The other part was obsessed with planning this Festival, and recalling those of the past.

The ceremony had not always been such a massive production. In fact, it began as a simple meeting between Kefali, his lone handler Arateus, and a woman known to history as Mary the Hebrew, in a cave deep in Mount Taygetus, located in southern Greece.

"Madam," Arateus announced, "I present to you my master, who begs your wisdom."

After a moment of surprised silence, Mary said, "You do have a unique problem."

"My master begs for your help," Arateus added as he knelt on one knee.

"Oh, get up, this isn't a temple," Mary said. She was dark-haired, middle-aged, and had the wry bearing of someone used to being the smartest person in the room. "Leave us so we may discuss matters in private."

Arateus nodded and scampered away toward the light at the cave's mouth. Mary shook her head. "Wish I could find a servant that devoted."

"He is that," Kefali agreed. "I genuinely couldn't manage without him. Now…can you help me? I can pay you."

"Pay me?" she repeated, and then her laugh rang throughout the cavern she used as her home. "I can turn lead into gold, what need do I have for payment?"

"I thought I should offer it, at least."

"If I decide to help you, and if I *can* help you, then the work itself will be payment enough." She knelt close and examined him, studying every inch of his exposed skin. "Do you have any idea how this happened? Not how you ended up as you are; even I heard about that. But why it affected you this way?"

"None. Unless it's the story my mother told me."

"Which was?"

"That my father was a god."

Mary didn't laugh at this but considered it for a long moment before saying, "My people believe in only one god, and considering how our priests and rabbis argue about him, I can't imagine what they'd be like with a whole pantheon. But it's as good a reason as any as to why you're still among the living."

"So can you help me? I know of your work with homunculi."

She smiled again. "Ah, you think I can simply alter that process to help you."

"It occurred to me."

"And that's why you sought me out?"

"Not entirely. I read some of your purported sayings. They seemed relevant."

"Let me guess. 'It rises from Earth to Heaven and descends again to Hell, thereby combining within Itself the powers of both the Above and the Below.'"

"That's the one."

"I never said that."

For the first time, Kefali seemed caught off guard. "My sources—"

"Just want to seem clever. But don't get your laurel leaves askew, it's a valid principle. As above, so below. Balance. That's the simple idea they're trying to hide in their poetry. That's the goal of my alchemy." She moved close and met his gaze. "You, my friend, don't balance. At all. Yet. That will be my challenge. A challenge worthy of the greatest alchemist of them all."

And from this challenge came the Festival.

Which was coming up again in two days.

A buzz drew his attention, yanking him from the distant past back to the moment. Darren was calling from his car. Kefali answered with, "Yes, Darren?"

"Hey, boss. How are you?"

"Same as usual."

"Just wanted to give you a progress report. I'm going to stake out the place I expect Artie's killer to be tomorrow morning."

"Good thinking. Do you need additional men?"

"Me? Nah. I'm indestructible, you know that. The last time I was in Europe, France surrendered to me just to be on the safe side."

Stavros laughed. Darren was one of the few people who truly amused him. "Very well. I trust your judgement, Darren."

"I don't suppose Artie's head has shown up yet?"

"Not yet. But it will. And I'll let you know."

"Boss, I hate to ask this, but do you have *any* idea who hired Apocalypse Joe? Anything you haven't told me?"

"No, Darren."

The open line hissed for a moment before Darren spoke again. "So… I'm sorry for not stopping in and saying hi when I was at the HQ. B.J. and I got distracted."

"I'm sure you both needed it."

"Yeah, I know, but I just wanted to tell you, I wasn't trying to avoid you."

"I'd never think that, Darren."

"Good. Anything else? Because I'll be out of touch tomorrow until I have something to report."

"Just be careful. There's a formidable mind behind all this, and it won't be easy to discover its identity."

"Will do, boss. And same back at you." Two beeps indicated the call's end.

Stavros closed his eyes. This had to be just the start of another turf war with some upstart gang. *Had* to be. And he'd deal with it in his usual efficient ways.

Because the alternative—if it turned out his suspicions were, in fact, correct—was more than he could bear.

12:01 A.M.

Apocalypse Joe stood at the hotel room window. Seven stories below on the streets of Bay View, approaching headlights glowed white on one block, while red taillights illuminated the next. It reminded him of the blood flow to and from the heart, and he wondered what the heart of this city could be.

Behind him, the room was in darkness. Delilah sat on the edge of the bed, hands demurely in her lap. "What are you thinking about?" she finally asked.

"Stavros Kefali," he said. "He's a real mystery."

"Why?"

"The Kefali family has been at the top of the city's organized crime for longer than anyone can remember. And Stavros Kefali has always been the head of the family. He must be in his nineties by now, at least."

"So he has a son or daughter who'll take over when he dies?"

"No one knows. Very few people even know what he looks like. He has no internet presence. Do you know how rare that is? How hard to accomplish? There's not a confirmed photograph of him to be found anywhere."

"Maybe he's shy?"

"No, there has to be a tactical reason. And I'm betting it has something to do with that man we killed this morning."

"Well, yeah. He was Kefali's lawyer, wasn't he?"

"It's more than that." He turned from the window, his lean form silhouetted against the lights outside. "Killing the man was one message. It says that you're vulnerable, that we can hit you whenever we want. But taking his head…that's a whole other level."

"But we're done, right? We're leaving tomorrow?"

"Yeah, right after I get my new kill ink."

She got to her feet and put her arms around him. "Let's just leave now. You can get your ink anywhere."

He kissed the tip of her nose. "Delilah, that's the point—you get your kill mark in the city where you made your kill. It means you've done your job so well, you have no worries about being caught. It's how you maintain your rep."

"I think your rep is solid."

He stroked her hair. "A rep has to be constantly tended, like a garden. You know that."

"I know. I just worry."

"Have I ever let you down?"

"That's not what worries me. I'm worried that one time, we might step into something bigger than we can control."

He kissed her gently on the lips, and they stood in the dark in each other's arms. But her words echoed in his head.

Something bigger than we can control.

12:06 A.M.

Ibis, the oldest surviving member of the Mendicant's gang, noticed the white-haired woman first.

The six kids now clustered in the cellar beneath a tenement had survived the gas station massacre because they were out working their scams. Upon their return, they had seen either the bodies or the police; and, following protocol, they hid here until further instructions arrived. Even the ones who'd seen the Mendicant dead on the floor waited here, so hard-wired was their programming.

This was the closest they had to a central hideout. They spent most of their time at one of the other temporary locations, only returning to this one for either a major group meeting or following a crisis.

But instead of the Mendicant, a woman stood at the bottom of the stairs. No one had heard her approach. She was tall, slender, and had spiky white hair. Most disconcertingly, her eyes were blank, like the eyes of an animal after it's decided you are prey. "Hello," she said. "Is everyone all right?"

"Who are you?" Ibis asked. Ibis was short, squat and looked like she'd be out of breath before she ran a block. She was actually one of the fastest kids in the gang.

"I'm here to take you somewhere safe," Lobotomy Eyes said. "The Mendicant sent me."

"The Mendicant's dead."

"He made arrangements beforehand."

"You have a name?"

"You can call me Loby."

"Yeah, well, Loby, I ain't never heard the Mendicant mention you. Besides, we're safe here." *Or we were,* she thought but didn't say.

"Where's everyone else?" a younger girl called Sandpiper demanded. "They didn't kill that many of us."

"The police arrested several. But I'm not with the police or social services. I'm here to help you get out of sex trafficking and into somewhere safe."

The kids all snickered. "Lady, we're not into that," said a little boy named Grouse.

"None of you?" the woman asked. "He hasn't pimped any of you out for pedophiles?"

"None," Ibis said proudly. "Anyone tries to touch one of us, the Mendicant would take care of them but good. But if the Mendicant really sent you, you should already know that."

Lobotomy Eyes smiled, but it was purely a mechanical movement, with no emotion involved.

12:15 A.M.

Laura Slade parked on the street and made her way past the sawhorses toward the abandoned gas station. A dozen marked and unmarked police cars, light bars flashing, encircled the building, and uniformed officers stood guard in a ring around the crime scene. Around that, a crowd of Ratway folk milled about, muttering and seething.

The crowd's hostility was palpable. They weren't just rubbernecking; they chattered and glared and held out phones to film the scene. In turn, the cops were tense with suppressed violence, ready to crack heads. This was 89th Precinct territory, where the two allegedly corrupt officers had been injured by the Lightning Girl, and everyone felt on edge.

Laura flashed her badge and ducked under the yellow tape. She spotted Cole standing outside, watching two men carry out a stretcher. The body on it was much smaller than it should have been.

"Holy shit," she said when she joined him. "How many kids are dead in there?"

"Six, plus one adult male."

"Murder-suicide?"

"No. I think the same killer did them all."

"Jesus. How did you even hear about this?"

"Anonymous tip from a concerned citizen," he said dryly.

"Come on, man. I'm your partner."

"We'll talk about it," he said, then lowered his voice. "But not here."

A large Black man in a long coat came out of the building and joined them. He offered a hand to Laura. "Detective Stan Rampede. If he's Slaughter, you must be Slade. The two detectives voted Most Likely to Have a TV Show Named After Them."

Laura said, "This is your case, I take it?"

"Yes. Because luck runs downhill. I told your partner that we had it under control, so I don't understand why he called you down here." Rampede's eyes narrowed with the same suspicion any cop would have if their territory was invaded.

One of the CSU techs said, "Excuse me, Detective Rampede?"

"Yes?"

"This is quirky. The adult male was shot six times, small-caliber rounds, but one bullet has already been dug out of his body."

Rampede's wide forehead creased. "What? Where is it?"

"Beats me. Someone wanted a bullet for a souvenir, maybe."

"Or as proof," Cole suggested.

Rampede turned to him. "Is there something you're not telling me, Detective Slaughter?"

"Just a moment." Cole turned to the technician. "Make getting those slugs to Loomis in Ballistics a priority. I need to see the report ASAP."

The technician looked at Rampede, who said, "Ballistics reports are for everyone, aren't they? Do as he says."

"Will do," the technician said, before running back inside.

When they were relatively alone again, Rampede said, "I'd like that explanation now, if you don't mind."

"There was a murder this morning on the East Side," Cole said. "A man was shot, then his head was cut off."

"I heard. Some big-time lawyer."

"Yes," Laura said. "Arthur Shawcross."

Rampede let out a long whistle. "You think this was related? Hard to get farther apart, in any sense, than a tony shyster in a private East Side parking garage and a bunch of street urchins in a closed-down Ratway gas station."

"I know," Cole agreed. "But both are totally over the top. Both could be intended as messages. And both could be strikes in an impending gang war. That's why I want to see the ballistics, to see if it's the same shooter."

"Seems reasonable. I'll let you know." Rampede nodded at them both, then went back inside.

Barely moving her lips, Laura asked quietly, "Did you seriously get an anonymous tip?"

"I honestly have no idea who it was." And that technically wasn't a lie, since he genuinely didn't know who was under the Lightning Girl's hood.

"Okay." In a normal voice she said, "I have something interesting on our actual case."

"Really? Do you *ever* go off duty?"

"Says the guy at a crime scene at midnight in another precinct. And you're assuming I don't enjoy tracking down clues."

"You need a hobby."

"I will if you will. Do you want to hear what I found?"

"Sure."

"I got to thinking, what could you use to take off a man's head quickly? I mean, it wasn't sawed off, or chopped, it was cut. Clean, neat, and fast."

"And?"

"There's a thing called a bone cutter. It's used in amputation, or autopsies. It's basically a big pair of scissors spring-loaded to close with the bite force of a great white shark."

Cole nodded. "I think I saw one of those in a horror movie once."

"Here's the interesting part. You can only get them through medical supply companies, and then only with authorization."

He slowly smiled. "So we need to check all the places that are authorized to have them and see if one's missing."

"That's the plan," she agreed. They fist-bumped.

Then another stretcher bearing a dead child came out, and the momentary sense of accomplishment dissolved into the night.

                            12:52 A.M.

The City Free Clinic technically closed at midnight, although Saraya wouldn't leave until she'd seen every waiting patient. Rebecca put the last of the wet scrubs into the dryer and turned it on. The steady thump as the clothes rolled around in the drum filled the little laundry room. She turned off the light and went back to Saraya's office, where the doctor was entering patient notes into her computer.

"You need an office manager for that," Rebecca said with a yawn.

"I can't pay one. You volunteering?"

"I've done my charity work for the night." The clock said it was almost one o'clock, and Rebecca was fading fast. She yawned, then asked, "So will she call, or knock, or…?"

Saraya continued to type. "Take out the garbage."

Rebecca's eyes narrowed. "Hey, I—"

Saraya looked up and spoke with clear urgency. "Take… out… the garbage."

Rebecca felt a little thrill of excitement. "Ah. Gotcha." She stuck her reporter's notebook in the back pocket of her jeans, then removed the trash bag from the can beside the desk, did the same with those in the exam rooms and lobby, and put them all into a common bag. She carried it to the back door. She stopped and took a few deep breaths, trying to calm her pounding heart. It took a lot to rattle the newswoman's cool, but this did.

She unbolted the back door and pushed it open. A large dumpster sat just outside, and she took a careful look in both directions before stepping out. She kicked in the wooden wedge to hold the clinic door open then deposited the bag. Something in the dumpster scurried out of the way.

Rebecca waited beside the dumpster, arms crossed, listening. The only sounds were traffic from the streets around her. Except for the rectangle of light coming through the open door, the alley was pitch black. None of the windows in the buildings on either side were lit, and security lights were nonexistent. It was warm and humid, and the smells from the dumpster made her want to gag. When was the last time it had been emptied?

With no warning, a bright flash of light appeared beside her, momentarily blinding her. It gave off a sudden, searing heat that drove her back a step. Ozone overpowered all other odors.

When she could see again, she was not alone.

The Lightning Girl stood not five feet away. The first, and biggest, surprise was that there was nothing that unusual about her: she didn't wear a spandex costume, she didn't put her hands on her hips in a heroic pose, she didn't glow with electricity. She was just a girl in a hoodie pulled low over her face, in stature both shorter and slighter than Rebecca.

"So, you're a reporter," the Lightning Girl said. Rebecca could tell nothing from her voice except that she was female. The girl added, "People I trust say you're trustworthy, too."

"I do my best," Rebecca replied, clicking automatically into journalist mode.

"And you want to know all about me for your newspaper."

"Whatever you'd care to tell me."

"I'm not sure I want to tell anything."

"Well, if you're trying to stay anonymous, I have to tell you, you're doing it wrong."

Beneath the hood and the black paint makeup that covered the upper half of her face, the Lightning Girl smiled. It only lasted a moment. "Ask your questions."

Rebecca took out her phone. "Just so I can get the quotes right, I'd like to record this."

"Won't work."

"Why not?"

"Because I don't want it to. Just like I don't want you to get any pictures."

At that, the screen went blank. "These things are expensive," Rebecca said, annoyed.

"Recharge it and it'll be fine."

Rebecca put away the phone. "Okay. Do you mind if I take notes, then?"

"Why not?"

She took out her reporter's notebook and flipped to a blank page. With her pen poised, she asked, "I guess the obvious first question is, who are you?"

"Just a concerned citizen of Ratway," she said.

"Do you have a name?"

"Not that I'd tell you."

"How about a *nom de guerre?*"

"What the fuck is that?"

"A fighting name. Like Maverick or Rambo."

"Rambo was the guy's actual name."

"You know what I mean. Do you?"

"No. They call me the Lightning Girl, which is as good a name as any. Go with that."

"Not Lightning Woman?"

"I'm not that nit-picky."

"And you can control electricity?"

"So they say."

"Can you?"

"Anyone can. All you need is a switch."

Rebecca scowled. "You're evading."

"And you're either dense or rude."

Rebecca was starting to dislike this woman. She switched to a new page, refocused, and set pen to paper again. "How did you acquire this ability?"

"My parents were shot in an alley. No, wait: a radioactive spider bit me. Or I'm the last survivor of an alien planet sent to earth and raised by kindly farmers. Or maybe it's none of your damn business."

"Is it all a trick, then?"

"Ask those two asshole cops in the hospital."

Rebecca sighed. "Look, a news interview depends on real answers, not just evasive snark. Otherwise, it's just a PR piece, and we're both wasting our time."

"All right, then. Suppose you could do this." The Lightning Girl held up her right hand. Little arcs of electricity traveled up between her fingers to finally flare out at the tips. "Never mind whether you were born with it or got it later. If you could make electricity do whatever you wanted, what would you do with it?"

"You tell me."

"I will. You've basically got two choices. You can be selfish or selfless. One might make you a ton of money, maybe even make you famous. The other means you can sleep at night."

"So, you're guided by your conscience?" Again that small, enigmatic smile. Rebecca fervently wished she could see the girl's eyes. She flipped back through her notes and said, "If you don't mind, I'd like to follow up on something you said earlier. You called yourself a 'concerned citizen of Ratway.' Is that why you do what you do?"

"I do it because no one else will."

"No one else will stop corrupt cops?"

"No one else will protect Ratway."

Rebecca finished scrawling on her pad, then paused and looked at the girl skeptically. "Not to be rude or anything, but if you're not here to cooperate with me, why *are* you here? Just because Saraya asked you?"

The Lightning Girl folded her arms, then said carefully, "I'm here to make my intentions clear. I know people wonder about that."

"Your intent being that you'll help where no one else can."

"No. I said no one else *will*. Plenty of people could do what I do: cops, politicians, people in the media. For some, it's even their job. But they don't. So I have to."

"Why is Ratway so important to you? There's crime in Bay View, Bowland, the East Side..."

"Because Ratway needs it the most."

"And you only operate in Ratway?"

Again that little smile. "So far."

It gave Rebecca the perfect segue into the real question of the hour. "Did you assault those two police officers last night?"

"Yes," the Lightning Girl said with no hesitation. "They deserved it. They've been terrorizing people here for months."

"Can you prove that?"

"I don't have to. I'm not a fucking district attorney."

"You know they'll come after you for that."

"I know they'll try."

"Are you declaring war on the police, then?"

"I'm declaring war on anyone who wants to hurt Ratway."

Rebecca scribbled the answer, then studied the Lightning Girl for a long moment. Was she for real? She carried no visible weapons, and except for the hood and black greasepaint, she wore no disguise. Could this all be an elaborate trick, done with smoke, mirrors, and devices?

"You're staring at me," the Lightning Girl pointed out. "Are we done?"

Rebecca snapped back to the moment. "Is there anything else you'd like to say to the rest of the city?"

"Yes. Ratway has been your garbage dump long enough. From now on, if you come in here looking to sell drugs, or traffic in sex, or run gambling, or squeeze protection money out of people just trying to get by, then be sure and look behind you, because one day I'll be there. And you'll burn."

Before Rebecca could ask a followup, another flash blinded her. When her eyes returned to normal, she was alone in the alley.

"Did you get what you wanted?" Saraya asked from the doorway.

"She's a lunatic," Rebecca said. "Do you *condone* her?"

Saraya shrugged. "I don't condemn her."

Rebecca followed her back inside the clinic. "Do you know how she does that stuff with electricity? Is it real, or just an elaborate trick?"

Saraya made sure the back door was closed and locked. "Ask those two rotten cops if it's real."

"That's what she said." Rebecca rubbed her eyes. "You have any saline drops?"

"Of course."

As she followed her friend down the hall, Rebecca considered anew whether Saraya could be the Lightning Girl. But even though she hadn't seen them together, it just didn't work: Saraya was taller, curvier, her voice was different, and she wouldn't have had time to make the switch, even with Rebecca temporarily blinded. No, wherever she came from, whatever her intent, the Lightning Girl was for real.

And now Rebecca had the interview of a lifetime.

1:02 A.M.

Darren once slept completely buried in mud, with only a rubber tube to provide air, to avoid the lackeys of a South American drug lord who would very likely have fed him his own testicles had he been discovered. That was his gold standard for uncomfortable, so the dismal room with its germ-factory mattress was practically a luxury suite in comparison.

"Expect you two gone in the morning," the portly hotel manager had said as he handed over the key. He shifted his cigar to the other side of his mouth. "This ain't no Mar-a-Lago."

"We'll be gone," Darren said. "Right, babe?"

Beside him, the tawdry young woman with tired eyes said, "You're the boss."

In the room, Darren locked the door behind them, and the woman's slack expression vanished. Now her eyes sparkled with intelligence and amusement. "Wow," she said. "It smells like piss and Pine-Sol. You take me to such classy places."

Maria was a professional actress, and like all actresses had auditioned many times for roles as a prostitute. Darren befriended her at the bar where she worked between gigs, and he'd offered her the equivalent of six months' worth of tips to pose as his paid escort for the evening. He turned off the light, then gestured at a battered recliner visible in the neon illumination that shone through the window. "Have a seat."

She raised an eyebrow. "I wouldn't sit in that chair with your ass."

He took off his old, threadbare sport coat and hung it up, then put his valise, with duct tape on three worn corners, onto the wobbly table. He opened it and removed a small metal cage with a white mouse inside, then a can of industrial disinfectant. He sprayed the bed, scowling at the antiseptic smell. Then he sat on the edge; it creaked like the cry of the world's largest tree frog.

"Guess they know when a working girl is working," Maria said. She waved her hand in front of her face to fan away the cleaner's odor. "That stuff stinks almost as bad as the scent of old jizz."

"Glad you said, 'almost.'"

"And what's with the mouse?"

"He keeps me company."

She went to the window, opened it a bit, and lit a cigarette. "So how long do I need to stay here?"

"Forty-five minutes should do. That'll make it seem like we had a good time."

She gave him a provocative look. As an actress, she could really convey it, too. "It doesn't have to just 'seem' like it."

"That wasn't what I paid for."

"And it's not what I'm selling. You're a good-looking man, and more, you're an honest one. This is strictly a personal offer."

Darren smiled at her. He had no particular aversion to trans women, but after his encounter with B.J. earlier in the evening, he doubted he was up to the, er, *challenge* again this soon. "And I appreciate it. But even if you're not, tonight *I'm* on the clock. Raincheck?"

Through a puff of smoke, she said, "If I'm not under someone else's umbrella by then."

He went to her and kissed her gently on the lips. "If you are, then it's my loss." He looked past her out the open window, at the Ink Ink Nudge Nudge tattoo parlor across the street. Its windows were dark, and its neon sign extinguished.

"Planning to get a tattoo?" Maria said over his shoulder.

He tensed. Maria was no dummy. "Just getting some comparatively fresh air."

She leaned against a wall, which creaked even with her insubstantial weight, and took her phone from her purse. He considered killing her just for security, but that seemed extreme. There was literally no way she could guess why he was here, and she knew better than to ask.

He closed his eyes. The sounds of the city night filled his ears.

"I like it when it's quiet like this," Maria said absently. "Like if you want noise, you have to make it yourself.

"It's not quiet," Darren said, his eyes still closed. "You know where it's quiet? Tokyo. It's a bigger city, but it's downright serene."

"Never been," Maria said through a puff of smoke.

1:15 A.M.

Laura drove Cole back home. Neither spoke; the worst thing any law enforcement officer, no matter how jaded, could encounter was murdered children, and it left them both beaten into muteness. They crossed the Smoke River on the Fumo Bridge and cut through Bowland neighborhoods to reach the expressway into Bay View, where Cole lived.

Finally, Laura broke the silence, "You said we'd talk about it, but not back there."

"I know," Cole said flatly.

"So tell me about this anonymous tip."

The "anonymous concerned citizen" bit was a catch-all for confidential sources that either had to be protected or wouldn't stand up in court anyway. "I shouldn't say."

"I'm your partner," she pointed out.

"I know."

They rode in more silence. The radio crackled with reports of other crimes for other cops. At last Cole said quietly, "It was… her."

"'Her'?"

"The Lightning Girl."

"Ha, ha. Very funny."

"I'm serious."

She glanced at him. "Shit, you are. So you know who she is?"

"No, but we have… an understanding."

"That's what men say they have with their wives, when they want to get someone else in bed."

"You're funny." At least she couldn't see him blush.

When he didn't continue, she prompted, "You can't just drop it at that. How did you even meet her?"

"It's kind of late for—"

She cut him off. "I can get on the interstate and take us all the way to Atlanta if I need to."

"All right, all right." He blew out a deep breath; this had been a long, stressful night. Then he told her about how he met the Lightning Girl, leaving out the whole matter of his crush.

"I reached an agreement with her," he finished. "We'd swap information that we thought the other could use."

"Holy shit. You're a reverse narc."

"From a certain point of view, yeah. Look at it another way, and it's… justice."

After another heavy silence, Laura asked, "Does she pay you?"

"What? No!"

"Do you pay her?"

"No. None of this is about money." He sighed. "You need to meet her. Talk to her yourself."

"I think I do," she agreed. But her reasons were very different from Cole's. If she met this so-called mutant vigilante, then she could put a stop to this before someone else got hurt.

1:2O A.M.

The night watchman poked his head inside the office. "Security," he announced. "Anyone here?"

"I'm here," B.J. said from her desk.

The watchman had once been a leg breaker for a Kefali loan shark, but age and disease had withered him. Stavros kept him on out of pity, giving him a job that really didn't exist since the building's security was all automated. "Pulling an all-nighter, Ms. Burr?"

"Hope not," she said without looking up. After a shower, B.J. had gotten back into the police department computer system to pick through the reports of Artie's death, searching for anything she didn't already know. So far, she'd found nothing.

"Can I get you anything? The all-night bakery's just around the corner."

"No, thanks. I'm fine."

"Then I'll leave you to it. Good night, Ms. Burr."

"Good night," she said distractedly.

She watched the night watchman toddle off on the security pop-up screen and saw nothing suspicious; it would be a long shot if he was the mole who provided Artie's killers with access to his building—as far as she knew the night watchman had no idea where Artie lived—but right now everyone except her, Darren, and Stavros was a suspect..

She returned her attention to the computer. Detectives Slade and

135

Slaughter seemed competent, if uninspired, but oftentimes the sheer repetitive drudge work broke a case. Nothing in their personnel files indicated they were on the take or amenable to it. But they were no slouches when it came to diligence; both had worked at the location of the multiple murder at the Ratway gas station. Would the cops make the connection with Artie's murder as quickly as Darren?

She stumbled into the crime scene photos. The small bodies at the feet of the various adults choked her up, and the text comments that identified the victims as "orphans" brought up memories of her own childhood before Artie and Stavros had taken her in. Before that, she'd lived on the street for as long as she could remember; her mother was just a vague, dark-haired memory and she had no idea who her father even was. Other kids had helped her at first, but then she became a threat, competition for territory and resources. She'd learned to run, to lie, and when necessary, to fight.

With Kefali's resources she could've found out what happened to her mother and, perhaps, even identified her father. But she'd never done so. As far as she was concerned, Stavros and Artie were her only parents.

Still, six orphans killed. Six children like her, living by their wits and satisfied with a meal and a flat surface to sleep on. Tears welled in her eyes.

She let herself cry it out, understanding that a big reason for tears was just weariness. By the time the last of the tears left her exhausted body, she was more than ready to go home. She called down for a car and gathered her things.

Darren yawned and stretched in the chair. Maria had departed some time ago, and he'd sat in the dark, watching the tattoo shop across the way. A couple of cars had driven by slowly, and he wondered if one of them was Apocalypse Joe, casing the place. If so, he'd never spot Darren in the window, and even if he did, he'd have no idea who he was.

He looked up and down the street. The difference from the views on the East Side was always surprising. There, every window sported a light, the street was bumper-to-bumper until well past midnight, pedestrians filled the sidewalks and clustered at the intersections, headed to fancy bars, restaurants or hotels.

Here in Johnson Loop, the last neighborhood in Bay View before the waterfront, it was different. The gentrification that overran Bowland had only gotten an intermittent purchase here, putting new and renovated buildings between the old ones, like silver teeth set in a grin. Some optical illusion made their shadowy forms appear to lean together, like great fingers about to pinch off the paved arteries running between them. The traffic moved in clumps, leaving empty blocks behind them, and the people lurking on the sidewalks were definitely not on their way to anything fancy. They were more like the scavengers that picked the last of the meat off a carcass's bones.

Now that he was still and quiet, Darren could finally dwell on his emotional response to Artie's gory murder. The last time they spoke, Artie had called to ask Darren to go fly-fishing with him.

"I'm terrible at fly-fishing," Darren had protested. "Can I shoot them instead?"

Artie never got annoyed by these protests. "Oh, come on, Darren. It'll be fun. Beer, sun, fresh air."

"I'm addicted to airborne carcinogens."

"You know what Thoreau said, right? 'We need the tonic of wildness.'"

"Thoreau didn't have to chase down pimps who are shorting the boss. Or convince two bodegas to pay protection."

"I'll pick you up Friday night. We'll drive up and get a start bright and early Saturday."

"I don't know those words 'bright' and 'early'. What language is that?"

But as always, he'd given in and had been actually looking forward to it. If Stavros was Darren's father figure, Artie was the cool uncle.

He gazed up at the water stains on the ceiling. Artie had been the one who brought him to Stavros in the first place, back when he was a teenage delinquent with a junkie mother and no clue about his father. Artie worked as a public defender, even though he was already on the Kefali payroll; later Darren discovered Stavros had insisted on it, so that Artie would learn the city's legal system from top to bottom, and from both sides.

He had met Artie in an interrogation room down in a Bay View precinct. Darren was seventeen, used to the juvenile justice system but scared to death of the adult one. He tried not to let it show.

"I'm your lawyer," Artie said as he sat opposite him and put his briefcase on the table. "Tell me what happened."

"Those cops planted shit on me. I never did nothing."

"Yes, you did. You used a rather clever device to skim credit card numbers from the cash machine inside the Deep Hurting nightclub. There's no point in denying it, especially to me."

"Oh, yeah? And what makes you so special?"

Artie leaned across the table and spoke softly, but with emphasis. "That nightclub is under the protection of the Kefali organization. That means you stole from them. And they don't like that."

Darren turned white. On the street, the name 'Stavros Kefali' was legendarily ruthless. "Oh, shit, man. You gotta help me."

Artie sat back. "Do I? And why is that?"

"You're, like, my lawyer, right?"

"I am. But just so you know, Stavros Kefali put me through law school. So I look out for his interests as well."

Darren could think of nothing to say. His eyes filled with tears.

"Oh, Jesus, kid, take it easy," Artie said with a laugh. "I have a deal for you."

"Wh-what?"

"First, answer a question. That cash machine is inside the club. How did you get past the doorman in the first place? There's no way you'd pass for 21."

Darren sniffled and wiped his eyes with his fingers. "There's an air vent right behind the machine, that's attached to the air conditioner on the roof. I used a plumber's snake to get the sensor down there. The sensor had a magnet on the bottom, so it just snapped into place."

Artie nodded, impressed. "Not bad. Here's my deal: I'll get you off on this charge, and in return, you come work for Mr. Kefali."

Darren had to blink a few times for this to register. "Are you serious?"

"You've got no family to speak of, no adult record yet, and what we call a genuine entrepreneurial spirit. I think he'll like you."

At the time, Darren felt he had no choice. But later, he understood how lucky he truly was. Stavros had given him a purpose, a guiding philosophy, and a thorough education. And he owed all that to Artie.

He wiped the tears from his eyes again, just as he'd done that day in the holding cell.

TWO DAYS BEFORE THE FESTIVAL

6:10 A.M.

As always, the sun struck the East Side first, glinting off the glass and metal of its buildings, sending unwanted reflections into neighboring apartments. Throughout those unfortunate dwellings, people woke up surly, annoyed, or downright angry at the intrusion.

Three years earlier, one tenant, an investment banker who'd gone off his meds, tried to shoot out windows in the Kefali building with an AR-15. Luckily the double-paned glass was bullet resistant, so no one was injured. The shooter spent a year in an institution at Kefali's expense and now worked in their accounting department. His loyalty to Kefali was total.

Sammartino, the doorman at the Kefali Building, hated his uniform in the summer. When the humidity rose, the collar always felt just a hair too small, making his face continually red and chafing his neck. He kept intending to have a uniform custom made but always chickened out; he had issues with his own sexuality, and the thought of being measured—especially *down there* for the inseam—made him sweat and tremble. So he suffered in mostly silence, smiling and holding the door for the dozens of employees who filed in every morning.

On this morning, though, there were few smiles in return. Arthur Shawcross's death had been on the news all day and night, and by now almost everyone had heard about it. The lawyer had been popular with the Kefali rank and file, most of whom, like Sammartino, worked entirely legitimate jobs for the company.

"Good morning," he said as Stefan Carr approached.

"Morning, Sam," Carr replied with a weary smile.

"Sorry to hear about Mr. Shawcross."

"Me, too," he said as he went inside.

Head of security Pawson had warned Sam to be alert; a package was expected, and while no one told him so, Sam knew it had to be connected to Shawcross's death. He also didn't know that Shawcross was beheaded, which was a lucky thing, as it turned out.

Because just then, yawning, the bike messenger rode up.

"I ask you, who wants a package delivered at six-thirty in the goddamn morning?" the skinny messenger said as he handed over the clipboard for Sammartino to sign. Then he gave him the cardboard box.

Darren had finally dozed, but his phone alarm woke him at six a.m. with B.J.'s voice purring, "Time to kick ass and take names, Mr. Flaxstone." She'd recorded it as a joke, but he'd kept it because he could think of no better sound to start the day.

The tattoo shop was still locked up across the street, and there was little traffic; people in Johnson Loop didn't tend to get up with the sun. A pair of intoxicated men wove their way down the sidewalk and stopped to peer in through the bars at the shop. Was one of them his quarry, casing the joint? No, this Apocalypse Joe was too cocky to be that devious. They continued on down the street, and he lost sight of them after three blocks.

Darren showered, wincing at the tepid water, and dressed for his job. He'd learned the hard way to prepare for any eventuality, including the chance that his quarry knew he was coming. The scars he bore all spoke to situations where he'd failed to anticipate something, and he'd just as soon not add any more.

The mouse, in its cage, looked up at him. "Sorry for what I've got you into, little pal," he said softly, then put the cage in his valise and left the room.

There was no one at the front desk, only a lock box with *Room Keys Here* written on the side by a Sharpie. His key rattled as it landed atop others. He waited inside the lobby doors, watching the tattoo parlor and the street for anything that felt out of place. Nothing did.

"Expecting an Uber?" a gruff voice said.

He turned to see a different man behind the counter. This one was long-haired and stubbled, clad in a t-shirt beneath an old sweater. He looked, Darren realized, exactly like he smelled.

"Nah, just waiting," Darren said. "I'm in no hurry."

The desk man grumbled something, then turned on the old portable TV. He couldn't see the screen, but Darren knew the voice: Magnum York, whose mellifluous tones gave even the worst news a subtle touch of Barry White-esque sensuality.

"...which means order your steak well done, Walter. In local news, seven bodies were discovered in an abandoned gas station in Rattaway last night. Police say the victims, an adult and six children, were killed sometime earlier, execution-style. Currently there are no suspects, but police ask anyone with any knowledge to please call or text their anonymous tip line."

"Mm-mm," the desk man said, shaking his head. "Ain't that a shame. You heard about it?"

"No." Darren turned back to the door but was aware the man continued to look him over. Darren mentally kicked himself; he should've simply left. Now the desk man might remember him.

To be truly secure, he should kill the desk man and then leave, and any other time, he might. But with seven fresh corpses already in the news, it might have the opposite effect and attract more attention. So he pushed open the door and walked out onto the street.

I t arrived by bike messenger," Sam told Pete Pawson in his office. The package sat on the security chief's desk, a box large enough to hold a bowling ball, tied with string and with no return address.

Pawson nodded. "Thank you, Sam. You can go now."

"Does this have something to do with Mr. Shawcross?"

Pawson's gaze grew hard behind his glasses. "I said you can go."

"Yes, sir," Sam said and quickly departed.

When the door clicked shut behind him, Pawson immediately punched the line to B.J.'s office. Stefan Carr answered.

"I need to speak to B.J.," Pawson said. "It's urgent."

"She's not here yet," Stefan said.

Pawson wasn't privy to B.J.'s personal contact information. "Then please let her know the package she expected has arrived."

"She left instructions. I'll be sending some people down. Don't open it."

Pawson eyed it warily. "Not a chance."

7:00 A.M.

By the time Laura Slade arrived at the 6th Precinct, Cole Slaughter was already there, working on the perpetual backlog of paperwork and reports. The smell of fresh coffee filled the squad room, and she stopped to refill her travel mug. Cole glanced up, nodded, and returned his attention to his work.

Laura's desk faced Cole's so the partners could easily communicate. She put down her bag, settled into her seat and said coolly, "Good morning."

"Morning," he said without looking up.

"Did you have a good night?"

"Sure."

"Did you think any more about our discussion in the car?"

"Nope. Said my piece. You?"

"It's hard to say. I'm still mulling it over."

He stopped typing and peered at her over the top of his monitor. "I trust you, you know. That's the only reason I told you."

"Yeah, that's not the sticky part. It's the whole 'helping-a-vigilante-kill-people' part that I'm having trouble with."

Cole looked around to make sure no one else heard. "Christ, Laura, post online about it, why don't you?"

"I *should* be in there telling Captain Evans what you told me."

"Then why aren't you?"

"Because you're my partner, and my friend. I'm waiting for you to convince me I'm wrong to want to do that." She paused, still seething. "Did she threaten you, Cole? Or Anna? Is that it?"

"No, nothing like that."

"Does Anna know?"

"No one knows except you, me, and her."

"And whoever *she's* told."

He acknowledged the point with a shrug.

"I've really got to think about this, Cole. It's not covered in the manual." She sighed and sat back. "But we can talk about it later. How's the paperwork coming on the Dodger?"

"Already done. Just waiting now to see if there's a connection between Shawcross and that massacre last night."

Laura's stomach dropped at the memory of those tiny bodies on stretchers. She sipped her coffee, grateful for the way it burned her lip, keeping her in the moment, and not back at that desolate crime scene.

7:05 A.M.

Sparrow opened his eyes and lay very still. He'd slept buried in the garbage overspill from a long-neglected dumpster, in between discouraging curious rats who sniffed around to see if he was dead. Despite what he told the Lightning Girl, after what happened to his friends and the Mendicant, there was no way he could return to any of his usual haunts; for the first time in his young life, he was truly on his own. And since Ratway was no longer safe, he'd relocated to the back alleys and vacant buildings of Bay View until he could figure out his next move.

Satisfied no one was watching, he climbed out into the open. His stained, threadbare clothes—jeans too short, a tie-dyed t-shirt too large, miss-matched tennis shoes—looked none the worse for wear, and his ragged, unkempt hair fell into place with a vigorous shake of his head. He leaned back against the brick wall, his empty stomach gurgling in the gray dawn light.

He sensed rather than heard someone approaching and slid silently behind the dumpster. Peeking out from behind it, he watched a man in a long coat, carrying an old suitcase, come down the alley. The man was unshaven, his hair was mussed, and he looked like any other vagrant, most likely passing through on his way to Ratway.

Something held Sparrow's attention, though. The man's eyes were crystal clear, not red or heavy-lidded. No vagrant would be awake and stone sober at this hour.

And then he recognized the man: Darren, who'd questioned him about the Mendicant at the gas station. Yesterday, he'd been clean and well-dressed; now he was a bum. Was he in *disguise?*

Sparrow had so many other pressing concerns, but he was only ten, and despite the unusual maturity his hard life had granted him, he was still prone to childhood impulsiveness. So, using all the skills the Mendicant had drilled and beaten into him, he followed Darren.

The sheer coincidence of it all didn't even occur to him.

The package sat on a stainless-steel table, inside a soundproof, bombproof chamber. B.J. and two Kefali "technicians" who were really veteran explosives experts, one trained by Interpol and one by the IRA, stood outside the thick observation window.

"I found no evidence of electricity indicating a timer," one tech said.

"And I got no trace of explosives," the other added.

"So you're saying," B.J. said, "that it's not a bomb."

The Irish tech shrugged. "A bomb's like a banjo solo, lass. By the time ye hear it, the damage is already done."

"All right, gentlemen, thank you. If you hear a big boom, you'll know you were wrong."

The techs exchanged a look. "Don't you want us to open—"

"That's been taken care of. Now, if you please?" She gestured toward the door. Puzzled, the two men departed, leaving her alone.

She touched her Bluetooth. "Did you hear all that?"

"Yes," Stavros said in her ear.

"I suppose you want me to open it?"

"Unfortunately, we don't have robots to do it remotely."

"Put that on my tombstone."

B.J. went into the room with the box. She put on a respirator, pulled on latex gloves, then cut away the string with a box cutter. She sliced the tape holding the paper and unwrapped it to reveal a plain cardboard box, recycled from an Amazon order.

She opened the lid. Inside was a plastic ice chest.

"Here we go," she said softly, for Stavros's benefit. She knew he watched everything.

She removed the lid.

Arthur Shawcross's gray bloodless face greeted her. Thankfully, his eyes were closed.

She swallowed hard. Nothing had prepared her for the reality of this. Still, her voice was steady when she confirmed, "It's him."

"I see," Stavros said. "See if there's anything else in there."

"Jesus, Stavros, are you serious?"

"This is a message, B.J. We wouldn't want to overlook part of it."

She took a deep breath and slowly blew it out, the warm air momentarily filling the respirator. She reached into the cooler, around Artie's head. She felt the limp strands of his hair, the cold softness of his skin, and tried not to vomit. Then her latex-clad fingertips encountered something hard. She withdrew a small card in an envelope, protected by a plastic sandwich bag.

"You were right," she said, not waiting for his instructions to open it. The envelope was pastel green, and inside it was a simple white card that said, *In sympathy.*

Only one line, in Greek, had been written on the otherwise blank interior. The sight of the language gave her a jolt, and it was even stronger when she translated the words in her head:

Hell has frozen over. I'll see you at the Festival.

There was no signature. But there didn't need to be.

It took her a moment to get her voice working. "Is that from who I think it is?"

"Yes, it must be," Stavros said. "Did you find Arthur's ring?"

"No." B.J. put the card down on the table. "What do we do, then?"

"Nothing. We continue to plan the Festival just as we always do."

"And if…?"

There was a long silence. "It had to happen eventually, B.J. That's the problem when you deal with the eternal."

9:41 A.M.

A s he put the finishing touches on the report, Cole's cell phone rang. He answered without looking at the number. "6th Precinct, Slaughter."

"Hey," his wife Anna said.

"Hey, honey," he replied, forcing his brain to snap out of work mode. "How are you?"

"I'm good. The shop's kind of slow today, so I wondered if you might like to meet for lunch, since I barely saw you yesterday."

He tried to think of a reason to avoid it but couldn't. "Uh... sure, sweetheart. Where?"

"Too much trouble for you to come down here?"

"No, not at all. I can hop the D train and be there in twenty minutes."

"Great," she said, and he could hear the bright smile in her voice. "I'll meet you at Calvin's, around the corner from the shop. Twelve-thirty?"

"It's a date. Love you, honey."

"Love you, too."

When he ended the call, he caught Laura looking at him. "What?"

"Is Anna working again?"

"Yes, at the flower shop."

"Full-time?"

"Half-time. They're being really supportive. If things get too rough, she can leave without getting in trouble."

"How's she bearing up?"

"Fine, so far. I think it hurts when people come by with babies, but she manages. She hasn't missed a shift."

Laura smiled sadly. "She's brave."

"Yeah." Since their infant son died three days after birth because of a heart defect, Anna had been fragile, to put it mildly. The least little thing could set her off on an hours-long crying jag. Cole didn't blame her, and he was totally sympathetic, but he was also at the end of his own rope, emotionally. Because of her, he'd yet to really mourn himself. Seven months of choking down grief wore on him. He dealt with it by avoiding Anna whenever he could, making his job the priority. He wasn't proud of it, but sometimes survival demanded it.

And then, of course, there was *her*. The more he tried to avoid thinking about the Lightning Girl, the more she crossed his mind.

Before he could say more, his desk phone buzzed. He picked it up with a clipped, "Slaughter." He listened for a moment, then said, "Thanks," and hung up.

"Ballistics?" Laura asked.

"Yep. The same gun that killed the Dodger also killed that man and those kids. Now we just have to figure out if it was in the same hands when it did it."

Laura passed him a printout. "Got an I.D. on the dead man from his prints: John Wilson, a.k.a. Jack Warding, a.k.a about a dozen other aliases over the years. Known in the city's criminal circles as the Mendicant."

Cole rubbed his eyes. "Remind me what a 'mendicant' is?"

"It means a beggar."

"So, he was a professional bum?"

"Not a bum, exactly. At least, the word means more than that. Some religious orders exist by begging. St. Francis was a mendicant."

"Was this guy a priest?"

"According to his rap sheet, more of a Fagin."

"What's a 'Fagin'?"

"Not what, who. Fagin had a band of children he trained as thieves in *Oliver Twist*. You know, like the Artful Dodger? The musical *Oliver*?" In a terrible cockney accent, she said, "'Please, sir, may I have some more?'"

"I have no idea what you're talking about."

"You should really read something besides James Patterson, you know."

He rubbed his eyes again. "Okay, so you're saying this guy had a gang of kids."

"Yes, but there were only six killed with him. He had as many as twenty-five. So there might be nearly twenty kids out there who might still be in danger."

"Does that Ratway detective we met know all this? What was his name, Stampede?"

"Rampede. Yes, I'm sure he knows."

"We should meet him and compare notes, then."

"Before or after lunch?"

Cole sighed. "I guess I better cancel—"

"*No.* Not on your life. I'll talk with Rampede and see what we can piece together. You have lunch with your wife."

"But this is—"

She stood up and grabbed the car keys. "Shut up, Cole. You've been a terrible husband lately, and you know it. Anna needs you. I can handle things for a few hours. If anything urgent comes up, believe me, I'll call."

"Don't hesitate, okay?"

"Stop it. For the next two hours, you're a husband, not a cop." She held his gaze until he looked away. Then she put her purse over her shoulder and headed for the elevator.

Captain Evans came out of his office and strode over to Cole's desk. "Where's Slade going?"

"We've got a ballistics match. The same gun that killed the Dodger also killed a man and six children in Ratway."

"Yeah, I heard about that. Shit, what a nightmare. Come into my office, will you?" Evans said this casually, but Cole knew a summons from on high when he heard one.

Once behind the closed office door, Evans gestured at a chair and took his own seat behind his desk. "The Dodger was part of the Kefali gang, wasn't he?"

"As far as we know. He was Stavros Kefali's *consiglieri*, or whatever that's called in Greek."

"That's right, Kefali's Greek," Evans said.

"And?"

"Have you ever heard of Kefali hosting something called, 'The Festival'?"

"Festival of what?"

"Just 'Festival.' '*The* Festival.'"

"Is it like Coachella for Greek music?"

"No, nothing like that."

Cole sat back, puzzled. "Captain, I don't follow."

Evans leaned on his elbows and spoke so softly Cole had to really pay attention. "The only thing we really know about this Festival is that it exists. We don't know where it's held, how long it lasts, what purpose it serves. The fact that it's so fucking secret, and allegedly put on by the head of a known criminal organization, makes it troubling. And the fact that I have reasonable certainty that the mayor, police commissioner, and chief of detectives are on the guest list make it downright worrisome."

Cole was silent for a moment, then asked, "What happens at this Festival?"

"No one seems to know, or they're not telling. I understand guests are sworn to secrecy and have to present special tokens to be admitted."

"Is it like the Illuminati or the Masons?"

"The Illuminati is a myth, and the Masons are just old guys who like role-playing that they're special. This is something else."

"So why are you telling me all this?"

"Because the Festival happens in two days, and it seems reasonable to suspect that the Dodger's murder so close to it might be a prelude to something larger, not to mention those kids."

"You think there'll be more killings?"

"I don't know, and that's the problem. The last thing I want is a gang war with our mayor, commissioner, and chief right in the middle of it. Ever hear of the St. Valentine's Day Massacre?"

"That was bad guys killing bad guys in a turf war, as I recall."

"It was people lured to a certain place at a certain time to be wiped out. I'd rather the mayor, commissioner, and chief not be this year's model."

"What do they say about it?"

"Fuck, Cole, I can't say anything to them. I like this job."

Cole thought for a moment. "If they attend, will it be as city officials or private citizens?"

"At that level, nothing they do is as private citizens."

"Again, Captain, why are you telling *me*?"

"I want you to know, in case you run across something relevant in your investigation of the Shawcross homicide. I wouldn't mind losing the mayor, honestly, but the commissioner is all right, and the chief is a friend."

"I'll tell Slade, and we'll keep our eyes open—"

"No. This is just between you and me. You report only to me on this, in person. No paper, no emails or texts, no phone calls. Understood? Regular reports, but only in person from you to me."

"You want me to keep this from my partner?"

Evans grinned wryly. "Son, if I could make it work, I'd like you to keep it from *me*. But I need to know, and given my position, I can't do the digging myself."

"Yes, sir," Cole said. What else could he say? But after the Lightning Girl, if Laura found out he'd kept another major secret from her, she might just shoot him on general principle. He couldn't blame her, either.

Rebecca Hutchcraft waited at her *Daily Standard* desk, nervously scrolling through the wire service postings. She'd been up all night writing her story on the Lightning Girl, transcribing the conversation from her notes, shaping the story into something that would keep people reading past the first page, onto the pages with the advertising that was so important. Most people would read it online, she knew, and hopefully many would subscribe in order to get past the paywall.

"You look beat," Eli Caruso said. "What committee meeting did you have to cover last night?"

"I did an interview," she said, looking past him at Ransom's office, where he sat gazing thoughtfully at his screen. She had no way to know if he was reading her story, and that made it pointless to interpret his expressions. It didn't stop her from trying.

"Oh, yeah? With who?"

"I can't say. It's an exclusive, though."

"Can you at least tell me if it was a sports, entertainment, politics...?"

Ransom sat back in his chair and clasped his hands behind his head, revealing sweat stains in his armpits. He continued to stare at his screen.

"Can't say," Rebecca repeated absently.

Eli realized she was looking right past him and turned. "Ransom reading it now?"

"I don't know. I hope so."

"Huh. You know you can't tell anything by his face. I'm glad I've never played poker with him."

"I know."

Caruso wasn't kidding about Ransom's poker face. Nothing stronger than mild curiosity ever registered on his features. He cut his eyes toward her, and she quickly returned her focus to her own screen. She flushed red at being caught.

Her desk phone buzzed. "Yes?"

"I suppose you want to know what I think," Ransom said. "Or are you just mesmerized by my strong jawline?"

"It *is* hypnotic. But yeah: what do you think?"

"Come in here and I'll tell you."

She went to his office, aware that every eye in the newsroom followed her. Once inside, he said, "Close the door."

She did and folded her arms. "Well?"

"You can sit down."

"Yes, I learned early."

He glared at her. She took a seat.

He tapped his screen. "This is a real interview, right? I mean, you didn't just get high and make this all up as some practical joke?"

"I don't get high. And yes, it's real."

"Do you have a recording?"

"Recorders don't work around her. Neither do cameras, which is why I don't have pictures. But I have notes."

"So you have the notes to back up every quote?"

"Yes."

He thought this over. "Then this goes front page, above the fold tomorrow morning. But it goes on the website today. Right now."

Her eyes opened wide. "For real?"

"For real. I don't know how you did it, but damn, Rebecca: good fucking job."

She felt the rush of pride swell in her and was about to laugh with joy when he brought it all crashing back down again. "So, when can you do the follow-up?"

10:09 A.M.

By mid-morning, Darren had circled the Ink Ink Nudge Nudge tattoo parlor for three hours, taking a different route each time, spiraling out several blocks and then coming back to walk right across the street from its front door. No one followed, and no one noticed. The parlor didn't open until noon, and no one had come in early.

So now it was time to go to work.

He slipped through the bodega whose rear entrance stood opposite the tattoo parlor's own back door. He crossed the alley and crouched by the locked, faceless outside door. It was the kind of security entrance that could only be opened from within, or at least that was what the manufacturer swore. The truth was considerably less reassuring.

From the satchel, he took out what looked like a metal handle taken off some cabinet door. He pressed a small switch on the shaft, which turned the handle into an incredibly powerful horseshoe electromagnet. The handle stuck hard to the metal door with a quiet *clank*. The magnetism was so strong that it pulled the panic bar inside closed, which popped the latch. He held open the back door and shone a flashlight through the gap.

There it was; Legs, the ironically-named "stay away snake" that guarded the parlor's back door. A bad-tempered boa kept perpetually hungry, it had injured three different would-be burglars. Now, hanging from a towel rack on the wall, it swung its head slowly around to stare at Darren with blank, emotionless eyes.

"Hey, Legs," he whispered. "Brought you a treat."

He took out the mouse's cage, opened it and shook the mouse out onto the floor just inside the door. The snake moved before the mouse even realized it was free and struck in an instant.

The snake withdrew, the mouse's rear end hanging from its mouth. Then it made a slow swallowing motion that pulled the mouse in the rest of the way. Darren grabbed his valise and slipped inside.

He could've killed the snake, of course, but that would tip off Wingo. He could've also given it bigger prey, like a rat or even a rabbit, but those would've left telltale bulges on the snake's body. This way it was occupied with digesting something so small it left no outside trace but still made the animal lethargic.

Except for light coming through the front window the place was dark. A check of his watch told Darren he had twenty minutes before Crespa arrived to open up, and ninety minutes before Wingo's appointment with Apocalypse Joe.

He went into the first tattoo room, the one Wingo preferred. In one corner, covered by a hanging velvet tapestry of Jimi Hendrix, there was a small supply closet. He moved the tapestry and took out a small power drill. He installed a fisheye peephole, the same kind you'd find in someone's door, at his eye level. A quick check assured him that he could see through the tapestry's weave enough to cover the whole room.

Then he unscrewed the air-conditioning vent near the ceiling and placed a small canister inside. He put another in the front of the store, and a third near the back door, hidden in a shadowy corner.

He carefully entered the closet and, before closing the door, tugged the tapestry back into place. Then he settled in to wait.

10:13 A.M.

In the alley outside, Sparrow approached the parlor's back door. He tried grabbing the edges with his fingertips, but he couldn't move it. He stepped back and folded his arms, wondering why this Darren guy would go to so much trouble to make sure he wasn't followed, just to rob some cheap-ass tattoo place.

If Sparrow was curious about him before, he was fascinated now. Whatever went down, he wanted to see it. He looked up at the fire escapes, saw one with its ladder within jumping reach if he did a wall scramble, and started his run.

T hanks for meeting me," Laura said to Rampede.

The Black officer stood at his desk and offered his hand. "When someone's so desperate to talk that they come all the way down here, I figure I better talk to them. Come on, let's go in here."

She felt every eye in the bullpen on her, not in a curious "who's that?" way, but more suspicious, even hostile. The 89th Precinct radiated a siege mentality.

She followed Rampede into an interrogation room. He indicated the lone chair. "Take a seat, if you'd like."

"That's okay. Why was everyone staring at me like I shot their dog?"

"Morlette and Hogan. Internal Affairs has been all up in our business ever since they were hurt."

"Do they think it was an inside job?"

"Who knows what they think?" he muttered. "We know who did it. There were even witnesses, but not a damn one of 'em tried to help. And now everyone's saying that they might've deserved it."

"They were dirty?"

"Beat cops in Ratway? *Of course* they were dirty. That doesn't mean they deserved to have their balls burned off, certainly not by some fucking vigilante weirdo." Rampede paused and rubbed his eyes. "I'm sorry. It's been stressful. I have to talk to I.A. myself right after lunch, even though I was nowhere near it."

"I understand." She gave him a moment, then asked, "Did you see the ballistics report on your shooting last night?"

"I did indeed. Same gun as your fancy East Side lawyer."

"That's why I'm here. Whoever killed Arthur Shawcross also disabled a very sophisticated security system long enough to get in and out without being seen. To me that says 'professional.'"

"And whoever killed the Mendicant and his kids did so in broad daylight, apparently unconcerned with witnesses around the crime scene. In and out, unseen in both cases. Also sounds like a pro. Has to be the same shooter."

"So how do we find him?"

"The Mendicant had a whole lot of other kids who ran with him, and I know social services rounded up a few of them. I planned to talk to one of them and see what that old bastard was up to for the last few days." He gave her a little smile. "Care to join me?"

"Don't you have to talk to I.A.?"

"It appears that appointment is going to slip my mind."

She smiled. "Then let's roll."

11:05 A.M.

The conference table in B.J.'s office held three dozen neatly addressed envelopes, all holding identical invitations to the Festival. For security reasons, she'd done all the addressing herself, and she was proud of her calligraphy. The *Métoikoi* had no idea how honored they should feel; once they would never have been invited to such an event.

Stefan stood ready to distribute the invitations for personal home delivery. He knew the Festival existed, but that was all; he most definitely had no idea what it was about. He was impressed with many of the names: famous musicians, actors, politicians, online influencers, sports figures. Many, though, were people he'd never heard of. "Looks great," he said.

"Thanks. Have you arranged the messengers?"

"Yes, ma'am. Twenty, all under thirty, all—by my standards at least—quite attractive. Handsome men, sexy women."

"Perfect."

B.J. ran a fingertip lightly over the expensive paper of the envelopes. Did one of these carefully vetted people send the package with Artie Shawcross's head? Would they laugh at the irony of being invited to the Festival by the very man they'd tried to threaten?

"Something wrong?" Stefan asked, after B.J. had been silent for a long moment.

"No. Nothing's wrong. Everything's right on schedule."
"I hope so."
"Have my car brought around. I want to go inspect the venue."
"Yes, ma'am." Stefan departed to attend to his duties.

Crespa came in right on schedule, fifteen minutes before the tattoo parlor opened. She put on the coffee, turned the radio to an all-nineties-grunge channel, and made sure all the equipment and ink was in order. Finally, she took Legs and put him back in the big aquarium where he spent his days. She also tossed in a mouse but didn't stick around to see if the snake consumed it. She'd always been squeamish about that.

Darren watched her through the peephole and fabric; she had no inkling he was there. He smiled at his own inadvertent pun. *No inkling* in a tattoo shop.

An hour later Wingo arrived, kissed Crespa on the cheek and prepared his room for his first customer. From the way he set up, it seemed the design had already been decided. Darren wondered if, despite what Wingo had told him, the artist had worked on the killer before.

The electronic chime over the front door announced an arrival. The words were indistinct, but the tone was genial, and in a moment Crespa appeared at the room's doorway. "Your ten o'clock is here," she announced and stepped aside.

Now Darren got his first look at Apocalypse Joe. Like Darren, he knew how to blend in and not attract attention. He also had the straight posture of someone with military training. That wasn't a surprise; if a combat veteran didn't become a black ops mercenary or a cop, assassin was a natural third choice. When the other option was living homeless under a bridge somewhere, it was no surprise many chose to continue killing for money.

"Wingo," Joe said. His accent was carefully neutral, giving away nothing. "How are you this morning?"

"All set up," Wingo said. "Just take off your shirt, sit down, and get comfortable."

Joe removed his t-shirt, revealing a lean torso already covered with ink. Darren recognized many of them: a military unit, a prison skinhead gang, a motorcycle club's colors. In and around them were small five-pointed stars; they stopped abruptly below his left pectoral muscle. As Wingo wiped an alcohol swab across the bare skin, he realized they were his kill marks.

"How many?" Wingo asked professionally.

"Eight."

Artie, the Mendicant and six kids, Darren thought. *The motherfucker counts the kids.*

Wingo pulled the surgical mask onto his lower face, settled onto his stool, and began to work. The ink gun's wavery buzz filled the air.

Joe's companion stuck her head in the room. "Dude, I think your snake's sick," she said to Wingo.

He didn't look up. "Yeah? How so?"

"He's ignoring that mouse."

"Maybe he's not hungry."

"Maybe. You care if I take him out and look at him?"

"Okay with me."

"Be careful, Delilah," Joe said, with a sincerity that surprised Darren.

The girl gave a little *hmph* of annoyance, then left.

Darren put his thumb over the radio switch in his palm. He pressed it and waited.

The planted devices dispensed an expensive formulation of odorless, colorless gas that would render unconscious anyone exposed to more than a whiff of it. Luckily it was also easily counteracted and blocked by the long-acting pill Darren swallowed earlier. He waited for it to take effect.

There was a loud crash from the front, and Wingo looked up. Darren realized with a start that the surgical mask might keep the gas from working on him. "Crespa?" he called. "Hey, Crespa? You all right?"

When there was no reply, he stood up and went to the door. He pulled down the mask and shouted, "Hey, Crespa!" Then his knees wobbled, and he slid to the floor, holding onto the door jamb until the last moment.

The man in the chair, fingers laced across his bare belly, did not move. His chest rose and fell in slow, rhythmic breaths. Still Darren waited; he was always alert for the chance he'd been outsmarted.

At last he risked opening the closet. Cooler air dried the sweat on his face. After another wait, he slid back the curtain and stepped out. Apocalypse Joe didn't move.

He wasted no time. He gave Joe a quick injection to keep him under, then found his companion. She lay on the floor with Legs the snake beside her. A quick shot also rendered her helpless.

He searched Joe and found a small .22 automatic–the same caliber as the bullets that killed the Dodger. The smug bastard was so sure of himself that he hadn't even ditched it.

They'd brought a satchel-type bag with them as well. He took out a heavy, oddly-shaped object wrapped in a hotel towel. When he saw it, he actually winced.

It was an enormous scissor-like bone cutter. The one, no doubt, that had beheaded the Dodger after he was dead.

He took out his phone and opened a very specialized app created by Kefali's software team. Using it, he scanned Joe's fingerprints and sent them to B.J. He closed the app, made a call and when someone answered, said merely, "Ready."

Sparrow, huddled small on the third-floor fire escape landing, watched an old, rust-spotted SUV come down the alley and stop outside the tattoo parlor's backdoor. A man in coveralls got out and opened the back doors. A moment later Darren came out of the tattoo parlor carrying a shirtless man, either dead or unconscious, over his shoulder. He placed him roughly in the back of the SUV, then returned to the shop.

With a cold jolt of fear and fury, Sparrow realized the shirtless man was Apocalypse Joe, who had killed the Mendicant.

Sparrow silently crept down the stairs to the second-floor landing. He froze when Darren returned, this time carrying the limp form of Joe's girlfriend, Delilah. She too was placed in the SUV. Darren went back inside; the SUV's driver started the engine but didn't leave.

Sparrow reached the ground without the driver noticing. He knew Darren would return soon, and the vehicle would depart. He had to make a quick decision.

Darren returned to the alley carrying his valise and Joe's bag. Crespa and Wingo would awaken soon, with pounding headaches but otherwise none the worse for the experience. They would either assume Joe and Delilah had drugged them, or that someone out to get the two strangers had done so. Either way, there was nothing to tie it to Darren, and through him, to the Kefali organization.

Darren climbed into the passenger seat. "Go," he said to the driver, and within moments they were lost in the traffic.

12:16 P.M.

Anna waited for Cole on the restaurant's outside patio. Tierney's was a nice neighborhood eatery in the fashionable part of Bay View. Many who worked on the East Side commuted from this borough due to its bucolic normality; as the old haunt of Irish and Italian immigrants, it had that sense of place other parts of the city had lost. It had also, so far, avoided most of the gentrification eating up Bowland and the rampant crime of Rattaway.

Cole emerged from the subway station down the street from Tierney's and stopped behind an organic fruit kiosk to observe his wife before she saw him. She was still the pretty, charming woman he'd met on the C train, but her eyes no longer sparkled with mirth; instead they were gray and dead, even when she smiled. Cole wondered what visible marks, if any, the death of his newborn child had left on him.

He took a deep breath, put on a smile and strode into the open. She waved at him, and he nodded that he would enter through the front door. The lunch crowd was heavy, and it took him a few moments to work his way through and join her.

"Hey, honey," he said as he kissed her. "How's your morning been?"

"Pretty good," she said brightly, with just a hint too much emphasis. "The shop's very busy. Lots of summer weddings, and one really weird event I'm not even sure about. How about yours?"

He sat opposite her and took her hand across the table. "Not quite as life-affirming. Eight bodies in twelve hours."

"Oh, my God. All from the same case?"

"No, two different cases, but all related. Probably all over the news."

"Not today. Have you seen the news?"

"No; why?"

She took out her phone, called up the *Daily Standard* web page and handed it to him. The headline read, *She's Real!* and, below that, *Exclusive Interview with Rattaway's "Lightning Girl."*

"Huh," Cole said noncommittally. He fought to keep any reaction from his face, while inside he thought, *What in the holy fucking hell is this?* His first response was to chalk it up to a joke or publicity stunt, but Rebecca Hutchcraft had the byline. She wouldn't be fooled, and she wouldn't knowingly write a lie. So what was Sparky up to, going public like this?

"That's all you've got to say?" Anna said, yanking him back to the moment. "The city has a real superhero."

He handed back the phone. "I don't know if I'd go that far. It could still all be a hoax."

"Don't you want to read it?"

"I'll read it later. Right now, I just want to visit with you."

"It's all anyone at the shop can talk about."

"And I'm sure it'll be all over the station when I get back."

She put away her phone, and they ordered lunch. The salads arrived quickly, and as they ate, an uncomfortable silence settled over them. Once they could barely stop talking to each other, wanting to share everything; now it seemed their mutual silence was all they had in common.

"How's Laura?" Anna asked finally.

"She's fine. She sends her best."

"Please give her mine. Didn't she have a birthday recently?"

"I have no idea."

She sighed, teasingly. "Do you even remember *my* birthday?"

"No, but I remember where I have it written down."

They both smiled, then laughed, and for that instant they became their old, pre-tragedy selves. Then Anna frowned as she watched something over his shoulder, in the street behind him.

"Now who is *that?*" she asked.

He turned to look. A silver stretch limousine had stopped in front of the old Catholic Church, long shuttered but recently the site of renewed construction and renovation.

"The new priest?" Cole suggested.

"In a limo?"

"Then maybe it's the bishop," he asked with a shrug. He scooted his chair around to see who got out.

He expected a man in a cleric's collar, or at least someone in a suit and tie. But when the driver held the back door open, a tall woman in an expensive suit and sunglasses, her black hair pulled severely back, emerged. Her skirt was short enough that every straight male and gay woman within eyesight was riveted to her legs, including Cole. For a full twenty seconds, it kept him from realizing he knew her.

"I'm pretty sure that's no priest," Anna pointed out dryly.

"No," he said. "She works for Stavros Kefali." *Belinda June "B.J." Burr, senior vice president of the Kefali Corporation. Why would she be here, checking on an old church?* Once the city's mobs had deep ties to the church, or at least the Italian and Irish mobs did: both groups were known for their heavy Catholicism. Kefali was Greek, and while there were plenty of Greek Catholics in the city, there had never been that sort of entanglement with his organization. But maybe there was now?

He realized Anna had said something, but he'd ignored her. "I'm sorry, honey. What?"

"I asked if you knew her." The hint of jealousy, something else that was new to their relationship, colored her words.

"One of the people killed yesterday worked for her. We met when we went to search his office." He turned back in time to see B.J. climb the steps and enter the building.

He noted the signs that announced the companies working on the renovation. He didn't recognize the names from the list of Kefali holdings, but that didn't mean the organization didn't control them.

"Hello? Earth to Cole?"

He forced his attention back to Anna. Once he wouldn't have had to use force. "Sorry, hon. Have you heard anything about the work they're doing in the church?"

"Only that we're doing centerpieces and arrangements for some major shindig there tomorrow night."

"It wouldn't be some kind of 'festival,' would it?"

"I don't know, Loraine handles all that, I just do the work."

Their lunches came, but neither had much appetite. Anna picked at hers, while Cole ate with mechanical efficiency, barely tasting anything.

"I'm sorry," Anna said at last, not looking at him.

"No, honey, it's me. I need to learn when to turn off the job. Any chance we can salvage this?"

"The lunch, or the marriage?"

Her words sent a fresh jolt through him. "Is the marriage in danger of sinking?" he asked quietly.

"You tell me."

He forced down his annoyance, a trick that grew harder and harder with each passing day. "I think we should do what the grief counselor said. We should see a couple's therapist."

"You think I'm crazy?"

"Not at all. I think that we both are feeling things we don't know how to express, and they're coming out as attacks on each other. You know damn well I'm not seeing anyone else, just like I know you're not cheating on me. But we snipe about it when other things get too hard to figure out."

"So, you *did* pay attention in the counseling sessions."

He gritted his teeth. "I'm doing the best I can here, Anna."

"What if that's not good enough, Cole?" she shot back.

He froze in mid-bite. With careful deliberation he put down his fork, slowly arranging it perpendicular to the edge of the table. He put his napkin atop his plate, then stood. Without making eye contact he said, "I'll see you at home," then turned and walked out of the restaurant.

Raging inside, he started toward the subway station, anxious to get back to work, where at least he knew what to do and say in most situations. But he stopped at the corner, turned, and looked at the big old church. How long had it been empty? At least five years, maybe as many as ten. Settlements in the church's pedophilia scandals had closed it, like many others. So why was it re-opening now? Who was paying for it? And what did Kefali's senior VP have to do with it?

Was it the site of the mysterious "Festival?"

"Dammit," he muttered and crossed the street toward the church.

12:35 P.M.

B.J. stood in the center of the great open nave. In place of the pews, the floor now shone with dark polished granite, covered with plastic while other work progressed. Around the edges of the sanctuary, Doric columns made of gleaming white marble rose toward the ceiling. They were all that had been saved from the last five Festivals.

"We got yer extra roof supports going in, and the sound system is being wired," said Joe Kecias, the construction foreman, gesturing with his clipboard as he spoke.

"Very good," B.J. said approvingly. "You're ahead of schedule."

"Yes, ma'am, a bonus like you promised gives us a lot of motivation."

"Have there been any unforeseen problems?"

"We had to reinforce the foundation to make it strong enough to hold all this marble and granite. Been easier and cheaper to tear the whole thing down and start from scratch."

"That's not the job, Mr. Kecias."

"Oh, I know. Sacred ground and all that."

"Is the special studio also ready?"

"It will be by the time your folks get here tomorrow to set it up." He smiled and puffed out his chest, proud to recount his accomplishments for this beautiful woman.

"And the green room? Does it have access to the power needs we discussed?"

"Yes, ma'am. Except I don't think the building inspector will sign off on that."

"That's not your worry, Mr. Kecias."

"You know, I once installed the electric lines for a fancy particle accelerator lab, and it was a lot like this. What are you planning to hook up in here?"

B.J. gave him her hardest stare. "Mr. Kecias, if you want that bonus, you'll stop looking for mysteries and just do the job. Am I clear?"

Kecias swallowed hard. "Yes, ma'am."

B.J. walked away from the man and tried to visualize what the place would look like when finished. There would be curtains of sheer silk, soft cushions and well-padded hammocks. It would recreate something that had not truly existed outside this Festival in five thousand years, and it would serve a purpose none of those invited could truly guess.

And it would burn to the ground the day after.

She ran a hand along the smooth white stone. It seemed so wasteful to destroy such beautiful work, yet part of the Festival's power was its impermanence. So this place would be reduced to powder and fragments, along with everything else installed for the occasion. Only the columns might survive, to be stored for another century.

Her cell phone buzzed. She touched her earpiece and said, "Burr."

"We've got 'em," Darren said. The road noise in the background told her he was in motion. His words told her he had the people responsible for Artie's death.

"Excellent," she replied. "Let me know what they've been up to as soon as you can."

"Will do."

The call ended.

"Miss?" Kecias called.

When she turned, she was startled to see Detective Cole Slaughter beside her foreman. He was such an out-of-context presence in this place that she simply stared for a moment, trying in vain to put together a chain of reasonable circumstance that ended with him here. "Detective Slaughter," she said at last.

"Ms. Burr."

"This is a little off your usual stomping ground, isn't it?"

"Actually, I live in Bay View not far from here. I was on my way to the subway when I saw you going into the church. I wasn't aware it was being renovated, or that Mr. Kefali was involved, so I thought I'd poke my head in."

"I told him it wasn't safe," Kecias said.

B.J. ignored him, and said to Cole, "What do you think?"

He looked around. "Not exactly Vatican standard, is it?"

"It's no longer being used as a Catholic Church."

He nodded as if that made perfect sense. "And Mr. Kefali's footing the bill?"

"That's a private financial matter."

"Of course. Well, I'm sorry to interrupt, Ms. Burr. I'll let you get back to it."

"One moment, Detective, if you please. Do you have any more information on my friend's murder?"

She said this so plaintively that, for a moment, he thought she was putting him on. But her expression was so genuinely sad he realized she was serious.

"We've got some leads. And I'm not just saying that. His murder seems to be connected to another one, in another part of the city. That's all I can say right now, but as soon as we make an arrest, you'll be the first to know."

"Thank you, Detective."

He nodded, turned and departed. B.J. took a moment to compose herself, then said to Kecias, "Now I'd like to see the security office."

Again he gestured with the clipboard. "Right this way, ma'am."

12:40 P.M.

The girl was, as near as anyone could tell, eleven or twelve years old; she claimed not to know her birth date. She'd been scrubbed clean and now wore a neat t-shirt and new blue jeans. Her hair, still unruly and long, was at least parted straight down the middle and clean. It put Laura in mind of Tom Sawyer after Aunt Polly got her hands on him.

The girl sat on the very edge of the couch in a Pigeon Hill brownstone. The couple who owned it, the Mohleres, were compassionate veteran foster parents who'd endured pretty much anything a child could throw at them. They also knew the routine when the police needed to question one. Mrs. Mohlere stood in the kitchen and watched through the archway, wary but not interfering.

"So, your name is Thrush?" Laura asked gently. "Is that first or last?"

"Just Thrush," the girl said.

"Okay, Thrush. Where are your parents?"

"Beats me. Don't even remember them. They dumped me at some group home when I was three or four."

"And that's where the Mendicant found you?"

Thrush said nothing.

Detective Rampede, who'd remained standing so that his physical size could be used to intimidate the girl if needed, said, "I'm sorry to have to tell you, the Mendicant is dead."

"I figured," the girl said flatly. "The cops already grilled me when they first caught me."

"He was your father in everything but name, wasn't he?" Laura asked. The girl didn't look away, or respond. "Someone murdered him."

She shrugged. "Shit happens."

"Along with some of your friends."

That got her attention. It took her a moment to find her voice. "You mean other kids?"

"Yes."

Her lower lip trembled, and the practiced hardness vanished. "Wh-which ones?"

"We're waiting on identifications," Rampede said.

Thrush swallowed hard. "Was...was one of them a little boy named Sparrow? Or maybe an older boy named Corvus?"

"We honestly don't know," Laura said. "How many kids were in your gang?"

"F-fifteen," she said shakily. The effort it took not to cry showed in her face.

"We were hoping you could help us find the killer. We think it was someone the Mendicant helped get a job, and that he was killed to eliminate anyone who knew about it."

"Why did they kill the other... the kids?" she asked. Her eyes gleamed with unshed tears, but she remained perfectly still.

"We think they were just in the wrong place at the wrong time."

Thrush looked down and let out a sigh. "Ain't that a kick in the head?"

"Where did you hear *that* phrase?" Laura asked.

"The Mendicant used to say it."

"So can you help us?"

She turned her head toward the wall so she wouldn't have to look at Laura. "I saw him talking to some guy he called 'Mummadabba.' And then, a few days later, a scary guy and his weird girlfriend came by."

"Did the scary guy have a name?" Rampede asked.

"Pickle Hips something." She appeared to be thinking hard. "Pickle Hips Joe."

"'Pickle Hips Joe?'" Laura repeated.

"Yeah. That was it."

"What did he look like?" Rampede asked.

"Average. White guy, brown hair, not too tall, not too short."

"What was scary about him?"

Thrush shrugged. "Just a feeling. You learn to trust those."

"You said his girlfriend was 'weird'?"

"Yeah. She was twitchy, you know? Like she couldn't sit still. Or maybe she was retarded."

"Thrush," Mrs. Mohlere gently scolded from the archway. "People don't use that word anymore."

"How many times did he meet with the Mendicant?" Laura asked.

"I only saw him once, and he didn't stay long. But he and the Mendicant had a very serious talk about this Mummadabba guy."

"Any idea what about?"

She shook her head, which dislodged the tears. They ran down her cheeks, and her lower lip trembled.

Laura wanted so badly to give her a hug, but before she could, Rampede knelt in front of Thrush and put one large hand on the girl's shoulder. "We'll get them," he said, his voice a low rumble. "And when we do, I'll personally let you know." He gently patted Thrush's cheek then stood. "Thank you, Thrush."

In the car outside, as Laura pulled away from the curb, Rampede said, "Pickle Hips Joe. What the hell kind of hit man goes by that?"

"You don't believe her, then?"

"No, I totally believe her. If she'd made it up, it would've made more sense."

"If this Pickle Hips was a pro, he's probably long gone," Laura said.

"Maybe. But there's gone, and there's gone. We've got a name and a description, and it's almost a guarantee that somewhere, he's got a record. That might point us in the right direction."

"She said there were fifteen. Six are dead, two are in custody. That leaves seven still unaccounted for."

"Ratway's a big place," Rampede said.

12:58 P.M.

Rebecca Hutchcraft sat at the bar in the Bullpen, a sports bar that served as the de facto watering hole for the *Daily Standard*'s staff. She nursed a beer and scrolled through her article's comments on her phone. As with all online forums, it quickly turned into a shouting match about politics, with Russian bot accounts arguing with each other just to keep the flames stoked. How the story of some weird mutant vigilante had anything to do with Obama's legacy was beyond her. But then she reached a unique comment posted two hours earlier.

I know who she is. I see her all the time. I'll tell somebody, if they'll pay me. The crazy bitch needs to be stopped.

The username was Angelyne223. Rebecca clicked on the name, and saw that whoever she was, she'd posted a lot, and for a long time. Most of her posts were on articles about city government, where she displayed Libertarian leanings that frequently drew the ire of the more liberal commentators. But there was enough variation to convince Rebecca that, if nothing else, this was a real human being who lived in the city.

Most of the responses to this particular comment were foul-mouthed variations of the opinion that Angelyne223 was the crazy one. Surprisingly, she engaged with none of them, apparently content to let her original comment stand on its own.

Rebecca clicked to send her a private message. *I'm interested. Let's talk.*

Just then a familiar voice said at her elbow, "The woman of the hour. Reading your fan mail?"

She put her phone facedown beside her drink, embarrassed at being caught doing exactly that. "They're not all fans, I promise."

Assistant District Attorney Max Gilsan took the stool next to her. Max was smooth, in every sense: in addition to his deep voice and ability to navigate any social situation, he was also born with congenital hypotrichosis, which meant he had no hair anywhere on his body. It did not affect his attractiveness. If anything, it was the icing on his smooth, smooth cake.

"That was some article," Max said. "Everyone at the courthouse is reading it."

"Thanks," she said.

"Tell me, did she discuss the two injured officers?"

Rebecca's guard went up. Choosing her words carefully, she said, "Only in passing. Claimed they had their own little reign of terror going. It's all in the article."

"Huh." He took out his phone and patted his pockets one-handed. "Shit, where'd I put that? Here." He handed her his phone, found what he sought, took back his phone, and before Rebecca even realized it, she was holding a subpoena.

She looked from it to the A.D.A. "What the *hell*, Max?"

"A grand jury has been convened to consider charges in the assault on those two officers. Your new friend is a vigilante, Becks, and we need to find her before she injures anyone else."

She scowled at him. "I thought we were friends."

"We are. Which is why I know you understand."

She put the subpoena in her purse. "I'll have the paper's lawyer get back to you."

"Actually, you can call him on the way." Suddenly two uniformed officers stood behind her, one a fireplug of a man with a crewcut, the other a lithe Black woman. "Officers Miller and DeMars will escort you to the courthouse."

"What, *now?* Max, come on."

He spread his hands in a shrug. "The grand jury is in session. We don't want to wait and have to convene another one."

Rebecca looked at the two stern officers, then back at Max's apologetic but still serious face. She stood and put her purse over her shoulder. "This is way out of line, Max. And you know I can't testify about a source. We have a shield law."

"That's between you and D.A. Sakamoto," he said. The four left the bar, to the puzzled gazes of the other patrons. Miller held the back door of the patrol car for her; it wasn't a true perp walk, but it was close enough. Fuming, Rebecca pulled her phone from her purse and hit Ransom Wade's number as the car eased away from the curb and into traffic.

When he heard what had happened, Ransom said, "Jesus H. tap-dancing Christ. All right, I'll get a lawyer down there ASAP. In the meantime, take the Fifth on anything they ask you."

"I will. This is nuts, Ransom."

"It's not nuts at all. It's because of those two cops, which all the other cops take as a personal insult. And since the D.A. depends on the cops, well… there you go."

Rebecca ended the call. She glanced through the back windshield and saw Max following in his own car. Fascism had crept into law enforcement for years, and now it wasn't afraid to step into the open. If the police could snatch a reporter off the street like this, then it wasn't much of a step to holding her indefinitely and keeping her incommunicado.

Rebecca was angry but also a little frightened. She sat back, folded her arms, and stared straight ahead.

1:01 P.M.

B.J. inspected the security room, and then the "special" room with its unusual power needs. It was indeed loaded with electrical outlets of all designs, from regular to extremely heavy duty. She imagined the equipment in place, and was satisfied with it. "Very nice, Mr. Kecias."

"Thank you."

The other room, for Stavros, was also acceptable. Kecias had been chosen for both his skill and discretion, but she had to wonder if he suspected the true purpose of any of these rooms. If he did, he kept it to himself, which is what kept him alive.

"Some special equipment will arrive for installation tonight. Our own people will take care of it. Once it's in place, these rooms will be locked, and armed guards placed outside them. Please inform your crew, so that they don't get the wrong idea."

"Yes, ma'am."

"And if that policeman, or *any* policeman, starts poking around asking questions, please call me immediately at this number." She passed him a business card.

"Yes, ma'am," he said with a jaunty little salute. He tucked the card in his pocket. "You can count on me."

1:03 P.M.

H ey. *Hey.* Joe. Wake up."

Darren had injected the sleep gas antidote five minutes ago, and the expected effect should be kicking in. Sure enough, Apocalypse Joe's eyes opened. He said nothing, but just cut his eyes around, taking in as much of his current situation as he could.

He was in some kind of deserted, high-ceilinged industrial building. Wind whistled through the broken windows and cracks in the walls, and pigeons fluttered in the rafters. A distant dog's barking echoed off the bricks. The room stretched away on either side farther than, at the moment, he could see.

He sat in what felt like an old-style barber chair; duct tape held him by the wrists, biceps, ankles, thighs, head and neck. The edges of the tape bit into his skin and cut off circulation, making his hands tingle and his face flush.

Darren wore a white lab coat, a fresh surgical mask, and latex gloves. "Good morning, Joseph McGillicuddy Clifford."

At the sound of his real name, Joe glared.

"Believe me, I understand," Darren said. "If that was my name, I'd go by Apocalypse Joe, too." Once Darren had scanned the man's fingerprints, the Kefali tech crew had been able to forward page after page of information about the assassin, from his birth in Missouri to his juvenile record, on up to his court-martial plea-bargain for second-degree manslaughter.

187

There were no surprises in it, and nothing Darren could really use against him. But it took away a lot of the intimidation factor of knowing him only by his admittedly-cool nickname.

"I'm going to ask this just to get it out of the way, since I don't expect you to answer at this point, and I wouldn't believe it if you did. Who hired you to kill Arthur Shawcross?"

"I give up," Joe said. "Who?"

Darren smiled behind the mask. "Oh, you're a caution, aren't you?"

"What makes you think anyone hired me?"

Darren ran a finger across the tattooed kill marks, and Joe suddenly realized he was naked. Like any man, he felt particularly helpless with his genitals exposed; but unlike most, he understood it for the tactic that it was. Darren watched these thoughts play out across his face, impressed with the self-control. He tapped the half-finished tattoo from earlier and said, "Because you're a pro. You don't kill without getting paid."

"If you know that, you know I'm not going to say anything."

"That's my challenge, isn't it?" Darren walked to a table, where several instruments of torture lay neatly arranged, again mainly for theatrical effect. He picked up Joe's own immense bone cutter. "This do the job?"

"Did you find his head?" Joe shot back.

Darren pulled the blades open, then let the powerful spring snap them shut. The loud metallic *schick* sound echoed around them. "So we know this works on the big head. Wonder how it'd work on the little one?"

He pulled it open again, held it over Joe's groin, and let it slam shut inches above. The bound killer, despite his best efforts, still jumped.

Darren smiled and put the cutter aside. "You haven't asked about your friend Delilah."

"I'm not friends with any 'Delilah.'"

"Oh, sure you are. Delilah Elaine Johnson, from Milwaukee. In and out of mental institutions her whole short life, until she finally just disappeared. I'm guessing that was around the same time she took up with you."

A flicker of something momentarily flared in the killer's eyes. Fear? If so, it wasn't for himself. "Okay, fine. She's my partner. But she has nothing to do with my job."

"Aren't you a little old for her?"

"She's working through daddy issues." He tried unsuccessfully to turn his head. "Is she here...?"

"She is," Darren said and stepped behind the chair. He raised the back enough that Joe could see down the length of his body. Delilah, still unconscious, was strapped into an identical chair that was upright and facing him. She was stripped down to her matching Hello Kitty underwear.

"Is she hurt?" Joe asked.

"Oh, no. Well, not yet. See, I understand that you're tough, and that getting information out of you would probably be pointless. You can endure anything I can think of to inflict on you; that's a given. But it'll take a mighty hard man to watch his girl go through the same things." Darren held up a hypodermic needle half-filled with an amber liquid.

"What is that?" Joe asked darkly.

"It's commonly called *magnum sentire*. Comes from the vaults of an old Soviet lab in the Ukraine. It's used to enhance physical sensation. It's very popular with wealthy older men; they say when it's combined with Cialis or Viagra, it's mind-blowing. I've never tried it, so I can't say."

He stood beside Joe's chair, the hypo held upright. He pushed the plunger enough to send a stream of fluid shooting into the air. "A lesser-known use," he continued, "is that it also magnifies the sensations of pain. It can make the slightest pinch feel like the grip of an industrial vise."

"And you think that'll get me to talk?" Joe said.

"You're not paying attention. I'm not going to give it to you." He turned to Delilah in her chair and, with no preliminaries, injected it into her arm. Almost at once, she began to stir.

"You motherfucker," Joe snarled.

Darren used the table's control to move the chair until Delilah lay flat on her back. From the tray, he took a four-inch-long acupuncture needle, so thin it was almost invisible. He looked back at Joe and said, "Let me explain how this works."

1:31 P.M.

Back at the 89th Precinct, Laura watched over Rampede's shoulder while he searched the police database for anyone with the alias, Pickle Hips Joe. Surprisingly, one man actually used it, but he was in prison, which ruled him out.

"I'm astounded that two people chose to call themselves 'Pickle Hips Joe,'" Laura said.

"Maybe the kid heard it wrong," Rampede mused. "What scary word sounds like 'Pickle Hips'?"

Laura thought it over. "'Apocalypse'?"

Rampede typed in "Apocalypse Joe."

A name popped up. *Joseph McGillicuddy Clifford.*

"Think that's him?" Rampede asked Laura.

Clifford's mug shot showed him to be truly generic, a face that would vanish from your consciousness an instant after you saw him. "Former army sharpshooter," Laura read aloud. "Won medals for it. Also proficient in electronics and computer science. That could explain how he disabled the security system in Arthur Shawcross's building. Charged with an Article 119 at his court-martial. Served two years. Subsequently arrested three times for murder one, but each time charges were dropped for lack of evidence."

"No current address, no employer, no trace in seven years," Rampede muttered. "Could be. So now all we have to do is find him."

She thought for a moment. "He's been entirely off the radar for seven years. If he's so damn smart, though, why is he still using the same alias?"

"Mark of pride," Rampede said. "Every man has one, and it comes out in unexpected ways sometimes."

"And you think women have no pride?" Laura challenged.

Rampede smiled. "I think women are smart enough to come up with a different alias."

Suddenly, a fresh voice interjected, "Hi."

"Detective Slaughter," Rampede said.

"What are you doing here?" Laura said to Cole.

"I called the precinct, and they told me you were down here, so I took the subway. Figured I could ride back with you." He nodded at Rampede's screen. "Who's that?"

"Our assassin," she said, then added, "Maybe. How was lunch with Anna?"

"It was fine," he said noncommittally. "But I stumbled across something odd while I was there. Remember B.J. Burr, the Kefali VP we spoke to yesterday? I saw her going into an old, closed-down Catholic church in Bay View. They're turning it into some kind of event space."

"In Bay View?" Rampede said, puzzled.

"I know," Cole agreed.

"Why is that odd?" Laura asked.

"I checked around. They do a lot of the work at night, and the neighbors have complained about the noise, to no avail. When I asked a guy I know in one of the Bay View precincts, he said that the orders came down from on high to disregard any complaints."

"How high on high?" Rampede said.

"Any higher, they'd come with a choir. Which makes me wonder if it has anything to do with our murder."

"Why would it?" Laura asked.

"Well, think about it. Who would've handled all the paperwork for Kefali getting permission for these renovations?" Cole said.

Laura slowly smiled. "And someone from the neighborhood might see his name on those forms and think he was responsible."

"And this same someone killed those seven people in Ratway?" Rampede asked. "That makes no sense."

"We know it was the same gun," Laura pointed out, "not necessarily the same trigger finger."

"And we know Artie was killed first," Cole added. "If our killer tossed the gun, then your killer might've found it."

"Wonder if there had been any threats Kefali just happened to 'forget' to mention?" Laura said.

Rampede got to his feet, the sudden motion reminding Cole and Laura how huge he really was. "We should ask," he said with a chilling smile.

1:35 P.M.

Rebecca's police minders preceded her out of the courthouse elevator. Almost at once a male voice said, "Rebecca! Over here!" A harried-looking middle-aged man with a long ponytail waved.

"That's my lawyer," she told the two officers.

They stepped aside. Rebecca shook hands with Farber Kelly, the newspaper's attorney. "This is nuts," he said at once.

"Tell me about it."

"I've tried to get an emergency hearing on the subpoena, but none of the judges are either available, or willing to touch it. The police commissioner is on a tear over these two cops, and he doesn't care whose rights he has to trample. Man, I miss the days when they had to at least pay lip service to the Constitution."

"So, I have to testify?"

"I'm afraid so."

"Come on, Farber. You know that's not right."

"Of course I do. But when the judiciary doesn't care about 'right' or 'wrong,' what can a lawyer do?" He lowered his voice and pressed a card into her hand. "Just answer the questions that feel right and take the Fifth on the others. Here's the text to use."

"*That* won't make me look guilty," she said dryly. "Can't you come with me?"

"They don't let lawyers into grand jury hearings. Remember, Rebecca, you're not a suspect. They don't think *you* killed anyone. They want that vigilante. They want what you know about her."

"Everything I know is in my article."

"Then use that as your guide. If you wrote about it, answer. If you didn't, refuse."

She nodded resignedly. "All right."

Farber looked at the two stone-faced officers and said snidely, "That all right with you two? Meet with your approval?"

Before either of them could answer, A.D.A. Gilson came out of the grand jury room. "Ah, here you are. They're ready for you."

Rebecca grabbed Farber's arm. She hated to admit it, but she was truly scared. "Don't leave me hanging here."

"I'm doing my best to get you off the gallows, I promise."

1:36 P.M.

Delilah, semi-conscious and sweating, tossed in slow motion as much as her bonds allowed. She hadn't quite registered her situation; as the sedative wore off, the *magnum sentire* took effect.

"Don't do it, you bastard," Joe hissed. "She's got nothing to do with this. It's between you and me."

Darren almost barked a laugh. "Don't tell me you're actually trying '*mano a mano*' on me. That's a beginner's mistake, Joseph. You should know better. None of this is personal. It's all business."

He put his left thumb down on the soft skin just above the lacy cup of Delilah's bra and positioned the acupuncture needle against her skin. "You had to know someday she'd be used against you. You get too close to someone in our business, that's bound to happen." He paused. "This needle is solid gold, did you know that?"

"Hey, what are you doing?" Joe protested, straining uselessly against his bonds. "That's not a pressure point."

"Pressure point?" Darren repeated. "Oh, you actually know about acupuncture? That's funny. Because I don't know a thing." With that, he pushed the needle in.

Delilah's eyes opened wide. In the hands of a trained practitioner, she would've felt nothing, but Darren was totally unskilled. However, he was knowledgeable about anatomy and knew that the needle's point would penetrate down to, and into, her lungs. The *magnum sentire* made the sensation almost unbearable.

Her scream echoed throughout the big dark room. Joe rattled his chair with his efforts to free himself.

Darren left the needle in place, and Delilah thrashed against her own bonds, her screams vapor-locking in her throat. He picked up another, shorter needle.

"Stop!" Joe said. "Take it out. I'll tell you."

"Tell me, and I'll consider it."

Joe opened his mouth to speak, then clamped it shut. Delilah continued to make noises like she was being disemboweled.

"I know what you're thinking, Joseph," Darren said, having to shout over Delilah. "If you tell me, and by some miracle escape from me, then you'll always know your limit. A wise man once said, 'A good man always knows his limitations,' but that's not true, is it? People like us, we depend on *not* knowing how far we can go."

He poised the second needle over her right thigh.

"Mummadabba!" Joe roared. "The motherfucker's name was Mummadabba. He's a fence in Bowland. Sells high-end electronics. It's where we got the jammer for the security system. The Mendicant put me in touch with him!"

"Now why would a fence want you to kill an East Side lawyer?"

Joe's whole body was taut, and the duct tape bonds creaked as he fought them. "I don't know! He was a middleman, like the Mendicant." Then Joe fell back against the chair, exhausted.

Darren took out his phone. "Excuse me for a moment."

Delilah continued to moan in pain.

"Come on, man, take out the needle!" Joe cried.

"*Doveryai, no proveryai,*" Darren said with a wink. "'Trust, but verify.'" He walked into the darkness and out of Joe's view.

Joe struggled anew. The tape was solid, but the fabric had just enough give that he could almost free his right hand. He lay back again, taking deep breaths and mustering the strength for another try.

Then he realized Delilah was now silent.

She was limp on her table, no longer writhing. Something dark dripped from the table to the concrete; her throat had been neatly cut.

"No!" he cried, and renewed his fight. "No, Delilah! *Delilah!*" Then his anguish turned to rage. "Motherfucker, when I get hold of you, you'll understand what pain is, you bastard! I promise you!"

"You shouldn't do that," a small voice said beside him.

The tape across his forehead was too tight for him to turn his head. He cut his eyes and just made out the dirt-smeared face of a little boy he'd never seen before.

"Who the fuck are you?"

"I said, you shouldn't do that."

"Do what?" he said through clenched teeth.

"Make promises you can't keep," the boy said. And then he cut Apocalypse Joe's throat, too.

The boy was still standing there, bloody knife in his hand, when Darren returned and almost dropped his phone at the sight.

I'm sorry, detectives, but I'm not clear on what you're asking me," B.J. said. She sat behind her desk, the three detectives standing opposite. Rampede's physical presence dominated the room as he loomed behind and over Cole and Laura, but B.J. was as cool as ever. Politicians, lawyers, and royalty had tried to intimidate her before; this was nothing.

"We're asking if the late Arthur Shawcross had anything to do with that church you're renovating in Bay View," Cole said.

"He's not a contractor," she said with a laugh, as if the idea of Artie Shawcross getting his hands dirty was absurd. Then her expression fell. "I mean… he wasn't."

"But did he handle the legal paperwork? The sale, the zoning, that sort of thing?" Cole pressed.

"He would've been in charge of it, yes. But it was all routine, so I doubt he did much personally."

"But it would've been his signature on everything, right?" Laura said.

"Well, yes. Oh, my God, do you think that's why someone killed him?"

"It's a possibility," Cole said. "May we speak to his staff?"

Before she could answer, the cell phone on her desk buzzed. She saw the caller, said, "Excuse me," then answered coolly, "This is Ms. Burr."

"It's me," Darren said. "Since you're being so formal, I assume you're not alone?"

"That is correct."

"Got a name for you. 'Mummadabba.' Apparently, he's a fence for fancy stolen electronics, but he moonlights by setting up hits. Once I get rid of these two, I'll need to pay him a visit. When your company leaves, can you look up where to find him?"

"Will do. Thank you." She ended the call and turned back to the detectives with a cool smile. "I apologize for the interruption."

"Was that your boss, Mr. Kefali?" Rampede asked. It was the first time he'd spoken, and his deep voice rumbled around the room.

"No, it was an unrelated matter," B.J. said. She put her finger to her Bluetooth. "I believe you wanted to speak with the legal staff?"

"That's right," Cole said.

She pressed the button. "Stefan, would you ask the legal department to meet me in conference room five? Yes, the whole department. Thank you." She stood and came around her desk. "If you'll follow me?"

They filed out, Rampede bringing up the rear.

The grand jury room in the courthouse was a big, old space with a high ceiling, paneled walls and the jurors seated in a tiered semi-circle of padded chairs. There were sixteen of them, the usual group of registered voters who couldn't talk a judge into letting them get out of jury duty. They looked tired and bored, like most juries, but Rebecca was pretty sure they'd perk up soon.

Max Gilson sat at a table with a laptop open before him, but he wasn't doing the interrogating. That fell to his boss, District Attorney Valerie Sakamoto. Dressed in a power suit, her black hair pulled back in a flawless bun, she made up in presence what she lacked in height. She was more feared than most cops, and the city's criminals dreaded her seemingly inevitable appointment as a judge. If anyone could shake the somnambulistic jurors out of their stupor, it was her.

Now she stood before Rebecca, hands clasped behind her back. Rebecca sat in a wooden straight-backed chair in the center of the room, conscious that every eye was on her.

"Please tell us your name," Sakamoto said, "and spell it for the court record."

"Rebecca Elaine Hutchcraft." She then spelled it out.

"Have you appeared before this grand jury in the past?"

"No."

"So none of these people are known to you?"

"No."

"Did you come here voluntarily?"

"No, I was subpoenaed and brought here immediately after I was served, so I had no chance to consult legal counsel."

Sakamoto ignored her. "You work for the *Daily Standard* newspaper, correct?"

"Yes."

"In what capacity?"

"Reporter."

"What sort of stories do you cover?"

"Usually crime-related."

"And in your capacity as a reporter of crime-related stories, did you meet and speak with the person known as the 'Lightning Girl'?"

"Yes," she said. She kept telling herself, *short answers. Volunteer nothing. Be alert for traps.*

"And what did you discuss?"

"It's in my story."

Sakamoto turned to the jury. "Please take a moment and refer to the copies distributed earlier." The jurors each picked up a printout from the paper's website.

"Thank you," Sakamoto said to them. To Rebecca, she said, "Did the Lightning Girl mention anything about the assault on officers Morlette and Hogan?"

"Not by name."

"But she did admit to assaulting them?"

"What she said is in my story."

Sakamoto smiled. On anyone else, it might've been a kindly, reassuring expression, but on her it had the look of a predator who knows her prey has absolutely no chance of escape. "Ms. Hutchcraft, this vigilante assaulted and seriously injured two policemen. There's no telling what she'll do to an average citizen who engenders her ire. I could have subpoenaed your notes as well as yourself, but I refrained because I respect the freedom of the press. But that freedom has limits."

Rebecca couldn't resist. "Freedom with limits isn't really 'freedom,' is it?"

Sakamoto's smile didn't waver, but her eyes burned with anger. "This is no place for flippant comments, Ms. Hutchcraft," she snapped. "Do you feel that the officers in question deserved what happened to them?"

"Of course not."

"But you believe they were corrupt."

"I have no knowledge either way."

"But that's what your story said."

"That's what the subject of my interview said," Rebecca corrected.

"Do you know how to get in touch with this 'subject' again?"

"No. As my story said, I was volunteering at a friend's clinic when she appeared."

"It wasn't a planned meeting?"

Rebecca began to sweat. She was being maneuvered but couldn't tell toward what. "No."

"And when you first encountered her, your first instinct was not to run, or to call 911, but to chat?"

"My first instinct was to do my job."

"Yes. And were you assigned to this story? Did you go down to the City Free Clinic with the express purpose of interviewing the vigilante?"

Shit, Rebecca thought. She'd fallen for the trap like an explorer tumbling into a pit of spikes. *If I tell the truth, I might get nailed, and if I lie, she might have proof.* "I prefer not to answer."

"Oh? And why is that?"

From the card Farber had given her, she read, "I respectfully invoke my rights under the Fifth Amendment of the U.S. Constitution on the grounds that answering this question may incriminate me."

Now Sakamoto's eyes gleamed with triumph. "A truthful answer would, in fact, incriminate you?"

From his table, A.D.A. Gilson cleared his throat. Sakamoto glanced at him, and said, "I withdraw the question." She paced for a moment, then added, "And I have no further questions."

Rebecca started to rise.

"One moment, Ms. Hutchcraft," Sakamoto said. "I do have a question from the jury."

A thirtyish man in jeans and a flannel shirt passed Sakamoto a piece of yellow paper torn from a legal pad. She read it, folded it away and said, "Ms. Hutchcraft, did you give the police a description of the suspect after your meeting?"

"No. As I said, I did not contact the police. And until your officers frog-marched me here, I had seen no police in connection with this."

The man scrawled out another question and passed it to the prosecutor. This time Sakamoto read it verbatim. "If you saw her in this room, or out on the street, would you recognize her?"

That hadn't occurred to Rebecca. "I don't believe so. We met in the dark, and she wore a hood that hid most of her face."

Sakamoto looked at the juror, who held up his hands to show he was done. "Now you may step down, Ms. Hutchcraft," Sakamoto said.

In the hall outside, Farber Kelly jumped up from the bench where he'd been waiting. He fell into step beside Rebecca as she practically ran for the elevators and asked, "How'd it go?"

"How the hell should I know?" Rebecca snapped.

"Did you have to take the Fifth?"

"Only once, when they asked me if I went to Ratway with the express purpose of doing the interview."

"Did you?"

They reached the elevator, and she pushed the button. "I'd hoped I would, sure. But I had nothing scheduled. It was a leap of faith on my part."

"You probably should've taken the Fifth from the start," Farber scolded. "Sakamoto is notorious for getting confessions out of people who—"

"People who what, Mr. Kelly?" Sakamoto said right behind them.

Rebecca and Farber turned, startled. Sakamoto and A.D.A. Gilson stood behind them, waiting for the same elevator.

"People who don't have benefit of counsel," Farber finished. "You gave her no time to consult with me before her testimony."

"And yet here you are."

"Uh-huh. She called me from the police car bringing her here. That's right on the edge of fascist, Valerie, not to mention unethical. I should bring it up with the bar."

Again, Sakamoto smiled that cold predator's grimace. "Do what you think is right, Farber. I'm always prepared to justify my conduct. Come on, Max, we'll take the stairs."

She nodded at Rebecca, turned and walked off down the hall, her heels clicking on the tile. Max, following, looked back with a *what can you do?* shrug.

"I used to think he was a friend," Rebecca fumed.

"An attorney is never your friend," Farber said.

"Not even you?"

"Not even me. At best, I'm the lawyer least likely to screw you over."

The elevator doors opened, a few harried attorneys and clerks got out, and Rebecca and Farber got in. They rode down to the first floor alone, in silence.

1:45 P.M.

A different batch of attorneys and clerks sat around the conference table in the Kefali building. They could not have been a more diverse group had they tried: Black, White, Latino, Asian, and some whose racial origin couldn't be visually assessed. Men, women, and some whose gender identity wasn't clear. They looked at the three detectives with open, honest faces, ready to do their civic duty and help find out who'd killed their boss.

But not one of the three cops believed that.

"Thank you for gathering on such short notice," B.J. said. "I know some of you haven't had lunch yet, but detectives Slaughter, Slade, and… I'm sorry, I've forgotten your name."

"Rampede."

"They believe Arthur's murder might be connected to the church renovation in Bay View, since his signature would be on much of the paperwork. They'd like to ask you all some questions."

She stepped back and stood quietly against the wall.

Laura and Cole exchanged a glance. They knew B.J. had announced the company's party line, and they doubted anyone would cross it. The questioning had just become pointless.

Until Rampede asked, "Any of you know a man named Mummadabba?"

The people at the table all looked, first at each other, then at B.J. She appeared as surprised as they were, almost aghast.

"He's lower in the ranks, under Grimy Tim. You've heard of him, surely? I bet one of you fine upstanding legal minds has made sure Tim got off with a wrist slap at least once."

Again there was silence. B.J. said, "Do you mean as pro bono work? We encourage all our—"

"No, I mean for people directly employed by the Kefali organization to distribute drugs and run prostitutes in Rattaway. Because I have to tell you, both are thick on the ground down there."

Again there was a long pause. Both Laura and Cole considered interrupting but decided to let Rampede keep going. Sometimes shaking the cage is the only way to get the bird to sing.

B.J., still non-plussed, said, "Detective Rampede, I don't appreciate you impugning the company's name this way."

His glare could've melted steel. "And I don't appreciate having to clean up yet another dead Black kid thanks to your boss, either. Your lawyer was probably killed as payback for some real or imagined slight; dealers make a big thing out of honor."

"I assure you, you none of us—"

"No, of course *you* didn't. You sit in this big tower and make phone calls that leave six dead children in Rattaway. And I bet not a one of you loses a bit of sleep over it."

He stepped close to the table and pointed across it to a young, slender man with a deer-in-headlights expression. "You. Tell me, have you ever dug up dirt on victims to help exonerate the scum that victimized them?"

"Detective Rampede, that is quite enough," B.J. said. The surprise had worn off, and she stepped close to the big detective, unintimidated and angry. "This meeting is over. Any subsequent questions you have for the staff will come through me or through a court order."

"Didn't really expect an answer," Rampede said, smiling for the first time. He told Laura and Cole, "I'll wait for you downstairs. All this rarified air makes me dizzy."

"Lois," B.J. said to a young woman at the near end of the table, "please escort Detective Rampede downstairs."

She stood and smoothed her skirt. "Certainly. If you'll come this way?" The big detective followed her out.

B.J. turned to Cole and Laura. "The Kefali organization has cooperated at every step of this investigation. I will not allow this type of slander in our own building." She folded her arms, clearly expecting an apology.

"Well, then," Cole said. "I guess there's no point in taking up more of your time. Good day."

He followed Rampede out the door. Laura followed him. B.J. watched them go, her mind awhirl. Of course it was no secret, especially among law enforcement, that Kefali ran a crime empire in the city. But millions of dollars was spent to keep the police in their place. These street cops might not be on the take, but their higher-ups certainly were. Had the corruption reached critical mass, to where the grunts felt they had nothing to lose?

She needed to talk to Stavros.

1:46 P.M.

Darren froze when he walked back into the light and saw Sparrow and the dead bodies. He was speechless for a moment, looking from the bodies to the blood-spattered, knife-wielding boy. Finally, he managed, "Did you *kill* them?"

"They killed my friends," Sparrow said unapologetically.

Darren still couldn't believe it. "You're that kid from the gas station."

"Yeah."

Darren checked Delilah, but she was dead, her skin already turning that distinctive blue-white shade of pale. Her throat no longer bled, although crimson streaked the table and pooled at its base on the concrete.

Joe, though, still held on. The blood at his slashed throat bubbled with air as he tried to breathe, and his eyes flicked around in desperation. Darren sighed in disappointment. "Too bad for you, man. You might've lived another hour if I had my way. Fuck the rotten luck."

Joe's eyes locked on Darren's, and he saw the rage in them, cold and snake-like. Then that faded, along with the ineffable light that indicated consciousness. With a weird, soft burble, he followed Delilah to Hell.

Darren turned his attention back to Sparrow. Annoyed, he said, "I wanted to get more information from them, you know."

"Fuck the rotten luck."

He fought the urge to laugh at the way the words sounded in Sparrow's child's voice. His irritation was overwhelmed by an amused appreciation of the kid's sheer nerve. "Shouldn't you be running away?"

"If you want to kill me, go ahead. I've done what I needed to do." He finally let the bloody knife drop to the floor.

Darren couldn't believe the weary resignation in this little boy's voice. What had he seen in his few years to age him so much? "If I wanted to kill you, you'd have been dead before you even knew I was around." He narrowed his eyes. "Your name's Sparrow, right? What happened to the rest of your gang?"

"You saw what happened."

"Come on. I knew the Mendicant too, remember? He had a lot more followers than just the ones who were killed."

"They went their own ways."

"You were the only one that cared enough to get revenge?"

"I was the only one who saw what you did at the tattoo parlor."

If nothing else, the kid was definitely on the ball. "And what do you think you saw?"

"You broke in, and a while later, you carried these two out to an SUV. Then you brought them here. Pork Lips Joe told you he worked for someone named Mummadabba."

"'Apocalypse,'" Darren corrected. "Apocalypse Joe. And back up. How did *you* get here?"

"Held onto the bottom of the SUV. Those things ride so high, it's easy when you're a kid. Just have to make sure your clothes don't catch on something, and you don't burn yourself on the exhaust system."

He laughed out loud. "Sparrow, you're something. There's not a kid in a million who would do what you did for a jerk like the Mendicant."

"Family avenges family."

"So you wanted revenge?"

Sparrow turned and looked at Joe's body. "I wanted for nobody else to have to feel like I do." Then he calmly looked back at Darren, ready to face any consequences.

Darren knelt to be on his eye level. "Do you remember my name?"

"Darren."

"That's right, Darren Flaxstone. Do you know who I work for?"

He shook his head.

"He's a very powerful man named Mr. Kefali. Did the Mendicant ever mention him?"

Again, he shook his head.

"Well, he took me under his wing when I was just a little bit older than you. He sent me to college, made sure I had the training I needed, and then gave me a job with his organization. Do you know why he did all that?"

Another shake of his head.

"Because he saw that I was quick. Quick-thinking, quick-acting. It meant I had good instincts, and that is one thing you cannot be taught." He picked up the knife; the boy shivered once but didn't retreat. "I think you're quick, Sparrow. I think you have very good instincts. I'd like to take you to meet Mr. Kefali."

He said nothing.

"If you want to," Darren added.

"If I don't," he said calmly, "then I suppose you'll have to kill me too, won't you?"

He nodded, sad but honest. "Nothing personal. One of the things Mr. Apocalypse and I have in common is that we don't leave witnesses."

"'*Had*' in common."

"Had," he agreed with a nod.

Sparrow thought for a moment. "Then I guess I want to meet your friend."

"Good choice." He stood. "But I still have some things to do here."

"Get rid of the bodies?"

This time he did laugh. "Sparrow, you are the high point of my year."

"Do you dissolve them in lye, or just dump them somewhere?"

He held up the bloody knife. "Since I've got a murder weapon to plant, I think I'll just leave them where they can be found. And where word can get around that this is what happens when you mess with Mr. Kefali."

"Then this Mummadabba will know you're onto him."

"Oh, no worries there, Sparrow. I plan to visit him long before he hears anything about this."

The Erstatt Clinic was so exclusive, it didn't even have a sign. You needed a referral, which you only got after a strenuous background check. Security, too, was tight. The clinic offices were on the top floor of its building, reached by an express elevator. The rest of the floors were given over to biomedical research.

And Stavros Kefali funded the whole operation just so he could be ready for one night every hundred years.

B.J. stood beside the clinic's namesake, Dr. Frederick Erstatt, as the physician demonstrated the advances and improvements made to his equipment since the last visit. B.J. took it all in, then said, "So this will be faster?"

"Considerably," Erstatt assured her. "And the donor?"

"He's enjoying his remaining hours as he requested. The truck will be here to pick all this up in an hour. Let me know when you've arrived and gotten everything set up."

"Of course."

B.J. shook hands with him and departed. It was getting late in the day, and she had one more stop before returning to the Kefali Building.

ole and Laura waited at the subway station with Rampede. He hadn't asked them to drive him back to the 89th, and they hadn't offered. In fact, none of them had really spoken. Around them, commuters ready for an early ride home began to gather on the platform.

Finally, Rampede said, "Thank you for chauffeuring me around today."

"Our pleasure," Laura said. "Thank you for your intimidation back at the Kefali building.

He caught her tone. "You disapprove?"

"I don't think it was the most diplomatic approach."

"She said, diplomatically," Cole added.

Rampede chuckled. "Just so you know, I wasn't just raging for the sake of rage, although I was genuinely pissed off. I can't tell you how many overdoses I investigate in a year. And no one is ever held accountable, because of people like them."

"I'm sure you meant well," Laura said.

"Don't fucking condescend to me, woman," Rampede said. He stood closer, using his size to intimidate and overpower. People waiting on the subway platform instinctively gave them more room.

Laura almost reflexively backed up, but at the last instant held her ground. She looked up at him. "I'm not condescending to you, detective.

I'm expressing my opinion that your tactics might be effective in Rattaway, but here they're heavy-handed and off-putting."

"Well, excuse the fuck out of me," Rampede said. "It might interest you to know that I bet someone at that conference table thought I was talking straight to him. He's having second thoughts right now and considering calling us with some intel. Those fuckers were lawyers, which means they had to go to law school, where they learned right from wrong. Then they had to bury that knowledge beneath whatever it is they do for Kefali. But there's always one who second-guesses himself."

Laura and Cole exchanged a look. Did that even make sense? Laura finally said, "I hope you're right, then."

Before they could continue, the train pulled in and drowned out all conversation until it came to a stop. As the commuters disembarked, Rampede said, "I'll look into this 'Mummadabba' character and let you know."

"Thank you," Laura said.

Rampede nodded to them and entered the car. The doors closed, and the train jerked forward.

As the subway noise faded, Cole said, "That guy's either a genius, or a lunatic."

"We shall know him by his fruits," Laura said.

"Are you quoting the Bible at me?"

"Not quoting. Paraphrasing."

He raised an eyebrow. "Is that allowed?"

She chuckled. She attended church regularly, but she knew Cole eschewed all religion. Neither ever tried to change the other's mind. She said, "Any God that would be okay with this city won't mind a little rewording."

The hotel suite was the height of luxury, with unlimited room service, a fully-stocked (and re-stocked) wet bar, a hot tub, and a bed large enough for a half dozen people. Five now occupied it, all slender young men with blond hair, none of them over twenty-five, all of them naked.

They all watched the dark-haired young Greek man who, clad only in a silk robe, poured himself some more champagne. He was sleepy-eyed and had a contented, stoned smile on his face.

B.J. ignored the men on the bed. In Greek she asked, "Are you being well-treated?"

The young man, known as Karan, replied in the same language, "Oh, yes. Everything is wonderful."

"How do you feel?"

"A little weak, but otherwise fine."

"Good. I'm glad to hear it. Mr. Kefali sends his regards as well."

At the name, Karan's eyes seemed to clear, and he suddenly looked apprehensive. "Will I see him before the Festival?"

"No."

"He's so legendary. I hoped we'd get a chance to talk."

"I'm afraid not."

He shrugged. "Ah, well." He picked up a small amyl nitrate bottle, took a whiff, and his smile returned. He was now visibly erect beneath the robe. He crawled back among the young men, all of which pawed eagerly if lethargically at him.

B.J. observed this clinically for a few moments, then left him to his fun. After all, this was all part of the deal.

It was twilight by the time her car emerged from the hotel's parking garage, and all the buildings sparkled with light against the fading red and yellow sky. Karan would have been dead three months ago, if not for the treatment paid for by the Kefali organization. As it was, he got some borrowed time in return for his help with the Festival. Karan had this final night to indulge his vices before he was prepared for the Festival tomorrow. As always, she wondered if he really comprehended what would happen to him.

As her car joined the flow of traffic, B.J. called her office, where Stefan relayed the information they'd found on the man Darren sought, Mummadabba. She thanked him for his thoroughness.

Tomorrow night, she thought, gazing idly out at the crowded sidewalks. *It all happens tomorrow night. If we can keep whoever killed Artie from fucking it up, that is.*

ONE NIGHT BEFORE THE FESTIVAL

The clear sky was black behind the city's tallest buildings when B.J. stepped into Stavros's private chamber behind her office. "Everything is on schedule," she reported. "And Karan is more than satisfied with his treatment."

"Good," Stavros said. "And the venue?"

"It'll be gorgeous. Except…"

"What?"

"The police are being… pestersome."

Stavros chuckled. "Is that a word?"

"It is now."

"What are they doing?"

"While I was there at the church, one of the detectives investigating Artie's death showed up. He said he lived in the area, which was easy enough to confirm. But it's still a bit jarring. Knowing that he's even tangentially aware of the venue makes me anxious. And then there's what happened in the conference room. Did you watch?"

"I did," he confirmed. "That Black detective is interesting."

"How so?"

"He's got a personal stake in this somehow. You could tell it from his vehemence. Nobody acts like that unless they're emotionally involved."

B.J. knew better than to second-guess Stavros on his judgement of people. "Any idea what it is?"

"He works out of the 89th Precinct in Rattaway. He's the one investigating the murders of the Mendicant and his brood. To choose the obvious, perhaps he has a thing about child killers."

"I can understand that," B.J. said. "But he can't think we had anything to do with it."

"We *are* a criminal organization."

"Yes, but there are some lines we won't cross. And that's known. And don't we pay his superiors to keep him in line?"

"They have to know about it to prevent it. He strikes me as a man who goes his own way."

"That makes him dangerous."

"Indeed," Stavros agreed. "He's out of the same precinct where those two officers were attacked by that 'Lightning Girl' person. Working down there has to foster a foxhole mentality, in addition to the usual 'thin blue line' nonsense. An attack on one is an attack on them all."

"Oho," B.J. said, suddenly seeing the connection. "Then the whole 'dead kids' thing might be a smoke screen. He might think that *we* had those cops set up."

"He might. Were they ours?"

"No. They were in the Marleys' pocket, not ours."

"Have you heard from the Marleys?"

"Just the one call, when Harrison told me they weren't behind the hit on Artie. Should we worry?"

"We should always worry when the police are involved. Have you heard from Darren?"

"Yes. He wants information on someone called Mummadabba. It's waiting on my desk."

"Mummadabba," Stavros mused. "That's interesting."

"Do you know him?"

"Like Detective Rampede said, he's a small-time fence who handles mainly stolen electronics. He's one step up from the thieves he buys from, and several rungs below most of his buyers."

"Affiliated?"

"Freelance. He pays us, he pays the Marleys, probably pays the smaller families as well. But he's not officially tied to anyone."

B.J. was now more puzzled. "Then how is he involved?"

"Only on the fringes. *She* is the ultimate power behind it. The master moving the pieces, including Mummadabba."

B.J. felt a chill. Somehow, not using her name made her seem even scarier. But she understood why Stavros wouldn't want to. That name, *her* name, must feel like a knife to the heart.

"She wouldn't have hired that assassin herself," he continued. "She's smart enough to make sure there were several levels of intermediaries, all of whom are expendable."

B.J. sighed. "And all this right before the Festival. Do you think *she'll* try to crash it?"

"That's why she took the ring."

"It's just a piece of jewelry, Stavros, just because somebody wears it doesn't mean we—"

"Anyone with a ring gets in," Stavros said firmly. "It's as much a part of the tradition as all the other aspects, and to disregard it would affect everything else."

"But—"

"Belinda," Stavros interrupted. He never lost his temper, but he did get vexed, and when he used her actual name, she knew he was. "I love you and I value your perspective and advice, but believe me, the rules of the Festival must be followed. And you don't know anything about *her*."

"I'm sorry," she said sincerely. "Sometimes I forget how far back you two go."

"So do I," Stavros admitted. "Not to traffic in clichés, but it often feels like it was just yesterday."

8:11 P.M.

The bodies of Apocalypse Joe and Delilah, rolled up in plastic, were tucked into the back of Darren's battered SUV, now parked between two old buildings on the Pigeon Hill waterfront. The area might serve as the nesting place for the city's old money—it was also called Tuxedo Hill—but its waterfront was in the last stages of urban decay, abandoned since ships grew too large to use it. Now, in addition to being an eyesore, it was a handy place to drop corpses when you wanted to confuse the police.

"Call from… B.J.," the automatic voice said, and Darren answered through the SUV's Bluetooth hookup. He said, "Talk to me."

"I have your intel," B.J. said. "This Mummadabba is non-affiliated. He works for both us and the Marleys. Probably others as well."

"So when he's working for us, who's his *capo*?"

"Grimy Tim."

Darren made a face. A man didn't get that nickname for no reason. "Any hint Mummadabba might be making a move against him?"

"None that registered. As far as Tim knows, Mummadabba is a model soldier. You don't stay on the edge like that unless you're really good at balancing."

"Did Mummadabba have any connection with Artie?"

"Not that I can find. But something else weird happened today."

"What?"

"Remember when you called, I couldn't really talk? That was because three cops working on Artie's murder came by, wanting to speak with his staff. I got them all in a conference room, and the cops start berating them, telling them they're criminals and they're implicated in the deaths of murdered children. They also knew about Mummadabba, *and* Grimy Tim."

"Jesus Christ."

"I know. I got our people out of there as fast as I could, and I've authorized a bonus to them all, to cover their hurt feelings and remind them about their non-disclosure agreements. But I can't believe the police would be so blatant about it."

"Three days ago, we didn't believe anyone could touch the Dodger."

"But that's not all. Before that, this afternoon while I was inspecting the venue, one of the cops showed up there. He said it was a coincidence, that he lived in the neighborhood and just happened to see me arrive. He does live there, but as for the rest...I don't know."

"What did Stavros say?"

"He says the Festival goes on as planned. End of discussion."

"Yeah, that sounds like him. If you talk to him again before I do, tell him I've got somebody I want him to meet."

"You do?" B.J. said, surprised.

"Yes. A young man named Sparrow." The boy looked up at his name, and Darren winked at him.

B.J. understood; it was, after all, her history as well. "I'll tell him. It'll need to be after the Festival, of course."

"Of course. Text me this Mummadabba's latest address, will you?"

"Have done."

"Great. Thanks, B.J."

He ended the call and put away his phone. Through the windshield, they watched the harbor as big commercial ships, mere outlines sparkling with safety lights, moved in and out of the port.

"Did you follow any of that?" Darren asked Sparrow.

"I wasn't listening."

"Don't lie to me. It's disrespectful to me and dangerous to you."

The boy's tone did not change. "The cops are closer than they know to something you want to keep secret. And the guy we're looking for works a little bit for everyone, which means he's not loyal to anyone."

"Very good." He resisted the urge to tousle Sparrow's hair; once he'd been the one in the passenger seat, listening to the Dodger detail his plans. "Now, let's deal with our cargo. We could wait until it's darker, but I don't think it'll matter, since I've got you to act as lookout. Are you ready?"

Sparrow nodded once. He had been taught, or learned from experience, the dangers of excess: excess words, excess gestures, excess thoughts. He gave out only the bare minimum needed for clarity.

"Let's go, then," Darren said and opened the door.

It took less than ten minutes to place the bodies under the old wharf, and to toss the knife into the surf right at the water's edge. They wanted it found; it would help sell the illusion that Joe and Delilah had been killed here. To provide motive, Darren sprinkled cocaine powder on their clothes, just enough for a CSU team to detect, and then tucked the .22 automatic back into the man's waistband, where he'd found it. Then he got some spray paint and tagged the nearest wharf pylon with the symbol for the Hawkclaws.

His torture and murder of a pair of assassins thus became yet another drug deal gone bad that claimed the lives of Joseph and Deborah, two Midwestern losers overcome by the big city. Under that guise, it would barely raise a ripple.

"What do we do now?" Sparrow asked.

"Do you think you can stand watching me work some more?"

"If I can't, I know how to turn my head."

Darren looked at the address B.J. had texted him. "Then let's go dancing."

8:15 P.M.

Harrison Marley, Jr. stood in the upstairs hallway. His father's bodyguard, heavy-set and almost comically Italian, sat reading the day's paper outside the old man's bedroom door.

"Need to see Pops," Harrison said.

The bodyguard nodded. Harrison knocked softly then opened the bedroom door. "Hey, Dad. Got a minute?"

His father's nurse, a very attractive young woman with red hair, rose from her seat. "Mr. Marley?" she said to the man in bed. "Your son's here to see you."

Harrison Marley, Sr., or what was left of him, stirred awake. His skin had drawn tight against his skull, and his sparse white hair formed a dandelion-like nimbus around his head. He still wore his mustache, though, and tugged one corner of the facial hair into his teeth for chewing.

"Harry," he said, the word riding on a rattling breath.

"Hi, Dad," Harrison said. He knew at once that whoever his father saw standing in the room, it wasn't his son as he was now. He'd never seen Harrison for what he really was.

"Come here, come here," he said, gesturing with one gnarled hand.

Harrison swallowed hard. He was no wimp—he'd gotten plenty of blood on his hands growing up in the organization—but seeing his father this way fundamentally creeped him out. The roaring, terrifying giant of his childhood was reduced to a mere skeleton covered with pale, papery flesh; not even his brain functioned reliably. He wanted the old man to finally die, if nothing else just to be rid of the smell, a miasma of antiseptic, perfume, cigar, and decay. But Harrison Sr. held on to life by his metaphorical fingernails.

The old man looked at the nurse. "Leave us alone for a moment, sweetheart."

She nodded and left without protest. Harrison wondered if his father requested she wear a uniform at least one size too small, or if that was just her style.

When the door was closed, the old man said, "I understand somebody took out the Dodger."

Harrison had no idea how he'd gotten that information, but he was used to that sort of thing by now. "Yeah."

"Somebody wants a war." It was not a question.

"Not if I can help it. I didn't order the hit. Monte's out trying to find out who did."

"It's Kefali," the old man wheezed. "Kefali's at the root of it."

"He killed his own consiglieri?"

"Not the murder!" The exclamation made him cough for a long moment. "That's just a pawn move. Do you know what happens tomorrow night?"

"No."

"The Festival!"

Harrison had heard of the Kefali-sponsored Festival of course, but before now his father had never spoken of it directly. "So?"

He swung his palm at the side of Harrison's head. The younger man had plenty of time to move, but let his father have his moment. The slap was a mere shadow of the blows the old man once dispensed.

"Use your damn brain, son! Is this how you plan to run things when I'm gone?" He took a couple of deep, wheezy breaths, then said, "The Festival happens every hundred years. A murder like this, so close to it, has to be all about the Festival. Someone is planning something, and if it's not us, and it's not Kefali, then it's a someone new trying to muscle in by taking Kefali out."

"What's the big fucking deal about this Festival?"

The old man managed a smile. Once, not so long ago, Harrison Senior's smile alone could break a man's will. It was still cold, but lacked most of the wattage.

"Do you remember how your mother took you to Mass every weekend? Sometimes twice, Saturday night and again on Sunday. Did you ever look around and think about how old the thing was? Not the church building, but the ritual?"

Harrison had no idea where this was going. "Uh… no."

"Two thousand years. The first Pope was Saint Peter, and he knew Christ personally." Again he paused to catch his breath. "Kefali's festival comes from before *that*. Before Christ. Your grandfather went to the last one."

"Then why have you never told me about it before?"

"Because you don't *talk* about it, you moron!"

"The first rule of the Festival is you don't talk about the Festival?" Harrison said dryly.

He thought the old man was going to hit him again, but the last blow had exhausted him. He paused for several wheezy breaths, then reached into his pajamas and pulled out a small key on a neck chain. He tried to jerk it hard enough to break a link, but lacked the strength.

Harrison calmly unfastened it. "What's this?"

"Look in my middle desk drawer," the old man wheezed. "There's a small velvet box."

Harrison did as instructed, working the key into the lock with difficulty. The middle drawer had never been opened in his presence, and he truly had no idea what it held. He found the box nestled among mysterious old papers, photographs, and .45 pistol. He returned with it to the bedside.

"Open it," the old man instructed.

Inside was a thick, heavy man's ring. It was made of gold and encrusted with jewels that formed a strange design Harrison didn't recognize. "What is this?"

"Your ticket to the Festival. Your grandfather left it to me, but I'm too sick to use it."

"Why would I go to Kefali's shindig?"

"Two reasons. One, to see who's trying to start this war. You can be sure they'll be there."

"How will I know who it is?"

Again Harrison accepted the weak blow, this time to the other side of his head. "Can you really not think on your feet?"

Harrison's own temper simmered, and he grabbed the old man's twig-fragile wrist before it could boil over. "First, if you hit me again, I'll fucking hit you back. Second, you're talking nonsense. Or bullshit. For all I know, this is one of your little 'tests' to see how gullible I am." Harrison had endured those repeatedly as a teen, to the amusement of his father and the family's *capos*.

"It's not bullshit. Didn't you ever wonder why I never seriously tried to muscle in on Kefali? It wasn't because I was afraid of a war, believe me. It was because of who Kefali is, and *what* he is."

"And what is he?" Harrison asked skeptically.

"Go to the Festival and figure it out."

"Fuck, Dad, just *tell* me!"

"You're running the family now. You have to find your own answers." With great effort, he rose to a seated position and snarled, "But if you get the chance, you put that Greek sonuvabitch down, you hear me? This town'll be a whole lot better off without him and his weird mumbo-jumbo."

Harrison senior fell back onto his pillow and drifted into sudden sleep with that same cold smile stretched, *risus sardonicus* style, across his face. His breathing was rapid and shallow.

Harrison looked at the ring. It was heavy enough to be useful in a fight, if nothing else. He slipped it on and held it close to study the strange design, but could make no sense of it. It wasn't a coat of arms, or any school symbol he'd ever seen.

"Yeah, Dad," he muttered to his sleeping father. "I'll go to your stupid party. And there better be a goddam open bar."

Laura Slade stopped off at the Bullpen on her way home. She didn't usually drink, but the day had been a stressful one, and she knew a gin and tonic would help calm her down. She sat at the bar, gave the bartender her order and waited. The place wasn't yet full of the hipster crowd; it was quiet enough to actually hear the background music. Unfortunately, it was Kid Rock's "All Summer Long." It came over some satellite radio station, so there wasn't even a jukebox to fantasize about shooting.

As she took her first sip, Rebecca Hutchcraft took a seat two stools away. "Hey," Laura said.

Rebecca turned. "Oh, hey, Laura. Didn't see you. Want some company?"

"Sure."

Rebecca relocated to the adjacent stool, and the bartender moved her coaster and placed her beer on it. She and Laura clinked glasses. "And how was your day?" Laura asked.

"Well, lemme tell ya. I was sitting right over there at lunch when Max Gilson—you know him, right?—serves me with a grand jury subpoena to talk about the Lightning Girl."

"Because of your interview?"

"Yeah."

"Your lawyer should be able to get that quashed."

"That's just it—they gave me no time. They took me immediately to the grand jury. I mean, they had two uniforms ready and waiting."

Laura scowled in disbelief. "You're kidding."

"I wish I was. I think I got out okay, but I don't mind telling you, it scared me to death." She held up her hand with its still-trembling fingers. "I plan to drink until that stops."

"I don't blame you," Laura said sincerely.

"What about your day?"

"Still working on the Dodger case," Laura said, then paused, suddenly reminded that she was speaking to a journalist. "This is all off the record, okay?"

"Of course."

"The same gun that killed him also killed seven people down in Ratway. Six kids and an adult."

"Jumping Jesus on a pogo stick, that's awful. Do you have any leads?"

"Everything ends up back at the Kefali organization. And they're too big, too well-connected, and too good at stonewalling." She smiled and narrowed her eyes. "I bet you have contacts at Kefali, don't you?"

Rebecca sipped her beer. "I can neither confirm nor deny."

"Well, if you do, I bet you can find out what the internal scuttlebutt is, can't you?"

Good-naturedly, Rebecca teased, "Why should I?"

"Maybe I can help you with your story on the Lightning Girl."

"I already wrote that."

"And the news *never* runs a story to death, do they?"

Rebecca laughed. "All right, then. I'll see what I can find out. But it's all on the *quid pro quo*; you get nothing until I do, and vice versa."

"Deal." They shook hands. Laura downed the rest of her drink and said, "I better get home. The cat calls all the emergency rooms if I'm half an hour late."

Rebecca knew better than to ask about a boyfriend. Or girlfriend, for that matter. Although she'd never confirmed it, Rebecca was pretty sure her friend was an "ace"; she never dated, never talked about sex, lived alone with her cat, and seemed perfectly happy that way.

Rebecca nursed the last of her beer and pondered the day's events. It surprised her to realize she actually worried about going to jail; although her situation was not as bad as a cop, she could end up housed with the subject of one of her past news stories who might not have appreciated the publicity.

Her phone buzzed. She opened it and found a notification from the paper's site that she'd gotten a personal message. She clicked on the link.

It was from Angelyne223. *How do I know this is really you?* she asked.

Rebecca answered, *Why would someone pretend to be me?*

She was about to put down her phone when she got an immediate reply. *To catch me in the open.*

Rebecca sighed. She'd hoped it might be for real, but clearly this was some lunatic craving attention. She typed, *No time for games. Want to talk? Let's meet somewhere public.*

Again, the reply came almost at once. *Riverwalk at 14th and Brannigan. 8 tomorrow morning.*

The riverwalk was a wide paved path used by joggers, parents with strollers, and people on bikes. There were dedicated spaces for fishermen, although these were all posted with warnings not to eat anything they caught. It was, indeed, a very public place.

She checked the time. She wanted to get home to her husband and son, although Tim would probably be asleep by the time she did. Still, she'd earned her meager salary today for sure.

C ole Slaughter unlocked his front door and dropped his keys in the bowl. They'd bought this house with the intention of starting a family, but the universe had other ideas, some of them particularly cruel. It was too much room for a couple, but the thought of selling it was exhausting. So they stayed.

He heard the TV in the other room, and found Anna curled up in a t-shirt and sweatpants, mechanically clicking through thumbnails on the streamers. "Nothing good on?" he said as he sat beside her.

"How can there be this many options and nothing worth watching?"

"If I figure it out, I'll let you know." He leaned over for a perfunctory kiss.

"So did you find out who was renovating the old Catholic church?"

"A big East Side firm. Might tie into a case that seems to have as many threads as a sewing machine factory."

"I, uh… I'm sorry about how I acted at lunch," she said with real regret.

"Me, too. I should be able to turn it off for an hour."

"And I should be more understanding." She cut her eyes at him. "Sorry you married me?"

He put an arm around her shoulders. "Never."

He started to pull her close but realized he still wore his weapon in his shoulder holster. He took it off and placed it carefully on the coffee table.

Then he did snuggle against Anna. This chaste embrace was as intimate as they ever got these days.

11:30 P.M.

W hat're they waiting for?" Sparrow asked.

He and Darren peeked around a building's corner and watched the people queued outside a closed door in a decrepit building. There was no light except the icy glow of cell phones, but very faintly, the steady beat of music came through the sidewalk.

"That," Darren said, "is what the kids call a squat rave."

"You're old, aren't you?"

He laughed. "Ancient. You ever been to one?"

"I'm ten."

"You seem to be wise beyond your years."

"Yeah, well, the Mendicant kept us away from drugs and stuff. Said they made you sloppy."

"He was right. But you know what a rave is?"

"Sure. People dance, get high, get laid."

He looked down at the boy. "Are you sure you're only ten?"

Sparrow gave him a broad, beaming smile. "How did you know where to find it?"

He pointed to the brick wall of a nearby tenement, where a security light illuminated an elaborate graffiti tag that announced, *Dance or Die.* "There's a code in the design that, if you know how to read it, tells you where the party will be."

Sparrow tilted his head. "I don't see it."

"That's why it's a code. I'll explain it later. For now, follow me."

He led the boy around the block to the opposite side. Between a boarded-up kosher butcher shop and a rundown liquor store was the entrance to a long-closed beauty salon. He had to shove hard to get the door open.

Inside, the remains of old-style hooded hair dryers loomed in the shadows like alien brainwashing pods. Unseen rats scurried to their hiding places. Behind him, Sparrow said, "Are you sure this is the right way?"

As if on cue, a burst of bass rattled the room, making the abandoned equipment clatter.

"Okay, okay," the boy said. "But who exactly are we trying to find?"

Darren crouched to Sparrow's eye level. Gently but firmly, he said, "I believe that the Mendicant put Apocalypse Joe and Delilah in touch with a guy named Mummadabba, because someone wanted them to kill my friend. Mummadabba may or may not know why; he *does* know who hired them. So, I'm going to ask him nicely first, since he theoretically works for the same people I do. If he can't or won't answer, then things… escalate." He looked at Sparrow hard. "We do *not* kill him unless and until I say so. Are we clear on that?"

Sparrow shrugged. "Sure. Whatever."

He patted the boy's head. His efficiency in throat-slitting still made Darren shiver inside. He held out a butterfly knife. "Do you know what this is?"

"Yeah."

"It's for emergencies, or if I tell you to use it. Got it?"

Sparrow expertly twirled it to expose the blade, then twirled it again to nestle it back inside the handles. "Got it."

"Good. Initiative is a great thing, but sometimes we all have to just follow orders. This is your chance to show me you can do that."

Darren used the flashlight app on his phone to light their way. Their feet crunched on broken glass and debris. At the back, they found another door marked *Employees Only*. When he pushed it open, the bass grew louder; both felt it deep in their chests.

"Stay close," Darren told the boy. "It'll be hard to hear, so don't wander off."

Another door opened on a stairwell. The thumping music grew

painfully loud as they descended, until they reached a final door at the bottom.

When they opened it, the music smashed them in the face, along with the strobing lights and the reek of heat, body spray, weed, and alcohol. Darren edged out of the door and hugged the wall, waiting for his senses to adjust. He smiled inwardly as he felt Sparrow tightly grip his hand. *He's a kid after all.*

The basement was long, with a concrete floor and a low ceiling. The DJ worked from a table at the far end, and strobes and other lights had been mounted in each corner. Hanging in the center, barely above the dancers' heads, was an old-fashioned disco ball.

The dance floor was packed with dancers burning through huge amounts of energy to keep up with the rhythm. Along the walls, a few chairs held people either making out, getting high, or doing business. Darren was interested in the third one.

He edged along until he spotted Mummadabba seated with a girl beside him. Mummadabba wore a shimmery green polyester shirt open to his navel. A sweaty White kid gestured as he explained something, probably why he couldn't pay Mummadabba's price for the Ecstasy he needed to keep going. Mummadabba was unmoved.

Darren pushed his way through the crowd. If anyone thought it odd that he had a little boy in tow, no one said anything. He elbowed the still-begging kid aside and waited for Mummadabba to recognize him. When he did, Darren indicated they should find a place they could hear each other talk.

If he was surprised or nervous, Mummadabba hid it well. The dealer led them out another door into a hall where assorted couples used the comparative privacy to get intimate. At the far end, where the music was bearable, Mummadabba said, "Hi. Good to see you again." He nodded at Sparrow. "Your son?"

"My backup. How's business?"

"Steady. The rich White kids who like to live on the 'edge,'" he said with air quotes, "have lots of money to spend. And don't worry, I make sure Mr. K. gets his share."

"And the Marleys as well?"

He shrugged. "Render unto each Caesar what is each Caesar's."

"I also understand you put people together. A man needs a burglar, you hook him up with one. Someone wants a bodyguard to look tough, you can arrange it."

"I know all sorts of people. Seems foolish not to take advantage of it."

"What about assassins?"

That got the first reaction from him, a nervous chuckle. "Sure. Does Mr. K. need one? I figured he handled everything in-house."

Darren put a hand on Mummadabba's bony shoulder. "I'm more interested in one you already found. You put out the word, and the Mendicant sent him your way. He's called Apocalypse Joe."

Mummadabba had a world-class poker face, but the rest of his body wasn't so great at keeping his secrets, and Darren felt him start at the name. "So… you want to hire the same guy? He comes highly recommended."

"He's pursuing other interests, I'm afraid. Permanently."

It took Mummadabba a moment to process. "*You* killed him?"

Darren nodded at Sparrow. "No. Him."

This broke through the practiced nonchalance, and Mummadabba's brows rose in surprise. "I don't want any trouble with Mr. Kefali. Or you. Or him, apparently."

"Glad to hear it. Answer one question, and you won't have any. Who asked you to find them an assassin?"

"Come on, man, I can't tell you that. Word gets around, I'm toast."

"My friend here tortured Apickle...puck...*Apocalypse* Joe's girlfriend with acupuncture needles," Sparrow said. "I've heard a lot of screaming in my life, but never anything like that."

His words worked on Mummadabba more efficiently than Darren's actual torture might. He ran a hand through his hair and said, "Okay, look. I didn't know the hit was on Mr. Kefali's attorney. If I had, I—"

"Would've charged more," Darren finished. "I don't care. I care about a name. Give it to me, and we're done."

Mummadabba made no attempt to hide his terror. "How 'done' do you mean?"

"Look, Mummadabba, Apocalypse Joe not only killed Mr. Kefali's lawyer, who was like a son to him. He also killed the Mendicant, as well as six *children* who made the wrong-place-wrong-time mistake. I'm not real patient tonight, so you can either help us, and hope you don't die, or *not* help us, and ensure you do."

"All right," he said with a defeated sigh. "You ever heard of Wide Justice? The computer game company?"

Darren shook his head. "I don't have much time for games."

"Yeah, well, they make all those games about historic battles. Gettysburg, Iwo Jima, the Siege at Troy, you know."

"He's stalling," Sparrow said.

"No!" Mummadabba said quickly. "What I'm saying is, the boss of Wide Justice is who hired me."

"I still need his name," Darren said.

"Not 'him.' Her. Helen Pappas."

The name meant nothing to Darren. "And you're certain she's the end of the chain?"

"No, but that's who paid me, and who I delivered—" He stopped suddenly, realizing what he was about to reveal.

Darren's eyes narrowed. "What did you deliver to her?"

"You said if I gave you a name, you'd leave me alone."

"Come on, Mummadabba."

"All right. I delivered a box. I didn't pack it myself."

"What was in it?"

"I assumed it was that lawyer's head. I didn't check. Like Jason Statham says, 'Never open the package.'"

"That *is* good advice."

"There was one more thing. She also wanted his class ring."

"And where did you deliver these things?"

"At her company's office in Bowland. One of those new gentrified buildings."

Darren nodded. "Thank you, Mummadabba. Is there anything else I should know that I haven't thought to ask about?"

"I was just the middleman, Mr. Flaxstone. She hired me, and I got the Mendicant to get me Apocalypse Joe. I didn't do the actual killing."

"I know."

"I mean, I didn't even know who the target *was*."

"I believe you."

"So… are you going to kill me?"

"What will you do the next time someone wants to hire an assassin through you, Mummadabba?"

"Tell them no?"

"Wrong. Tell them yes." He handed him a business card with only a phone number. "Then contact me and tell me all about it."

"Y-Yes, sir. I'll definitely do that next time."

"Good night, Mummadabba."

"Good night, Mr. Flaxstone."

"Oh, and Mummadabba? If anyone were to warn this Helen Pappas that I was asking about her, I'll know who it was. And then I *will* kill you. With great creativity and relish."

"Believe him," Sparrow said. "I've seen him in action."

Mummadabba could only nod.

11:43 P.M.

When he was sure Darren and Sparrow were gone, Mummadabba took out a cigarette and lit it, which took a few tries with his trembling fingers. He leaned against the nearest wall, suddenly exhausted. He had more business to conduct inside the rave, but first he needed to calm down.

The door beside him, that led to a stairwell to the street, opened. A man reached through and put a gun to his head, pressing the end of the barrel hard against his temple.

"You said you weren't going to kill me," Mummadabba said, hoping he sounded at least somewhat defiant.

"I didn't say nothin' to you," a deep voice growled. "Now keep your hands where I can see 'em."

Mummadabba didn't move. He glanced down the hall, at the other people either fucking or getting high. None of them looked his way.

The man pulled him through the door and slammed it behind them. Another pair of hands roughly patted him down.

"I never carry," he volunteered.

"Shut up," the gunman said.

The other man put a blindfold on Mummadabba, yanking the ends tight. Then one of them took his arm and guided him out of the alley, to a car waiting on the street. They pushed him inside and drove away.

11:47 P.M.

On the street outside the old beauty shop, Sparrow said, "I thought for sure you'd kill him."

"I probably should have," Darren said.

"Why didn't you?"

"This may be hard for you to believe, but you can get sick of anything, even killing people who need killing. And sometimes it's better to leave them alive, so that they can tell others what happened."

"Do you think he'll warn this Helen person?"

"I'm not worried about it. Whoever she is, she clearly wants Mr. Kefali's attention, so she'll be expecting someone."

They passed a stoop where several teens lounged, sharing bottles in paper bags. Around them, graffiti covered every inch of available surface. Darren ignored the challenges and calls, including those who impugned his masculinity and implied things about his relationship with Sparrow.

When they were out of earshot Sparrow said, "You going to let them get away with talking to you like that?"

"Of course."

"Why?"

"Because a man is only as big as what makes him mad."

"Mr. Kefali teach you that?"

"He did." Darren chuckled at the memory. "With great difficulty. I wasn't as smart as you seem to be."

They turned into the alley where he'd parked the SUV in the empty garage of a firetrap owned, through a dozen intermediaries, by Kefali. Gang signs painted on the concrete by bangers on the Kefali payroll kept away the riffraff.

Sparrow looked up at the sad building. "You said Mr. Kefali owns this?"

"Yes."

"Then why doesn't he fix it up?"

"Because there's more money in leaving it the way it is."

Sparrow looked at him, his little eyebrows drawn down in thought.

"Look, Sparrow, you have to understand–Mr. Kefali runs a criminal organization. Yes, a lot of it isn't, and there's a shiny East Side building for those parts of it. But he hurts people. *We* hurt people. If you have a problem with that, maybe we should part company right now."

Sparrow's expression didn't change. "Would you kill me?"

"I'd give you a head start," Darren said honestly.

A sizzling *pop* noise rang out above them. Instinctively Darren stepped in front of Sparrow as both looked up. He got a brief impression of a figure standing on the edge of the roof eight stories above. Then another pop and flash of light right before them momentarily blinded them both. Darren backed up, pressing Sparrow into the wall behind him. He kept blinking, willing his vision to return.

A woman's voice said, "You almost look like you belong here, like you're down on your luck and out of options. You got the clothes right. But that's a two-hundred-dollar haircut."

"Two-fifty with the tip," Darren said. "Never go cheap for your barber or your dentist." Now he could make out the silhouette of a woman in a hoodie.

"You don't have to hide the little boy; I'm not going to hurt him."

"I don't get that same assurance?"

"Ha! No."

He could see her now, or at least the lower part of her face. Of course, he knew who she was. "So," he said calmly. "You're real after all. Up until thirty seconds ago, I would've sworn you were either an urban legend or a practical joke."

"No one's laughing, I promise you."

Sparrow stepped into the open and said, "Hi, LG."

"Sparrow," the Lightning Girl said. "You turn up in the strangest places."

Darren was rarely taken aback, but this connection did so. "You two know each other?"

"Yes," Sparrow said. "And whatever you do, don't call her 'Sparky.' She hates that."

"This guy bothering you?" she asked the boy.

"No, he's cool."

Sparrow pointed a finger at her, and the Lightning Girl touched the tip. There was a small spark of connection, and Sparrow's hair all stood on end with static electricity. He giggled, and she smiled.

"I'm here because of him," the Lightning Girl said as she broke the contact. "His friends were killed in cold blood. I have reason to believe a man named Mummadabba knows who and why. Then I see the two of you."

"Mummadabba does know," Sparrow confirmed.

Darren frowned at him. "There's such a thing as too much information, Sparrow."

"Hey, she's my friend," Sparrow said. For the first time in Darren's presence, he really sounded like a little boy.

"So you know who killed the Mendicant and the kids?" the Lightning Girl asked Darren.

"He does," Sparrow said.

"*Stop* that," Darren scolded. To the Lightning Girl, he continued, "If you're here to avenge the Mendicant and those kids, you're a bit late. The ones who killed them are dead."

"By your hand?"

"Mine," Sparrow said proudly. "I cut their throats this afternoon."

"He's not kidding," Darren said.

"And yet you're both here. If you don't need this Mummadabba to tell you who the killers were, then you must be trying to find out who employed them. Which brings up the question, why do you care?"

"Nothing gets past you, does it? Look, I'm Darren Flaxstone. I work for Stavros Kefali."

The Lightning Girl's voice grew hard. "That puts us on opposite sides, then. Kefali, Marley, and the rest are the reason Ratway is the way it is. I'm going to clear them out."

"So you can take over?"

"So people won't have to be scared all the time."

"People will always find something to be scared of."

"Ooh, clever. Did you read that somewhere?" Then she said, "Wait a minute. Why are *you* interested in who hired the Mendicant's killers?"

Before Darren could answer, Sparrow said, "Same as me. They killed a friend of his. He wants revenge like you and I do."

"Not revenge, little man," she corrected. "Justice. So what did Mummadabba tell you?"

Again, Darren considered whether to be honest. "I have a lead, that's all."

"Who?"

"I'd rather not say."

He could almost see her eyes in the shadow beneath the hood as she pondered this. Her disguise was both simple and amazingly effective: with the cap's shadow and black greasepaint covering her upper face, it was impossible to discern her real appearance. In fact, it was more effective than any mask would've been, because you had to be this close to even realize it wasn't merely the cap's shadow. Finally, she said, "Someone in Ratway?"

"No."

"Then I'll leave you to it. You can tell me about it when you're done."

"And why would I do that?"

"Because I won't stop asking."

Darren chuckled. "Are you always this charming, or is it just for my benefit?"

She opened her mouth to respond, then closed it and just stared at him. Darren guessed not too many people flirted with her.

Oblivious to this, Sparrow asked, "Have you seen the rest of my friends?"

She blinked back to the moment and shook her head. "No, I haven't. I'll keep an eye out, though." To Darren she said, "We may be on opposite sides, but Sparrow is a mutual friend, and I trust his judgement. So we have, what did they call it with the Russians? *Détente*."

They both looked down at the boy. He gazed back, placid and impassive. If he could hang onto that skill, Darren realized, he'd be one hell of a poker player. "Sure," Darren agreed. "It's a cold war, then. And in the spirit of that *détente*...Helen Pappas."

"Your lead?"

"Yes."

She nodded her thanks. "And take a message to your boss for me: I want Ratway safe, and I'm willing to do whatever it takes to make it that way. Including applying the heat to our cold war." She held up her right hand, and arcs of electricity ran up and down between her spread fingers. "I don't care what happens in the rest of the city. But this place is mine."

Another flash blinded him, and when his eyes adjusted, the Lightning Girl was gone.

"You've got to be ready to close your eyes fast," Sparrow said, apparently unaffected.

"Any idea how she does that?"

"Electricity," Sparrow said with a shrug. After a moment, he added, "I don't think she likes you."

"Some guys play hard to get; I play hard to want," Darren said with a wink.

A new voice said belligerently, "Hey, motherfucker, this your ride in here?"

A trio of young toughs now blocked the parking garage entrance. They gave no indication they'd seen the Lightning Girl. If they had, they clearly had sense enough to wait until she was gone.

Darren didn't know them personally, but he certainly knew the type: vicious, territorial and high-strung little carnivores capable of taking down prey twice their size. Addicts, probably diseased, certainly free of anything like empathy. They would, as the cliche said, just as soon kill you as go fishing.

But Darren knew a rule they probably didn't: don't wound what you can't kill.

So, he answered, "Yeah. That's my ride."

"You gotta pay to park here," the second one said. "Gimme your wallet."

"No," Darren said.

His cool, unafraid tone gave them pause. He wondered if the Lightning Girl might intervene, but she was either gone or uninterested. He glanced down and whispered, "Sparrow, get—" But the boy had vanished.

One of the punks danced forward, an automatic loose in his hand. Darren knew that the recoil would make his shots go wide, but that didn't mean he still wouldn't hit someone. "You think you're fucking Chuck Norris or something, man? Maybe Bruce Lee? Because I'll put a bullet right up your ass and watch you dance to it."

He considered telling them who he worked for, but he doubted these bottom-feeding scavengers would know the name or care. Saying he worked for Kefali would have the same effect as saying he worked for Nixon.

Instead, he said, "Last chance."

The two other toughs exchanged a look and laughed. "The dude's fucking crazy, man," one said.

Darren sighed. "Yeah."

Then he threw himself forward in a roll, and at the same time drew and snapped open his switchblade. He slashed under the gunman's arm, through the soft flesh and tendons in his armpit, and opened his axillary artery.

The man screamed, dropped the gun and clapped his other hand over the wound, the blood pulsing out between his fingers.

Darren picked up the gun and shot one of the others in the forehead. *Not bad in this light,* he congratulated himself.

The third one tried to run, but a small figure shot from the shadows and slashed him across the lower calf, severing the Achilles tendon and cutting into the posterior tibial blood vessel. The man fell, the small shadow jumped on his chest, and his cries ended with a sharp gurgle.

The first man tried to run, but he collapsed from blood loss after a few steps.

Darren surveyed the alley. He wasn't even breathing hard.

He examined Sparrow's handiwork, while the boy deftly closed the butterfly knife with a flick of his wrist. "Nicely done," Darren said.

"You, too," he replied, as if this was the most normal thing in the world.

"It's been a busy enough day," Darren said. "Let's go clean up a little and get something to eat. There's a great all-night diner not far from here."

"Wait," he said. "Can we go check on my other friends? The ones who didn't get…" He trailed off.

"I thought your sparkly pal was going to do that?"

"She doesn't know where to look; I do." He looked so pitiful that Darren felt a pang of sympathy; then he immediately wondered if it was all an act. There was only one way to find out if it was a trap, though: walk into it and see if it sprang shut.

Then Darren got it. "Is there a *particular* friend you're worried about?"

Sparrow nodded. "His name's Corvus."

"Corvus. That means 'crow,' right?"

"I guess."

"Sure," Darren said. "Let's go." As they entered the building where their vehicle waited, Darren scanned the nearby rooftops for movement but saw none.

12:06 A.M.

Laura Slade, in pajamas covered with sloth designs, was curled up on her couch, deep into the latest J.D. Robb novel. Her one-eyed cat lay across the back, alternately sleeping and watching her read, one paw dangling down to bat at a strand of her hair.

She jumped when her phone rang. The number told her it was for Detective Slade, not Laura, and a professional call after midnight was never good news. "This is Laura Slade," she said crisply.

"Detective," the dispatcher said. "Two bodies were just found in Bowland. The officers on scene think it might be connected to your murder case."

"I'm on my way." She looked around for her pants as she hit Cole's number. He answered on the second ring. "Hey."

"Hey. They found some bodies in Bowland, and they think they might be connected to the Dodger's murder and the massacre at the gas station."

"Let me get my—"

"They don't need both of us until we know for sure. I'll go down and check it out."

"You did it last time. It's my turn."

"Shut up. How's Anna?"

"Asleep."

"I'll be in touch. If it's legit, I'll call. Otherwise, I'll text. Just be a husband tonight."

"Thank you," he said sincerely.

W here's your partner?" Detective Rampede said when Laura had gotten through the police barrier. Unlike the Ratway gas station, at this time of night, down by the water, there were few onlookers.

"Home with his wife, where he needs to be. They lost a baby last year. Their first child. Only lived three days."

"Damn," Rampede said. "I'm sorry to hear that."

"They called you, too?"

"Yeah. They think it's all tied in with my dead kids and your beheaded lawyer."

"Based on what?"

"Based on the caliber of weapon found on one victim, along with a rather specialized bit of evidence." A tall, willowy Native American woman with a badge clipped to her leather jacket emerged from the night. "Detective Sergeant Wilhelmina Two Wolves. Please, call me Mina."

She shook hands with Laura and Rampede.

"That is one unpleasant smell," Rampede observed with a nod toward the water.

"Shit, literal and metaphorical, has been dumped into that river for a hundred years," Mina said. "It's the smell of history."

They followed Mina down onto the rocky semi-beach, and then beneath an old wharf that stuck out into the river, its length twisted almost like a DNA strand. Portable halogens directed their bright light onto the edge of the water, where crime lab technicians worked around two plastic-wrapped bodies.

"Two victims with their throats cut," Rampede said. "One male, about thirty-five, the other a girl about a decade younger. Found a bloody knife down at the edge of the water, almost like it was left there for us."

Laura nodded. There was no denying the scene looked staged, but for whose benefit? "What makes you think they're related to our case?"

"Two things. The man had a .22 automatic on him. That's an odd weapon to carry. You have to really know your stuff to use it."

"Like whoever shot the Dodger and the Mendicant. He got his throat cut even though he was carrying?"

"He's sporting quite a fine set of duct tape adhesive residue as well. Might not've been able to draw it."

"It was planted," Rampede said. "If I was going to tie someone up, I'd definitely disarm them."

"What's the other thing?" Laura asked.

Mina went to an old half-soaked satchel at the edge of the surf. "Because in that bag, we found this." She picked up an enormous medical bone cutter.

"Shit," Rampede said, impressed.

"Ballistics will tell us if it's the gun. Crime lab will tell us if this was used to cut off your lawyer's head. Fingerprints will tell us who *they* are. Then maybe we'll see if they're all connected."

"They are," Laura sighed. "These are the killers."

"How can you be so sure?" Mina asked.

"Like the man said, the first rule of assassination is, 'kill the assassins.' These two killed the Dodger, then the Mendicant and those children. Then *they* were killed by whoever put this all together in the first place."

The head of the CSU unit joined them. To Mina he said, "There's some residue on both of them that I'm pretty sure is cocaine. I'll confirm it back at the lab."

"Thanks," Mina said. The CSU head returned to his work, and she said to Laura and Rampede, "It's a plant. This isn't drug-related."

"It could be," Rampede said. "No reason a pair of professional killers couldn't also be addicts."

Mina chuckled. "No reason at all. But this is a fucking Christmas present: dead bodies, murder weapons, and now a motive. We're meant to believe this was drug-related."

Laura looked across the river at the lights of the East Side, all clean diamond-points in the dark. It was, of course, a dangerous place as well, but it was also a wonderful one, with culture and food and opportunity. Pigeon Hill, though, still had rot around the edges, and Ratway was *all* decay, abandoned by the city at large.

"I'll be in touch," Mina said. "Pleasure meeting you both, and sorry to drag you out in the middle of the night."

As they walked back to their cars, Rampede said, "Well, back to Ratway."

"Do you live there?" Laura asked.

"Yeah. Third generation Ratway Rat."

"And you like it?"

"It's what I know," he said with a shrug.

When they reached their cars, Rampede said, "You want to go get some coffee?"

"Where did you have in mind?"

"I know an all-night place in Ratway that makes the best coffee you'll find at this time of night."

"That's not exactly a glowing recommendation."

He chuckled. "No, but at least it'll get the smell of the river out of your nose."

She considered it carefully. Was Rampede coming on to her? Was he setting her up in some way so that he could use her as a source later? He was short-tempered and intimidating, but she'd seen no sign he was dishonest or corrupt.

"Okay. I'll follow you there."

1:10 A.M.

Mummadabba, blindfolded, was pushed into the waiting car outside the rave. The rumbles of a bridge's expansion joints told him when they'd left Ratway, and he knew they'd passed through the East Side when they no longer had to stop every block for traffic lights. The smell of too much expensive cologne and cigars meant he was probably in the company of Marley family foot soldiers.

His encounter with Darren Flaxstone had burned away most of his panic adrenaline, so he was numb. *Just be cool,* he told himself. *If they wanted you dead, you'd be dead. They want something from you, which gives you all the cards.*

He smelled salt water for the last few minutes of the ride. The car stopped, and his mysterious abductors yanked him out. They marched him along a wooden dock, onto a boat, and down some stairs into a stateroom. They slammed him into a chair and then yanked off the blindfold.

Someone shook the collar of his open shirt. "Polyester must be hard to button," said a man's voice.

Mummadabba laughed nervously.

"Mr. Mummadabba. Do you know who I am?"

The speaker was in his thirties, good-looking and sharply dressed. Behind him was the shadowy form of another, larger man.

"No," he answered honestly.

"No reason you would, I suppose. I'm Harrison Marley, Jr."

The blood drained from Mummadabba's face. Harry the Less. The man who ran, in everything but name, the Marley family.

"Nice to meet you," Mummadabba managed. "Sir."

"No, it's not, and I don't want you to pretend it is. Ordinarily I wouldn't even be talking to someone like you. But this is a special occasion, because you're involved in something I don't know enough about. I want you to enlighten me."

"Sure...sir."

Harrison stepped closer. "I know that you put a contract killer in contact with someone. I know that this specialist took out Arthur Shawcross. I don't care who he is, but I'm *very* curious to know who asked you to find him."

Mummadabba swallowed hard. First Flaxstone, now this. He had very little reserves of calm left. "I didn't find him, the Mendicant did."

"Again, pay attention. That's not what I asked. I asked *who* contacted *you.*"

He swallowed hard. "Helen Pappas."

"Who?"

"Some chick over in Bowland."

"Now why would 'some chick over in Bowland' want Arthur the Dodger dead?"

"Beats me. I don't ask questions like that."

Harrison pondered this. At last he asked, "Why did she want his head?"

"Didn't ask about that, either."

"You don't ask much, do you?"

"That's my motto. 'If the money's there, I do not care.'"

"Fine words to live by," Harrison agreed. "I'm sure you know how this sort of thing usually ends, don't you? I ask you questions, you give me bad answers, or no answers, and then I have someone shoot you in the head. After they shoot you in the kneecaps."

Mummadabba managed a smile. "I'm being straight with you, man...sir."

"No, you're answering my questions, which is very different from telling me what you know." After a moment, he continued, "You're not affiliated, Mummadabba. You don't work exclusively for us, or Kefali, or the Chodian Mad Dogs, or anyone. You pay your insurance to all of us. That makes you fairly unique."

Mummadabba chuckled nervously.

He indicated the large, shadowy figure behind him. "See this man? His name is Monte. Say hello to Mr. Mummadabba, Monte."

From the shadows, the big man said coldly, "Hello, Mr. Mummadabba."

"Monte has a cell phone. And this is the number." He held up a piece of paper with a phone number on it. Then he pressed it into Mummadabba's damp palm. "If you learn anything new about the killing of Arthur the Dodger, I expect you to contact him."

"Sure," Mummadabba said.

"Now put that in your pocket before your sweaty hands make the ink smear."

Mummadabba did so.

To the men who'd brought him, who Mummadabba had still never seen, Harrison said, "Take him back where you found him."

1:17 A.M.

D r. Saraya Parashar took off her glasses and rubbed her eyes. She'd worked a split shift, napping for five hours on the cot in her office while a volunteer physician worked off part of a DUI community service sentence. She really needed the help of another full-time doctor, but had nothing to offer one, and so far she hadn't run across anyone with the right combination of altruism and masochism. But she never gave up hope.

She looked over the last of her notes on her computer, made some corrections, then closed the file. The wallpaper photo of her sister back in Istanbul now filled the screen.

The back door opened and softly closed. Footsteps came quietly down the hall. She put her hand in her desk drawer and closed it around the taser she kept for emergencies. Every muscle was tense as she watched the shadow approach.

"It's just me," the Lightning Girl said.

Saraya sighed with relief. "Don't sneak up on me like that. Make the lights flash or something."

The Lightning Girl leaned against the door frame. She pushed off the hood and removed the cap to reveal long, wiry curls held back in a scrunchy, and the black greasepaint that covered the top half of her face. "Why are you so tense tonight?"

"I don't know. Something in the air. Is the moon full?" She put on her glasses. "Did you see the paper this afternoon?"

"Yeah. What did you think?"

"I thought it was good. Certainly made you sound mysterious and dangerous."

"You were right about that whole 'answer-with-no-answer' thing."

"I'm usually right about everything. That's why I'm a doctor." She paused. "What's wrong?"

"The murder of those children has gotten complicated. I was on my way to burn the truth out of a low-level fence named Mummadabba, but one of Kefali's people was already there."

"A Kefali goon? For real?"

"Well, sort of. He wasn't a goon, and he was with one of the Mendicant's former gang, a little boy I know. He told me that the kids' murderers were already dead, and that he was trying to find out who actually hired them because they also killed some high muckety-muck in the Kefali gang. This Mummadabba, and the Mendicant, were both just middlemen."

"Did he know who was behind it?"

"He gave me a name. Helen Pappas."

"Helen Pappas?" Saraya sat back in front of her computer and typed in the name. The first hit caught her by surprise. "Wait, you mean *this* Helen Pappas?" She clicked on the link.

The Wide Justice Games website popped up. A banner showcasing images from their games automatically scrolled across the top, while in the *News* section, the first headline read, *Wide Justice founder Helen Pappas honored with award from historians.*

Saraya clicked on the link. The woman identified as Helen Pappas looked too young to be a CEO: she had black hair, olive skin, and a Grecian nose. She was also beautiful, in that hard-lined classical way, and even the tweedy historians gathered around her to present the award seemed to notice that.

Saraya clicked through to her company bio. Where most people in similar positions would trumpet their education and accomplishments, hers was surprisingly vague:

Born in Greece, Helen came to the U.S. and thrived in its mix of technology, new media, and game culture. Her first game, The Battle of Arbela, created a new sub-genre of immersive historical play. She launched Wide Justice Games a few years later, and remains involved in its day-to-day operations, designing and coding alongside her employees to ensure each game lives up to her exacting standards.

"And *that's* who hired an assassin to kill the Mendicant?" Saraya said in disbelief.

"Not to kill the Mendicant," the Lightning Girl corrected. "She used Mummadabba, and he used the Mendicant to find the assassin, who then killed that Kefali lawyer. Killing the Mendicant was just...housecleaning."

Saraya shook her head. "Six children dead for no good reason."

"*Is* there a good reason?"

"You know what I mean. What now?"

She shrugged. "The housecleaners have been housecleaned. Technically, I suppose, that's that. This Helen is over in Bowland, and that's not my territory."

"It could be."

"No. I work in Ratway. The Kefali guy, Darren, promised to tell me what he finds out about her. I suppose I just wait."

Saraya leaned back. The Lightning Girl put her hands on Saraya's shoulders and sent a tiny charge into the doctor's sore muscles. Saraya sighed with relief. "Thanks."

"Anytime."

Saraya stood. "I'm going to the diner to get something to eat before I go home. Want to join me?"

"I have work to do."

"Oh, come on. It'll take an hour at the most. It'll do you good to be around people you're not angry with."

"I'm not dressed for it."

"I keep a change of clothes. You can borrow the blouse and shoes." She took the Lightning Girl's chin in her hand and looked into her eyes. "Doctor's orders."

The Lightning Girl gave her a skeptical smile. "All right, fine. Let me go wash up and change."

Imitating Billy Joel, Saraya crooned, "'Don't go changin' to try and please me...'"

"I don't want clever conversation," the Lightning Girl sang back.

1:20 A.M.

The Mendicant's hideaway, or headquarters, or Mendicave was in a cellar beneath the crumbling remains of one of the hundreds of old tenements in Ratway. Squatters occupied the apartments with intact floors, and this late at night, candles and open fires flickered in the windows. Somewhere a generator hummed, providing electricity to the top two floors.

Darren followed Sparrow down the stairs, past the walls of debris that appeared impassible but in fact moved smoothly on hidden hinges. Whoever designed and installed it was pretty damn clever.

But the basement gathering spot was empty. None of the other kids waited there.

Darren used his halogen flashlight to inspect every corner. Neat cots ran in rows along one wall, and a wobbly pair of picnic tables spoke of communal meals. It was, he realized, surprisingly homey, and no doubt gave the kids the illusion of family they so desperately craved.

"Nobody's home," he said.

"No," Sparrow agreed. He looked confused, worried, and frightened; Darren had not realized a child's face could be so eloquent. "And their stuff is gone."

"Including Corvus's?"

"Yes. This was his spot." He patted one of the cots.

"Where did you sleep?"

"Under here," he said, indicating the spot beneath Corvus's cot.

"He looked out for you, huh? Like a big brother?"

"Yes."

"They must know what happened," Darren said. "Maybe they're afraid to come back. Probably waiting until the whole thing quietens down."

"Yeah. We can go."

"As long as we're here, do you have anything you want to bring with you? Any books, or toys, or anything?"

"No. The Mendicant said those things made you weak."

Darren imagined the Mendicant raging, Immortan Joe-like, at his adoring flock about the dangers of attachment. Then he realized that the shifty bastard had been exactly right; with nothing to lose, the kids were free to run and keep running if danger got too close.

Which it definitely had. He hoped Sparrow's missing friends were safe, wherever they were.

"Come on," he said, putting a hand on his bony little shoulder. "I'm starving, and I bet you could use a bite yourself. I know the perfect spot."

1:21 A.M.

Harrison Marley, Jr. stood on the deck of his father's yacht, the *Penny Ante.* He'd grown up on it, learning the ins and outs of seamanship as well as the finer points of smuggling, evading the Coast Guard, and being cool when caught. Now the night wind blew off the ocean and tousled his hair as he looked down at his phone.

Down the coast, flashing lights showed where the cops and fire department clustered around one of the old, crumbling piers. When Monte came up the gangplank, he reported, "Two bodies found down there, wrapped in plastic. Looks like a drug thing."

"One of ours?" Harrison asked without looking up from his phone.

"Nah."

"Who's in charge?"

"Two Wolves."

That got Harrison's attention. Mina Two Wolves was sharp and honest, two qualities he hated in cops in general, and cops in his own backyard in particular. "Keep one ear on it."

"You bet," Monte assured him.

Harrison tapped his phone screen. "The internet says the only Helen Pappas in the city runs a software gaming company out of an office in Bowland," he said.

Monte, who as always stood quietly nearby, asked reasonably, "Why would she want the Dodger's head?"

"That's the big question," Harrison agreed.

"Want to go see her now?"

"No. Bowland's not like Ratway; we can't just grab whoever we want without attracting attention. But find out everything about her tomorrow."

Monte nodded. "There's always the possibility that Mummadabba just pulled the name out of his ass."

"Maybe," Harrison mused. "But 'Pappas' is a Greek name and so is 'Kefali.' That's a big coincidence. Of course, the Greeks have their own organized crime. You think this is some old-country vendetta?"

"*Ventetta*," Monte corrected.

"What?"

"It's 'ven-TET-ta in Greek, not 'ven-DET-ta.'"

"How the fuck do you know that?"

"You'd rather I was a moron?"

Harrison shook his head. "I don't know *what* the fuck is going on, but handing over the head of the person who took the Dodger's would be a good way to maintain the peace. Show Kefali for sure that it wasn't us." He looked hard at Monte. "It wasn't, was it?"

"I checked with everyone, boss. All our people are accounted for. None of them did it or know who did."

Harrison sighed and put his phone away. "It's late, Monte. I'm going to bed here on the boat. Wake me at six a.m."

Monte nodded. "Yes, sir."

THE SHOOTOUT
AT MISTY'S DINER

Misty's Diner, at the corner of Hamilton and 95th Avenue in Rattaway, had originally been opened as George's Eatery back in 1931, the waning years of Prohibition. The basement had more square footage that the diner, the better to accommodate the Spit N' Varnish speakeasy that was the *raison d'être* for its existence. It had changed hands (and names) some thirty times but never closed and currently stayed open 24 hours to provide one of the few safe late-night places to eat in Ratway. The gangs considered it neutral territory, like a church.

Four big men in a back booth gave Darren and Sparrow a once-over as they entered. A young couple on stools at the counter glanced up, then returned to their meals. Even the cook narrowed his eyes at them from behind his window. The price of Ratway was eternal vigilance.

"It smells really good here," Sparrow said.

"That's because it might be the one place in Ratway that's not a front for something else," Darren said.

Darren stopped here often, always in some sort of disguise. It didn't have to be much: a garish baseball cap, a phony cast on his arm, and once a fake mustache that fell off in his coffee, luckily when no one was looking. The trick to a good disguise, he knew, was to give people something to remember other than your face. Let the cops look for the guy in the red windbreaker, for example, and Darren would be completely incognito once he'd discarded that garment.

Tonight, his disguise was Sparrow.

"Can I get you and your son something to drink?" the server asked as they took a booth near the door. She was middle-aged, heavy and cheerful, a veteran who could handle sick drunks and petulant foodies with equal aplomb. Her name tag said *Leah*.

"I'll take some coffee," Darren said. He asked Sparrow, "Would you like a Coke, or some chocolate milk?"

"Chocolate milk sounds good, Daddy," he said innocently.

When Leah left, Darren reached across the booth's table and playfully squeezed the boy's nose. "Don't bury yourself in the part, kid."

"I'm just glad I got my good looks from Mom," he deadpanned back. Darren barked out a surprised laugh, and it made Sparrow smile.

The diner's fluorescent light really accented the boy's disheveled condition. Not only was his hair unkempt, but dirt streaked his face, and his fingernails were black-edged with filth. Darren couldn't even imagine what he'd look like cleaned up and properly dressed.

"Why are you staring at me?" Sparrow asked.

"I'm not staring, I'm evaluating. When's the last time you had a bath?"

"I dunno. What year is it?"

"Ha. Maybe I'll just strap you to the top of my car and run you through a car wash." He paused. "So now that we've got a minute, tell me about yourself. Where did you come from?"

Before Sparrow could answer, Leah returned with their drinks. "And what are you doing up so late at night?" she asked Sparrow, carefully looking him over for signs of abuse.

"Daddy works at night," he said brightly. "It's the only way we can do 'Take Your Child to Work Day.'"

"Oh?" she said to Darren. "And what sort of work do you do? Must be one that gets you dirty," she added with a glance at the boy.

"Animal control," Darren said. "I clean up roadkill."

"Really?" she said skeptically.

"Somebody has to. I have some pictures on my phone if you'd like to see. You'd be surprised which animals you find splattered on the street."

"That's okay," she said quickly, with a little shudder. "Now: what can I get you?"

Darren ordered bacon and eggs, and Sparrow asked for French

toast. When they were alone again, Sparrow said, "You still want to know about me?"

"I'd like to. If you don't want to tell me, though—"

"No, it's okay." His eyes got a little unfocused as he spoke. "My mom was a junkie—that's what they called it at the group home—and the state took me away from her. I don't really remember her. I was farmed out to foster parents. And that's where the Mendicant found me."

"Your foster parents abused you?"

"No. They were fine."

"Then why did you leave?"

"They were boring. That whole life was boring."

"And this kind of life is more exciting?"

"Oh, *hell* yes."

"How old were you?"

"Seven."

"And you're ten now?"

"Ten and a *half*."

Darren wasn't surprised by the story, only by the boy's strange, unsettling maturity as he told it. Darren himself had been the aimless son of a low-level thug, whose death sent his mother into hiding and left him on his own at age twelve. Luckily, he'd drawn the Dodger as a public defender. He wondered if Sparrow would consider himself as lucky in twenty years.

The bell over the door jingled. Two people, a large Black man and a lean White woman, entered. Darren instantly made them as cops, even before he saw their shields and glimpsed their weapons. *Detectives*, he thought, given their plain clothes. There was no way they could be looking for him...was there?

The four men at the back booth, as well as the couple at the counter, tossed down money for their checks and heads down, scurried past the two officers into the night. Just a lone older man, sleeping with his arms on the stained Formica, remained.

Laura Slade watched the others leave the diner with weary amusement. "If we're not careful, we might bankrupt this place."

Rampede grinned. "Everyone feels guilty about something."

"Even you?"

"Even me."

Laura took quick stock of the remaining diners, a man and his son, both rough and dirty-looking. *Perhaps they're homeless*, she thought. *It is awfully late for a child to be up.* But the boy looked happy, and his father seemed sober. Being poor wasn't yet against the law.

Rampede led her to a corner booth. He had to scoot the table closer to Laura to make room for his bulk.

"You come here a lot?" she asked.

"More than I should," Rampede said. "Beats going home and cooking after a long night."

"You're not married?"

"No. Tried it once, but it didn't take."

"I'm sorry."

"Don't be. It was for the best. What about you?"

"I don't need a husband, I have a cat."

Leah arrived, put down silverware and menus, and said, "Why, Detective Rampede, I didn't know you had a girlfriend."

"Neither did I. Leah, this is Detective Laura Slade from the 6th Precinct on the East Side."

Leah's eyebrows rose. "You're a long way from home."

"I go where the crime is," she said with a smile.

They ordered coffee. Over Rampede's shoulder, Laura couldn't stop watching the man and the little boy. Something about them seemed off, and she couldn't quite place it. Certainly, the child seemed under no duress; in fact, both were laughing. But she knew to never ignore her cop's spider-sense.

"What are you looking at?" Rampede asked quietly.

"There's a man and a little boy in a booth behind you."

"I saw them when we came in."

"There's something about them. Do you know them?"

Rampede discreetly checked them out. "Never saw them before. Want to talk to him?"

"No. Got no probable cause."

He chuckled. "Man, you East Side cops must go through a whole different kind of training."

Leah brought their coffee. "We've got the safest diner in Ratway tonight. You two police officers, and that gentleman from Animal Control."

"The one with the little boy?" Laura asked.

"Yes. Now, what can I get you?"

Laura ordered a short stack, and Rampede picked the steak and eggs. Laura insisted on separate checks. When they were again alone, Laura said quietly, "The little boy looks street-urchin-y. Could be one of the Mendicant's missing kids."

"Then why is he with a guy from Animal Control?" Rampede asked sensibly.

"Why is a guy from Animal Control taking his son out for breakfast past midnight? That's awfully late."

Rampede sighed. "It's also awfully late to go looking for trouble when we've got plenty right in our laps."

"You're right. I'll stop." After a sip of the strong yet smooth coffee, she said, "What made you decide to become a cop?"

"Why? Is it that weird that I am?"

"Can I be blunt?"

"Please."

Laura organized her words before she spoke. "You grew up Black in Ratway. Your experience of cops couldn't have been good."

"So because I grew up Black, it was inevitable that I have bad experiences with cops?"

"You said I could be blunt."

"Actually, I was never arrested as a kid. It's hard to believe, but I was a skinny little runt until I was fourteen, and people pretty much overlooked me. By the time I'd filled out to the magnificent specimen you see here—" he said this mock-seriously—"I was already on the honor roll at school. A cop came and spoke to us on Career Day, and the rest is history."

"Really?"

"There *might* have been an element of seeing three cousins killed by the police, and deciding I'd rather be on the other end of the gun."

"I'm sorry."

"Eh. One was a car thief, one stole a jar of change from a bodega, and the other just looked like someone who'd done something bad. Happens all the time."

"Doesn't make it right."

"What about you?"

"Me? Family tradition. My mom was a cop, all my aunts were cops, my grandmother was a cop. I was already a beat patrolman before I ever knew there were other jobs out there."

The bell over the door jingled again, and two young women entered.

One was Indian, her dark hair loose around her shoulders, wearing black-frame glasses. The other one was pale, her skin blotchy like it had just been scrubbed, her hair held back in a ponytail. They waved at Leah like regulars.

"Hey, Dr. Parashar," Leah said. "Hey, Devon."

⚡

"Hey," Saraya replied to Leah. She looked around. "Wow, it's busy for so late at night."

Leah nodded toward the man asleep with his head on the counter. "And except for Henry there, none of them are drunk."

"I'm not drunk," said Henry without raising his head.

"And Hell's not hot," Leah said dryly. "Sit wherever you like, Doc. I'll be right with you."

Saraya turned to her friend Devon. "Want to sit at the counter? It always feels more authentic that way."

Devon shrugged. "Sure, if authenticity's an important part of your dining experience."

Devon began to sit, then saw the man and little boy. She started so hard she nearly missed the stool, and Saraya had to grab her arm to keep her from falling. "Whoa, are you all right?"

"Yeah, just slipped," Devon said quickly. Making sure her back was to the pair, she leaned close and whispered, "That's *him*. The Kefali guy I told you about."

Saraya surreptitiously checked him out. "Are you sure? He's got his son with him."

"That's not his son. That's Sparrow, one of the Mendicant's bunch."

"Sparrow, as in the one who told you about the murders?"

"Yes."

Leah stopped in front of them. "Coffee tonight, ladies?"

"Yes," Devon said.

"Hot tea?" Saraya asked.

"Of course. Coming right up."

When she was gone, Saraya said softly, "Well, don't have kittens. There's no way they can recognize you."

Devon mock-slapped her arm. "That's not what I'm worried about! He was going to check into this Helen Pappas, and now I find him here. What's he up to?"

Saraya risked another glance. "Eating an early breakfast?"

Devon sighed. "You think I'm being paranoid, don't you?"

"I think you need to switch off the LG for a while. Just be Devon. Enjoy the company of your smartest friend."

"Where?" Devon said with a mocking look around.

Leah brought their drinks. "Busy night at the clinic?" she asked Saraya.

"Busy as a mosquito at a nudist colony."

"Any more irate husbands try to bust in?"

"No, I think word's gotten around about Tinley ever since she broke that one guy's jaw."

"Good. Nice to see somebody standing up for them. You do good work, Doc."

"Thanks."

"I don't know if I ever asked, but what do you do, Devon?"

"I'm an electrician," Devon said with a straight face.

Leah nodded. "Now what can I get you?"

Saraya ordered eggs and toast, and Devon chose a southwestern omelet. Leah put the order on the carousel and spun it back for the cook.

"Why is he here?" Devon said with quiet urgency, watching Darren and Sparrow in the reflection on the polished napkin holder.

"Will you—" Saraya stopped, then whispered, "Oh, shit." She spun back around to stare at the counter.

"What?"

"Look over there behind us," she said, barely moving her lips.

Devon followed her gaze to the booth where a large Black man sat with a White woman. Both practically radiated that they were cops. The Black one saw her looking and stared back. She turned away.

"What about them?" Devon whispered.

"The guy," Saraya said with quiet urgency. "He's the one."

Devon risked another quick glance. "Are you sure?"

"He pointed his gun at me, Devon, of *course* I'm sure."

As they ate, Darren watched the two women at the counter out of the corner of his eye. He knew the Indian one, at least by reputation: Dr. Saraya Parashar, whose clinic was a haven for battered women and children. But there was something about the White one with the ponytail that seemed familiar. "Sparrow," he said, "you know a lot of the people around here, don't you?"

"Sure," he said around a mouthful of French toast.

"Take a look at the two women at the counter. Specifically, the one with the ponytail. Do you know her?"

He wanted to see how discreet Sparrow could be, and he wasn't disappointed. The boy picked up his unused spoon, polished it with his napkin, and used it as a mirror. "Nope."

"Are you sure? She looks familiar to me."

"Not to me."

"Okay. Thanks." He ate a mouthful of eggs. "How's your French toast?"

"It's great."

"Do you order it a lot?"

"No, I've never had it before. I just liked the name. 'French toast.' It just sounds like it would be sweet and delicious, doesn't it?"

He raised his coffee in salute. "It does indeed."

"I take it you know them," Laura said.

Rampede blinked back to the moment. "I'm sorry, what?"

"Those women at the counter. You didn't look happy when they came in. Who are they?"

"I know the Indian one," Rampede said with forced casualness. "Dr. Parashar. She runs the free clinic a few blocks over. I've had occasion to stop by now and again."

"That's got to be a tough job, down here."

"It can be, that's for sure. But if anyone can stand up to it, she can. Although she gets in the middle of things sometimes that are none of her business."

Leah brought their food, and Rampede waited until she'd gone to resume speaking. He continued, "She was an army medic and served two tours overseas, right in the thick of things. She even once ran directly into a sniper's fire to reach a fallen soldier. Got hit, got a medal."

"Wow," Laura said. "So, did she grow up here? Is that why she opened the clinic?"

"No. I honestly don't know why she's here." His voice carried an unmistakable simmering resentment.

"You don't like her," Laura said.

"She can be pushy, and that tends to rub people the wrong way. She could stand to learn when to step back, you know?"

Laura had encountered plenty of men who resented forceful women—"pushy," as Rampede called them—simply because they felt it was inappropriately un-feminine. She had no patience with it. "I think, given everything else you've told me, that 'pushy' might be a necessary part of the job."

Rampede shook his head. "I'm sorry. I try to be modern, but sometimes the old-fashioned slips out."

"No worries," Laura said and turned her attention to her plate. She didn't see Rampede glance back at Saraya with cold, hard malice that he made no attempt to hide.

"He's staring at me, isn't he?" Saraya asked softly.

"He's looking," Devon confirmed. "Do you want to leave?"

"No," Saraya said through clenched teeth. "He's not going to run me out of here any more than he did the clinic. Just ignore him."

"I *am* ignoring him."

"I was talking to myself."

Devon watched her friend closely, seeing the fury in every small movement. Not many people could angrily sip coffee, but Saraya could. "Okay. It's your call."

Leah brought their plates. "Here you go, ladies. Hope you enjoy it."

"I'm sure we will," Devon said, unrolling the napkin to get the silverware.

Saraya hadn't moved or acknowledged Leah. "Is something wrong with the eggs?" the server asked. "Did you not want them scrambled this time?"

"Hm? Oh, sorry. No, that's not it. Just a lot on my mind."

"You're sure? I can get them redone, you know. It's no problem."

Saraya managed a smile. "No, Leah, they're fine. Thanks."

When they were alone again, Devon said, "Are you sure you don't want to leave?"

"I'm sure," Saraya seethed. "He's not running me out of someplace I like."

"No!" yelled a male voice from the kitchen. "No, wait, don't—"

And a gunshot rang out.

⚡

At the sound of the shot, Darren reached under the table, grabbed Sparrow's leg and yanked him from his seat. His head banged on the table's edge and he cried, "Ow!"

Darren wedged himself under the table as well. "Stay down!" he hissed and pulled the Beretta Pico he wore on his ankle.

⚡

Laura and Rampede both jumped to their feet, weapons drawn. The noise from the shot still echoed in the room.

"Everyone, *down!*" Rampede yelled to the other patrons. Laura held up her shield, as if anyone in the place didn't already know they were cops.

They approached the kitchen's swinging doors and flanked either side.

From this angle, Laura made eye contact with Leah, crouched behind the counter. She put a warning finger to her lips.

The kitchen doors burst open, and a skinny guy came out in full, street-tough swagger. He waved an automatic wildly about and shouted, "Let me see some hands, motherfuckers!"

"Mine are right here," Rampede said and put the barrel of his gun to the man's head.

"Ain't you the hero, big man?" another voice said. The second robber emerged from the kitchen, his gun leveled on Rampede. He was far less twitchy than his partner. "Drop it, Mr. Tibbs."

Laura put her gun at the base of the second robber's skull. "You drop it, or I'll drop *you* where you stand."

The second man grinned but kept his gun on Rampede. "Well, goddam. Cops everywhere."

"Drop it!" Laura repeated.

"You're gonna have to shoot me, baby," the second man said with a grin. "Got the balls for that?"

"What are you two shitheads doing?" Leah demanded as she got to her feet. "Nobody comes in my diner and tries to rob it. Everyone in Ratway knows that!"

⚡

"Uh-oh," Devon whispered. "I know these guys."

She and Saraya sat perfectly still, hoping the police could handle this. These were the same two losers, Seamus and his squirrelly friend Antonio, that she'd chased out of that empty apartment the previous night. She was certain they'd fled Ratway, but here they were.

She felt the electrical energy swelling in her, ready to be deployed. But she couldn't risk it, not without her disguise, not with witnesses. At least, not unless it became life or death.

"Just be cool," Saraya whispered back. "Let the cops handle it."

"Stay down, Leah," Rampede ordered.

"Aw, fuck this!" Antonio cried, almost a shriek of panic and excitement. He ducked away from Rampede's gun and fired at Laura.

The shot was incredibly loud, and Laura heard the sizzle as the bullet burned a strand of hair on its way past her head and into the wall. She ducked, stepped close and hit Antonio in the nose with the full weight of her own gun. He rocked back on his heels but didn't fall.

Now that Antonio was the focus of both officers, Seamus pointed his gun at Laura.

Rampede spun and fired point blank at Seamus. The impact blew the robber back against the door jamb; his knees wobbled, but like Antonio, he stayed upright. Dazed, the hole in his t-shirt smoking as blood soaked out, Seamus still managed to raise his gun at Rampede.

Devon yelled, "Watch out!" then shoved Rampede aside. He fell awkwardly to the floor, the young woman atop him as the robber fired.

They hit the floor, and Devon's head conked solidly against the tile. As he fought to get out from under her, not knowing who had body-blocked him, Rampede heard two more shots.

Darren watched the girl with the ponytail leap smoothly from the counter stool and knock the big Black cop out of the way. The bloodied shooter fired at her, an instant before Darren shot him in the head from beneath the table.

Not fast enough, he berated himself. The pony-tailed woman had to have been hit at such close range.

The punk the lady cop had smashed in the nose tried to raise his own gun. But before he could, the Indian woman jammed her fork hard into his inner thigh, puncturing his femoral artery. When she yanked it free, he let out a wild shriek of pain, dropped his gun and tried to staunch the thick stream of blood pulsing out. But before he could bleed to death, Darren shot him in the head, too.

Sparrow yanked on his sleeve. "Give me the gun!" he whispered. Darren passed it to the boy, and he quickly tucked it into the space between the bench seat cushion and the base. Only then did Darren realize he'd trusted Sparrow without a second thought.

As if reading his mind, the boy grinned and winked.

"Stay down and look scared," Darren told him quietly. "And be ready to move."

1:49 A.M.

Echoes of the gunshots hung in the air, along with the odors of gunpowder, blood, and oddly, ozone. For a long moment no one moved or spoke.

Rampede stood up. The two robbers lay on the floor, both dead from head shots. He checked their pulses just to be sure.

"You all right?" he asked Laura.

"Fine," Laura said and put away her weapon.

Rampede took out his phone and called his precinct. "Multiple gunshot injuries, 312 in progress, Misty's Diner, corner Hamilton and 95th. Send backup and buses."

Laura looked over at Dr. Parashar, who knelt beside Devon. "How bad is she hit?"

Devon was out cold. Saraya pressed her fingers against her friend's neck, then pulled up one lid and saw the eye rolled back in its socket. Something made a soft sizzling noise; faint electrical arcs flashed in the spaces between Devon's limp fingers.

Saraya grabbed Devon's hand and winced at the mild shock that traveled up her arm. "Wake up!" she whispered urgently. "You're sparking!"

The current faded, and Devon opened her eyes. She said flatly, "Ow."

"She's not shot," Saraya said and released her. Her palm ached from the minor burns. "I think she just hit her head."

274

"'Just,' my ass," Devon groaned.

"Are you sure?" Rampede pressed.

Saraya gave him a hard stare. "I *am* a doctor. I know what a gunshot wound looks like."

"She's right, I'm not shot," Devon said, and tried to rise. "But I do see three of you."

Saraya put a hand on her friend's chest and gently pushed her back down. "You need to get checked for bleeding in your skull. Just lie still and wait for the ambulance."

She draped an arm over her eyes. "You're the doctor."

Rampede walked away. Saraya whispered, "You were sparking between your fingers while you were unconscious."

"What?"

Saraya showed her the burns on her palm. "Don't worry, no one saw."

"Shit, Saraya, I'm sorry."

"I didn't know you did that when you were knocked out."

"I didn't, either. I've never been knocked out before."

The two friends looked at each other, choking down all the comments and questions for a later, more private time. Then Saraya said, "I'm going to see if anyone else needs help. You stay put."

Rampede went over to the man and his son. "Are you two all right?"

"I think so," the man said, his voice shaking.

Rampede knelt to talk to the boy, still under the table. "It's all right. It's all over. You're safe."

The little boy whimpered, his eyes wet with tears and his lower lip a-tremble.

Rampede gave the father a reassuring shoulder pat. He rejoined Laura, who leaned against the counter and waited for the adrenalin rush to fade. Quietly he said, "Can you keep a secret?"

"Sure."

He nodded at the dead men. "Those head shots aren't mine."

It took a moment for the implications to register on Laura's adrenaline-soaked mind. "What?"

"I put one in that guy's chest, but that's it."

"*I* didn't do it. So who did?"

Before he could answer, Rampede noticed the father and son were gone. He stared at the booth they'd occupied.

Leah emerged from the kitchen, helping a heavy-set man with a red stain on his apron. "Emilio's hurt," she said.

Instantly the Indian doctor was there, helping Leah guide the man into a booth. "Stay the fuck on the goddamn floor," the doctor barked to her friend, who again tried to rise. She examined the cook's wound, then bunched up a corner of his apron and pressed it against the hole. He moaned in pain.

"Keep pressure on this," the doctor said to Leah.

"Buses are on the way," Rampede said, as the first siren grew louder. "Leah, did you know that man and the little boy who were here?"

"No, never saw them before," she said. "Where are they?"

"They're gone." Rampede looked back at Laura. "It must've been him who shot these guys. Whoever he was, he saved us all."

"Then why," Laura asked, "did he run?"

Once the paramedics took over caring for Emilio, Saraya returned to Devon, who still had her arm over her eyes. "You did what someone told you to," Saraya said dryly. "You *must* be hurt."

"Now I know why you don't get Christmas cards."

"Because I was raised Hindu?"

"Because you can't pass up a chance to say, 'I told you so.'"

Saraya felt gently under Devon's hair. Her friend had conked herself pretty good, and a lump was already forming. She leaned close to Devon and asked quietly, "Are you sure you're not shot, too?"

"I think I'd notice," Devon said. "Besides, I vaporized the bullet in the air before it hit me."

"I didn't know you could do that."

"Neither did I. Seems to be a night of firsts."

Saraya looked around. Rampede was outside talking to some uniformed cops, while the female officer showed the forensics team where to work. "This is going to get complicated," she said quietly.

"We'll deal with it. Oh, and next time? *I* get to pick the restaurant."

As they drove across the bridge to the East Side, Darren felt the comforting presence of the gun back on his ankle. Before they'd slipped out of the diner unnoticed, Sparrow had retrieved it, then followed without question into the men's room and out through the window. They'd ducked into an adjacent doorway just as the police cars and ambulances arrived, both of them well-versed in how to be overlooked. Now they drove toward his place at the end of a spectacularly long day.

"That was some quick thinking back there," he said.

Sparrow said nothing but did sit up a little straighter.

"You're a pretty good partner," Darren added.

"The Mendicant never thought so. He said if I was any dumber, I'd need to be watered twice a week."

"He was wrong."

The boy beamed with pride. And by the time Darren pulled the old SUV into his reserved parking spot, Sparrow was asleep against the passenger door.

St. Bibiana's Hospital was a hundred years old, filled with equipment twenty years out of date, tending to patients who couldn't possibly afford it, and staffed by doctors and nurses who had the blank, blasted look of people who'd seen the worst the world could throw at them. It was also where Saraya had hospital privileges, since none of the more upscale facilities had any use for her mostly-indigent patients.

Saraya made sure Devon was X-rayed instead of MRI'd, since she knew that Devon's abilities, without her constant conscious control, might screw up the MRI machine. She was relieved to see no sign of bleeding on Devon's brain. The ER physician recommended overnight observation, as they always did, but Saraya overruled him. Sometimes it was useful being a doctor.

In the Uber back to the clinic, Devon rested her head on Saraya's shoulder. "Thanks for watching my back."

"Thanks for watching mine. At least your friend won't have to worry about Seamus stalking her anymore."

"She'll be glad to hear that." Devon yawned. "I still need to go back out tonight."

"Not a chance. You need rest. And before you go back to work, we need to talk about what happened while you were knocked out."

Quietly so the driver wouldn't overhear Devon said, "If I don't go out on patrol, somebody might notice that when Devon got hurt, LG went MIA."

"Like who?"

Devon just looked at her. "I hate it when you're logical, you know that?"

Laura stood on the sidewalk outside the diner, gazing at the East Side lights across the river. She finished a long text to Cole, telling him what had happened. Rampede was still inside, patiently explaining the sequence of events to a short-tempered Internal Affairs investigator who didn't appreciate being awakened this late. Soon it would be Laura's turn as well.

The crime scene technicians examined things in their methodical way. Leah paced on the sidewalk, side-stepping cops and CSU's, waiting for a ride to St. Bibiana's to check on Emilio.

She stopped beside Laura. "I wish my sister would get here. Have you heard anything from the hospital?"

"No, ma'am, I'm afraid not."

"I hope Emilio will be all right. He's such a good man. He just got his first grandchild, did you know?"

"They'll do all they can," Laura said mechanically.

Leah nodded toward Rampede and the IA officer. "Will you two get in trouble?"

"No. I mean, we didn't do anything. That man with his little boy, though—are you sure you didn't know him?"

"I swear, I've never seen him before."

"Thanks."

Rampede emerged, scowling. "He's ready for you, Slade."

Laura went inside, careful to avoid the splashes of blood and discarded shell casings. The IA officer was thin, with sharp features and cold, tightly-focused eyes that left no room for sympathy. She noticed he wore a wedding ring and instantly felt sorry for his husband or wife.

"Detective Slade," he said in a dark, cold tone. "You're a long way from home."

"Yes."

"Let me see your weapon."

She handed him the gun. He looked it over, sniffed the barrel, and noted the serial number. "None of these shots were yours?"

"No."

He returned the gun and said, "So tell me what happened?"

She gave him a concise report, careful not to describe anything she didn't personally witness. He listened impassively. When she finished, he said, "And no one knows this man and his son? They're not regulars?"

"Not according to Leah, the waitress."

"Yes, she gave us a pretty detailed description. Said he told her he worked for Animal Control, picking up dead animals hit by cars."

"He might."

"Yes, except Animal Control doesn't employ anyone to specifically do that."

Laura sighed. "Then I can't help you, Sundance."

"Hm. You can go."

"Am I on desk duty?"

"Do you want to be?"

"No, of course not."

"Then it's your lucky day. You didn't fire, and no civilians were injured by your inaction. Plus, this is Ratway."

"What does that mean?"

"It means that if you walked out in the street and shot the first three people you saw, you could probably get away with it because they'd all have rap sheets."

Laura started to protest this profiling but caught herself in time. "I see."

"Stay away from this investigation, though."

"Gladly."

Outside, she joined Rampede down the block, far enough from the diner that they could speak freely. He asked, "Did they nail you?"

"No. They didn't even give me a hard time."

"Me, neither." He paused thoughtfully. "What the fuck happened in there, Slade? Who *was* that guy? Was he on the job?"

"Beats me. Even if he was, why'd he bring his son along?"

"And did you smell electricity? You know, like something was burning?"

"I did. I just figured it was something in the kitchen."

"Yeah, that makes sense," he said with a sigh.

That's the only thing that does, she thought.

THE DAY OF THE FESTIVAL

6:37 A.M.

The transport will be here shortly," B.J. told Stavros in his private room behind her office. "Dr. Erstatt will be waiting for you on site."

Most of the screens around the room were dark, so his face was hidden in shadow. "How is the volunteer?"

"Under sedation, so it's too late for him to change his mind."

"Thank you. Any further news about…?"

"No."

"I'll be indisposed for the rest of the day, so whatever Darren turns up, you'll have to handle on your own."

"I know." B.J. tapped her fingernail against the nearest metal monitor bracket. "I'd be lying if I said I wasn't worried about this, Stavros."

"There's nothing we can do. So worry is pointless."

"We can postpone it. What's the worst that could happen?"

"I will die," Stavros said simply.

"You don't know that."

"I do. It's not a certainty I can explain or put into words, but it's a certainty nonetheless. If the Festival doesn't occur on the appointed date, in the accepted way, then I…will…die." He had not told anyone, ever, what would happen after that.

"And if *she* shows up tonight?"

"Her mere presence won't end it. But her actions might. And there's nothing to be done except to prepare for it."

"Why not just let Darren kill her?"

Stavros's smile was eloquent in its sadness. "If only it were that easy, B.J. If only that was possible."

The bathroom's bright, clean light and gleaming white surfaces accented Sparrow's accumulated grime. He said, "Wow. This is a big bathroom. How many people pee in here?"

Darren laughed. "Only one at a time, I promise."

"And this whole apartment is just for you?"

"It's not an apartment, it's a condominium."

"What's the difference?"

"A landlord owns an apartment. The tenant owns the condo."

The boy nodded, filing that information away. "Don't you get tired of cleaning all this white?"

"I have a housekeeper who comes in. Plus, I'm pretty neat."

Sparrow looked him up and down; Darren still wore the shabby disguise clothes he'd worn to question Mummadabba. Then the boy frowned. "Umm… why are you looking at me like that?"

"Trying to decide if I should just tuck you into the dishwasher instead. Didn't the Mendicant ever let you bathe?"

"Once a week, at the Boys and Girls Club. He said being dirty helped with our work. Made us look more pitiful. But you're not the freshest flower in the garden yourself, you know."

The boy's quick wit amused Darren. "I agree. But you first. Oh, and just put your clothes in the trash."

"Then what'll I wear?"

"I took care of that while you were asleep in the car. Take your time, all right?"

Sparrow looked into the shower stall, also shiny white tile, with a shower head as big as a Frisbee. "That won't come loose and fall on me, will it?"

"No."

He tentatively turned on the water.

Halfway out the door, Darren stopped and said, "I don't know what may have happened to you in the past. And I don't expect you to believe it yet. I know I wouldn't. But...you're safe."

Sparrow's gaze was older than any child's should be. "Okay," he said in a small voice.

If he hadn't been covered in days' worth of street detritus, Darren might've scooped him up into a reassuring hug. He closed the bathroom door, took a deep breath, and carried his laptop to the couch.

The sky was light, but the sun hadn't quite crested the nearby buildings. He'd been awake for almost forty-eight hours now, and his thoughts were growing fuzzy. He did a line of cocaine that cleared the cobwebs, at least for a while. But he'd have to sleep soon. His attendance at the Festival tonight was mandatory.

But he also had to get to the bottom of this Helen Pappas thing, find out why she killed Artie, and what she had against Stavros. So he took the usual first step: he Googled her.

He read through it, then enlarged her picture and gazed at it thoughtfully. Could it be... *her?*

He called B.J. and put it on speaker. "You awake?" he asked.

"It's the day of the Festival, of course I'm awake. How was last night?"

"Eventful." He gave her the run-down, including the name he'd gotten from Mummadabba.

"Helen Pappas," she repeated. "Never heard of her."

"Me, neither. She runs a software gaming company, believe it or not."

"Let me pull it up," B.J. said.

He gave her a moment, then asked, "So what do you think? Could it be... *her?*"

"It could be. She certainly looks Greek."

"Only Stavros would know for sure. Can you show it to him?"

"No, he's already busy preparing for the Festival. I can't see him until tonight."

"Okay. Then I guess I'll pay her a visit later. Ask her flat-out what she wants."

"If it is… *her*… is that a good idea?"

"Time's a factor. If she's a threat to the Festival, we don't have long to sort it out."

"Be careful. Keep me posted."

The genuine concern in her voice made him smile. "I will."

He ended the call, and the intercom buzzed. He walked to the door, pushed the reply button and said to the doorman, "Yeah, Stevie?"

"You've got a delivery, Mr. Flaxstone. Since it's from a kids' clothing store, I wanted to make sure you were expecting it."

"I am, Stevie. You can send it up. And thanks for your diligence."

Darren poured some coffee while he awaited the delivery. In the morning silence, he heard Sparrow's voice from the bathroom. He jumped up, afraid the boy was in trouble, and was about to rush in when he realized what he heard.

He was singing to himself. A children's song about a family of sharks. Happily.

He bit back his laughter and stepped quietly away from the bathroom door.

7:55 A.M.

Rebecca Hutchcraft sipped her coffee and watched the sun rise above the river, a hot bright spot between two skyscrapers. She hadn't seen the sunrise in months, and yawned anew at the thought. She was *not* a morning person. Angelyne223 had better be fascinating if she wanted to keep Rebecca awake.

She'd walked down from the newspaper offices; none of her fellow journalists were in this early, not even Ransom Wade. Copies of the morning's paper, with the hard-copy version of her story, lay scattered around. By now Ransom would have heard from Farber Kelly and put together some sort of legal strategy. One that, Rebecca hoped, didn't involve her going to jail to defend her right to shield sources. But she would if she had to.

There was a parking lot for the River Walk at 14th and Brannigan, packed with small, fuel-efficient cars that cost more than her yearly salary. If Angelyne223 drove one of those, she was awfully well-off for someone who frequented Ratway often enough to know the Lightning Girl's true identity.

True identity, secret identity...Rebecca never thought about these things in the context of real life. They belonged in comics and movies. But the Lightning Girl was, by the accepted definition, a superhero: she wore a mask, she fought crime, and she had *fucking superpowers*. Or rather, she had at least one: the ability to control electricity. Or appear to control it.

Rebecca sighed and yawned again. Her jaw stretched to its limit.

"Don't swallow your tongue," a voice said.

It took her a moment to spot the source: a bearded man in a wheelchair. One leg was missing below the knee. He had the look of a typical panhandler, and Rebecca opened her purse to find some change. She'd been close to homelessness herself in the past and always made sure to pay it forward because her chosen field wasn't known for its security.

"Naw, I don't want your money," he said. He had one of those wet, gravelly voices. "You're here to meet me."

"I am?"

"I'm Angelyne223."

She regarded him skeptically. "Oh? Am I supposed to know that name?"

"Come on, don't be coy."

"'Coy'?" she repeated archly.

"Would you prefer, 'smart-ass'?"

"All right. What are we meeting about?"

He checked around to make sure none of the joggers or mothers with strollers were close enough to overhear. "You want to know who the Lightning Girl really is, and I can tell you."

Rebecca kept her face neutral. "How would you know? She never leaves Ratway."

"She doesn't, but *I* do. No place to get dialysis over there on that side of the river." His eyes narrowed. "Are you wired?"

"No. But I would like to record this." She held up her phone.

"Not a chance. This is all off the record."

"Then why are you going to all the trouble to tell me?"

"Roll with me," he said, turned his wheelchair and headed west down the river walk. Joggers dodged around them, a few giving them disapproving glares.

"Damn East Siders," he muttered. "I served in Afghanistan, did you know that? Lost this leg to an IED over there. Ungrateful bastards."

"Where are we going?"

"Nowhere, I just like to move when I talk."

He stopped suddenly when he saw a mounted cop under a tree a few hundred yards away. "Is this a trap?" he said darkly.

"You must think a lot of yourself if you think one crazy email rates an elaborate scheme to trap you."

He laughed. "You're a pistol, aren't you?"

"Yeah, and my clip's getting empty."

"All right. Here's what I got. I live over in Ratway; I use the old V.A. clinic to get my methadone, and I have a room in a group home. I take the bus over here most mornings for my dialysis. I have a hard time sleeping, so sometimes at night I go out and just...roam around."

"Isn't that dangerous?"

"Eh. Nobody tries to rob me, and if anyone fucks with me just for the hell of it, I have ways. Anyway, so one night I'm rolling along, in the shadows 'cuz the streetlights are for shit, and I see this flash of light from the alley behind that free clinic, the one run by that Indian lady doctor. I roll close enough to see what caused it, and there's a woman standing there. She's wearing boots and a hoodie. Sound like anybody you know?" He paused to gauge her response. "You believe me?"

"So far," Rebecca said.

"Anyway, I'd heard stories about the Lightning Girl, but you know, I also hear stories that vampires and zombies are roaming around, or that there's an old house in Pigeon Hill built over a portal to Hell. So I didn't give it much thought."

He paused to let a pair of elderly, slow-moving people get out of earshot.

"Okay," he continued. "So she goes inside through the clinic's back door. I scoot around to the front, and a few minutes later she and the doc come out. Only she's not wearing a hoodie."

"If you didn't see her face, how did you know it was her?"

"She's still wearing the same boots."

"Then what?"

"Well, as you can imagine, I'm pretty damn fascinated by then. So I follow them. It's hard to be stealthy in a wheelchair, though, so they spot me and stop. They wait for me and then offer to help. I got a real good close-up look at her."

"If it *was* her."

"Okay, fine, be all Doubting Thomasina. You've seen her up close, right?"

"Yes," she said guardedly, hyper-careful so that she admitted to nothing that wasn't covered in her article.

"Then tell me this ain't her."

He pulled out a creased pencil sketch, done in great detail. It showed a pretty but unremarkable face, framed by tight waves of curls.

"Tried to take a picture with my phone," he added. "But the damn thing wouldn't work. Every picture was just static."

Rebecca didn't respond. She was totally engrossed in the picture. *Was it her?* She tried to match it up to her memory of the girl's lips, jawline, and chin. Had the makeup and hoodie conveyed an artificial hardness and assurance? Was she really, under it, merely this sweet-looking young woman?

"I don't know," she said honestly. "Could be. Where did you learn to draw like this?"

"Hell, I used to be a police sketch artist."

"Why'd you quit?"

"It was cheaper to fire me than to put in a wheelchair ramp."

Rebecca continued to look at the drawing. "Did you happen to get her name?"

He smiled triumphantly. "See, that's where the money changes hands."

"Ah. And what's the going rate for a superhero's secret identity these days?"

"Let's say...five hundred?"

"Let's say one hundred."

"That'll barely cover my bus fare."

"Not my fault you take the fancy bus."

"Two hundred?"

"One-fifty. And that includes the picture."

He sighed. "All right. But show me the money first."

She'd made sure she had bribing cash, so she took it from her purse. She held it up, then counted it out into his hand.

"Pleasure doing business with you," he said as he tucked it away.

"Now the name."

"I didn't catch it that clearly, but it was something like 'Dylan,' or 'Devon,' or 'Della.'"

"'Something like?'"

"Hey, no refunds or returns. But you know she's friends with that lady doctor, and there's her face right there. Aren't you supposed to be good at tracking stuff down?"

"All right, fine." She gave him another fifty. "This buys your silence."

He mimed zipping his lips.

"I have one more question. Why do you call yourself 'Angelyne223' online?"

"Name of a girl who broke my heart, and the apartment number where she did it. You never would've guessed it was some hairy old crippled vet, would you?" He spun the chair around and said over his shoulder, "Don't sweat the petty things, and don't pet the sweaty things, Ms. Hutchcraft. Have a good day!"

She watched him roll west, the walkers and joggers parting around him.

Obviously, it was no surprise that Saraya knew the Lightning Girl; but it was a surprise that they were, apparently, such good friends that the doctor knew her true identity. Saraya hadn't mentioned that.

And now that Rebecca knew it...what would she do with it? Could she really put Saraya on the spot and demand the information? And then what? Write about it, and risk that bitchy D.A. hauling her back in front of the grand jury? Not to mention whatever would happen to the Lightning Girl?

Rebecca tossed her empty coffee cup into a nearby garbage can and leaned against the rail overlooking the river. A barge chugged slowly upstream, its deck covered with wrecked cars. This was a tough one, all right. It would certainly raise her esteem in Ransom's eyes and increase the circulation even more.

For a minute.

Then it would pass, another drop in the river of news that never slowed, never dried up and never ended. Just like the river.

Shit, she thought. *Shit, shit, shit.*

Preoccupied, she headed back to the newspaper office.

8:03 A.M.

C ole Slaughter finished knotting his tie, a task that always took him at least three attempts even after fifteen years. Then he sat on the edge of the bed and kissed Anna, still asleep, on the cheek. She stirred and asked sleepily, "Hey."

"Hey. Heading to work."

"Will you be late?"

"I don't think so, honey. I hope not."

She smiled and burrowed down into the blankets.

He crept quietly from the house and made his way toward the subway station. On the way, his phone rang; Laura's name popped up.

"Hey," he said.

"Did you get my text?"

"I did. I assume you're all right?"

"I'm fine."

"What happened with that call to the Pigeon Hill waterfront?"

"A John Doe and a Jane Doe, so far. Rampede thinks they're related to the Mendicant killing, which means they're also related to the Arthur Shawcross murder."

"First rule," he said dejectedly. "Now tell me about this shootout."

"It wasn't a shootout, dumb-ass. We just went for coffee, and while we were there, a couple of losers tried to rob the place. They got taken out."

"By who? You or him?"

"Neither. Some guy who was in there with his little boy. And they skipped out before we could question them. And the real kicker? He got both the perps with perfect head shots."

Cole, like every other cop, was trained to shoot for the middle of the body, where there was more target. A head shot could easily go astray. "That's some shooting."

"It is," she agreed. "Where are you?"

"Almost at the train sta—" He looked around and realized he'd walked right past it. "Shit. I overshot. I'll have to take the next train. See you at the precinct. Cover for me."

He ended the call, then took in his location. Coincidentally, he stood across the street from the renovated church where he'd encountered Stavros Kefali's CEO.

Even this early it was a hive of activity. At least twenty workers carried boxes and crates into the building, while discreetly armed guards stood watch. It reminded Cole of the preparations he'd seen at the mayor's mansion, back when, as a uniformed officer, he'd been detailed to security. His presence was mainly to deter anyone who tried to sneak in; were these rent-a-cops doing the same?

He tried to connect things. Stavros Kefali funded this remodeling, and was throwing the first party in it. Kefali's top attorney had been gunned down three days beforehand, by a hired assassin. The renovation had obviously been in progress for a while, so the Dodger's murder didn't affect it. But was the murder an attempt to stop, or delay, this upcoming event?

He hadn't considered that before. Who might want this Festival stopped bad enough to kill? And since the initial killing had failed to stop it, who might be next?

9:10 A.M.

Cole arrived at the 6th Precinct, waved to the captain in his glass-walled office, and sat down opposite Laura. She looked up from a mug shot book on her desk. "You made it," she said. "I was about to call in an 805. I emailed you a copy of the report on the Pigeon Hill bodies."

"Thanks. And you're okay?"

"I told you I was."

"I repeat the question."

"*Yes*, Mr. Overprotective. I'm fine. So is Rampede. So is everyone at the diner, except the cook who took a slug to the belly and a bystander who hit her head. But according to the hospital, they'll both be okay, too."

He indicated the mug book. "What are you doing?"

"Looking for our hero."

"In there?"

"No one who can shoot like that is a civilian."

"Any luck?"

"Not yet. There just wasn't anything memorable about him, except that he was there after midnight with a little boy."

He waited a moment, then said, "On an unrelated case, there's something happening at that church Kefali bought down in Bay View."

"More remodeling?"

"No, looks like they're done and they're setting up for some kind of event. It got me thinking…what if the Dodger was killed as a warning to Kefali not to go through with whatever event they're planning?"

She thought that over. "It didn't work, then."

"No. So they might try something else."

"Go after Kefali himself?"

"I doubt they could get to him. But the next in line is B.J. Burr."

"Should we warn her? Offer her protection?"

"If we figured it out, so did she."

"Bring her in for questioning?"

"Then whoever's behind this will know that we know."

"Then they know that we know that she knows." She closed the mug book. "I know *you*, Cole. What's your plan?"

"We watch. We watch her at the office, and then watch the party tonight. Assuming IAD doesn't pull your gun and badge. Do you have to talk to them?"

"No. I didn't discharge my weapon. They cleared me last night."

Cole tapped his fingers, deep in thought. "I need to talk to the captain. I'll be right back."

He closed Captain Evans' door without asking for permission. "I've got something on that special thing you mentioned."

Evans gestured at a chair. "For god's sake, Slaughter, keep your voice down."

"I think I know where the Festival is going to be held," Cole said softly. "Kefali's been renovating an old church in Bay View. Not far from my house, actually."

"How sure are you?"

"At least eighty percent. But I want to stake it out with Laura, and I need your permission to bring her up to speed."

Evans thought this over. "No. Make up whatever you need to, but this stays between you and me."

"I'm not real comfortable with that, Captain."

"I know. But that's the way it is. Understand?"

With a sigh, he said, "Yes, sir."

At mid-morning, Darren stepped out of an Uber in front of the Wide Justice gaming company. He was dressed in his favorite bespoke suit, unarmed and immaculate. He looked prepared to discuss annuities and offshore banking.

"Wait for me," he told the driver.

"I'm not a cab, dude," she said.

Darren gave her two twenties.

"That gets you twenty minutes," she said, and tucked the money inside her blouse. "At twenty-one, I'm gone."

He smiled at her. "I hope your day is filled with people like you."

The guard at the door swiped him with a metal detector wand and waved him through. The lobby had a high ceiling, big windows, and a series of desktop computers set up with some of Wild Justice's games. Everything was shiny and new, the perfect first impression for a cutting-edge tech company.

The receptionist behind the front desk, a beautiful Asian woman, looked up. "May I help you, sir?"

"Yes, I'm here to see Ms. Helen Pappas."

"Do you have an appointment?"

"Do I need one?"

"Ms. Pappas is extremely busy." She looked at her screen. "She has an opening on—"

Darren tapped a Kefali business card on the desk. "Please tell her who it is, and who I'm representing. I think she'll see me."

The name clearly meant nothing to the receptionist, but she dutifully called up to the office. Darren stepped away to give her some privacy, studying the games on display. A surprising number of them were based on Greek and Roman battles. He wondered how well those really sold.

"Mr. Flaxstone?" the receptionist called. "Please take the third elevator to the ninth floor. Ms. Pappas is expecting you."

He nodded his thanks. In the elevator, aware he was being observed, he spritzed breath spray and checked his hair in the door's polished surface, playing the part of the unctuous flunky. The door slid aside and deposited him on the ninth of ten floors, where a sign informed him to turn right to find Helen Pappas's office.

Like B.J., she had a male secretary, young and model-handsome. He stood and offered his hand. "You must be Mr. Flaxstone. Ms. Pappas is expecting you. Would you follow me?"

Darren took in the layout as they walked down a short corridor. Four other doors opened off it, two of them closed, one open to an empty conference room, the last showing a security office with multiple screens.

At the end of the hall, the secretary knocked. "Ms. Pappas? Mr. Flaxstone is here," he said, then opened the door.

She looked like her online photograph, but that image had not captured her innate, disconcerting *stillness*. She stood behind her desk, in a crisp blouse and designer jeans. Wavy jet-black hair fell loose to her shoulders, and her skin was a pale olive complexion. "Good morning, Mr. Flaxstone."

She had a slight, nonspecific European accent; she'd done either a bad job at eliminating it, or a good one at fudging its origin.

"And to you, Ms. Pappas." He walked, not to one of the guest chairs, but to a framed poster from the game *Armada Meltdown*, based on the defeat of the Spanish Armada. "When does this come out?"

"Seven months, if beta testing is done on schedule." She joined him, and he was startled by how tiny she was; he'd guess a little over five feet. She wore low heels, so she wasn't self-conscious about it. "It should be the biggest game of next year. Do you play games?"

"That's a loaded question. I assume you know most of the reasons I'm here?"

"You work for Stavros Kefali, and you're here because you believe I had his lawyer killed and beheaded as a message to him."

"Almost. I do believe that, but I think the real reason he was killed is so you could get his ring."

"And why would I want that?"

Darren took a seat opposite her desk. "You didn't want it. You *need* it. There's no other way you can crash the Festival."

"What Festival?"

"The one that Stavros holds every hundred years that allows him to continue to exist."

She was silent for a moment. "His real name isn't Stavros, you know."

"I know. And yours isn't Helen, either."

"No. But my real name is too hard for Americans to pronounce."

"'Helen' is still properly epic."

"Thank you."

"We have a problem. The Festival is very important and needs to go on without a hitch. You're a hitch."

"And you're here to unhitch me?"

"I'm here to negotiate."

That was when he noticed it—Helen Pappas did not blink. Only one other person in his experience did that—his boss.

He felt a strange jolt of fear, and surprisingly, the first thing he thought of was how disappointed Sparrow would be if he died before seeing the boy again. But he had plenty of experience at not letting it show.

"Will you be at the Festival?" she asked,

"I will."

"Then you'll be a witness to what happens. I should warn you not to get your hopes up, though. It won't be a big, dramatic ending with car chases and explosions. It'll just be a simple closing of eyes that will never again open." She paused, then asked, "Was it difficult to accept the truth about what he is?"

"Sure, at first. But the reality is rather undeniable."

"And let me guess: you came to him as a child, and he raised you to be his lackey."

"He made sure I learned useful skills, and he's kind enough to employ me."

Helen laughed, as humorless a sound as Darren had ever heard, like the wind through gnarled branches on a distant Mediterranean island. "Do you have any idea how many came before you?"

"Quite a few."

"The first one was a young boy, barely a teenager, who happened to find him there in the forests of Greece. He believed the gods had guided him to this new master, and he fell under his influence. And when he grew too old, he brought new acolytes to take his place. And so it has been since the beginning. And that doesn't bother you?"

"Why should it? They have nothing to do with me."

"He wouldn't hesitate to kill you if it made things easier for him."

"Then I'll have to make sure I'm not hard to be around."

She stood, and so did he. She walked around the desk with the grace of a dancer in an emperor's court assured of the ruler's favor. She looked up into his eyes. "Remember this exactly as I say it. *Τίποτα δεν διαρκεί για πάντα*," she said, the words molding themselves to her accent. "*Ούτε καν εμείς.*"

"Is that Greek?"

"You know it is. I assume you speak it."

"*Με μια φοβερή προφορά*," he said.

Again she laughed. She turned and went back behind her desk. "I'm surprised you haven't tried to kill me, Mr. Flaxstone. That would solve so many things. It's the eyes, isn't it? I've been told they unsettle people. I spent years trying to learn to blink again, but I never could." She sat and crossed her legs.

"Then I'm free to go?" he asked.

"You were never a prisoner."

"Thank you for your time," Darren said with a little bow.

"And thank you," she said, "for your graciousness. That's a rare commodity among young men these days."

"You can thank Stavros for that."

He walked out, past the receptionist, expecting at any moment to feel bullets strike him in the back or the head. And yet he departed unmolested and climbed into his Uber untouched. He sagged against the backseat and let out a huge sigh of relief. He held out his right hand and chuckled at his trembling fingers.

"Damn," the Uber driver said. "That must've been some stressful job interview."

Lobotomy Eyes sat in the oily motel chair, one leg draped over the arm, clicking through the porn channel previews. She'd been awake all night, keeping watch, and yet felt no desire to sleep. If money was involved, she could wait until doomsday.

Her phone buzzed, and she answered as soon as she saw the name. "Yes?"

"Checking in," Helen Pappas said. "How are they?"

She looked around at the children. The four youngest slept in pairs on the twin beds, while the other two lay on the floor under blankets. None of them stirred at the sound of the phone. "They're fine," the dead-eyed woman said. "I gave 'em something so they'll stay asleep all day. I'll have them there on time."

"Good. Any of them give you any trouble?"

"No."

"See you there, then."

"With the other half of the money."

"Of course."

After the call ended, Lobotomy Eyes unfolded like some large, pale stick insect and stepped over the sleeping boys to get to the window. She had both the shades and curtain drawn, and a narrow glow shone around the edges. She pulled it open enough to peer outside, squinting against the bright glare.

The motel parking lot was mostly deserted, and cars hummed past on the overpass, oblivious to the decrepit building below. From the room above, she heard a woman bellowing in Spanish, and the TV in the room to her right was tuned to an old western.

This room smelled of triumphant mildew and defeated bleach. She picked up the bottle of Jim Beam and turned it up. In the closet, the row of white gowns that the kids would need that night hung neat and straight.

Rebecca looked up at the newsroom's old-fashioned analog clock, a relic of another time. Once there had been a row of them, each set to a different time zone; the un-faded circles of paint they'd left behind were still visible. She'd reported last year on a school that had discarded all clocks with hands, because kids raised on digital could no longer read them. It made her feel old, knowing she had a skill that was dying out. Probably the way her father did when cable first came to his building, replacing three channels (and PBS) with an unending list of options. Or, as Bruce Springsteen said, with "57 channels and nothin' on."

On her desk, Angelyne223's original drawing lay beside a photocopy, on which she'd drawn a hood and dark makeup on the upper face. No matter how long she stared at them, though, she couldn't make up her mind. Yes, it might be the Lightning Girl. And it might not.

She found Saraya's clinic page on social media and scrolled through her friends list, looking for one of the possible names: Dylan, Devon, or Della. There was no female Dylan, and no Della at all. There was a Devon; Devon Moraine. But her page was set to private.

Rebecca smiled. *You can hide now,* she thought, *but the internet is forever.* Using that name, she searched the net in general.

There wasn't much. Her name turned up in a list of supporters of a homeless shelter, another among those arrested at a protest against police brutality three years ago. She found a picture from that demonstration, but the woman identified as Devon Moraine was half-hidden behind a man screaming at someone.

But if she'd been arrested, she was probably booked, and the police would have her in their system. She thought it over, then called Cole Slaughter.

"Hey," he said. "I bet you want to talk to Laura."

"I can, but you won the coin toss."

"I wasn't even there."

"'There' where?"

"Oh, you haven't heard. Laura was involved in a shooting at a diner in Ratway last night."

"Oh, my God. Is she all right?"

"Extra cranky from lack of sleep, but otherwise, yeah."

"I'm not cranky," she heard Laura protest.

"Thank goodness." She paused, struggling with this new information. It was certainly hotter than what she'd called about. "I guess I'd better talk to her, then."

"Hang on."

There was a brief moment of hold music, then Laura said, "Sixth Precinct, Slade."

"It's Rebecca. How are you?"

"I'm fine."

"Can you tell me what happened?"

"Of course I can. My lips work as well as they ever did."

"And who's not cranky?"

Laura laughed. "I'll tell you about it, but you can't quote me. You need to talk to Stan Rampede at the 89th. It was on his turf."

Rebecca wrote down the name. Something about it rang a distant bell in her memory; had she written about him before? "I'd still like to hear about it. Off the record."

Laura related the events in typical cop fashion. Rebecca took efficient notes, already formulating the follow-up questions she'd ask this Rampede.

But the story Laura told was so strange, Rebecca finally had to interrupt. "Wait, so some guy there with his little boy shot both the robbers?"

"Yes. One head shot each."

"Was he on the job?"

"He didn't identify as an officer. And he skipped out as soon as our backs were turned."

"But he was a pro?"

"Some kind of pro. It's a miracle with all those bullets flying that nobody else was hit. And that a doctor was right there."

"Which doctor?"

"She runs a free clinic nearby."

Now Rebecca sat up straight. "Saraya Parashar?"

"Indian, maybe, or Middle Eastern?"

"Yeah."

"Must be her."

Rebecca's heart was pounding. "Was she hurt?"

"No. The perps shot the cook, but he'll be okay. The bad guys were the only ones who got their checks cancelled. Although we thought the doc's friend had taken a couple."

"Friend?"

"Yeah. Didn't get her name. Rampede might know."

Rebecca had encountered coincidence before, but this had to take some kind of prize. Saraya gets her an interview with the Lightning Girl, Angelyne223 shows her a drawing of Saraya's "friend" the Lightning Girl, and now Saraya and a "friend" are involved in a shootout. "Are you going to be at the station for a while?"

"Yeah. Lots of paperwork."

"Can I meet you there? I want to show you something that came to me from a whole other direction but might have some bearing on your case."

"It's not my case."

"Okay, whatever. I'd still like to show you."

"Sure, I guess. But anything I say is still off the record."

"Yeah, me, too."

When the call ended, Rebecca sat back and let out a long breath. *Don't get excited,* she warned herself. *You have no evidence of anything.*

She looked at the drawing. The lips and chin could be anyone's; there was no scar, or dimple, or anything distinctive about them. Hopefully the mug shot taken at Devon Moraine's arrest would make things clearer.

10:54 A.M.

Absolutely not," Dr. Erstatt told B.J. and Darren, his breath a cloud in the cold, dry air. "The process has already begun, and it cannot be slowed or delayed."

"We understand," B.J. said calmly. "But this is important, too."

Complex, computer-operated equipment filled the little room beneath the renovated church. The young man B.J. had visited during his all-male orgy lay sedated on a table, his nude body exposed to the chill air. Every bodily function was monitored, and three technicians in full environment suits watched to ensure no surprises. The dash lines for upcoming incisions already marked his skin.

Erstatt said, "You may have five minutes. No longer."

"Five minutes," B.J. confirmed. She led Darren to a corner of the room, where Stavros, also connected to the equipment, waited.

"Hey, boss," Darren said.

"Darren," Stavros acknowledged. "B.J."

"I wanted you to hear about Darren's meeting with Helen Pappas first-hand," B.J. said.

"I told you to handle everything," Stavros said. The tone was mild, but the scolding stung nonetheless.

"It was my idea to barge in," Darren said, and before Stavros could chide him as well, he gave a quick account of his encounter.

He was silent for a long moment, then asked softly, "Do you have a picture?"

B.J. pulled up the website photo from her phone.

"It's her," he said, his voice a sigh on an ancient breeze.

"She, ah...also gave me a message for you," Darren said. "*Τίποτα δεν διαρκεί για πάντα. Ούτε καν εμείς.*"

"'Nothing lasts forever,'" Stavros translated. "'Not even us.' I suppose the Festival affects her as much as it does me; I never considered that, because I thought she was still...where I left her." He let out a disappointed sigh. "I don't understand, though, how she's been this close for this long, and never crossed our radar. Wide Justice is a major player in the gaming world; we *should* know all about it."

"We do," B.J. said. "Just not that one little detail about who runs it. I would imagine she's gotten very good at hiding that in plain sight."

"Evidently. Well, we have one thing in our favor. To end the Festival requires things she's unlikely to have. Namely the blood of six virgins."

Darren looked up sharply. "Six virgins? Exactly six?"

"Yes, Darren. Why?"

"Would children count?"

"Oh, yes. They were often honored this way."

"Do they have to be willing?"

"No. Just virgins."

Darren's growing excitement made B.J. nervous. "Why?"

Darren said, "Because six kids from the Mendicant's gang are still missing."

They were silent for a moment as this sunk in.

"Excuse me a moment," Darren said, and stepped out of the room to make a call.

To B.J., Stavros said, "Have the police released Arthur's body?"

"Not yet," she said sadly.

"Perhaps at the Festival tonight, you can buttonhole the police commissioner and speed the process."

"I'll certainly try."

"The *ekphora* is supposed to take place three days after death." Stavros was silent for a moment. "Damn. Poor Arthur. Screwed over in this world *and* the next."

"Time is up," Dr. Erstatt said. "We must begin."

"See you soon," B.J. said to Stavros. She and Darren departed.

A t her desk in the squad room, Laura Slade looked at Angelyne223's drawing. "Yeah," she said with no hesitation. "That's the friend who was with the doctor last night. Cracked her head knocking Stan Rampede out of harm's way and got taken to the hospital. Where did you get this? It looks like one of ours."

"Unnamed sources," Rebecca said and waggled her eyebrows.

"So why did you want to know?"

"It connects up with something else I'm working on," Rebecca said evasively.

"If it involves a crime, you should tell us now," Laura said seriously.

"As soon as I'm certain, I will. But right now, it's only hearsay and rumor."

"Uh-huh," Laura said knowingly. "You can't fool me, Becky Hutch-craft. You just don't want to get scooped."

"Of course I don't want to get scooped. But I also haven't got all the ice cream together."

Cole, in the men's room when Rebecca arrived, joined them and peered over Laura's shoulder. "What have you brought us?" he asked as he looked at the drawing.

For an instant Rebecca thought she saw a mix of recognition and panic on his face. But it quickly vanished behind his normal cop neutrality. "Friend of a friend," Rebecca said.

"She was at the diner last night," Laura added. "We thought she was shot, but luckily, she hadn't been. Who is she again?"

"Her name's Devon Moraine, I think," Rebecca said.

"Yeah. I remember the doctor calling her, 'Devon.'"

"Huh." Cole went to his own desk and casually returned to work. Perhaps, Rebecca thought, a bit *too* casually. "So why are you showing it to us?"

"Can you see if she's in the system?" Rebecca asked.

"Sure. That's a great use of our time and resources, helping the press who won't include us on what they have," Laura said.

"You sure you're not cranky?" Rebecca shot back.

"Shut up," she said and typed in the name. The screen announced, *Not Found.* "Sorry."

"You sure you spelled it correctly?"

Laura gave the reporter a withering glare. "You were watching. Did I?"

"I just thought for sure she'd be in there."

"Why?"

"I heard she'd been arrested at an environmental protest once."

"Arrested, maybe, but not arraigned. Not under that name, at any rate."

"Slade!" Captain Evans bellowed from his office. "Get in here!"

"He finally heard about last night," Laura said as she stood. She went into the office, and the door closed behind her.

"Is she in trouble?" Rebecca asked Cole.

"Nah. The captain just likes to look like a hardass. He's probably congratulating her on not getting shot and not making it our case."

"Can I ask you something, Cole?"

"Sure. But it's off the record, right?"

"Christ, *yes.* Have I ever quoted you without telling you ahead of time?"

"Just making sure."

"I might have been imagining things, but it seemed like you recognized the woman in this sketch."

"Me? Nah."

"Are you sure?"

"I'm sure."

"Okay," she said dubiously. "Guess I was seeing things. Thanks." She turned to go.

"Hey, aren't you going to leave the sketch?"

"Ha! No way."

Once Rebecca left, Cole could think over what he'd seen. He recognized the woman in the sketch, of course; he'd studied that chin and mouth as closely as he'd ever looked at anything. There was still a hair of doubt—he'd have preferred a photograph—but if the drawing was accurate, that was her. The Lightning Girl.

Devon Moraine. Now, she had a name. A few simple keystrokes and he could search all sorts of records for her, find out who she was and where she came from. But wouldn't that be a betrayal? They'd agreed to exchange information on crime in Ratway, and to keep each other's secrets. Would an honorable man violate that trust, for nothing more than his own curiosity?

Another man stood as Laura entered Captain Evans' office. He was thin and harried-looking, and his eyes had dark circles.

"Detective Slade," Evans said, "this is Captain Tom Asiago, my counterpart from the 89th."

"Hello," she said, and they shook hands.

"Sit down," Evans told her. "Captain Asiago was just telling me his detective's version of what happened last night."

"Is it different from mine?"

"Well...you tell it, Tom."

"Detective Rampede said that the doctor from the free clinic, Dr. Parashar, I believe, kept him from apprehending the two robbers. Her and her friend knocked him to the ground. It was only the intercession of an armed patron that stopped the suspects from killing him, you, and everyone else."

Laura kept her expression neutral. "That's not exactly how I remember it. Have you read my report?"

"Yes," Asiago said. "That's one reason I wanted to have this meeting."

"Shouldn't Detective Rampede be here as well?"

Asiago looked a question at Evans, who nodded. Asiago said, "The 89th is a very different beast from the 6th. It's harder to keep good people. New officers who start there can't wait to transfer out, and the experienced ones usually have...questionable histories."

Laura's eyes narrowed. "What are you getting at here?"

"Last year, Detective Rampede was part of an...incident at the Free Clinic run by Dr. Parashar. His ex-wife sought an abortion there, without telling him. Being the suspicious type, he followed her and tried to force his way in. Luckily some beat cops caught up with him before he managed to do it. He put one of them in the hospital." Asiago paused. "He'd been drinking."

"The beat cop?" Laura asked archly.

"No, Detective Rampede. Oh—that was a joke."

"Not a good one. I apologize."

"Your report," Evans interjected, "states that the doctor's friend in fact saved Rampede's life, knocking him out of the line of fire, and that Dr. Parashar rendered aid to the injured."

"That's what happened," Laura said firmly.

"Then Detective Rampede is lying," Asiago said.

"Now, wait," Laura said. It was second nature to defend a fellow officer. "Maybe that's what he *thought* happened. I mean, it happened very fast and he *was* knocked to the floor. I had a view of the whole scene, he didn't."

"I appreciate your loyalty," Evans said. "And this isn't an investigation. Captain Asiago and I wanted to ask if you thought this was more than bad timing; if you thought the gunmen could've been targeting Rampede."

"No," she said with absolute certainty. "If that was the case, they'd have shot him first thing. They didn't react until after he did. This was a robbery that got out of hand."

"Speaking of reacting," Asiago said, "you said that one of the perps fired at Rampede from less that fifteen feet, and Dr. Parashar's friend pushed him aside. Is that right?"

"Yes."

"Then can you explain where that bullet went? Because the CSU couldn't find it. It didn't hit the wall, the ceiling, or anyone else. It just vanished."

Laura blinked. "That can't be right. There was no trace of it?"

"None. Do you have any idea what happened to it?"

"I honestly don't know. It should be there."

Asiago and Evans exchanged another look.

Evans said, "Detective, this next bit of information doesn't leave this office. I mean it. And that includes Detective Slaughter. Am I clear?"

"Perfectly, sir."

Again, Evans nodded for Asiago to continue.

"There were, however, traces of the same metal as the cartridges, on the floor beneath the spot where Detective Rampede went down. Except those traces were of metal that had melted and then cooled."

Laura stared blankly. "I'm sorry, I have no idea what you just told me."

"What he told you," Evans said, "is that the bullet melted in mid-air before it hit anyone."

"That's not possible," Laura said skeptically.

Asiago and Evans exchanged another look Laura couldn't interpret.

"Thank you, Detective," Evans said. "That'll be all."

Laura stood, as did Asiago and, belatedly, Evans. She shook hands with the visiting captain and returned to her desk. *Melted?* she thought. *How could a bullet melt in mid-air? Where did the heat come from?*

When she reached her desk, Cole was gone. That irked her; she just assumed he would stick around to find out what happened.

He'd left her no message, so she tried calling him, but it went to voice mail. She said, "Where are you? I just got out of that meeting. Call me back."

She had an email from her friend at Stilstand College about the strange scroll they found in Arthur Shawcross's office. She opened it, read it through, then re-read it.

"What the *fuck?*" she whispered to herself.

In the Starbucks across from the Kefali Building, Darren looked up as Emmett and Emma Cross, twin freelance operatives who were the absolute best in discreet following, appeared beside him. It was a tribute to their skill that, despite being on the lookout for them, he hadn't seen them approach.

"Thanks for coming on such short notice." Darren stood and held Emma's chair, while Emmett seated himself. They were as identical as opposite-gender twins could be, and he suspected that their cultivated androgynous appearance meant either could stand in for the other in an emergency.

"Always glad to hear from you," Emma said.

"You said this was urgent," Emmett added.

"It is. Do you know where Wide Justice Games keeps its offices?"

Emmett took out his phone. "Easy enough to find."

"What about it?" Emma asked.

"The woman who owns it is named Helen Pappas. It's extremely important that I know where she goes after she leaves work today. She's holding some children hostage, and I need to know where."

"Does she know she's being watched?" asked Emma.

"She isn't, at least not yet. But I'm pretty sure she knows someone will pick her up eventually and act accordingly."

Emmett and Emma exchanged one of those looks only twins can

manage, where lots of information gets passed but no one else can tell precisely how. "Is this on behalf of Mr. Kefali?" Emmett asked.

"It is."

"Because we wouldn't want to cross him," Emma added.

"I assure you this has his total approval."

"All right," Emmett said. "We'll call you when we have something. Same number?"

"Yes. Thank you. I know this is short notice."

"You said that already," Emma said.

They stood. And again, even though Darren was watching, he'd lost track of them before they were halfway across the room. They were like chameleons or octopi, changing to blend into any background.

Good afternoon," Anna Slaughter said cheerfully. "Welcome to Bloomerangs. May I help you?"

"I'm B.J. Burr," the other woman said as she removed her sunglasses. She was dressed in the kind of simple, elegant style that whispered money rather than shouting it. It intimidated Anna despite her best efforts to stay calm, to remember that *I'm just as good as she is.*

The woman continued, "I've got an order for an event at the old church tonight, and I wanted to check on it."

"Oh, yes, of course. Everything's on schedule, we just need to know which entrance to use for the delivery. I was going to call you about that in a few minutes."

"Then I'm glad I stopped by," the woman said and smiled. Anna could imagine it being described as "lighting up a room," in a way she knew her own never would. It depressed her anew. The woman continued, "There's a service entrance on the north side of the building. Your van or truck can back in and carry them straight into the main hall. We'll have some people there to show them the way."

Anna wrote that down. "I'll pass it on. 4:30 still the right time?"

"Yes. How many people will you be sending?"

"How many?"

"How many delivery men. Security is going to be very tight, and they'll want to know who to expect."

"For an order this size, we usually send three."

"Do you have their names?"

"I'm sorry, it sort of depends on who's available."

"When you know, please text them to this number," she said and put down a business card. "Thank you. Now may I see one of the arrangements, just to verify that it's correct?"

Anna's own professional smile faltered a little; was this woman implying they'd mess up her very specific instructions? It might have been a small shop, but everyone here was a pro and took pride in their work. If they could satisfy bridezillas and their mothers, they could certainly handle this order. "Of course. Follow me."

In the back, a dozen identical centerpieces waited to be loaded for delivery. Two florists worked quickly and efficiently to finish the rest.

"Beautiful," B.J. said. "And I love what you've done with the snowdrop blossoms."

"Our pleasure." B.J. had provided the plants, a specific variant that bloomed in summer instead of the more common winter flowering. "It's not often our customers supply their own flowers."

"I knew they'd be hard to find." She paused, then said, "Well, these are terrific. Thank you. This is a big night, and I'm so stressed out, I'm glad I have one less thing to worry about."

Anna beamed at the compliment. "Glad we could help."

Anna watched her get into her big car, the door held for her by her driver. When she was younger, Anna imagined a life like that for herself, but then gradually downscaled until she was satisfied as a wife and mother.

But now she was only a wife. *Merely* a wife. Defined by all the things she wasn't, such as a mother. The big car blurred as it pulled into traffic, and she watched through her tears.

Mr. Kefali? It's Dr. Erstatt. Can you hear me?"

"Yes," Stavros answered. His voice, though, was ragged and gravelly, as if his vocal cords only partly worked. The special medical room below the Festival site was even cooler now, and the air was as arid as a desert. Soft, regular beeps and clicks announced the steady life functions of the body on the table.

"Don't attempt to move," Erstatt said. "Just concentrate on breathing." He watched the chest rise and fall in a steady, unhurried rhythm. "Any discomfort?"

"No," Stavros said.

Erstatt gestured to one of his assistants, who dialed back the oxygen and let the room's cool air flow into the mask. "How about now?"

"No," Stavros repeated, his voice stronger.

"Wonderful. Now, I want you to raise your right index finger."

On the table, Stavros's finger obeyed the command.

"Can you make a fist?"

He could and did.

"I'm cold," Stavros said but not with discomfort. If anything, he sounded pleased.

"That's just what we wanted to hear. Do you feel strong enough to sit up?"

"Yes."

The two attendants unstrapped Stavros' legs and helped him swing them off the side of the bed. Erstatt quickly tapped both knees to verify the reflexes. He then put a stethoscope to Stavros's chest.

"I feel great," Stavros said.

"You sound great," Erstatt confirmed. "Bring Mr. Kefali's clothes." One of the assistants scurried to obey. "Remember what we discussed. Take it slow, stay alert for any problems, and don't hesitate to alert me at the slightest concern. We've come a long way since the last Festival."

"And unbelievably far since the first," Stavros said. "How long will it last this time?"

Erstatt sighed. "There are so many variables. But you should be able to make it through the Festival with no issues."

Stavros smiled. "That's all that matters. Will you join me in a drink, doctor?"

Erstatt poured wine from a waiting Greek *oenochoe* into two glasses, then handed one to Stavros. He watched closely as Kefali's right hand rose and took the glass in firm fingers.

Stavros raised it in a toast. "To the Festival."

"To the Festival," Erstatt echoed, and they touched glasses.

Stavros recalled all the other Festivals, with all their variations of the procedure he'd just been through. Magic, mechanics, and alchemy had all been tried in the past, but it took the advent of medicine and microtechnology to truly achieve what he sought and needed: a genuine recreation of that first Festival.

Erstatt stepped aside as the assistant returned with Stavros's clothes. With slow, methodical moves, Kefali pulled on the loose shirt and drawstring pants. He ran a hand through his hair and let out a satisfied sigh.

3:16 P.M.

As he rode up alone in the brownstone elevator, Darren's cell phone rang. He recognized the number. "Well?" he answered.

"We found her," Emmett said, his phone clearly on speaker. "She left her office half an hour ago."

"Great. Where did she go?"

"We lost her," Emma said.

"You lost her?" Darren repeated in disbelief.

"We're not proud of it, but there it is. We saw her leave, we followed her car, but when she got to the building, a man got out. And yes, we verified it wasn't her in disguise. We're not beginners. But we have no fucking clue how she did it."

"Any sign of the kids?"

"No," Emma said.

"We won't charge you for this," Emmett added.

"And please give our apologies to Mr. Kefali," Emma concluded.

When he entered his apartment, Sparrow waited on the couch with the TV remote in his hand, flipping through streaming movies. "Hey!" the boy said brightly.

"Hey, yourself." And to Darren's surprise, Sparrow jumped up and hugged him.

The boy looked so young now that he was clean and dressed in a new t-shirt and jeans. They sat on the couch, and Darren asked, "You get some rest?"

"Yeah. This place is huge. Are you rich?"

"I'm well-subsidized."

"I don't know what that means."

"Mr. Kefali owns this building and lets me live here for free."

"Wow. *He* must be rich."

"More than you can imagine."

"So where did you go?"

"I was seeing to some last-minute details. My boss is throwing a big party tonight."

"Can I come?"

"No, I'm afraid it's a grown-up party."

"Dang." Sparrow scrutinized him. "You look worried."

"I am, a little. You're a tough kid, right?"

"You bet," he said proudly.

"Then I'm going to be honest with you. I think your missing friends are in danger of being killed by an uninvited guest at my boss's party tonight. I want to stop it, but I'm not sure how. I have other things, duties I can't get away from tonight, you know?"

"What the fuck kind of party kills kids for fun?"

"One, that's a very good question, and I wish I could answer it. And two, try not to say 'fuck' so much."

"You do."

"Yes, but I'm an adult. Nobody thinks anything about it. But if a kid does it, everyone automatically thinks things about him."

"Like what?"

"Like, his parents aren't very good at their job. Or he's so wild they can't control him."

"So?"

"So? Come on, I know the Mendicant taught you better than that. People shouldn't form opinions about you unless it's the opinions *you* want them to have. The rest of the time, you want them to look right past you."

"Okay," Sparrow said, chastened. Then he was back at full strength with, "But you can't let my friends just get killed!"

"I don't intend to. But I need someone I can trust to keep an eye out for them while I'm busy, and for the life of me I can't think of someone."

"Don't you trust anyone?"

"I'm afraid all the people I trust will be as busy I will."

Sparrow was silent for a moment. Then he said, "I might know someone."

5:07 P.M.

As the sun set and lights twinkled on, Devon Moraine woke up in her apartment. She lay still for a moment, waiting to see if her head still hurt. There was a weak throb, but that was all. She wasn't nauseous or dizzy. *Yay, me,* she thought drily.

She snapped her fingers to turn on the lights, then sent a little spark at the coffee pot to turn it on. She lay back and stared at the water-stained ceiling while Spanish music came down from the apartment above; her wallmate's Italian prayers reached her through the plaster.

She'd overheard both neighbors discussing the Lightning Girl before, speculating on her origins and motives. None of them had any idea she was really the weird girl in apartment 712.

After last night, though, they might. She'd melted a bullet in mid-air, mere inches from her and the big cop, as a reflex. It was that, or get shot, and in the moment her self-preservation won out. But now there were clues, and someone smart might connect the dots.

And that someone smart might be Darren Flaxstone.

Holy shit, she thought, *he actually flirted with me—well, with the Lightning Girl.* And despite herself, she smiled at the memory.

Someone knocked on the door. "You decent?" Saraya called.

With a groan Devon got out of bed and went to the door. "I'm too tired to put on pants," she said. "Is anyone with you?"

"Who in God's name would I bring?"

Devon opened the door. Saraya entered, dropped her bag and hugged her friend. Then she took Devon's chin and examined her pupils. "Both the same size. Good."

"I am the poster girl for bilateral symmetry, you know," she deadpanned. "So did we make the news?"

"Just the crime blotter in the morning paper. Didn't even mention names, just that two men were shot at the diner during an attempted robbery."

"I think we finally found the one good thing about living in a high-crime zone. Want some coffee?"

"Sure. How's your head?"

"No one's ever complained."

"Har, har. Seriously."

"Sore where I hit the ground. Got anything stronger than aceta-minophen?"

"I'm not giving opioids to someone who shoots lightning from their fingers. Take 500 milligrams and quit bitching."

Devon handed Saraya a cup. "Just for that, I ought to make your hair frizz for the next 24 hours."

"Did you ice that bump like I told you?"

"Yes. I'm not an idiot."

Saraya reached over and tweaked her friend's nose.

Devon's cell phone rang. She pulled her static field in close, looked at the number, then sighed. "It's Robin. Fuck."

"Answer it."

"He'll just bitch about Mom."

"Yes. Answer it."

Devon flipped off her friend as she put the phone to her ear. "Hey, Robin."

"Hi," her younger brother said. He sounded tired. "I just wanted you to know that they moved Mom back into the secure wing."

"Why?"

"She punched an orderly in the balls. She said he was an agent sent to assassinate her. Anyway, she doesn't think I'm an imposter, so far at least. If you get a chance, could you drop by and see if she thinks *you* are? The doctors say it'll help map the progress of the Capgras."

"I'll see what I can do tomorrow."

"Thanks. I know you won't, but I appreciate you pretending."

Before she could snap back a reply, Robin ended the call. She scowled at the phone and said, "That boy."

"About your mom?" Saraya asked. "Is she getting worse?"

"Yeah. She beat up an orderly, so she's back in lockdown."

"You going to go see her?"

"No. I have too much to do here."

Saraya said nothing. Devon's mother was in a psychiatric institution about an hour north of the city. Her Capgras Syndrome caused her to suspect people close to her had been replaced by exact doubles with nefarious agendas. She'd been that way ever since that incident on the roof, and Devon often wondered how different she might've turned out if her mom had been diagnosed sooner.

Devon went to the window and looked out at the darkening city. "This time of day, Ratway seems almost as beautiful as the East Side."

"'Life is not measured by the number of breaths we take,'" Saraya said, "'but by the moments that take our breath away.'"

"Who said that?"

"Hell if I know. It was on a t-shirt."

Devon leaned her head on Saraya's shoulder. "Thanks for having my back last night."

"You've had mine often enough. We should talk about that whole thing with your fingers sparking while you were uncon—"

"Not now. Just...chill with me."

They watched the sky darken. The clouds were low tonight, so the city's glow reflected from them, casting a dim haze across it all.

With a sigh, Saraya said, "Time to go to work."

"Me, too," Devon agreed.

THE NIGHT OF
THE FESTIVAL

The Lightning Girl stood on the edge of the roof and looked out across Ratway. Her headache was down to a light roar, and the goose egg under her hair was small, if still really tender.

She'd started these rooftop vigils because it seemed like something a masked vigilante should do, and almost gave it up because, this far from street level, it was difficult to see any detail at night. But she discovered it served another purpose; it gave her a sense of the city as a whole. If she intended to dedicate herself to protecting Ratway, it helped to feel it was a single thing, like the tiny city inside a snow globe.

She watched lights come on in apartments and headlights make their way along the thoroughfares. She closed her eyes for a moment and listened to the city, *her* city, imagining it as a nocturnal beast coming to life.

Somewhere a child laughed, innocent delight in the midst of this cesspool. The thought of children brought up the survivors of the Mendicant's scattered brood. Where had they gone? Were they in danger?

She was no detective; she had no idea how to read clues or trick suspects into incriminating themselves. She'd have to ask around in her own crude way.

7:38 P.M.

Lobotomy Eyes looked at the children seated on the edges of the two beds. They were sluggish, glassy-eyed, still under the influence of the earlier sedative. Its effects would linger for a few hours more, rendering them pliable to suggestion. Which, she thought coldly, is exactly how children should be.

One by one they'd gone into the shower and washed off the last of the grime from their lives. The girls' hair was now brushed straight and shiny, and the boys' combed and neat. In their white robes, they resembled a midwestern choir gone awry during an ill-advised field trip to the big city.

Lobotomy Eyes checked the time, then stood by the door. "On your feet," she ordered, and they all obeyed. "Get in the van. No talking." She opened the door and watched as they filed into a nondescript Ford van parked just outside.

A normal woman would have at least some curiosity about what might happen to these kids. But not Lobotomy Eyes. In her case, once she was paid, she'd literally never think about them again.

Harrison Marley, Jr. studied himself in the mirror. His tuxedo was expensive, tailored, and still uncomfortable. He didn't mind dressing up, but only on his own terms; he hated monkey suits like this. As far as he was concerned, they made him look like the staff at a good restaurant.

Monte knocked on the door. "Boss?"

"Get your ass in here."

Monte also wore a tuxedo. His, though, was off the rack, and his bulky form strained the fabric at his shoulders and thighs. The bulge under his left arm where he carried his pistol was obvious.

"Ready?" Monte asked innocently.

"Ready to feel like an asshole?"

"It's what everyone wears, boss. It's the style."

"I paid forty grand for that custom-made navy blue suit from London. 'Bee Poke,' or some shit like that. Why the fuck isn't that good enough?"

Monte patted him on his shoulder. "You'll fit right in."

Harrison glanced down at the hand, which Monte quickly removed. "I better, Monte, or it's *your* balls that'll go in the Cuisinart."

Saraya Parashar stood with her arms folded behind the safety glass and iron bars that protected the clinic's front window. Across the street sat an unmarked police car. She couldn't see the officer behind the wheel, but she knew who it was.

Detective Stan Rampede had never forgiven her for helping his ex-wife escape his domineering influence.

She wasn't afraid of him, at least not for her own sake; her combat and medical training gave her confidence she could disable him in a heartbeat. But she did fear that his presence would cause people who needed her help to stay away, and *that* pissed her off.

The receptionist, Tinley, knew from her body language that Saraya was mad. "Careful, doctor, you'll pop like an aneurysm if you keep fuming like that."

"I just wish he'd try to come in," she seethed.

"Uh-uh. If he did, and you stopped him, you'd get arrested. And since your skin ain't white, you'd probably make the other cops who responded 'fear for their lives.'"

Saraya knew what that meant even without Tinley's air quotes; if she attacked Rampede, even in self-defense, other cops would execute her and use that tried-and-true defense. Like all non-White people in Ratway, she understood that cowardice excused anything, as long as the cowards wore blue.

Before Saraya could respond, all the lights dimmed for a moment. "Damn it," Tinsley muttered, rushing to hit save on her paperwork. "You'd think the city could get that shit fixed by now. They're probably ignoring it because it's us."

Saraya said, "I'll be in my office."

When she was out of Tinsley's sight, she opened the back door and went into the alley. The Lightning Girl was already there, and said, "Damn, you look angry enough to make NSYNC perform a New Kids on the Block song."

Saraya burst out laughing.

"I saw your friend across the road," the Lightning Girl continued. "We saved his ass last night; what's he doing here?"

"We also embarrassed him," Saraya pointed out. "You know how macho cops can be; they've probably been teasing him all day about how some girl had to come to his rescue. He's just out there looking for any excuse to show me how tough he is."

"Want me to heat him up?"

"No, let him think he's accomplishing something. At least when he's there, he's not out hurting anyone else."

"I need to ask you something. After the Mendicant got killed, I know Social Services rounded up about half of his gang. Any idea what happened to the rest of them?"

"No. I haven't seen any of them."

"Heard anything?"

"No."

"Me, neither. That worries me."

"I'll ask anyone around and see what I can find out."

"Okay."

"Both of you bitches, *freeze*."

Detective Stan Rampede emerged from the dark, his weapon drawn and held ready. He was breathing heavily, either from excitement or being out of shape. But his smile was entirely clear and vicious.

"Oh, for fuck's sake," Saraya sighed.

"I knew it," he said, practically hyperventilating with glee. "I *knew* you two were in this together, and that if I stuck with it, I'd catch you. I'm going to enjoy the hell out of this. Both of you, up against the wall. Now."

The Lightning Girl stepped in front of Saraya. "This is a really bad idea. Do you remember what happened to the last cops who fucked with me?"

"Shut up! Do as I say."

The Lightning Girl looked straight into his eyes. With no emotion, she said, "You do realize you're one of the bad guys, don't you? You don't represent safety or rescue or the law. The only authority you have is *bully* authority. Without that gun in your hand and that badge to cower behind, you're just another wife beater."

Rampede's expression darkened.

He intended to shoot; the message had already left his brain on its way to his trigger finger. But before he could, a bolt of electricity arced from the Lightning Girl to his gun, and it became too hot to hold. He yelped and dropped it.

"You could've cut that a little closer," Saraya muttered.

Sirens wailed in the distance, growing nearer. Rampede held his burned hand in front of him and practically shrieked, "You hear that? You'll never get away with this."

"Go," Saraya said softly. "I'll handle it from here."

There was a brilliant, blinding flash, and when it faded the Lightning Girl was gone.

Rampede glared at Saraya. "You're going to jail," he seethed.

"That may be," she said wearily, "but before then, I'm going to get my bag and tend to that hand, because unlike you, the oaths I took mean something to me. Even when every bone in my body wants to see your ass suffer." And she went inside, leaving Rampede to simmer, literally and figuratively.

From a nearby rooftop, the Lightning Girl saw police cars converge on the clinic. Things had escalated so damn quickly. If she intended to get Saraya out of this mess, and preserve her own secret identity, she needed assistance.

And she *hated* asking for help.

9:55 P.M.

From the usual rooftop, Cole watched the darkness for the Lightning Girl's approach. Sometimes he could spot her: a strange glow somewhere, a stray burst of light, the sound of something sizzling and the smell of ozone. But other times, she just appeared, as if she'd thrown off an invisibility cloak. He understood that she could control electricity, but he wondered if that sort of camouflage was also possible.

"It's like you read my goddamn mind," she said behind him.

His heart almost jumped up his throat. "Jesus, Sparky, I asked you not to do that!"

"And I asked you not to call me 'Sparky.' Looks like neither one of us gets what we want."

"All right, all right. Point taken." He ran a hand through his hair and blew out a deep, calming breath. "Look, I'm here to warn you: you've got trouble."

"More than you know. I need your help."

He blinked in surprise. "You already know that?"

"Don't sitcom me, Slaughter. I can tell we're talking at cross purposes. Here's *my* problem: my friend Saraya Parashar just got arrested by a crooked cop down at her free clinic. I need to get her out of their custody before she has one of those 'accidents' you cops are so fond of."

"I'm sure she's fine. This might be more urgent. That reporter who interviewed you? She has a picture of you, and she knows your real name."

The Lightning Girl displayed no reaction. "That's unlikely."

"Is it, Devon Moraine?"

She chuckled. "She thinks *that's* my name?"

"Is it?"

"I don't have time to talk about that. My friend is in trouble."

"What was she arrested for?"

"Knowing me."

"Do you know who arrested her?"

"Some big asshole named Rampede."

"Shit."

"You know him?"

"Yeah. He's formidable."

"So am I. I need you to go get her."

"And do *what* with her?"

"I don't know, take her to an East Side precinct where she'll be safe until she can make bail."

"It's not that easy. I don't outrank him."

She clenched her teeth. "Fine. I'll get her out myself. A lot of cops might suffer, but they're Ratway cops, so it won't bother me."

"You realize that's what they want, right?"

"Then I'd hate to disappoint them."

"They don't want to arrest you, Devon. They want to *kill* you."

"Sheesh, go back to calling me 'Sparky.' And they're welcome to try."

"'Sparky?'" a new voice asked, amused. "I know that's what *I'll* be calling you from now on."

Both Cole and the Lightning Girl turned in surprise. Cole's hand went automatically to the gun on his hip. "Who's there?"

Darren and Sparrow emerged from the shadows. Darren kept his hands in plain view, while Sparrow crossed his arms and tried to look tough.

"Does nobody in Ratway make any damn noise?" Cole muttered.

"Hey, Sparrow," the Lightning Girl said. Her smile was so genuine, to Cole it was like another whole face had appeared beneath the hood. "Look at you, all cleaned up."

Sparrow's tough act broke. "Hey, LG," he said happily and held out one finger to her. His hair stood out from his head when they touched, and he giggled.

"Darren Flaxstone," he said to Cole, extending his hand.

"Cole Slaughter." They shook. "I've heard of you. You're fairly legendary."

"Surely no more than notorious."

"What do you want?" the Lightning Girl said to Darren.

"My friends, the ones who didn't get killed with the Mendicant?" Sparrow said. "They're in danger. They're going to be killed tonight."

"By who?"

Sparrow looked up at Darren, who said, "Someone with a very long-standing grudge against my boss."

"Kefali," the Lightning Girl said, spitting the name. "And you expect me to help you?"

"No, I expect you to help Sparrow."

"Please," Sparrow said urgently.

"Who's planning this massacre?"

"Helen Pappas. She's going to kill them during a social event my boss is holding in Bay View."

"If you know who, why, and where, what do you need me for?"

"Because I'm going to be otherwise engaged."

She laughed coldly. "You've got a date that's more important than saving a bunch of kids from being murdered?"

"Maybe I can help," Cole interjected.

Both Darren and the Lightning Girl looked at him. "No offense," Darren said at last, "but this is far out of your league."

"I'm an East Side detective with twelve years' experience," Cole said defensively.

"And yet you didn't recognize the name 'Helen Pappas.'"

"Should I?"

"She's the woman behind the murder of Arthur Shawcross, which I think is your case?"

Cole hoped the darkness hid his angry red flush. "So you say. You're not exactly a reliable source."

"Please, you guys!" Sparrow implored. "Can you measure your dicks some other time?"

That shut them up, until the Lightning Girl said quietly, "I'd win."

They all burst out laughing.

With the tension broken, the Lightning Girl said, "So what exactly do you think I can do?"

"Be there when she shows up," Darren said. "Save the kids."

"In Bay View? Bay View isn't my problem. I'm only concerned with Ratway."

"These are Ratway kids."

Cole said, "Do you have any evidence against this Helen woman? Something to help me get a warrant?"

"I appreciate the offer, but you'd never find her in time," Darren said.

"I'm not an amateur."

While the men spoke, Sparrow took the Lightning Girl's hand and looked up at her with pure hero-worship. "Please, LG?"

"You know I only work in Ratway."

"But if you don't help them, who will?"

She scowled, sighed, and said, "Aw, fuck it. I'll help *you*. What time does this party start?"

Darren looked at his watch. "Midnight. Two hours."

"Then I want your help first. Help me get my friend out of jail here, and I'll save your ass in Bay View."

"An ass exchange, then?" Darren said with a smile.

"An ass for an ass," the Lightning Girl deadpanned.

"You're a saucy minx, aren't you?"

"And charming."

Cole rolled his eyes. "I should arrest you both before someone gets hurt. You can't just break someone out of jail anymore. This isn't the wild west."

"I'm afraid Officer Friendly is right," Darren said. "It's going to be a busy couple of hours. We need to hurry, and we need a plan."

10:14 P.M.

It wasn't much of a plan, and to be honest, none of them expected the first part to work. But it was all they had time to formulate.

A short time later, the Lightning Girl crouched on a rooftop across from the 89th Precinct. The police station was a squat, formidable structure, built to withstand full-out urban warfare. Yellow light shone through the glass doors and illuminated the steps down to the street.

That reporter knows my fucking name, she thought. *And she has my* picture? *How the flying fuckwads did* that *happen?*

She shook her head. No time for that, not while Saraya was still in trouble. She shut down her static field and switched on her phone; the plan would be underway, and she wanted to be sure and get any messages.

But waiting sucked, and she couldn't keep her mind from wandering. She'd promised Darren Flaxstone to go to Bay View to help rescue those kids. But she'd also promised herself, when she first took this on, that she would not become some city-wide righter of wrongs. Bay View, and the East Side, and Bowland, all had their own resources and infrastructure. Only Rattaway, isolated and abandoned, filled with people helpless to resist the unfairness, needed her kind of protection. And then only until the city lived up to its obligations.

So being the Lightning Girl wasn't a career. It was a temp job.

When she first started, she'd planned to be a myth, a rumor, like Bigfoot or Bloody Mary. She'd appear, do her work, then vanish. Word would spread, and hopefully people would be encouraged by her example to stand up against the city's evils. She'd realized almost at once that her initial plan was ridiculously naive. You couldn't go around shooting electricity at people without drawing attention.

Six kids from Ratway. She couldn't abandon them, even in Bay View.

But she also couldn't abandon Saraya, who was somewhere inside that ugly symbol of fascism below.

10:16 P.M.

Saraya Parashar sat in the interrogation room, a rancid cup of coffee before her. A thin Hispanic woman, Detective Carena Calderone, sat opposite and said, "I understand you resisted arrest."

Saraya took the bloody paper towel away from her lip. "If I'd resisted arrest, someone besides me would be bleeding."

Carena ignored the comment. "Let's go through this one more time."

"I didn't think cops really ever said that."

"We do when we don't get the answers we like in the first place."

"Look, you know damn well I didn't hurt Detective Rampede. I treated his injuries, but I didn't inflict them. Do I really have to stay here until Rampede gets back from St. Bibiana's?"

"You have to stay here until someone tells me otherwise. Look, I know what a jerk Stan Rampede is, believe me. I saw his wife's black eyes."

"I treated them."

"My point is, no one would blame you if you taught him a lesson. So, if you're the Lightning Girl, just tell me the truth about it."

Saraya laughed. "Honey, again, if I'd taught him a lesson, he wouldn't need another."

"Did you teach Morlette and Hogan a lesson, too?"

"No. But I'm sure they needed one."

"So, you're sticking to your story about the Lightning Girl being the one who injured Rampede, but not being you?"

"I'm sticking to the truth. Did you know Morlette and Hogan?"

"Just in passing, not personally."

"But you knew *about* them. Before everything happened, I mean. Just like you knew about Rampede."

"What's that got to do with anything?"

"If you knew about them, and Rampede, and did nothing, what does that make you, Detective Calderone?"

Carena's expression darkened. "I understand why that mouth of yours gets you in trouble, Dr. Parashar."

Someone knocked on the door then opened it. "Excuse me," Cole said. "I'm Detective Slaughter, from the Sixth."

"Good for you," Carena said.

"I'm working a murder case on the East Side, and I have reason to believe Dr. Parashar has crucial information we need. I'd like to take her back to the Sixth for further questioning."

This was so far out of the norm that it took Carena a moment to respond. "Wait, what?"

"You can have her back when we're done."

Carena stood. "Can we talk privately, Detective?"

"Sure."

She pulled him roughly into the hall, and when the door closed Carena held nothing back. "What the *fuck?* This woman's being held for assaulting an officer. Maybe three officers."

"All of whom are alive. I'm investigating an actual death."

People stopped to watch the confrontation. Working in Ratway came with a regulation-issue chip on your shoulder, so they all automatically resented the guy from the East Side, even before they knew what the argument was about.

Carena, so angry she almost spat the words, said, "You go talk to my captain, and if he says you can have her, you're welcome to her." She poked him in the chest. "Until then, you stay the fuck out of my interrogation." Before Cole could respond, she went back into the room and slammed the door.

"I wouldn't fuck with her," someone called. "She's so tough she can order a Big Mac at Burger King and get one."

Cole scowled in frustration, took out his phone and texted, NO GO. Then he left.

A moment later, the lights in the interrogation room dimmed and the air conditioner shut off. In the sudden silence, Carena and Saraya heard weary complaints of "Come on!" and "Not again!" After a moment, the lights returned to full power and the air conditioner kicked back on with a *thump*.

Saraya said, "I think we have more company."

The door opened, and a harried senior detective poked his head in. "Calderone? The captain says to get this woman outside."

"Outside?"

"Yes, *outside*. In the street. Now!"

"Stand up," she told Saraya, and cuffed her hands behind her back. Then she grabbed a handful of the doctor's hair, pushed her toward the door and snarled, "Let's go."

All the late-shift cops stood at the ground-floor windows. Carena shoved Saraya toward the main door, which two uniformed officers held open for her.

Outside, the Lightning Girl stood in the middle of the street. Four uniformed cops surrounded her, guns drawn, while a dozen others stood further back. Snipers positioned themselves in windows and on the station roof as fast as they could. Police cars screeched to a halt, blocking off both ends of the block.

She did not seem concerned.

When she saw Saraya, she called out, "What happened to your mouth, Doc?"

"Somebody didn't like the words it was making," Saraya answered.

"Did you bust her lip?" the Lightning Girl asked Carena.

"No," Carena answered. "But I'll bust yours if you like."

"It's your lucky night, then. The Doc did nothing. I heated up that detective's gun, after he threatened me with it."

"Then you're under arrest as well, for assaulting an officer. And for assaulting officers Morlette and Hogan."

"Do you know about how Detective Rampede used to beat his wife? Or about how those two other cops fucked up innocent people for kicks?"

"That's for a judge and jury to sort out," Carena said.

"In Ratway?" she said with a laugh.

"You're not above the law," Carena insisted. "And you're surrounded. So just stand down and surrender, and no one else gets hurt." Carena shook Saraya hard by the hair. "Including your friend."

"Don't do it!" Saraya said through clenched teeth.

The Lightning Girl grinned. "Not a chance."

Carena looked back at the harried-looking precinct captain. He took a deep breath and said loudly, "I'm afraid for my life!"

Immediately every officer drew their weapon and pointed them at the Lightning Girl. The sound of all those weapons being locked and loaded filled the air.

The Lightning Girl gave no warning, made no grand gesture, like raising her hands or sweeping her arms around. A great explosion of electricity burst from her in all directions, hair-thin bolts that struck every raised weapon. For an instant, the street looked like one of those plasma ball toys. Cries of pain, followed by the sounds of metal striking pavement, filled the night.

Protecting their stinging hands, the officers backed away. They hadn't been burned, but the jolt left them all numb.

"Your move," the Lightning Girl said.

Through teeth gritted so hard they seemed about to shatter, the harried-looking precinct captain said, "All right, Calderone. Uncuff the doctor and let her go."

"Are you serious?" Carena exclaimed.

"We all just heard a confession from this other...suspect," he snarled. "Now *do it!*"

Carena roughly unlocked the cuffs. Saraya rubbed her wrists and stepped out of reach.

The Lightning Girl pointed. "Hey, you. With the fancy haircut."

Cole, who'd lurked outside the station just for this reason, said with faux surprise, "Me?"

"Yeah, you. Take the Doc back to her clinic."

"But I'm not—"

"I didn't ask your fucking life history, pal."

"All right, all right. Calm down." He walked into the street. "After you, doctor."

They passed the other officers, none of whom knew exactly what to do, especially with their gun hands still numb.

When they were safely out of sight around the corner, the Lightning Girl announced, "Dr. Parashar and her clinic are off-limits to you starting now. And the rest of you fascist sons of bitches, and—" She looked straight at Carena. "—just plain bitches, you better take this to heart. Be honest and do your jobs, you've got nothing to fear from me. But act like Rampede, Morlette, and Hogan, and there's nowhere you can hide."

An immense blast of white light burst from the Lightning Girl, blinding them all, and when it faded, she was gone.

10:46 P.M.

Once Cole and Saraya rounded the corner and were out of sight, Darren picked them up in a stolen Pontiac and drove them the rest of the way to the alley behind the clinic. When they arrived, the Lightning Girl already waited for them.

"Thanks," Saraya said to Cole and Darren.

"My pleasure," Darren said. To the Lightning Girl, he added, "And I hope we can meet on better terms next time."

"Only if you stop working for Kefali," she said.

"I see electricity can be a harsh mistress."

The corners of her mouth turned up very slightly. "You can't start a fire without a spark."

Saraya rolled her eyes. "Dear god, they're talking in epigrams."

"Now that the doctor's safe," Darren said, "it's time to focus on saving the Mendicant's kids. Will I see you there?"

The Lightning Girl didn't answer for a long moment. "Yes. I'll do what I can."

"Good. Now, if you'll excuse me, I have to get ready for the Festival."

"I have to go, too," Cole said. "I do need to talk to you as soon as possible about the...thing I mentioned."

"No point," the Lightning Girl said. "Has nothing to do with me."

"Are you sure?"

"Absolutely certain."

When the men were gone, the Lightning Girl followed Saraya into the clinic. "Thank you," the doctor said as she looked for something to disinfect her lip. "Although when I told you to leave and let me deal with Rampede, I was trying to *avoid* a scene."

The Lightning Girl pushed back her hood. "You're really bad at that. And I'm really bad at taking hints."

"That's an understatement."

11:01 P.M.

Cole called Laura when he got off the train in Bay View. The sidewalks were still crowded with upscale bar-hoppers. "Hey."

"Hey, yourself. Where have you been? I got out of my meeting with Evans and you were gone, and you didn't answer your phone."

"I'll explain later. Right now, I need a favor."

"Sure," she said without hesitation.

"Don't get mad."

"Nothing good ever starts that way, does it?"

He gave her the quick version.

"Why the hell didn't you ever tell me you knew the Lightning Girl?" she practically bellowed.

He held the phone away from his ear. "It was part of the agreement. She told no one about me, I told no one about her."

"Oh, that makes it all better."

"You can be pissed off at me later."

"Want me to alert the Bay View cops?"

"No. *No.* I think we've stirred up enough other precincts for one night. This is just us."

"Because we're doing a favor for Stavros Kefali?" she said drily.

"No, because we're trying to save a bunch of kids."

"From this woman who runs a software company, who plans to kill a bunch of runaways to get back at Kefali."

"Yes. I know how it sounds."

"I'm not sure you do."

"Will you be there?"

"Of course I'll be there, dickhead. I'm still your partner."

"Thanks. I appreciate it."

"And I have something for you. Remember that scroll we found in the Dodger's office? It's...weird."

"Weird how?"

"I'll forward you the translation. See what kind of sense it makes to you."

She ended the call. Cole let out a sigh and headed for home.

11:20 P.M.

D arren checked the time. He was dangerously close to missing the Festival's opening, and there was no excuse for that. Still, he had one last task to complete before heading to Bay View.

"He's asleep in your guest room," Mrs. Miniver said. A professional babysitter from a top-flight agency, she had the air of a benevolent but iron-willed New England grandmother. "It's almost midnight; Are you sure you wish to wake him?"

He couldn't tell her the truth—that it might be his last chance to talk to Sparrow, if things at the Festival went badly—so he said, "I just want him to know I'm thinking about him."

He opened the bedroom door and quietly knelt at Sparrow's bedside. The boy slept with his mouth open, snoring lightly. He looked even younger now, and Darren felt a twinge of emotion deeper than he expected. The kid had left things to the two adults he trusted most, Darren and the Lightning Girl. He now slept the sleep of the just.

He touched Sparrow's cheek. "Hey. Sparrow. Wake up."

The boy yawned, stretched, and opened his eyes. "Hey, Darren."

"I just wanted to tell you good night."

Sparrow grabbed him around the neck and hugged him tight. "You'll save my friends?"

"You know it." Before he even thought about it, Darren kissed him on the cheek. Then Sparrow let go, rolled over and was asleep at once.

350

In the hall outside, Darren said softly, "I probably won't be back until dawn. If you need anything, the building manager will get it for you."

"Of course, Mr. Flaxstone. He's a sweet little boy. But if I might observe, you look as if you could use some rest yourself."

"Mrs. Miniver, tired isn't even a feeling for me anymore. It's a lifestyle choice."

Darren quickly put on his tux. As he left his apartment, he was genuinely surprised by how much his heart ached at Sparrow's absence. Was this how Artie had felt about him? Was this what a father felt for a son?

A Kefali car waited at the curb for him. The driver said, "Glad you made it, Mr. Flaxstone. We're going to have to book it to get you there on time."

"Then start booking, Elias."

H i, Laura," Anna said. "Cole said you'd be coming by."

Laura gave Anna a perfunctory hug and air kiss. "Yes, he's got something up his holster tonight." She paused for a deep breath. "It always smells so good in here."

"A perk of being a florist."

Cole came into the living room as Anna closed the door. He wore all black, including a Kevlar vest. He tossed an identical vest to Laura.

"I hate it when you wear those," Anna said with a little shudder.

"You'd hate it more if we didn't," Cole replied.

"Can I get you anything? Coffee, tea, water…?"

"No, hon. We'll be leaving soon."

Anna stepped close to her husband and looked imploringly into his eyes. "Be careful."

"I will. *We* will. Right?"

"I'll watch his ass like it was my own," Laura assured Anna.

Anna left them alone as they finished checking their gear. They each wore three guns: their normal duty weapon, smaller revolvers in ankle holsters, and a third unregistered semiautomatic tucked into their waistbands at the small of their backs. That last weapon served two purposes: an emergency weapon in case the other two failed, and something that could be used to justify a shooting if things went south.

"Did you read that email?" Laura asked. "The translation of that scroll?"

"No," he admitted.

"Well, do it. I think it might be important for tonight."

"Why?"

She slapped his arm. "Read it, smart-ass, and you'll see."

"Ow. All right, all right." He took out his phone. His frown deepened as he read. "Wait...what is this?"

"It's the standard story of Orpheus and Eurydice. Until the end."

"Oh, good, the standard story."

She gave him a disappointed scowl. "You have no idea, do you? Didn't you go to college?"

"My memory's a little foggy."

"Should you even be allowed to carry a gun? Okay, in ancient Greece, Orpheus was the son of Apollo, and he fell in love with Eurydice. She died, and he went down to the underworld to find her. He sang a love song about her for Hades, who was so moved that he let her leave with him and return to life, but only on the condition that Orpheus not look back at her until they reached the surface world again."

"But he did?"

"He did, so she returned to the underworld for good."

"And that's the standard story?"

"So far, yes. But that scroll had additional text that, according to my expert, has never been seen before. It said that Orpheus was subsequently torn to pieces by female followers of Dionysus, Apollo's opposite number in the Greek gods, who apparently were drunken, horny lunatics."

"So, he died and went to the underworld and got to be with his wife anyway, then."

"You'd think so, but no. Even though he was torn apart, he didn't die. Son of Apollo, remember? Half-god, like Hercules. His head remained alive, and conscious, and aware. He *couldn't* die."

"How in the name of holy fuck does this have anything to do with the Dodger?"

"I don't know. Maybe he was into history? But there's one last thing. Do you know what the word 'kefali' means in Greek?"

"No."

"It means, 'head.'"

They looked at each other. Finally, Cole said, "No way. That's just a fairy tale."

"Maybe."

"We saw him on that Zoom call."

"Which we both thought looked fake."

"Yeah, the background, not the guy." He paused. "Look, I'm not convinced, but suddenly we live in a city where a girl who shoots electricity is a real thing. Maybe there's always been stuff like this going on, and we just never saw it for what it really was."

They fell into an awkward, stunned silence, the kind that envelops people whose ideas of reality were being twisted and expanded. At last, Cole said, "So: are you ready?"

"As much as I'm likely to be," Laura said.

11:40 P.M.

Devon Moraine sat on the train, staring out at the city night, her own reflection superimposed over it by the glass. She wore the nondescript hoodie, cap, jeans, and boots that made up her disguise, and had a small container of black greasepaint in her pocket to apply before the action started. Except for two tired-looking middle-aged women and a trio of teenagers all on their phones, the car was empty, and that was fine. She was, unbelievably, *nervous*.

Devon had been to Bay View plenty of times. But the Lightning Girl never had.

Devon kept going back to Cole's warning. He now knew her real name, and if that was true, she had to assume he had her photo as well. She couldn't imagine how, though; there were no pictures of Devon Moraine online anymore, and no one could get a clear picture of the Lightning Girl unless, by some miracle, they used a non-electronic camera that shot with physical film.

So what the *fuck,* universe?

She also hated leaving Saraya alone for the rest of the night, but her friend would have it no other way. "Kids," she said. "They're asking you to help rescue kids. If you can't help children in trouble, you have no business claiming to be a superhero."

"I never claimed to be a superhero," the Lightning Girl protested. "Why do people keep calling me that?"

"Hm. You hide your face, you protect the weak, you only come out at night, and oh yeah, you have a *fucking superpower*." Saraya put a hand on her shoulder. "Now go save the kids, okay? I'll be fine."

She got off at the station closest to the church Darren had described. The renovated building was lit up like a cruise ship, and luxury cars lined up to deposit their guests at the entrance. A phalanx of tuxedoed guards, with discreet earpieces visible thanks to their crewcuts, watched over everything.

A shiny black Lincoln stopped, the driver opened the back passenger door, and a man got out. She couldn't quite tell at this distance, but she was pretty sure it was Darren Flaxstone. In a tuxedo.

Not a bad-looking guy, she thought before she could catch herself. *But after tonight, he goes back to being the enemy. Don't forget that, stupid.*

She saw no sign of Slaughter and his partner. *He knows your name*, she thought again, then pushed it aside. That whole problem was for future Devon. Tonight, it was all about saving a bunch of kids who'd done nothing except be poor. A bunch of Ratway kids, just like her.

What the hell is this Festival all about, anyway? she wondered.

There was only one way to find out.

THE FESTIVAL

I am scared to death," B.J. said as she checked herself for the millionth time in the mirror.

Her reflection did not reply. And since the newly remodeled dressing room was empty except for her, no one else commented, either.

She knew that, objectively, she looked great. If she was a stunner on an average day at the office, she was breathtaking now. The Grecian-style gown left one shoulder and her sides bare, and its shimmery electric-blue color brought out her eyes. Her dark hair was held back in a bejeweled diadem, and diamonds glittered at her throat.

And yet the gown would likely be torn and soaked in blood before the night ended, and she'd be lucky to escape without serious injury. And that was if everything went according to plan.

If it didn't, she had no idea what she'd look like by morning.

Above her, on the floor of the old church, the guests had begun to arrive, mingling into uncertain groups. The invitations had all been RSVP'd positively, so there would ultimately be around five hundred of the city's most powerful people gathered here, the one percent of the one percent. But while their money and influence may have marked them, they would not be asked to part with a cent of it tonight. The Festival had an entirely other purpose, and their participation was vital to the event's ultimate goal.

"All right," she told her reflection. "Bravery means being scared but going ahead anyway. And you're tough enough to squeeze orange juice out of a lemon. So, let's do this thing." She turned away from the mirror and left for the party.

The growing crowd inside the old church consisted of the rich and powerful from all the city's districts. The men wore tuxes, and the women were clad in their best and most expensive gowns, many of them designed and bought just for this occasion. The oddest part was that, were they to speak honestly, most of them would have no idea what this was all about; they simply came because they knew everyone else at their socioeconomic level was attending. The peer pressure of the powerful rivaled that of middle school.

There was also the cachet of rubbing shoulders with a known criminal. Legal lines blurred at the height of society.

Soft light now filled the former church and turned the marble the color of a demure girl's blush. Great swoops of fabric crossed the open space above the attendees, making a lattice between them and the cavernous ceiling. The flower arrangements Anna Slaughter's shop had worked on so hard were placed on small console tables against the walls and filled the air with their subtle scent. Servers in toga-inspired gowns drifted through, discreetly offering refreshments.

Mayor Bulac, with the pale skin and dark hair of his Eastern European ancestors, sipped his champagne as he scanned the room. The weight of the large ring on his finger, which had been scanned by burly security guards before his entrance, bothered him. He was also bothered that his assistant, the delectable Ms. Koenig, was not with him tonight. Instead Constance, his demure society wife, stood respectably by his side. She was from a proper Pigeon Hill family, had dutifully borne him two children, and had been raised at functions like this. But he sensed her nervousness and finally leaned down to say, "What's wrong now?"

"I'm anxious," she answered softly. "I don't know why. There's something in the air tonight."

"Did you take a Valium?"

"What? No."

"Maybe you should."

"I'll be fine," she said icily.

"Good. I don't want a scene."

He turned away after that to shake hands with a theater impresario, so he missed the unfiltered hatred in his wife's glance, or the relish with which she tossed down the champagne and gestured for another.

Across the street from the Festival, Laura and Cole watched the church entrance from an empty third-floor office suite that smelled like musty carpet and old turpentine. The keys were provided by Darren Flaxstone, because apparently if you dug through enough shell companies, Stavros Kefali owned the building. They worked in the dark, Laura monitoring the church entrance through binoculars on a tripod, while Cole checked the streets for anything unusual.

"I see Harrison the Less arriving," Laura said.

"How does he look?"

"Like somebody put a tux on a motel bed. You can dress up some people, but you can't class them up."

"He alone?"

"Yes."

Cole risked a quick scan of the nearby rooftops for the Lightning Girl. *Devon,* he thought. Could she really have such a mundane, positively girly name? And if so, how had the Lightning Girl emerged from this Devon?

"It's almost midnight," Laura said. "Flaxstone said that's when things kick off."

The final car in the line deposited its occupant, and the guards closed and locked the gates. If Helen Pappas intended to bring the six children to the Festival, Cole thought, she'd have to get them in some other way. Maybe parachutes? He looked up at the pinkish night sky, the stars lost in light pollution, and wondered if that was even feasible.

"I haven't seen a sign of any gate crashers," Laura said. "What do we do now?"

"Keep watching," Cole said. "What else can we do? After going to all the trouble of taking those kids—"

"Which we don't know for certain she did."

"Granted, but if she did, she'll be here. She has to be."

Laura was silent for a moment, then said, "Hey. Something's happening."

On her way to the main floor, B.J. stopped in the security control room, where a half dozen of the Kefali organization's most trusted technicians studied monitors and listened to audio streams from within and without the refurbished church. This was security at its most subtle, discreetly following every conversation and interaction long enough to determine whether it posed a threat. If so, it would be handled in an equally discreet way, and with no more force than necessary. The mood mustn't be disturbed.

"Ms. Burr?" a technician said. "Mr. Flaxstone is here. He's waiting for you upstairs by the entrance."

"Thank you." She left the security office, took the stone steps up to the main level and entered the former sanctuary. She felt the eyes of every man, and more than a few women, on her as she drifted gracefully through the crowd.

A hand touched her arm, and she stopped. "Why, hello, Mr. Zamitis," she said to the city comptroller. As the man who controlled the purse strings, Zamitis was possibly a more important contact to cultivate than even the mayor. He was in his early sixties, comfortable with his receding hairline and slight middle-aged paunch, which gave him an attractiveness his more youth-obsessed contemporaries couldn't match. His ring glittered on his long, thin finger.

"Good evening, Ms. Burr." He took her right hand in his left and kissed it, careful to maintain eye contact and not be caught checking her out. "You look lovely this evening."

"And you're quite the charmer." B.J. nodded at his wife. "Mrs. Zamitis, I hope you're both enjoying yourselves."

"Oh, yes," Zamitis said before his wife could reply. "And you?"

"Oh, like they say, no rest for the management."

"I thought that was 'for the wicked.'"

"Who has time to be wicked, Mr. Zamitis?" she said with a wink.

"Will Mr. Kefali be putting in an appearance?"

"He will indeed. It'll be worth the wait, I promise." She nodded at the champagne in his hand. "Drink up; it's a party, after all."

"I always do what a beautiful woman asks," he said and tossed down the contents of the glass.

Darren waited for B.J. inside the main entrance. Despite the tuxedo, which as always made him appear quite dashing, he looked tired and grim. But his face brightened when he saw her.

"You're here," she said, relieved, as he kissed her cheek. "Thank God."

"You look spectacular."

"It's the eye makeup."

"What have I missed?"

"Nothing out of the ordinary so far. Where were you?"

"Sorting out some things."

"Did you find her?"

"I didn't need to. We know where she'll be. And I have people ready when she shows up."

"Security? I haven't heard about it."

"Er...not exactly. Friends. Trustworthy ones."

"You're being evasive."

"Yes."

"Why?"

"Because if I tell you who they are, you'll doubt me when I say they're trustworthy, so I'll have to give you explanations. And there's no time for that."

She frowned at him. "I think I'm insulted."

"I don't mean to be insulting, just efficient. I'll answer all your questions once the crisis is past."

"I'll hold you to that."

"How's Stavros?"

"Everything went fine. It's really something to see."

Darren smiled. "Did you see the pictures from the last Festival? With that weird steampunk collar-thing he had to wear?"

"I did. He said it only held out for twenty minutes. This procedure should be good for hours."

He leaned close and squeezed her hand. "And you? Are you worried about your part in things?"

"I'm nervous," she admitted. "But I know what I have to do. I just hope nothing goes wrong."

"Nothing will. I'm here, remember?"

She gave him a sly smile and teased, "You think so highly of yourself."

"Hey, the boogey man checks under his bed for me."

They kissed again, lightly due to her lipstick, and she merged into the crowd.

From the top of an eight-story bank building on the next block, the Lightning Girl looked down on the remodeled church. She'd brought some binoculars borrowed from Saraya, Steiner 210 military issue with no electronics, that gave her a clear view of the roof and two of the building's four sides, including the main entrance.

The Lightning Girl was actually nervous about this encounter, and that worried her. Confronting the whole 89th precinct hadn't frightened her at all, but this Pappas woman scared Stavros Kefali, so it would be foolish to be overconfident.

But those kids wouldn't be sacrificed if she had anything to say about it. She'd promised Sparrow, and what kind of superhero breaks her word to a kid?

After all the buildup about this Festival, Harrison Marley Jr. was seriously disappointed. He'd expected some kind of orgy, maybe, or at least an opium den of hazy debauchery. Instead, it was like every other goddam function he had to attend to maintain whatever veneer of respectability the Marleys had left. And that meant he hated every moment of it.

He'd been among the last to arrive, and at the door, a man larger than Monte, with the look of an ex-soldier, said in a heavy Russian accent, "Your ring, please."

Harrison held up his hand.

The man reached for it, and Harrison snatched it away. "Hey, *hey*. What the hell?"

"I must scan your ring for authenticity." The man held up a small device with an ultraviolet glow at one end.

"Yeah, just don't get touchy-feely about it." Harrison held out his hand, curled into a fist. The blue light played over the ring, and the device chimed.

"Welcome to the Festival, sir." the guard said and held the door for him.

Now Harrison sipped champagne and watched the crowd. He recognized Jack Dorestine, head of the Dorestine crime family, across the room. He was only a little younger than Marley senior but unlike him was tan, healthy, and upright. Dorestine made eye contact, raised his glass in a toast and smiled that smug smile. *One day, Dorestine*, Harrison thought, *I'll rip that smile off your face and shove it right up your ass.*

Then he spotted the councilman from his district and sidled over. "Good evening, Sam."

Samuel Lanegan, battling his forties with a hair replacement and Botox around his eyes, said, "Hello, Harrison. How's your father?"

"In and out, I'm afraid. Won't be long."

"I'm sorry to hear that."

Harrison leaned close to whisper. "Sam, what *is* this bullshit?"

"It's a chance to butter up to a major campaign donor," Lanegan whispered back.

"Yeah, where is our mysterious host, anyway?"

"I'm sure he'll turn up." He finished the champagne with a flourish. "In the meantime, I plan to take advantage of his hospitality." He sauntered off to speak with the CEO of one of the city's largest banks.

Harrison looked down at the champagne glass in his own hand. The hairs on the back of his neck tingled, the way they always did when trouble was in his immediate future. He felt the sudden need to remain cold sober.

In the security room, Pete Pawson, dressed formally for the Festival, tried to watch every monitor at once over the technicians' shoulders.

"Hey," Pete said wearily when Darren entered. "Saw you arrive."

"Yes. I assumed you were stressing, so I came to check on you."

"Aren't you?"

"I'm trying to maintain the appropriate level of concern."

"And how's that working out for you?"

"Not as well as I'd hoped. What's the status?"

"Perimeter's secure. Well, except for those two across the street." He indicated a screen that, on its green night-vision display, showed Laura Slade and Cole Slaughter in the dark third-floor windows. "They've been watching all night. Figure they're FBI writing down license plates, except they're in tactical gear."

"Don't worry about them," Darren said.

Pete looked at him in surprise. "You brought in your own people and didn't tell me?"

"I didn't 'bring' them, they just...I'll explain later. But seriously, don't waste resources on them. They're with me."

"Okay..." Pete said dubiously.

Darren patted him on the shoulder, feeling the taut muscles. "Damn, man. You're as tense as a toothless mongoose at a cobra convention."

Pete burst out laughing. "Yeah, I am. I feel like it's all on me."

"Trust me, none of it is on you. If *she* shows up, just tell me or B.J. Don't engage and try to stop her."

"What about the boss?"

"He'll have enough on his plate."

Stavros Kefali didn't make a grand entrance to his own Festival; he just sort of appeared, moving through the crowd with the ease of a man in total control. He wore a tuxedo suit but, instead of a shirt and bow tie, wore an ascot that draped down over his bare chest.

"Good to see you, sir," Stavros said as he shook Mayor Bulac's hand. "And Constance, you're looking lovely."

"Quite the shindig you've put on," Bulac said.

"There's more to come."

As Stavros left to continue gladhanding, Bulac said quietly, "That's the first time I've ever met him in person. I thought he'd be taller."

When Constance said nothing, he turned to her. She followed the other man's movements with her eyes the same way a tiger watched a small child at the zoo, and with the same hot glare in them. It wasn't sexual desire; it was more primitive, more destructive, more *furious.*

He noticed other women around him follow Stavros with the same gaze. He finished his champagne and motioned for the server to bring him a new glass.

Police commissioner Frederic "Fair Freddie" Fairbourne wore his dress uniform, as expected at a function like this. His wife, Honore, also dressed formally in a long cocktail dress. They were both in their fifties, both in very good shape for their age, and both dedicated to maintaining his position in both the department and city society.

Which is why Fair Freddie scowled when Honore tossed down the last of her champagne, looked up at him, bared her teeth and *growled.*

"Honore?" he asked.

Darren glanced at the clock on his phone. Five minutes until midnight, and the true start of the Festival. The same thing that had happened every century would occur again tonight, and the combined release of energy would fuel Stavros's existence for another hundred years. Darren had seen the silent film footage of the last Festival, so had an idea what to expect.

He kept pacing to the front entrance, peeking out, and returning to his spot beside the champagne table. Helen Pappas must not mean to open the show; was her plan to crash it during the main event, when the blood was already flying?

"Hey! Flaxstone!"

He almost jumped. Harrison pushed awkwardly through the crowd. Anxiety creased his sweaty face, which he tried to cover with bluster. "I'm getting bored here. What's the big deal? When does the floor show start?"

Darren gave him his host smile. "Are you having a good time?"

"No, I'm not having a good time, I just said that. If I wanted to drink and schmooze, I could do that at home in some fucking comfortable pants."

Darren spotted Stavros through the crowd, smiling as he greeted some functionary. Seeing his boss this way brought him up short, and he gawked.

"Hey," Harrison prompted and shoved him with a meaty finger. "I'm talking to you."

"I promise you won't be bored for much longer," Darren said absently and walked away. When he reached Stavros, he could only stare.

His boss laughed and said, "You remind me of the woman who shaved off her eyebrows but then redrew them too high."

Darren blinked. "What?"

"You look *very* surprised."

"Oh. It's just…"

"I know," Stavros said. "Things will be back to normal soon." He took out his phone and carefully pushed a button on it, like a man whose fingers had fallen asleep. "It's time to begin."

The recessed lighting dimmed, and the gas jets supplying the flames in the wall sconces grew brighter, bathing the room in a fluttering faux-oil-lamp glow. Stavros patted Darren on the back and walked off, just as Harrison called, "Hey! Kefali! I want a word with you."

Darren held his arm. "I wouldn't do that right now."

"Oh, you wouldn't, would you?" Harrison said as he yanked out of Darren's grip.

"I'm just saying. You know that boredom you were complaining about? It's about to be over. Did you bring your wife?"

"What? No. Why?"

"Just checking. Either way, you might want to move out of the middle of the room."

The white van stopped at the closed gate, secured by a chain and padlock. A guard came out of the church and approached the fence. A dark-haired woman in formal dress got out of the passenger side.

"Sorry, ma'am, the event's already begun."

"That doesn't matter," Helen Pappas said and held up her hand. Arthur Shawcross's ring glittered in the headlight beam.

The guard spoke into his radio. "We have a late guest. She has the invitation. What do I do?"

Before he got any reply, the driver's door opened and another woman's arm pointed a gun at him. She fired two shots, both to his head. He crumpled without a sound.

Lobotomy Eyes put away the gun and climbed out. Unlike Helen, she was dressed casually and carried heavy bolt cutters. She made short work of the chain holding the gate shut, returned to the driver's side, then used the van to push it open. She made no effort to avoid the body of the man she'd just shot.

She drove to the entrance. No one emerged to welcome them. She got out again and opened the van's side door. The six children, dressed in the white gowns, stepped outside. Each wore a thin black collar with a small, blinking green light. Their movements were still lethargic.

"You can go," Helen said to Lobotomy Eyes. "Your money's been deposited."

Lobotomy Eyes pulled out her phone and checked her account. "All right," she said and walked down the drive and away into the night without another word.

Helen shook her head. Maybe the woman really had been given a lobotomy.

And then the double doors opened.

At the sight of the muzzle flashes from Lobotomy Eyes' gun, Laura jumped up. "Somebody's shooting. We're on."

She and Cole quickly left the empty office. They crossed the street quietly, hugging the shadows in their all-black gear. A taxi passed within six feet of them and never noticed.

"Excuse me."

Stavros stood in the middle of the room, and everyone turned to watch.

"I'd like to thank everyone for attending tonight's Festival," he said, his voice carried by the renovation's careful acoustics. "I promise you, it's something you'll never forget."

Then he paused, head down, and began to sing Roy Orbison's "Crying." And in his mind, he was drawn back into his past, to the time when the rules of his existence were established.

In a time when the gods walked (and did other things) with mortals, a Greek poet and singer named Orpheus descended into the underworld to retrieve his wife, who had died of a snakebite. Confronted by Hades, Lord of the Underworld, Orpheus did the only thing he could: he sang of his love for Eurydice. Because he was the son of Apollo, who among other things was the god of poetry and music, his voice broke even the heart of the ruler of Hell, who released Eurydice.

But there was that famous catch: Eurydice could follow Orpheus back to the land of the living, but only if Orpheus did not look back until they emerged from the Underworld. It was a simple challenge, doubly so for the half-human son of a god.

As they climbed, though, Orpheus began to think. Was Eurydice really the woman he wanted to spend his life with? She could be shrill, and vindictive, and even though he'd braved the underworld for her, inevitably they would quarrel. Were those qualities worth the others, such as her sublime beauty, her carnal enthusiasm, her quick wit and soft, silken skin? Now that he once again had her, did he really actually want her?

He spoke of none of this. In fact, as they climbed the steep underground trail toward the light, they spoke little. He knew she was there from her breathing and the scrape of her slippers, but he said nothing. And evidently that went both ways. If they'd already run out of conversation, what would the rest of their lives be like?

Famously, Orpheus blew it. At the last moment, he glanced back, and Eurydice returned to the Underworld for good. He was left with nothing, save the memory of his own failure.

Not quite nothing, though. Orpheus still had his voice and roamed ancient Greece singing of his sorrow to all who would listen. And any who heard were moved to tears. Because laced through the sorrow was guilt.

Which was why Stavros Kefali, formerly known as Orpheus, faced a room filled with sobs after the first chorus.

He sang *a cappella,* and it touched every heart that heard it, even the tiny rock-hard one inside Harrison the Less. To his chagrin and astonishment, he realized he too was crying. A couple of listeners had even fallen to their knees, and one woman slowly tore at her hair in mourning.

Over the music, he heard a soft tinkle of breaking glass. Ransom Wade, editor of the city's lone remaining paper, let his champagne glass slip from his fingers to the floor. His face had an odd slackness, like a sleepwalker. Harrison looked around; many of the men now had similar blank, neutral expressions, down which tears silently ran.

According to those same Greek legends, Orpheus died at last. There were various versions, but the true one originated, as so many things did in those times, in a petty disagreement between gods. Apollo, father of Orpheus, got into a snit with Dionysus, god of wine and revelry. As a result, much like social media mobs today, Dionysus urged his wanton female acolytes, known as the Maenads, to find Orpheus and rip him to pieces. Which they did literally, using only their teeth and bare hands, and left him shredded on the banks of a river. Legends say that when they went to wash off the blood, the river disappeared into the earth, shrinking away from their guilt.

But for Orpheus, this wasn't the end.

Stavros had tears on his cheeks as well. He kept his eyes closed while he composed himself enough to continue. Then, when he was able, he raised his face upward and began another song: "I'm So Lonesome I Could Cry."

It wasn't just the song, it was the way Stavros's high, clear, androgynous voice conveyed and embodied the words. Not even Hank Williams himself reached such heights of loss and sadness.

The men all watched, glassy-eyed and silent. The women grew more emotional and shuffled toward him. But this was no Beatlemania-style response; the mania in their faces was dark, cruel, and animalistic. These, the wealthiest and most poised women in the city, abandoned their perfect posture and hunched forward, their hands clenching into fists.

A few may have suspected that there were drugs or chemicals involved, and they were right. The champagne was laced with two compounds: the men were rendered immobile by a secret substance that deadened their masculine will, while another extract affected the women, filling them with the Dionysian rage that had surged through the Maenads thousands of years before. This was the opposite of an aphrodisiac; it transformed lust into bloodlust.

Orpheus was half-god but still mortal and being ripped apart by frenzied women should've been the end of him. But exposure to the Underworld had given him immortality of a sort. His consciousness survived in his severed head, which was found by a simple-minded country boy, Arateus, who fell under his influence all too easily. And as time passed, so did Orpheus pass into a succession of guardians, all of whom both protected him and did his bidding. He used them to build organizations that controlled society behind the scenes, relocating as each powerful nation-state was overtaken by the next. At last, he arrived in America.

But before that, while still with his simpleton shepherd, he crossed paths with Chalcomede.

$\frac{1}{2}$

Darren, flanked by Pete Pawson and two of the big Russians, stood outside the main entrance. No one had drawn a weapon, but the air tingled with possible violence.

If she felt that tension, Helen Pappas gave no sign. "Hello again, Mr. Flaxstone. I haven't missed the show, have I?"

Darren said nothing.

Helen stepped up to him and presented the ring. "Then I demand my right of admittance."

"That's not your ring," Darren said.

"That's not your call. Whoever bears this ring is allowed inside. Your boss's rules, not mine." She turned and gestured at the children. "And these are my guests."

"This is not an all-ages show."

"I should tell you that those are proximity collars they're wearing. If they get more than ten feet away from me, those little bombs detonate. And once one goes, they all go."

After a moment of silence, Pete prompted Darren. "Boss?"

"Let them in," Darren said.

Pete nodded and gestured to the two Russians, who held the door open for the woman and her charges.

$\frac{1}{2}$

"*You*," Orpheus almost snarled.

Chalcomede, one of the Maenads who had participated in his dismemberment, appeared in the door of his protector's hut. She wore full Maenad regalia: the skin of a panther, a live snake gently confined by a metal headband, and a staff with ivy leaves twined around the top.

She took a swallow from the bottle of sacred wine she carried and did not beat around the bush. "You remember me, do you?"

"I remember all of you," Orpheus said from the open pot on the table where his head rested. He vividly recalled the triumphant snarling smile on Chalcomede's blood-smeared teeth. "What do you want?"

"I bring Orpheus a message from Dionysus."

Arateus stepped in front of her. "You are not welcome here."

The snake in her headband hissed, and Chalcomede said, "Fuck off, boy toy." Or the ancient Greek equivalent.

"How did you find me?" Orpheus asked.

Chalcomede took another drink. "I was sent by a god. He knows where you are."

"What's your message?"

"You have a century. Then death will claim you and you will return to the Underworld."

Orpheus sighed with relief. "Then I'll be with Eurydice at last."

Her smile that day was as chilling as it had been when she ripped him apart. "Oh, no. You don't get all your parts back and die happily ever after. You go into a deep dark hole just as you are now. You spend eternity in the dark, in the silence, with no companionship and no hope."

"My father would never allow—"

"Looks like he did." She took another drink. "But he *did* give you one way to put off the inevitable."

The women made a wide circle around Stavros, as he finished the Hank Williams song. He drew breath to begin Joy Division's "Atmosphere" when movement caught his eye, and he turned toward the entrance.

No people living at this time had ever seen Stavros Kefali look surprised, let alone aghast, before. But now he did.

"Eurydice," he whispered.

In a form of Greek not spoken since before the gods vanished from the earth, with a smile as cold as the night in Antarctica, she replied, "Orpheus. The last time we saw each other, you had that same look on your face. So, the greatest bard in Greece is now a common criminal overlord."

He warily approached her. "I believe, all things considered, I at least qualify as an *exceptional* criminal overlord." After a pause, in English, he said, "How are you here?"

"You had to expect me."

"Yes, but..." *I expected you, but I never really* believed *you would come,* he wanted to say. But the words wouldn't form.

"Moly flowers," she said, nodding at the arrangement of snowdrops. "And in summer, too. I'm impressed. And look at all the *métoikoi.*"

The Greek word for foreigners made him smile sadly. "In this city, there's not much else to choose from."

"I don't suppose it matters, does it?"

"No." He choked for a moment and repeated, *"How?"*

"I convinced Hades to let me go. Well, to be honest, I spent thousands of years aggravating him, until he practically begged me to go. I used your example."

"How so?"

"I sang of my idiot husband. Incessantly."

His eyebrows rose. "You have a terrible voice."

"I know. Eventually Hades could no longer stand it."

Despite everything, Stavros chuckled.

"I also had Persephone on my side. Get a man's wife to help you, and you can get him to do anything."

"When did this happen?"

"Long ago. Before this city was even a crossroads."

"And you never sought me out?"

"I never wanted to see you again." She paused. "Now ask me why I'm here."

"I know why," he said. "Revenge."

She barked a laugh. "Revenge? *Revenge?* I would've thought eons of existence would have given you a bit more insight. You abandoned me to an eternity in the Underworld, Orpheus. And you *never tried again.*"

A tear trickled from one eye. "That's true."

"So believe me when I tell you that I could care less what happens to you. I'm here to save *me.*"

The first Festival was an exceptionally informal affair, held in a clearing deep in the woods where Pan's satyrs watched from the trees. Orpheus had followed Dionysus's instructions as relayed by Chalcomede. Under the ministrations of Mary the Hebrew, his head had been roughly bound to the body of a willing young man decapitated moments earlier. Orpheus had only the merest flicker of connection with the body, not even enough to move or take a real breath.

You must re-enact the attack of the Maenads every hundred years, Chalcomede told him. *If you fail, that hole in the Underworld waits for you.*

Not many things scared Orpheus. Certainly not death. But an eternity of darkness, solitude, and silence? That terrified him. And as the centennial of his dismemberment approached, he felt its pull growing, his life-force weakening with each passing day.

On this first occasion, the Maenads, summoned by whatever powers controlled them, arrived and, as they had done a century before, tore his head from the new body and ripped the dead man's corpse to pieces. Orpheus's latest servant, a former soldier with one eye, waded in and retrieved his head.

"How do you feel?" Mary the Hebrew asked him later. She was ancient now, and should have been long dead, but had her own secrets for prolonging life.

"Fine," Orpheus said, awash with relief.

"Then my job is done. If I can't achieve immortality, then at least my work will show the way."

And so it continued, for millennia, until the present. And with the unlimited funds provided by the Kefali corporation, Dr. Erstatt was able to improve on Mary the Hebrew's alchemy and connect blood vessels and nerves, allowing Stavros a genuine, feeling body for the first time since his own was destroyed. Erstatt was honest with his patient, though; it would likely only last a few hours before rejection set in. But it was enough to once again avoid that hole in hell.

"The lives of these six virgins," Helen said with a gesture toward the children, "will buy the end of my life, and yours. I'll return to the Underworld but not as before. As one who will be twice-dead, I will have no memory of my existence. I shall have what I most desire."

"Oblivion," Stavros said.

B.J. joined them, standing to one side of Stavros. "Is this...her?" she asked, watching Helen.

"Yes," Stavros said, but in a voice none of them had ever heard before. It was choked with emotion, with the agony of thousands of years of love and loss. "This is Eurydice."

B.J. gave her a thorough once-over. "I see. And you're here to kill Stavros?"

"I've already told them why I'm here," Helen said. "You can read the minutes of the meeting later."

Darren tried to ignore the kids, because each one reminded him of Sparrow. Only sheer luck had kept that boy from Helen Pappas's clutches, and from ending up in this group of sacrifices. Was one of them Corvus, the big brother who'd shielded Sparrow from the Mendicant? That infuriated him, but he did his best to stay calm. "This can end well for every-one, you know, if you leave the kids here and go on your way."

"This *is* my way."

"And you don't mind killing six innocent children?"

Helen gave him a look that might've melted iron. "Do you know how many innocent children die every day? No one helps them. These are street kids, unwanted orphans, the kind that have always existed, and always will. They won't be missed."

"They will by some," Darren said, and in one smooth move, he drew his gun and shot Helen Pappas between the eyes.

It was muffled by the building, but Cole and Laura recognized the sound at once. They jumped up from their examination of the dead guard, drew their own weapons and ran for the front doors.

There were no windows to see inside. Cole grabbed the handle, but the doors were locked. A quick check confirmed that their guns would make no dent in the heavy security steel. They ran to find another entrance.

The impact knocked Helen backward, and she sprawled to the floor. Darren instantly grabbed the hands of as many of the drugged kids as he could, making sure they didn't scurry away out of range.

Helen lay on her back, eyes open, blood spreading from under her head. The hole above the bridge of her nose still smoked.

Around them, the aroused women snarled, while the men just observed in silence.

"Here," Cole said, indicating a side door half-hidden behind a bush. It was locked, but unlike the main entrance, it was wooden and had not been replaced with a steel door. He stepped aside and let Laura kick it open. They entered the stairwell, guns drawn.

"Which way?" Laura asked. "Up or down?"

"Up," a new voice said. "That'll take you to the main floor."

The Lightning Girl stood on the landing above them. For Cole, who'd only seen her in the half-light of nighttime rooftops, the full illumination made her suddenly look small, and slightly ridiculous. The black grease-paint on her upper face glistened in the fluorescent light, and he was struck by how slight she seemed.

Laura instantly leveled her gun at her. "Don't move."

"Didn't you explain things to her?" the Lightning Girl asked Cole.

"He told me some things," Laura said, "but there's still a lot more explaining to do."

"Maybe, but not right now."

"She's right," Cole said to Laura. "We need to find out who's shooting."

"No, we need to rescue those kids," the Lightning Girl said.

Laura held the other woman's gaze then slowly lowered her weapon. "We're not done," she cautioned.

"Yeah, I'll add you to my calendar."

The Lightning Girl moved aside as Cole and Laura ascended the stairs. They reached the door to the main floor, crouched and listened. They didn't want to walk into a firefight.

Cole turned to the Lightning Girl. "Are you coming?"

Instead of an answer, there was another of those blinding flashes, and when their eyesight returned, she was gone.

"How does she do that?" Laura asked.

"Beats me."

"You didn't ask?"

He shrugged.

Without looking at him, she said, "You're a married man, Cole. Don't forget that."

He hoped he didn't blush.

Pete and the two Russians surrounded the kids to keep them close to the body, but it was unnecessary, since none of them showed any inclination to move.

Darren examined the collar attached to the tallest boy. It was electronically locked in place; any release mechanism would be part of the trigger device that Helen must possess.

She didn't carry a purse, and her gown had no pockets. He ran his hands under it, along her skin, searching for something taped or strapped in place.

And then Helen said with a chuckle, "You can feel me up, but at least buy me dinner first."

Cole risked opening the door to the main room. From their position, they saw the back of the crowd of dazed men all watching the events at the front entrance. The warm air, and the scents of flowers and incense, wafted in through the opening.

He looked a question at Laura, who nodded. They stood and slipped unnoticed through the door and ran smack into Harrison Marley, Jr.

In the security control center, one of the technicians pointed to the monitor that showed Laura and Cole and asked, "Who's that?"

"Shit, it looks like the cops," one of the others said. "I'll call the boss." He pressed a button to connect to Pete Pawson.

He yelped as a blast of static roared into his own earpiece, and all the monitors shut off. Before either could react, the lights blinked out and the door locked down. They were trapped.

Helen sat up, laughing, and gingerly touched the back of her head. "I thought you'd be smarter than that," she said to Darren. "If it was that easy for me to die, I would've done it already. But I can't die unless he dies, and I can't break the spell keeping *him* alive without sacrificing six virgins. Did you really not follow that?"

She extended a hand to Darren, and after a moment's hesitation, he helped her upright. She shivered at the touch of blood trickling down between her shoulder blades.

"Eurydice," Stavros said and stepped close to her. "Please. It's not just about dying. I would love to die and be with you again, even in Hell. But that's not what will happen to me."

"You were taller once," she said, meeting his eyes, their mutual unblinking gazes not wavering. "And your chest was broader. But these legs are definitely an improvement." Blood seeped through his ascot and oozed down his chest. "How long do you have before this body dies out from under you?"

"Not long," he admitted.

B.J. and Darren also exchanged a look. They had to stop her, but how?

The Lightning Girl made her way down the stairs past the security office to the lowest level. She peeked around the corner and saw the lone guard standing before an unmarked door.

They don't even have a sign saying what's in there, she thought. *If Kefali keeps it that secret, I definitely want to know.*

But that would be for later. Now, she had children to rescue.

"Cops!" Harrison gasped as he took in their gear. "You're cops, right? Thank fuck!"

Cole and Laura looked at each other. They recognized him, of course, although neither had met him before. And they certainly never imagined he'd be pasty white and sweaty with fear and panic.

"Listen, there's some weird shit going on here," he continued. "That Flaxstone guy just shot a woman in the head, and she fucking got up laughing about it! And look at everyone; the men are all acting like they're high, and the women like they want to rip him to pieces."

"Rip who to pieces?" Laura asked.

"Kefali, who else? And there's a bunch of stoned Mormon kids, too." Then he pushed past them through the door into the stairwell.

Harrison was right about one thing. The women were ready to get down to business. Stavros, and the others, had momentarily forgotten all about them.

News anchor Astrid Tuttle led the attack.

Screeching with inhuman fury, she charged at Stavros and yanked him away from the group into the center of the mob. She straddled his chest and ripped at his clothes, and the skin beneath them. Her voice was a high, keening rasp.

The other women pulled at his arms and legs, yanking them taut, ripping at his clothes and their own. This was completely asexual, though; no one wanted to fuck him. They wanted to fuck him up.

And they did.

"Not yet!" Helen screamed and clawed at her gown, digging for the hidden pouch that held the detonator. B.J. jumped forward and grabbed her wrists, and the two women fought for a few crucial instants.

Then Helen wrenched free, clasped the small device close, and punched the red button as hard as she could.

Nothing happened.

She looked up, her wide unblinking eyes confused and distraught. Punching it again and again she cried, "Come on! *Come on!*"

One of the nouveau Maenads screeched in delight, and B.J. remembered her job, her *one* job, in this chaos. She dove into the crowd of women, shoving and punching her way to the center where Stavros was being shredded.

Cole and Laura couldn't tell what was happening with the suddenly crazed women, but Laura noticed one crucial thing. "The kids all have bombs on their necks."

Then they watched Helen screaming at the detonator, hitting the button over and over.

"That must be the detonator," Cole said.

"Then why isn't it working?"

"Shoddy manufacturing," the Lightning Girl said from right behind them, making them both jump. Then came another of those blinding flashes.

Helen shrieked and dropped the detonator. They were all momentarily blinded by the Lightning Girl's arrival in their midst.

"Your detonator's dead," she told Helen. "And so is your plan to hurt these children." At that, the collars all blinked off, opened, and fell to the ground.

In spite of her thousands of years of existence and her experience with the immortal lords of ancient belief, Helen stared at the Lightning Girl just like everyone else did. "My god, you're *real*."

"Real as labor pains." When she saw the same look on Pete and the Russians, she added, "For fuck's sake, people, I was in the paper." To the kids she asked, "Are you guys all right?"

None of them responded.

"Are they high?" the Lightning Girl demanded.

"They're pacified. Not harmed. I don't want them to suffer."

"You did want them to die, though." She held up a hand, electricity sizzling between her fingers. "There's not much lower than a person who'd hurt a child."

"I wouldn't waste your time," Darren said. "I shot her in the head, and as you can see..." He nodded at the still-visible hole.

"That's a drop of rain," the Lightning Girl said. "I'm bringing the storm."

Bolts of electricity shot from her hand and struck Helen. This close, both the light and heat were unbearable. They all jumped back, and Darren pushed the children away.

Helen made no sound. She did not cry out or scream. But the smell of ozone and burning flesh filled the air.

It took less than fifteen seconds. When the lightning vanished, the clap of thunder was so loud it even made the Maenads pause in their fury.

But only for a moment. All of them were covered in blood, their expensive gowns in tatters, their jewelry scattered among the pieces of meat and viscera beneath their bare feet. Their husbands and significant others continued to watch.

All that was left of Helen Pappas, Eurydice of Greek legend, was a singe mark on the granite floor.

"You *killed* her," Laura gasped.

"She fucked with Ratway kids," the Lightning Girl said. She turned to Laura. "Don't try to arrest me, please. It'd just embarrass us both."

Laura looked at Cole, who shrugged.

The Lightning Girl nodded at the Maenads, reduced to low growling and lethargic, satiated squirming. "Do they have any idea what they're doing?" she asked Darren.

"Not really."

"So with Kefali gone, do you take over?"

It took Darren a moment to understand what she meant. To her, it appeared as if Stavros must be dead, even more so as one white-haired, blood-smeared matron of society raised a severed arm overhead. With a banshee cry of triumph, she waved it above her, then began to lick the blood from the fingers. "Not everything is what it looks like," he said at last.

A sudden commotion riled the group of women. B.J., blood-soaked and almost naked, writhed free with something wrapped in her arms. One woman, a tall Black model with enormous eyes, glared at her and cried out in a deep, unintelligible roar. B.J. roared back, her voice thinner but bolstered by the fact that she was cold sober. Before anyone could get a good look at what she carried, or any of the Maenads wrest it from her, she ran for a side door.

"What the fuck was *that*?" Cole asked.

"Did...did she just run off with his *head*?" Laura added.

In the stairwell, Harrison waited for the shakes to stop, grateful that he hadn't pissed his pants. He had to get out of here, get home, find out what the fuck had just happened.

A door opened above, and a blood-soaked woman carrying what appeared to be a *fucking human head* bounded down the steps toward him. He flattened himself against the wall, and she passed him with barely a glance.

He recognized her. And more importantly, he recognized the head she carried.

And then he pissed his pants.

In the small guarded room beneath the church, set up like his monitoring chamber back at the Kefali building, B.J. gently cleaned the blood from Stavros's face. When she'd found it in that tangle of Maenads, she'd been amazed at how light it was, and there was a moment when she feared those limpid eyes would never open again.

Until they did. And she sighed with relief.

"That was intense," she said as she daubed around his mouth. "They were still shredding the body when I left."

"They will for a while," Stavros said.

"What's it like when it's over and they realize what they've done?"

He smiled as she daubed his lips. "That's when it stops being about my eternal life and starts being about what I have to hold over their heads for the next thirty years. The security videos will guarantee my influence for quite a while."

"Is this what you did a hundred years ago?"

"Yes. It proved very useful then, as it will now. Only back then, I had to make do with blurry photographs and silent film. This digital era is a golden age of blackmail." He closed his eyes so she could wipe them. "Eurydice is dead."

"I couldn't see what happened. How do you know?"

"I feel it. I can't explain it, but I know."

"I'm sorry."

"Don't be. It's what she wanted."

She bit her lip before speaking. "Can I ask you something?"

"Did I ever think of making love to you while I could?"

She stopped in mid-wipe. "Yes."

He smiled. "No. You're my daughter."

"I would've let you."

"And I appreciate that."

"What about...her? She was your wife once, after all. There seemed to be a moment there..."

He chuckled. "There's not a mythology in the world where *that* would happen."

The screens around him came to life, one after the other, as he connected to the neural network that let him operate them. But all were blank, displaying *no signal* messages.

"Something's wrong," B.J. said.

"Go," Stavros said. "I'm fine."

The Lightning Girl turned to Darren and said, "I'm done here." She vanished with another flash.

After their vision returned, Cole and Laura faced Darren, Pete, and the two Russians. Behind them, the Maenads were down to growls and purrs; some of them were curled up asleep on the bloody floor, like contented and well-fed felines.

"What happens now?" Laura asked.

"Ideally," Darren said, "you two take these six kids in hand and make sure they get somewhere safe."

"And the two murders we both witnessed? And them?" She nodded at the bloody women.

"Murders?" Darren said. "No one's died here. I promise, tomorrow Stavros Kefali will be back in his office like any other day. And as for Helen Pappas…" He nodded at the burn mark. "You'll have a hard time finding any remains to make a murder charge stick, I suspect."

"We can't pretend it didn't happen," Cole said, mostly for Laura's benefit.

"Then arrest me. And B.J. And then explain why you were here in the first place."

He had them there. Laura threw up her hands in resignation.

They guided the kids outside, where Laura called for transportation. To Cole she said, "What just happened in there?"

He nodded at the children, who were coming out of their daze. "We saved them from certain death."

"And that'll look great on a report, but what about the woman shot in the head who got up as if nothing happened? And then got vaporized? And what about—"

"I say we get these kids squared away with social services, then go back to my house, have a drink, and hash out our story. Because if we put any of that other stuff in our report, we'll be pulling desk duty for a year."

Laura just looked at him.

"You said you trusted me," he reminded her.

"Yeah, I did." After a pause, she asked, "What happened to your other friend?"

"Sparky?"

"'Sparky?' You call her Sparky? To her face?"

"Yes, but she hates it. I don't know where she went, but if I had to bet, I assume it's got something to do with keeping Ratway safe."

B.J. reached the security office. The door was still locked, and the guards inside pounded on it helplessly. "I'll get help," she called out then went to find Pete.

Once he was alone again, Stavros let himself cry. There was no other way to get the impossibly deep feelings out. He certainly couldn't put them into words, or even a song. What song had ever been written that embodied this much sorrow, this much guilt, this much grief? Whose heart had ever been broken as his had?

Then he was dazzled by a sudden, bright flash.

"I've heard a lot about you," an unfamiliar voice said, "although one big detail got left out."

If Stavros could've jumped in surprise, he would have. "Hello," he said, trying to regain control of his emotions and blink the momentary blindness from his eyes.

The Lightning Girl stepped inside the circle of blank screens. "How the fuck do you even speak, anyway? You don't have lungs pushing air through your vocal cords, you—"

"The short version is magic," he said. "The details don't really matter, do they? Like it doesn't matter how you control electricity."

"So you know who I am?"

"Your reputation precedes you. Do you have a name?"

"My name is one of those things that doesn't matter. What does matter is what your organization does in Rattaway. Drugs, prostitutes, gambling, protection. It all stops now. Rattaway is under my protection and off limits."

"I think you have an unrealistic expectation of your people. My organization has never forced a father to gamble away his family's rent money, or a teenager to shoot heroin, or a young woman to undress for money. You're applying a moral standard to things that don't have one. People have vices, and if I don't supply them, someone else will, or they'll look elsewhere for them."

"Nice rationalizing. You do realize I could just vaporize you where you...well, 'stand' doesn't work, does it? I could vaporize you...where you're displayed. Just like I did upstairs."

"So you killed her."

"She threatened to kill some Rattaway children."

"I didn't ask why. But I am curious why you don't kill me."

"That'd leave a vacuum, and that means a war. And they won't fight that war here in Bay View or over in Pigeon Hill. They'll fight it in Rattaway. That's why I'm giving you this warning. If you take it, then you and I don't ever need to meet again, and your little secret is safe with me."

"This may sound like we're in some TV potboiler, but I'm serious when I say it: come work for me. Let me pay you well for doing what you already do." He paused, then added with a wry smile, "Besides, we're family."

"Come again?"

"I'm the son of Apollo, you're clearly the daughter of Zeus. If we continue to be on opposite sides, it'll be a war like no other."

"I'm the daughter of *who*?"

Stavros's smile slowly grew wide. "You don't know who you are, do you? You don't know how you got your abilities."

"And I don't care. What's important is what I do with them."

"You can't deny your heritage. Join me. Let's make it a family business."

"But then I'd have to do it how and why you say."

"Yes, that would be the agreement."

She shook her head. "Sorry. What I do isn't for money."

"Why, then?"

"I do it because no one else will." And with that, she vanished in a flash of light and a strong whiff of ozone.

THE DAY AFTER
THE FESTIVAL

5:02 A.M.

The Lightning Girl stood on a Ratway rooftop as the sky in the east changed from deep black to the faintest gray of impending dawn.

She was tired; the travel, the confrontations, and the sheer stress of the night had worn her down more than any physical conflict. Was it a sign that she wasn't cut out for this?

Who the fuck is? she asked herself.

But Kefali's words rang in her head. *We're family. You're the daughter of Zeus.* Was there even the slightest chance that could be true? Did the ancient Greek gods actually exist?

Seven years ago, on an otherwise clear day, she and her mother had ascended to the roof of their building. Her mother claimed to have something important to tell her and wanted privacy. But before she could reveal her secret, both of them had been struck by lightning.

It had felt like being hit by a car. The top of her head burned, and her body collapsed. She never lost consciousness, but she could not control her movements as her muscles spasmed repeatedly. She had no idea how long she and her mother had sprawled unseen, before Devon recovered enough to crawl down and summon help.

The doctors found that neither woman appeared to suffer any lasting ill effects. But almost at once her mother's Capgras syndrome manifested its first symptoms, and Devon's new abilities began to appear. So she never found out what her mother had wanted to tell her.

Had that literal bolt out of the blue been sent by Zeus? Was that even possible?

Somewhere below, a woman screamed, "Ow! Let me go Goddammit, stop!"

The Lightning Girl sighed. One more job for the night, apparently.

She ran to the opposite side of the roof and looked down at the street. A thick-bodied bald man methodically slapped a young woman around outside a parked towncar. Pimp/hooker, boyfriend/girlfriend, pusher/user? It didn't really matter. In another flash of light, she was on the empty street behind him. He froze in mid-blow.

"Come on, tough guy," she said. "Turn around and try that shit on me."

He did turn, but instead of the fear she expected, he had a huge malevolent grin. "I figured this would get you here."

"About damn time, too," the girl said, all fear gone, wiping the blood from her lip. "Now pay me my fifty."

"In a minute," the man said.

The Lightning Girl was instantly on full alert. "I'm warning you, pal. If you think I'm in the mood for tricks tonight, you're really not reading the room."

"When word gets around that I took you down," he said, "I'll be the top dog around here."

"Well, since you're already a son of a bitch, it'll be a short trip."

He pulled out a knife. "Come on, then."

She sighed and sent a short, low-energy burst of electricity at his hand.

He didn't react. At the very least, he should've dropped the weapon.

His grin grew so wide, it threatened to split his face. "Insulation's a wonderful thing," he gloated.

How tired was she that she missed his rubber-soled boots? "Okay, you got me," she said wearily.

"Oh, yeah," he snarled and charged at her.

She sent a huge surge of electricity not at him, but at the asphalt just ahead of him. It melted into a scalding hot sludge that, when he stepped in it, not only snagged his boots, but burned through them straight to his skin. He howled one of those high-pitched cries of agony and fell over, his feet stuck in the quickly cooling blacktop. His head hit the pavement with a solid <u>thunk</u>, and he lay still.

The Lightning Girl turned to his accomplice, but she was already fleeing the scene. "Keep the fifty!" she called over her shoulder.

"Wow," said a little girl pressed against the bars of a ground-floor apartment window.

"Shouldn't you be asleep?" the Lightning Girl asked.

"Who can sleep through that?" she said, indicating the now-whimpering man who struggled to unlace his melted boots. "Are you really the Flashlight Girl?"

She laughed despite her weariness. "It's *Lightning* Girl, sweetheart."

"Who are you talking to?" a male voice called from inside. "Get back to bed, it's five o'clock in the morning."

"That's my dad," the little girl whispered. "He's very good at telling time."

"Then you should do what he says."

She sensed movement behind her and spun around, preparing to strike. Instead, she faced a dozen on the street's residents, many of them awakened by the punk's screaming, all of them looking at her in a mix of fear and wonder.

Then they began to clap. Someone whistled, not lecherously, but with approval.

The Lightning Girl smiled in surprise. *This* hadn't happened before.

She gave them a jaunty little salute before vanishing in a flash of light.

6:20 A.M.

C ole. *Cole*. Wake up."

He swam up out of the semi-nightmare, in which a blood-stained, grinning Helen Pappas chased him and a group of teenage Mormons through Greek ruins, and opened his eyes. Anna stood over him. "What? he asked woozily.

"There's a bunch of police sirens outside."

He lurched to his feet and followed her to the front door. He passed Laura, still asleep on the couch, one bare foot poking out from beneath the comforter. Outside on their porch, his fuzzy brain sorted out the noise. "Those are fire trucks," he said. "A lot of them."

"Oh, my God. Look." In the distance, black smoke was visible over the trees and low buildings.

Everything clicked into place. "It's the church."

"What church?"

"The one where...the one they were renovating."

"What's going on?" Laura said sleepily, holding the blanket around herself as she joined them.

"The church where they held the Festival is on fire."

Cole and Laura exchanged a look that Anna missed, since she still watched the smoke.

Anna said, "I hope no one was inside it."

"There wasn't," Cole said, and if Anna thought his certainty strange, she didn't comment on it.

H ey," Rebecca Hutchcraft said, surprised. "You're up early."

"Haven't been to sleep," Saraya Parashar said. The *Daily Standard* bullpen was mostly empty; not even Ransom Wade had made it in yet. "Seemed like a good idea to vacate Ratway for a while after the scene at the police station."

"What scene at the police station?"

"May I sit down?"

"Sure."

Saraya pulled a nearby chair to Rebecca's desk and quickly filled her in on her rescue. "I figured I'd give the cops a chance to cool off. But I'll be there tonight for my usual shift."

"And if they arrest you again?"

She smiled. "If *you're* there, they might think twice about it. At worst, you'll get an exclusive. It'll cost you, though."

"Oh, yeah?"

"Yeah." Saraya's face turned serious. "Did someone tell you the Lightning Girl was really a woman named Devon Moraine?"

Rebecca's shields rose at once. *No one told me,* she thought. *I figured it out myself. But who told you that I had?* "I can't really discuss sources, Saraya."

"Devon's a friend of mine. So is the Lightning Girl, sort of. I can promise you, they're not the same person."

"Okay."

"If you print that they are, it'll make things very hard for both of them. So that's the trade. I give you an exclusive account of my rescue by the Lightning Girl, and you forget you ever heard the name Devon Moraine."

Rebecca continued to ponder this. "Do you think I could meet Devon Moraine? See for myself?"

"Sure," Saraya said casually. "Maybe we can all go out for a drink or dinner or something. With the understanding that it's all off the record, of course."

"Of course."

Saraya yawned. "I'm going to find a cheap hotel and sleep the day away. See you tonight for a volunteer shift?"

"A chance to handle medical waste *and* possibly see you arrested? Wouldn't miss it."

After Saraya left, Rebecca went back over the encounter. Saraya had never visited her at work before; it might as well have been a neon sign announcing that Rebecca was right, that this Devon Moraine *was* the Lightning Girl. But she'd given her word, and that was a journalist's bread and blood.

The elevator doors opened with a ding. As he crossed the room to his office, Ransom Wade shouted, "Hutchcraft! There's a church fire in Bay View! Looks like arson. Go check it out!"

"On it," Rebecca said and grabbed her purse.

She did not see the haunted disbelief in Ransom Wade's eyes as he relived the previous night.

9:51 A.M.

Harrison Marley Jr. had waited as long as he could. Unable to sleep, he finally went into his father's room, chased out the nurse and said, "Dad, wake up. We have to talk."

If possible, the old man seemed even more feeble. How much longer could he last? His eyes opened slowly, like a pair of heavy garage doors, and his intake of breath wheezed before he said, "What the fuck do you want now?"

"I went to the Festival last night. I saw a woman shot in the head from point blank range who got up like it had been a mother's kiss. And nobody else seemed too freaked out about it. I saw that fucking Lightning Girl appear and disappear in a flash of light. One minute she's there, the next, *poof!*"

"What the fuck are you talking about?"

"Those people are fucking *weirdos,* Dad. They tore Stavros Kefali's head off. I *saw* it."

The old man sighed, and in that ragged sound, Harry the Less heard all the disapproval and disappointment he'd endured his whole life. "You dumb shit," the old man breathed. "You can't even go to a damn party and get it right."

He couldn't say why, but that comment was the last straw. Harrison stood, pulled his gun, put a pillow over the old man's face and pumped three slugs into that brittle head. When the nurse rushed in and screamed, he shot her as well.

Monte, roused from a hard sleep and clad in his robe and pajamas, charged in with a gun in each hand. He stared at the corpses, still blinking awake.

"Get this mess cleaned up," Harrison said and stalked out of the room. "And then call my lawyer. We'll need to issue a statement to the press about poor old Dad."

1:15 P.M.

Darren Flaxstone gently shook Sparrow and said, "Wake up, sleepyhead." The boy rolled over, stretched and half-opened his eyes.

"You're back," he said. "You made it."

"I did."

"What happened to my friends?"

"They're safe."

That made Sparrow smile. "Can I see them?"

"Sure."

The boy got out of bed, dressed himself and joined Darren in the kitchen. "What time is it?" he asked as he sat down.

"A little after one," Darren said. He poured cereal in a bowl and pushed it toward Sparrow.

"Won't you get in trouble for skipping work?"

"I have a flexible schedule."

Sparrow nodded. "Me, too. Well...I did."

"Do you feel up to meeting my friend this evening?" Darren asked as he passed the milk.

"I guess," Sparrow said honestly. "He's your boss, right?"

"He is. Like I said, I met him when I was about your age, and he helped me get my life on track. I think he could do the same for you."

"He must be old," Sparrow said through a mouthful, "if he helped you when you were a kid."

Darren laughed. "Yes, he's old. But he doesn't look it. And he's very, very sharp."

"Okay, I guess. Do I need to dress up? Because I haven't got any dressy clothes."

"Actually, you do now. But you don't have to dress up. Just be polite, and if he asks you anything, answer him honestly."

"The Mendicant said we should never be honest with anyone but him."

"And look where he is now."

Sparrow met his gaze, and he could tell the boy was very seriously considering his words. At last, he said, "Does this mean I'll have to go to school?"

"If you decide you want to stay with us, yes. But I promise, it's not the kind of school you're thinking of."

3:12 P.M.

A couple of hours later, Darren and Sparrow stepped out of the company car in front of the Kefali building. "Afternoon, Mr. Flaxstone," the driver called before he pulled away from the curb.

Sparrow looked up at the Kefali Building like a tourist. He leaned so far back, Darren worried he might tip over. "I've never seen one of these buildings up close, just from over the river. And your boss owns all of it?"

"Every brick."

"Wow. You *work* here?"

"I get my instructions here. I do most of my work on the street."

"And how many other people work here?"

"A lot. All my friend's businesses are based here."

"He has businesses? Like regular ones?"

"He does."

"But I thought…"

"He also has businesses like the Mendicant's."

Sparrow shook his head. "He must be really rich."

"Oh, he is. Come on."

Sammartino held the door for them. "Good morning, sir. Who's your friend?"

"This is Sparrow. Sparrow, this is Mr. Sammartino."

"My friends call me 'Sam,'" he said with a smile.

398

Inside the lobby, Darren introduced the boy to the receptionist, and then to the guard in front of the executive elevator. When they reached the top floor, he let Sparrow stop at the water fountain and get a drink to help his ears pop. Then they went to B.J.'s office. Sparrow impulsively clutched Darren's hand as the people in cubicles all stood and greeted them.

"Good morning," Stefan said cheerfully. "I'm afraid Ms. Burr is taking the day off. The Festival and all, you know."

"I know." Darren said. "Stefan, this is my new friend, Sparrow. Sparrow, this is Stefan."

Stefan extended his hand. "It's very nice to meet you, Sparrow."

"Thank you," Sparrow said uncertainly. All this deference and politeness was beginning to freak him out.

Stefan buzzed them into B.J.'s office. When the door was closed, Darren said distinctly, "Call internal security program."

"What's that?" Sparrow asked.

"Security program to make sure we're not disturbed." When the automated voice announced it was ready, he added, "Begin protocol Flaxstone Five."

Darren went to the wall and put his palm over the hidden reader. The secret panel opened.

He knelt so he could look Sparrow in the eye.

"Sparrow, you're about to see something you've never seen before. I'll answer all your questions about it later. This is my friend, the man who helped me when no one else would, and who gave me the love and respect I never knew I was missing. So to put it simply, be cool. Okay?"

The boy nodded.

Darren took his hand and guided him into the chamber.

"This," he said, "is Stavros Kefali. Stavros, this is my friend, Sparrow."

"Hello, Sparrow," Stavros said.

"Wow," Sparrow whispered, then smiled. "Hi."

THE END

SPECIAL THANKS

Steven Stack
Melissa F. Olson
John Hartness
Stefan Rudnicki, Gabrielle de Cuir, and Alison Belle Bews
Andrew Vachss (RIP)
And as always,
Valette, Jake and Amelia

SPOTIFY PLAYLIST
https://open.spotify.com/playlist/62ljOvB2Af8rQ2nvms8pvy?
si=kuJfN3RLRrGkQfS4mIk9WA

C-I-T-Y (John Cafferty and the Beaver Brown Band)
Living for the City (Stevie Wonder)
Shadowplay (Joy Division)
Hot Child in the City (Nick Gilder)
In the City (Eagles)
You Belong to the City (Glenn Frey)
Sweet City Woman (Stampeders)
'Til the City's on Fire (311)
I Love Livin' in the City (Fear)

ABOUT THE AUTHOR

Alex Bledsoe grew up in west Tennessee an hour north of Graceland (home of Elvis) and twenty miles from Nutbush (birthplace of Tina Turner). He's been a reporter, photographer, editor, and Kirby vacuum cleaner salesman. He now lives in a Wisconsin town famous for trolls and tries to teach his kids to act like they've been to town before.

ALSO BY ALEX BLEDSOE

The Tufa Series:
The Hum and the Shiver

Wisp of a Thing

Long Black Curl

Chapel of Ease

Gather Her Round

The Fairies of Sadieville

The Eddie LaCross series:
The Sword-Edged Blonde

Burn Me Deadly

Dark Jenny

Wake of the Bloody Angel

He Drank, and Saw the Spider

The Zginksi novels:
Blood Groove

The Girls with Games of Blood

Standalone Works:
Dandelion

Give the People What They Want (audio only story collection)

FRIENDS OF FALSTAFF

Thank You to All our Falstaff Books Patrons, who get extra digital content each month! To be featured here and see what other great rewards we offer, go to www.patreon.com/falstaffbooks.

PATRONS

Dino Hicks
John Hooks
John Kilgallon
Larissa Lichty
Travis & Casey Schilling
Staci-Leigh Santore
Sheryl R. Hayes
Scott Norris
Samuel Montgomery-Blinn
Junkle
Vickie DeSantos
Quincy J. Allen
Allison Charlesworth

Thank You for Supporting Independent Publishing!

We believe that you should be able
to read your books, your way.
That's why this Falstaff Books
print edition includes a digital copy
at no additional cost!

Just scan the QR code with your device,
follow the directions on Prolific Works,
and enjoy!
You can also join our newsletter when prompted,
and never miss an awesome Falstaff Release!

www.ingramcontent.com/pod-product-compliance
Lightning Source LLC
Chambersburg PA
CBHW021952120726
47898CB00001BA/107